Nadine Gonzalez wr[...] [...]ies [...]ve featuring a diverse cast of characters: American, Caribbean and Latinx. A lawyer by profession, she lives in Miami, Florida, and shares her home with her Cuban American husband and their son. She networks on Twitter but lives on Instagram! Check out @_nadinegonzalez. For more information, visit her website, nadine-gonzalez.com

A former job-hopper, **Jessica Lemmon** resides in Ohio with her husband and rescue dog. She holds a degree in graphic design, which is currently gathering dust in an impressive frame. When she's not writing super-sexy heroes, she can be found cooking, drawing, drinking coffee (okay, wine) and eating crisps. She firmly believes that God gifts us with talents for a purpose, and with His help, you can create the life you want. Jessica is a social media junkie who loves to hear from readers. You can learn more at jessicalemmon.com

OH SO WRONG WITH MR. RIGHT

NADINE GONZALEZ

THE MAN SHE LOVES TO HATE

JESSICA LEMMON

MILLS & BOON

First Published in Great Britain 2023
by Mills & Boon, an imprint of HarperCollins*Publishers* Ltd
1 London Bridge Street, London, SE1 9GF

www.harpercollins.co.uk

HarperCollins*Publishers*
Macken House, 39/40 Mayor Street Upper,
Dublin 1, D01 C9W8, Ireland

Oh So Wrong with Mr. Right © 2023 Harlequin Enterprises ULC
The Man She Loves to Hate © 2023 Harlequin Enterprises ULC

Special thanks and acknowledgement are given to Nadine Gonzalez and Jessica Lemmon for their contributions to the *Texas Cattleman's Club: The Wedding* series.

ISBN: 978-0-263-31759-6

0523

This book is produced from independently certified FSC™ paper to ensure responsible forest management.

For more information visit: www.harpercollins.co.uk/green

Printed and Bound in the UK using 100% Renewable Electricity at
CPI Group (UK) Ltd, Croydon, CR0 4YY

OH SO WRONG WITH MR. RIGHT

NADINE GONZALEZ

For Ariel

One

Catch. That. Man.

Sasha had him in her sights. She took off, racing through the crowded airport, up an escalator and down a corridor, desperate to catch up with him before the crowd swallowed him up. The likelihood of that happening was slim. He was a striking Black man, taller than most. But he moved quickly, making long strides, smoothly dodging other travelers as he wheeled a smart carry-on suitcase behind him. Sasha was weighed down by her hefty luggage—a month's worth of clothes—and had to shuffle just to keep up. Was this reasonable, hunting down a stranger at an airport? No, but her options were few. She'd just survived an emergency landing on a plane that looked like it had been pieced together by glue and prayers. The idea of camping out at the airport gate, awaiting the next flight out, made her sick. He was her ticket out.

Wait. Where did he go?

Sasha reached an elevator bank. He was nowhere in sight. The acid in her queasy, empty stomach churned. She wanted to scream, but didn't quite have the energy. She gave up, and not just on pursuing him, on life altogether.

Screw this. She'd grab something to eat and sort it out. It had been a dumb idea from the start.

She located the nearest coffee shop on the airport map and steered her suitcase to Hot Cup of Joe, wondering if their breakfast sandwiches were any good. And that's where she found him. He stood at a counter-height table, a Styrofoam cup in one hand, his phone in another, brows drawn as he read.

She walked up to him and dropped her travel bag on a vacant seat.

He glanced up from his phone and their eyes met.

By God, he was gorgeous.

That shouldn't have been her first thought, but since it was she might as well unpack it. He was good-looking, emphasis on *good*—no bad-boy vibes here. He had warm brown skin, well-drawn features and the clearest brown eyes she'd ever seen. His short-cropped hair gave him classic boy-next-door appeal. Sasha was weary of those. Every girl's first crush, they stole your heart in junior high and carelessly tossed it back before taking off for college.

He raised a brow, questioning.

She straightened up and tossed back a long box braid over her shoulder. "Remember me? We sat on the same flight, same aisle. You might've forgotten, but you helped me store my camera bag in the overhead compartment."

He'd done more than that. When the plane lost altitude and started its tumultuous descent, he'd helped her with her seat belt. She'd rushed back to her seat from the restroom, where she'd gone to have a panic attack—for totally unrelated reasons—and had trouble clicking the parts together because her hands were shaking so much. He reached over and helped her, tugging on the end of the belt to make sure it was secure. To be fair, he'd checked on the elderly gentle-man seated in between them, retrieving his glasses that fell off while he hastily adjusted his oxygen mask. Looking back, he was the only one on the whole damn plane who'd kept it together throughout the ordeal, including the pilot.

He set down his phone. "I remember you," he said, his voice low and raspy.

"You have something I need," she blurted out.

His eyes narrowed with suspicion. "Is that right?"

"Yes. A ride." Sasha raised a finger to silence him even though he hadn't uttered a word. "Before you suggest that I rent a car, you should know that I tried. You scored the last one on the lot. How do I know this? I was in line at the rental car when they put up the NO AVAILABILITY sign. You were the last client they served. And, if you're wondering in what world that automatically makes you my driver, the an-swer is: This one, a world where I'm stranded in the middle of nowhere and you scored the last rental car."

She paused to catch her breath, suddenly light-headed.

"Are you okay?" he asked.

She wasn't. The emergency-landing trauma was the least of her issues. A tornado of gloom and doom had followed her from California to Georgia, where she'd made a brief stop for work, like an omen. Who was to say she wasn't somehow responsible for bringing down the plane?

He took her hand and pressed two fingers to her inner wrist. Her pulse leaped to his touch. He withdrew. "Wait here. I'll get you a water."

"Coffee, too!" she called after him. "And a biscotti!"

Sasha watched him go, as cool as ever. Nothing she'd said or done had rattled him, even though she was, by her own standards, pretty much unhinged. What must he think of her? In his suede jacket and jeans that fit just so, he was every inch the sophisticated traveler. She, on the other hand, in her leggings and oversized sweatshirt, a pair of massive head-phones dangling around her neck, looked as if she were on her way to the library to cram for finals.

He returned and set a short bottle of water and a tall cup of coffee before her. Hot Cup of Joe wasn't fancy—no milk substitutes and no latte art here—but as promised, the coffee was piping hot.

"Thank you."

"You're welcome." He gently placed a caramel brownie on a napkin. "Sorry, no biscotti."

She smiled gratefully. "That's okay."

There was a quiet stillness about him that she liked. It settled her. The coffee helped, too. As a seasoned traveler it was tough to admit that maybe, just maybe, the plane inci-dent had spooked her.

"They're servicing the car," he said. "Once it's ready, I'll take you where you want to go."

Sasha relaxed for the first time that day. This was far eas-ier than she'd anticipated. She didn't have to twist his arm or resort to blackmail.

"Thank you," she repeated.

"Was Royal your final destination, or—"

"Royal is fine," she said. "Drop me off at the county line. I'll take it from there."

He offered her an easy smile that killed any remaining ap-prehension. "I'll take you home."

"Royal isn't home," she said, quickly dispelling that notion.

"Where is home?"

His phone buzzed with a text message before she had a chance to answer. He read it and pocketed the phone. "They're ready for us."

Us. The little word wormed its way into her heart. Every-thing was going to be fine now. She had someone to rely on. Not that she needed a man to serve that purpose. She was independent and self-sufficient 99.9 percent of the time. Today was a fluke. Sadly, if they never met again, he would forever think of her as the woman who couldn't swim her way out of a puddle.

Sasha finished gobbling up the brownie. Hopping to her feet, she reached for her bag. He beat her to it. "I'll take it from here."

Her battered little heart leaped for joy.

Two

You like the wild ones.

Nik received his cousin's text and had every intention of returning fire. Then she showed up with her swinging braids, feline eyes, deep brown skin and brash attitude. *You like the wild ones*... Where was the lie?

Nik slowed down to keep pace with her. "I don't think I caught your name."

"It's Sasha."

"Hi, Sasha. I'm Nik."

"Thanks again for agreeing to this."

"Don't mention it."

At the lot, they were led to the last compact SUV. Come to think of it, he was lucky to have scored it. Catching a glimmer of sunlight on her long, frayed lashes, he believed his luck was only getting better.

Nik loaded the truck.

"Need help?" she asked.

"No."

She twitched, restless. "I'll drive! It's a long one, around six hours. We can take turns... And before you make a crack about women drivers—"

"Why would I do that?" Nik interrupted. "Is this 1973 or something?"

"I—I don't know," she stammered. "You wouldn't be the first man to—"

Nik shut the trunk. "Do you always do this?"

"Do what?"

"Argue against points no one's made."

Her expression turned sheepish. "Maybe."

Nik leaned against the back of the SUV. "My dad wasn't around when I grew up," he said. "My mother drove my Little League team all over the state of Florida in a rusty minivan. She did it all, changed the flats and jumped the battery. I don't make *cracks* about women drivers."

She nodded. "Understood."

It was his turn to feel sheepish. That got real deep, real fast. What had possessed him to share so much?

"The offer stands," she said. "We can take turns driving."

"I'll need to catch up on work emails later, so that's fine by me."

"And I won't interrupt," she said. "If you need to take a call, it's no bother. I've got noise-canceling headphones. You won't even know I'm there. I know you need to make it back in time for dinner, so we don't even have to stop for snacks."

It wasn't until he got behind the wheel, finger hovering over the ignition button, that it hit him. "How do you know I need to get to Royal by dinner?"

"Doesn't everyone want to make it home in time for dinner?" she said with a shrug.

He echoed her words. "Royal isn't home."

"Well...we've got that in common."

He waited. They weren't going anywhere until she fessed

up. It took a moment, but she relented. "I might've overheard you making plans over the phone. You asked to reschedule a lunch date to dinner."

"Uh-huh." Nik reached for a pair of sunglasses in his jacket pocket and tossed the jacket in the back seat. "I'm going to ask you a question. Don't get offended."

She let out a nervous laugh. "I can't promise that, but I'll try."

"Are you stalking me, Sasha?"

She met his eyes. "I am," she said, coolly. "Usually I'm more discreet. Today is an off day."

"Oh, really?"

"I'm a photojournalist," she said. "Observing people is what I do. It's my superpower. I catch details others miss."

Now this was interesting. "What else do you think you know about me?"

She flipped her long braids off her shoulder, readying herself for the challenge. "We boarded in Atlanta. But when you stood to help me with my bag, I caught a glimpse of your boarding pass. You're traveling from Florida. You spent most of the flight reading the *Royal Financial Times*. So I figure you're traveling for business. I can't imagine anyone doing that for fun. You're not wearing a ring. I don't think you're single, though. You're the type to be in a long-term stable relationship."

"Very good," he said, impressed. "Batman and Sherlock Holmes would approve." The last point, however, was news to him.

She raised her pointed chin. "If I'm wrong, tell me."

She had most of it right. No doubt her "superpowers" served her well in her profession, but he was fairly certain he'd spotted her first, well before they'd boarded the plane in Atlanta.

Nik first laid eyes on Sasha at their gate at ATL. In a holding pen full of anxious people, she sat with her headphones, a faraway expression on her heart-shaped face. To the casual observer she was lost in an audiobook or podcast, but he noticed how her cat eyes tracked all the moving parts, how she studied the people around her, taking in every detail. On the plane, when she took her seat at his aisle, he felt her gaze on him, assessing, measuring and pasting together every bit of information she gleaned for some later use.

"You're right about the *RFT*," he said. "No one reads it for fun."

She considered him a while, her expression inscrutable. "Before I forget. I need your full name."

"I'm surprised you don't know it already, along with my PINs and passwords."

She offered him a sweet smile. "It's not for lack of trying. Believe me."

"May I ask what you need it for?"

She held up her phone. "I'm sending your name and a photo of the license plate to my sister."

"Right," he said. "In case *I* turn out to be a deranged stalker."

"Do you think I'd climb into a stranger's car without some kind of plan?" she asked. "Before you call me paranoid—"

"I would never," he said. "Do me a favor and tell your sister I didn't lure you in with the promise of candy. You *asked* for this ride."

"The eye candy comes standard?"

Nik could not control his smile. "Is that your way of saying you like me?"

She slid him a glance, her expression sour. "Name, please."

"Nikolai Williams."

"Nikolai… Like Gogol?"

"Yes, but call me Nik. Everyone does."

She typed out the text message, attached the photo, and hit send. "Done."

When she looked up from her phone, she was decidedly calmer. "Listen," she said. "In my heart of hearts, I know you're a perfectly kind, loving and trustworthy human being. In this crazy world, you can't be too careful. You know?"

"I know it," Nik said. "Only wondering who I should text about the woman who carjacked me."

"Your girlfriend, maybe?" she suggested. "That sounds like a good place to start."

She was fishing. Having already figured out that he wasn't married, she wanted to know if he was single. That boded well for him, but he wasn't going to make it easy on her. She'd have to use her detective skills and find out.

"I'll take my chances," he said.

"Let's both focus on arriving in Royal in good spirits and good health," she said. "Sounds good?"

"Sounds great," he said. "I'd like to add one last thing, if you don't mind."

"Let's hear it." She rummaged in her bag for lip balm and dabbed it on her full lips with the tip of her finger. "No murder podcasts? No singalongs?"

"No to that," he said. "But do you remember when you asked me to help you with your luggage on the plane?"

"I'm recovering from a shoulder injury," she said. "It's hard for me to reach. Usually, I manage just fine."

"That's not my point, Sasha," Nik said. "Do you remember what you told me?"

She shrugged. "I don't know. *A little help, please?*"

"No," he said. "*Help me with this and I'll never ask you for anything ever again.*"

"Okay..." she said. "That tracks, but how was I to know the plane was going to plunge out of the sky from cruising altitude—"

"Sasha, that's *not* my point!"

"Well, what is?" she demanded.

"For the next six hours, it's just you and me in this car," Nik said. "I want you to be comfortable. I want you to feel safe. If you need something, if you want anything, even to stop for snacks or just to stretch, tell me. Ask for what you want. You don't have to barter or make promises we both know you can't keep. Just ask. The answer will be yes. Understood?"

Nik was pressed for time. This quick trip to Miami to finalize the sale of his condo wasn't supposed to interfere with that. He'd assured his business partner that he'd be back in time to meet a new client for lunch at the local country club. He hadn't counted on insane travel delays, a plane losing fuel midair and an emergency landing. He hadn't counted on Sasha strutting into his life and making demands on his time. But that's the hand he'd been dealt, and he'd play it.

Sasha fell silent. She looked at him, as if for the first time. Then a devilish glint lit up her eyes. "Careful," she said. "I'll ask for the moon."

"Go ahead," Nik said, and fired up the ignition. "I'll find a way to get it for you."

Three

Headphones on, Sasha stared at the narrow strip of road ahead. To one side of the road there was nothing but amber waves of grain as far as the eye could see. Was there time to stop to snap a few photos? She wouldn't ask. That would be inconsiderate on her part. He had to get back in time for that dinner meeting...no, dinner date? He was so tight-lipped about it. One thing was certain: Nikolai Williams wasn't the mild-mannered boy next door she'd made him out to be. That calm demeanor was steel. When he held her steady in his gaze, she fell to pieces inside.

She fidgeted now, restless, and tugged off the headphones. "The airline better reimburse us," she said. "I used travel points for this trip," she went on. "I'll need them back to book a vacation when all this is over."

"Where will you go?" he asked.

"Anywhere with a nice, calm beach."

"God, I'd like that."

His voice was raspy with yearning. Sasha pushed down the urge to give him all the things he wanted and would not ask for. She could take him away, get him to unplug, push him onto a bed of soft sand and force him to relax. Maybe his girlfriend could do that, if he had one. Why couldn't he confirm if he was single or not? Not that it mattered. In fact, her therapist suggested she swear off men altogether until she sorted some things out.

She deleted the image of Nik wearing close to nothing on a sandy beach. "If not the beach, somewhere fun."

"Royal is fun."

Sasha tossed him a quizzical look. "Is it, though?"

"I might not be the one to ask," he said. "I've only been there for work. Everyone else looks like they're having a great time."

Ever the reporter, Sasha resumed questioning him. "Where do you live? What kind of work do you do?"

"I'm from Florida," he said. "For the last ten years, I've lived in Miami. I just sold my place because I'm rarely there. And I'm in marketing."

Marketing...of course.

"Is Miami just one big ad agency?" she asked. "Because I'm starting to wonder."

When he smiled or even smirked, as he was now, at anything she said, Sasha felt such a sense of accomplishment. It was ridiculous.

"Okay," he said. "Tell me about your groundbreaking journalism."

"As I mentioned earlier, I'm a photojournalist." She pointed to the duffel bag in the back seat. "That's my gear."

"What are your subjects?"

"My last job was in Georgia. I photographed the aftermath of a flood."

The ring of a phone cut her off. It was coming from the back seat. Nik cursed under his breath, and mumbled something about forgetting to pair his phone with the car's Bluetooth.

"Want me to get it?" she asked.

He responded with a frown. "It's probably not important."

The phone kept ringing.

"Then why are you twitching?" she asked.

"I'm not."

The corner of his eye was definitely twitching. The phone stopped ringing, and started right back again. Sasha could see that it was torturing him. "I'm getting it."

Sasha had released her seat belt and crawled over the center console.

"What are you doing?" he cried. "Be careful!"

"It's fine!"

The ringing was coming from his jacket. She patted the pockets and found it. The ringing stopped just as she pulled it out. She read the screen. "You have two missed calls from someone named Oliver, and a text message from Krystal saying…" She blinked. "Saying you like wild women and it's no wonder you don't have a date—"

Nik circled an arm around her waist, and slammed hard on the brakes. Next thing, they were plunging nose first into a roadside ditch.

Sasha had landed on Nik's lap. She clung to him, breathing erratically. One minute they were driving smoothly, the next they were careening off the road. She grabbed his face between her hands. "Are you breathing? Are you okay?"

Nik gathered her close. "Don't worry about me. Are you hurt?"

There was such genuine concern in his eyes, his voice, his touch, she couldn't help but wrap her arms around his neck, almost choking the man to death. "I'm fine. What just happened?"

"I got distracted, and then a deer jumped out of nowhere."

"No way!" Sasha cried. "Is she hurt?"

He brushed her hair away from her face. "She's alright. Bambi lives to cause another accident."

"What?" Sasha pulled back and searched his face. He was serious as ever. She started shaking with laughter. "Oh God," she said, laughing. "You have a dark sense of humor."

"Don't laugh," he said. "This is my fault. A few missed calls from my business partner wasn't worth putting you in danger."

In the static of her brain, the text message resurfaced. *You like wild women.* What was that about?

"You ignored the calls," she reminded him. "I'm the one who couldn't let it go. Plus, let's not minimize the role Bambi played in this."

He gave her a reluctant smile. "You're right. Bambi's the wild card."

Sasha eased off of him and immediately missed his warmth. "This might be a good time for me to tell you that I'm cursed."

He looked at her closely. "Want to repeat that?"

"I'm cursed," she repeated. "It's probably my fault our plane crashed."

"Our plane didn't crash," he pointed out. "It lost fuel, and landed."

"We went plunging—"

"It *was* a little rough."

A little rough? Her heart was in her throat the whole time. "How are you so calm about it?"

"I was in the Air Force."

"Wait." Sasha sat kneeling on the passenger seat, hands planted on her knees. "You're a fighter pilot?"

Nik was staring back at her in bewilderment. "You hear what you want to hear, don't you?"

"You said—"

"I enlisted straight after high school, and mostly worked in tech. I do fly, though."

Before she could stop herself, Sasha blurted, "God, you're hot."

A bashful expression replaced the bemusement. Sasha revised her opinion. He was hot, smart and brave, but also a little shy about it. She went on teasing him.

"What do I care about airline points? You can fly me to paradise."

He brushed her braids out of the way to take a good look at her. "Sasha, did you hit your head?"

His fingertips skimmed down the sides of her face. In his eyes, she saw genuine concern for her well-being. She had trusted him from the start. Her trust hardened and solidified to something concrete that she could rest on. "Should we get out of here?" she said. "What if we sink into quicksand?"

"Doubtful," he said. "At the very least we should assess the damage."

The SUV was at a slant, leaning heavily on her side. "I don't think I can open my door."

Nik pushed open the door on the driver's side. He got out first and helped her follow him. Nik assessed the damage to the car, which was minimal except for one of the tires that definitely looked flat. They would have to get it towed.

A pickup truck slowed to a stop at the side of the ride. A woman wearing a floppy sunhat hopped out. "Hey, you two!" she called out. "Y'all okay?"

"We're fine!" Sasha called back. "Men drivers... Am I right?"

Four

Their Good Samaritan's name was Donna. She co-owned a barbecue shack down the road where they could wait comfortably for the tow truck. Nik loaded their bags into the back of Donna's pickup and turned to Sasha. She stood in the shade, looking uncomfortable.

"Are you alright?" he asked.

"Don't mind me." She fanned her face with her hands. "I'm having a heatstroke."

On the plane her heavy sweatshirt might have been a good idea, but it had now turned into a very effective torture device. "Do you want to change out of that? I'll get your suitcase."

"That's not necessary," she said. "The trick is to wear layers."

She slipped the sweatshirt over her head. Underneath she wore a simple stretchy tank top that clung to her curves. *Nice trick*, he thought and turned away. It was no use. The image of her rounded shoulders and full breasts was seared in his mind.

To distract himself, he pulled out the phone that had put them in this tight spot. Two missed calls from Oliver and a follow-up text.

Client can't make dinner meeting. Lunch is scheduled for tomorrow instead. Same time and place. There's no reason to rush. Take your time and enjoy the drive.

Oliver, who knew him well, had gone out of his way to encourage him to relax. His cousin, Krystal, in her own way, was doing the same. "Your work hard, play hard approach to life is killing you," she'd scolded him. He'd had the not-so-bright idea of stopping by her place to pick up his tuxedo while she was home, instead of waiting until she was at work. The Realtor had staged his condo to look appealing to buyers. Most of his clothes and clutter was stored in Krystal's spare bedroom closet. She'd eyed the garment bag with suspicion.

"What do you need a tux for?" she asked.

"A wedding in Royal."

"Ooh," she cooed. "A *royal* wedding?"

"Might as well be," he said. "Ariana Ramos and Xavier Noble are getting married in June."

"Shut up!" Krystal had leaped into the air like she used to when they were kids. "You're invited to that wedding?"

"Anyone who's anyone is invited," he said coolly.

"Lucky bastard," she said, grinning. "Who are you taking?"

"Would you like to be my date?"

"Sweet of you to offer, baby cousin, but I'll be in Italy perfecting a charcoal sketch of the statue of David by then."

Nik was younger by one year, yet she insisted on calling him "baby cousin."

"Cool," he said. "Suit yourself."

"You mean you can't get a date for one of the most talked-about events of the year?" she asked. "Where are all the women you date?"

"I live here, but I'm constantly on the West Coast trying to build Nexus," Nik said. "The wedding is in Texas. Try to connect the dots."

"Listen, smart-ass," Krystal retorted. "Women have traveled for way, way less. I once hopped on a plane to attend an indie band's show at a dive bar in Austin with a guy I didn't even like."

"That says more about you than anything else," Nik replied.

"You don't have a date because there's no one you can reach out to, is there?" Krystal said. "You like the wild ones. Trust me, I get the appeal, but those fiery relationships burn out quick. When you're sick, or lonely, or just want someone to talk to, they're no place to be found."

"I'm not sick or lonely," he said. "And I've got you to talk to."

She looked at him disapprovingly. "It's five p.m. somewhere. Let's go to my favorite spot and get margaritas."

Nik checked his watch. "It's five p.m. here."

She waved her hand dismissively. "Let's go. We've got a lot to talk about."

They'd spent the afternoon drinking and talking. Apparently, it wasn't enough, because Krystal had felt the need to follow up with the text message that Sasha had found and read aloud, distracting him to the point that he'd driven into a ditch. Okay, the deer was also to blame. Nik was an excellent driver. He'd never had an accident in his life.

Sasha approached him. "Was the missed call important?"

"No," he said. "Oliver is my business partner. He was calling to let me know that tonight's dinner was canceled. There's nothing to rush back to."

"Nothing?" she said.

"Not a thing," Nik said. "I'm all yours."

She grinned. "You better feed me, then. I've no other use for you."

"Y'all hungry?" Donna said. "You're in luck. Our pulled pork sandwiches are a favorite around here and today's special is boneless ribs with our signature sauce, your choice of tater tots, potato salad or fries, and freshly made churro sticks for dessert."

"Donna, don't tempt me!" Sasha wailed. "It all sounds so good!"

She turned to him. "How about you? Any preferences?"

"I eat everything," Nik said.

"That's what I like to hear," Donna said. "Hope you two don't mind squeezing in next to me. There's no back seat to speak of."

"We don't mind," Sasha replied. "And we're grateful for your help."

Nik held the passenger door open for Sasha. He climbed in after her. They were packed in so tight, she was practically back on his lap.

Donna got behind the wheel and focused on her driving. Meanwhile Nik couldn't tear his gaze away from Sasha. He liked how friendly and easygoing she was, even after all they'd been through. He wanted to turn things around, make the day better for her. If staying for delicious food was what she wanted, that was what they'd do.

"So let me get this straight," Nik said, once they were seated at a picnic table with sandwiches and a pitcher of ice tea. "You've got superpowers, but you're also cursed."

Sasha popped a tater tot in her mouth and winked at him. Warmth spread in his chest. *You like the wild ones.*

"How does that work exactly?" he asked.

"Let's not go there," she said. "It's such a nice day. How

about you tell me about the wild things you're into? What was that about?"

"Wild cats," he said wryly. "They're harder to domesticate than you think."

He'd expected her to bring up the text message, but he wasn't ready to talk about that.

"That's fair," she said. "Let's stick to simpler topics."

"Okay." Nik switched subjects. "Are you traveling to Royal for work?"

"For a wedding." She licked barbecue sauce off her fingertips. "My sister is getting married. Of all the places in the world, she chose Royal. So I'll be camping out there for a few weeks to hang out with her a bit, keep her sane, and get to know my future brother-in-law better."

"Your sister?" Nik leaned closer to study her. Those eyes, sharp cheekbones and smile... How had he not seen the resemblance before? "Sasha, are you Ariana Ramos's sister?"

She winced. "Should I have mentioned that earlier?"

"And that's the sister you sent my information to?"

"I only have one sister, Nik."

"She probably has me on a FBI watch list by now."

"If it makes you feel better, the text never went through," she said. "I checked earlier, and my phone was still in airplane mode."

"Your future brother-in-law is Xavier Noble," he said. "And I nearly killed you! You're precious cargo, Sasha. I have to get you there safely."

"I'm precious no matter who I'm related to," she said.

"You are to me," he said. "But I've got to deliver you safely to the official Royal wedding committee or they'll run me out of town."

"You have a point there," she deadpanned. "I'll put in a good word."

"You're Ariana's sister," he repeated stupidly.

"Calm down," she said. "I'm nowhere as amazing as her. She was discovered at our local mall when hanging out with friends in college. She started acting and now has her own production company. Between you and me, she was born a star."

"But you're the sun." Sasha did not meet his eyes. Was she shy, all of a sudden? He hadn't meant to put her on the spot, but he'd meant every word. Ariana, whom he'd met in passing, was brilliant. But Sasha glowed hot. If he stared at her long enough, he'd catch fire. "Does it ever bother you to have a famous sister?"

"Sometimes," she admitted. "Like when we just want privacy. I'd like nothing more than to meet my older sister for drinks after a long day at work, but it's always a production. We'd have to go somewhere really exclusive to be left alone, and where's the fun in that?"

Nik didn't have siblings. Hanging out with Krystal, catching up over margaritas, was his therapy. It got him through some tough times.

"Other times," she said, "it's useful, a shield, of sorts."

"How so?"

"Well," she said. "Whatever mistakes I make, however badly I mess up, my superstar sister acts like a lightning rod, drawing the attention to herself and away from me. You can't pay for that sort of protection."

"I'll protect you," he said. "So long as I'm around."

"Promises, promises."

She'd brushed him off, but there was that glow again. All he had to do was tell her exactly what he was feeling to get her to light up from her core. It did something to him.

"I'm invited to the wedding," he said. He might as well put it out there.

She perked up. "You are?"

"It's a work thing for me," he said. "My company just took

over the PR firm that handles Xavier Noble's press. We met a few times for business and we're invited to the wedding. I don't have to tell you that scoring an invitation is a big, eff-ing deal."

"No, you don't," she said wryly. "It's the Oscars of wed-dings."

"Are big weddings your thing?" he asked.

Was it his imagination or had she gone pale beneath her warm complexion?

"Definitely not," she said. "I don't think I'll ever marry."

"Really? Why?"

"My job," she said. "I'm on the road a lot and most men expect their wives to be home for dinner by five."

"You need to meet new men."

Her expression was inscrutable. Nik worried that he'd upset her. Those worries broke like clouds when his phone rang and she reached out and placed her palm over the screen. "Thought you were all mine."

Nik instinctively took her hand in his. At the airport, her pulse was racing and she looked out of sorts. Now she was calm, cool and playful. He wanted to believe that he'd done that for her—even though he'd driven her into a ditch.

"I fed you," he said. "What more do you want?"

She withdrew her hand. Nik wouldn't let her get away so easily. "Come on," he said. "I'm listening. Just tell me."

The most devious smile tugged at her lips. Nik resigned himself. There was no use fighting this thing growing inside him. He liked what he liked, and he liked her.

This time he had no trouble ignoring the ringing phone, but just like last time, it drove Sasha crazy. "Answer it!"

Nik took the call. It was the tow truck driver, confirming their location.

"We don't have long," he said, when he got off the phone. "The driver is twenty minutes away."

"That's a shame," she said. "It's so beautiful here."

"Did you want to stick around and take a tour?" he asked.

"Oh, no," she said. "Ari will worry if I don't make it to Royal by tonight. She's got a whole evening planned. Maybe we could come back sometime."

"Maybe," he said, even though he was thinking, *Definitely*.

She reached for her camera bag on the bench next to her. "Do you mind if I take a few photos? I want to remember this place."

"Please. Go ahead."

Hillside Smokehouse was located in a converted barn set in a field with no hills in sight. It looked like something out of a postcard and he could understand why Sasha would want to photograph it. When she pointed the camera lens at him, he was confused.

"Don't move," she said. "I don't want to forget you, either."

Five

The instant she pressed the shutter button, Sasha knew she could fall for this man. Not only was he strong, he was lovely and attentive. No one had asked how she felt about the big, fat Royal wedding. They only expected her to show up with a positive attitude, lines memorized, ready to play her supporting role. No one had suspected the fresh bout of anxiety it induced, but he had tactfully changed the subject. Sasha had discerned something in him then, something rare and precious. She wanted more of him, not less.

She hadn't come to Royal looking to get involved with anyone. Maybe he could be her date for the wedding. She hadn't thought she needed one. As the maid of honor, she was sure to keep be kept busy. The word *maybe* fluttered about her stomach like a caught butterfly, eager to fly free. Should she ask him? No! Hell, no! Not yet, anyway. She was jumping way ahead of herself. Was he even single? The jury was out on that, even though he was a Grade A flirt. And what was she to make of that text message from Krystal... *You like the wild ones...* That could be interpreted in a hundred ways. How artfully he'd dodged her question with that quip about wild cats! It was cute, but she wasn't fooled.

But what if he were single? What if Krystal was a horse breeder or something? It was possible. They were in Texas, after all. Either way, it didn't matter. That was the beauty of a quick fling. She'd be on a plane to San Francisco in a few short weeks, which meant their emotional baggage could stay locked in storage.

He'd left to take care of the car. She took a few photos of the restaurant and chatted with Donna for a bit. She got the history of the place and even a sneak peek at the kitchen. Donna let her take a few pictures, walked her through the process of smoking meat, and gifted her a jar of barbecue sauce. By the time Nik got back, Sasha had enough for a blog post. She'd pitch the story to a magazine or local publication.

"Packed up and ready," Nik said. "Also, it looks like rain. We should get going."

They thanked Donna and said their goodbyes. Just when they stepped off the porch, a fat raindrop fell onto the tip of her nose. Nik had parked the car in the restaurant's lot, but it was still some distance away. He reached for her hand and together they made a run for it. Sasha shrieked all the way.

They were panting when they made it to the SUV, shrieking and laughing, too. He unlocked the doors and they climbed in.

Earlier, Sasha had slipped on her sweatshirt and only had to take it off. The tank top she wore underneath was dry. Nik was not so lucky. He swore under his breath and yanked his wet T-shirt over his head. "Sorry," he mumbled. "Hope you don't mind."

Not unless he minded her watching.

Rain tapped on the roof and rushed down the windshield, blurring the world. All she saw was smooth brown skin, the cut of his muscles, the lines and grooves that all pointed downward.

The T-shirt came off faster than she'd expected and Sasha was caught staring.

Damn it.

Once again in only a few short hours, Nik questioned her with a raised brow. She turned away.

He reached for a bag in the back seat, pulled out a fresh T-shirt and slipped it on. "The answer is yes," he said.

"I don't know what you mean," Sasha said. "What's the question?"

"The one question you've been asking in a hundred little ways."

"In that case, I have a follow-up question. Who's Krystal?"

His soft laugh rippled down her spine. "My bossy, overbearing, older cousin."

Sasha tore her gaze away from the water-stained glass. His brown eyes were alive, swirling with heat and want. That heat radiated through the car, fogged the windows and walled them in. Sasha's pulse kicked up again. She just couldn't stand it a second longer. She reached for him, grabbing fistfuls of the soft cotton tee, and drew him to her. She raised her lips to his and whispered, "That's all I wanted to know."

"You," he said, his voice gritty.

"Kiss me."

He kissed her hard then withdrew, panting, and cupped her face. "If you distract me again and we drive into a ditch again it'll be your fault, Sasha."

"I'm not worried," she said. "It feels like I'm in good hands."

A strong knock on the car window jolted them apart. The rain had thinned to a drizzle and the world sharpened into focus. Donna stood under an umbrella outside her door. She cradled a jar of barbecue sauce. Sasha took a second to compose herself and lowered the window.

"You forgot this!" Donna cried.

"Thanks!" Sasha said. "I would have cried myself to sleep."

"I doubt it," Donna said with a cheeky little grin. "Drive safe, y'all!"

Four and a half hours later, Nik delivered Sasha to her sister's door. Actually, he delivered her to the lobby of the downtown high-rise where she and her fiancé had taken up residence. Rumpled and disheveled, they looked out of place in the sleek interior, but he didn't care. When he was with Sasha, everyone and everything faded. Nothing mattered.

He offered to take her luggage up, but a porter rushed forward and took care of it. Nik felt crazy territorial, as if the younger guy had stolen his job.

The porter called an elevator. Sasha turned to him with a lopsided smile.

"Thank you," she said. "You delivered me safe and sound. The wedding committee will appreciate it, I'm sure."

There was nothing left to do but say goodbye.

On the drive, they'd talked about everything, from favorite movies to ice cream flavors, but they hadn't discussed what would come next.

"I'd like to see you again," he said, shyness creeping into his voice. "Can I get your number?"

Relief transformed her, erasing worry lines he hadn't noticed before. Nik couldn't believe it. Hadn't he made his feelings clear?

Sasha went through her bag and produced a business card. "That's my number. My email, too, should you need it. Really, just text me."

The card read: Sasha A. Ramos, Photojournalist.

Nik pocketed it. "I'll text you so you'll have my number."

"Okay."

The elevator doors slid open. The porter rolled in the trolley. After following him in, she whirled around and blurted, "Ariana sent Xavier away a few days so we could have some sister time. When he gets back, I'm moving to a hotel near the wedding venue. I'll have a lot more time then."

She either couldn't or didn't care to hide her eagerness. "Alright," he said. "And thank you, too."

She stopped the sliding doors with a firm hand. "For what?"

The elevator sensors chimed. The porter said, "Ma'am." Sasha withdrew her hand. A shadow of regret clouded her expression as the doors slowly slid shut.

He'd promised her the moon, but she'd managed to capture the sun and put it in his pocket. And for that he was grateful.

Ariana flung open the door. "Sasha! Finally!"

Sasha was immediately enveloped in a perfumed hug. The feathered trim of her sister's silk pajamas tickled her nose. "Where have you been? Did you get my calls? Why didn't you return them?"

"It's a long story, Ari," Sasha replied with a heavy sigh.

"Poor little sister, what have you been through?"

"The plane lost fuel. We made an emergency landing six hours away."

"How did you get here? You took a bus?"

A bus? Why hadn't she thought of that? Carjacking an unsuspecting marketing executive from Miami seemed like the most reasonable option at the time.

"If it happens again, *please* make an effort to reach me," Ari said. "I was worried."

Ariana's embrace tightened. Sasha let herself be hugged and loved. When she closed her eyes, she could only think of Nik and the look he'd given her just as the elevator doors walled him out. Those brown eyes were so warm with feeling.

"I want to hear all about it." Ari yanked her inside, but urged her to take off her shoes before going any further. "No offense. You look...grimy."

Sasha stepped out of her sneakers. "None taken."

Compared to her sister, she probably looked like she'd crawled out from under a bridge. Ari looked immaculate. A trained actress, she was most at home on movie sets and had a flair for elaborate costumes. With her cropped hair, golden-brown skin and shapely figure, she was comfortable in the role of the rising star poised to marry an American literary icon.

"I'll give you the grand tour later," Ariana said. "This is the main room. It's comfy."

Not the word Sasha would have used. The furnished apartment her sister rented with Xavier for a couple of months before the wedding was minimal and modern. Floor-to-ceiling windows opened the space to a sweeping view. The low furniture took nothing away from it. Large mirrors and crystal vases added extra sparkle and shimmer. This was home for the next few days, until Xavier returned from a fishing trip with his cousin Tripp. Sasha had every intention of enjoying it, like a free spa getaway.

Her sister took her by the hand. "Let's go to your room."

The bedroom was small. The four-poster bed was not. Sasha couldn't wait to dive in. "Take a long, hot shower," Ari said. "The bathroom is to your right. You'll find a robe on the hook behind the door. Slippers are in the closet."

"Great. Thanks."

"Ice cream?"

"Uh...yes, please!"

Dessert before dinner was their way of acting out a childhood fantasy. Growing up, their mother would not let them so much as bite into a chocolate chip cookie before a meal. To this day, the ultimate act of rebellion was to scarf down cake, flan or ice cream before dinner.

Ari squealed. "Go shower, and I'll set up the sundae bar!"

"Yay!"

The long hot shower revived Sasha. She slipped on a plush robe. She found a pair of fuzzy slippers in the generous closet that housed Ari's designer luggage set. She couldn't believe her big sister was still encroaching on her closet space, and not just for accessories. A picture collage on poster board rested against the closet wall. Sasha picked it up and studied it. Cutouts from various bridal magazines painted a picture of a classic old Hollywood glamor wedding.

"That's my original vision board. I forgot it there."

Sasha jumped at the sound of Ari's voice. She'd entered the room without her noticing.

"It's beautiful."

Ari took the board from her. "We kept the color palette. Only we've added touches of blue. The bluebonnet is the Texas state flower. You won't believe the trouble we went through to find accessories to match just right. It's all in the details."

Sasha stepped into the slippers. "You can plan every detail and things still fall apart."

"What did you say?"

Sasha had muttered the words under her breath. Judging by the look on Ari's face, she'd caught every single one.

"Sorry," she said. "I hate weddings. You know that."

Ari looked aggrieved, as if Sasha had declared she hated kittens.

"You don't *hate* weddings," Ari asserted. "You're far too sweet and tenderhearted for that. You're still haunted by your canceled wedding, that's all."

Sasha let out a caustic laugh. "Is that all?"

"You were smart enough to back out of a marriage that would've ended in disaster," Ari said. "Now you're free to find the true love of your life. It's really not that complicated."

"Aren't you even a little scared?" Sasha asked, her voice shaky.

"Of what?" Ari raised a finger. "Don't you dare say that word."

The word exploded from Sasha's chest. "THE CURSE!"

"For the love of God, Sasha!" Ari grabbed her by the sleeve of her robe and dragged her to the bed. They sat side by side, shoulders touching. "There's no curse. No evil witch hexed us. We are *not* the Witches of San Bernardino Valley."

"What about Mom? And Grandma? How do you explain what happened to them?"

Ari's eyes skidded away. Sasha knew she was being unfair. Now wasn't the time to rehash all of this. If only her sister didn't insist on minimizing her experience to a soap opera plot point. There was nothing uncomplicated about a generational curse. Three generations of runaway brides... it boggled the mind.

"Okay," Ari said. "I hear you. It happens a lot in our family, but it ends now. I am not backing out of this wedding. You don't have to worry about that. Xavier is the love of my life."

The love of her life... Sasha wondered how it would feel to love like that, to be so sure, to leap forward and never look back.

"Nothing short of a typhoon could stop me from marrying him." Ari went on with her rant. "And, on the off chance I am visited by the curse, it's your role as the maid of honor to set me straight. Remind me that on the other side of 'I do' my whole life is waiting with that wonderful man."

"Fine!" Sasha cried, eager to drop the topic. "Can we still be witches, though?"

"Sure. Why not?" Ari said with a laugh. "So long as our witchcraft doesn't interfere with my wedding."

Sasha dropped her head on Ari's shoulder. "You're going to be the most beautiful bride Royal has ever seen."

"Damn right!" she cried. "Now let's go eat ice cream!"

Curled up on the couch with bowls of ice cream drowning in chocolate syrup, they were girls again, only in premium loungewear as opposed to matching pajamas sets. Sasha indulged Ari, and let her carry on about the wedding plans, starting with the venue down to the cake and flowers. When they exhausted the topic, they moved on to gossip. Ari's best friend, Dee, who'd flown to Texas ahead of time to lay the groundwork when Ari was stuck filming on location, had fallen for Xavier's cousin, a guy named Tripp.

"Love is in the air!" Ari proclaimed.

"In that case, I'm going to double-mask," Sasha quipped.

"Don't be a grump," Ari said. "When you're ready, you'll find love."

A phone rang from somewhere in the apartment. Ari sprung from the couch. "That's the doorman," she said. "Probably a delivery. I'm expecting loads of packages."

Sasha licked chocolate sauce off the back of her spoon. "You're going to have to find somewhere other than my closet to stash them all."

"You're too pretty to be petty!" Ari sang on her way to answer the phone.

She was back in a flash, eager to get on with her story. "In the beginning, Dee was all… *I don't have time for love. I'm focused on work.* You know how that goes." She mimicked her friend's tone and mannerisms so well Sasha couldn't help but laugh. "Now she's head over heels in love. There's just something about these country boys, you know?"

"With all due respect," Sasha said. "Royal doesn't qualify as 'the country.' Just look at where we are."

"Tripp is a rancher," Ari said. "He makes his living off the land."

"A rancher?" Sasha said. "Is that a real thing?"

Ari pinched her cheek. "Yes, sweetie, it is," she said. "And careful what you say in these parts."

The doorbell rang. Ari sprung off the couch once again. Sasha went to the kitchen and added another scoop of ice cream to her bowl. She desperately needed comfort food.

From the door, she heard Ari cry. "Nik Williams! What are you doing here? This is a surprise. I thought you were the delivery guy."

Sasha dropped her spoon. Nik?

"I have something for Sasha," he said evenly. "I told your doorman I had a delivery."

"How do you know Sasha? Are you friends?"

Ari's voice had stiffened with protectiveness. It was a tone Sasha knew all too well. The overbearing older sister was flexing her strength. She set down her bowl and rushed out to rescue him.

He stood outside the door, keeping a respectful distance. However, he towered over Ariana and was easily able to scan the interior until his molten brown eyes rested on her. Sasha shivered. The memory of their kiss rushed back to her, nearly bowled her over. How could she have tucked it away? The way he'd touched her, tasted her, tangled his fingers in her hair. She nearly cried; it felt so good.

"Let him in," she said.

Ariana turned to face her. "How do you know him? You just got here. *I* barely know him."

Sasha narrowed her eyes at her sister. "You're being very rude."

"I don't mean to be. I'm just confused," Ari said.

"Ariana!" Sasha snapped. "Who died and made you mom? Let the man in."

When Sasha entered junior high and the neighborhood boys started coming around, Ariana had taken it upon herself to protect her virtue. It wasn't cute then, and it wasn't cute now.

Ari moved out of the way. "Please come in."

Nik stepped into the entryway and the whole room filled with warmth. "I'm sorry for interrupting your night."

"Never mind that," Ari said. "You're welcome to stay. Would you like some ice cream?"

"No, thank you," he said.

He was so polite and polished; Sasha wanted to ruffle him up. "You have something for me?"

"I have your phone."

That simple statement triggered Ariana once again. "You lost your phone and didn't notice?"

"Apparently so," Sasha said.

Normally, she was glued to her phone, texting, responding to email inquiries, or updating her portfolio on three social media sites. The fact that she'd gone this long without noticing was a miracle.

He handed over the phone. "I found it on the floor of the car."

Ariana was well on her way to the kitchen when that last bit caught her attention. "What car? I thought you took the bus."

Nik cut Sasha a glance. Sasha took a breath. "I never said I took the bus. You assumed that I did."

"Oh, yeah?" Ari folded her arms across her chest. "And who let me go right on assuming?"

"I should go," Nik said.

This time, Sasha blocked his exit. "Don't go. Stay for dinner."

Unlike her, Nik hadn't enjoyed the luxury of a shower and a change of clothes. He wore the same rumpled T-shirt that she'd come so close to ripping off at the Hillside Smokehouse parking lot. He had to be exhausted from the drive. In the end, she hadn't been much help.

"Dinner?" he said. "Don't you mean dessert?"

Sasha's mind wandered. Yes, she meant dessert. Stay for the most delicious dessert.

"She means dinner," Ari cut in. "Don't let the ice cream fool you. That's just our weird sister thing. We've got *plenty* of food. I ordered tacos, all kinds. What are your preferences?"

"He eats everything," Sasha said.

Ari went silent for the first time that evening, taking in Sasha with a steady gaze. *"Vamos a la cocina."*

Great! Now she was being summoned to the kitchen. *"Porque? No hace falta."*

Nik cleared his throat. "Full disclosure: I speak a little Spanish."

He was from South Florida. There was a chance his Spanish was better than theirs. Ariana and Sasha were multiethnic and racial. Their father was half-Mexican and spoke mostly English at home.

Sasha smiled up at him. "Is there anything you can't do?"

Nik stifled a laugh, a shy smile spreading across his lips. Sasha wished they were alone.

Ariana granted that wish. She stomped into the kitchen, granting them a moment of privacy. Sasha watched her go. "You'll like her once you get to know her. She's going through some weird overprotective sister phase."

"I don't think she likes me," Nik said.

"You'll just have to charm her, like you charmed me."

Nik crossed the distance between them in two strides. "Is that what I did?"

"You know exactly what you did."

He pulled her to him by the tie of her robe and brushed a kiss to her temple. His breath fanned her cheek. Sasha closed her eyes and let the feeling take her. "Stay," she whispered into his neck. "Don't go just yet. Stay and have dinner with me and my oddball of a sister."

His grip tightened on the knot of her robe. "I can't. I'm behind on so many things."

Sasha tossed her head back and searched for his eyes. "Because of me?"

"Let's blame the deer," he said.

"Fair enough."

A clamor from the kitchen broke them apart. Sasha adjusted the flap of her robe. "Thanks for returning my phone. I would have noticed it was missing eventually."

"I was halfway across town when I sent you my number, and it started buzzing."

Ariana poked her head out of the kitchen. "Nik, will you have beer or wine?"

"I have to pass," he said, politely.

"Are you sure?" Ari asked. "Xavier bought a case at a local brewery. He says it's the best he's ever had."

"No doubt it is," Nik replied. "May I take a raincheck?"

"Absolutely. You put up with my bratty sister and brought her home safe," Ari said. "I owe you one."

"That was my pleasure," Nik said.

Ariana returned to the kitchen. Sasha could not hold back her smile. "You charmer," she said, and led him to the couch.

Six

Ariana pounced just as soon as Nik walked out the door. "I want the whole story and don't leave out a thing. Start talking."

Sasha loaded the dishwasher to keep busy and play for time. She had to be as forthcoming as possible, all the while withholding some crucial details. Sasha told her sister the story of how she and Nik had met on the plane and recounted his bravery in the face of danger. She peppered in anecdotes of their impromptu road trip, leaving out the accident, the parking lot kiss and the way he made her shiver just by whispering her name.

"Let's recap," Ari said. "He's handsome, smart, kind, heroic *and* trustworthy."

"He's all those things." Sasha rinsed a handful of utensils and shoved them in the basket. "What are you getting at? Don't you like him?"

It hurt her to her core that her sister, or anyone really, might not see how awesome Nik was.

"I like him fine!" Ari exclaimed. "I liked him well before you showed up. Nexus took over the company that handles Ex's book marketing. He was very impressed with them."

Nexus had a nice ring to it. Sasha would get him to talk more about his work when she saw him next. Right now, she focused on her sister.

"Did you have to be so rude to him?" Sasha demanded.

"Didn't mean to be," Ari said, contrite. "I've lived in Hollywood for too long. Protecting my privacy is key."

Sasha scoffed. "He's not paparazzi!"

"I'll send him a case of beer or a bottle of scotch," Ari said. "Or better yet, let's all go out to dinner when Ex returns. He's a member of the Texas Cattleman's Club. We'll go there—or somewhere else, someplace nice."

Sasha grunted her approval and went back to rinsing dishes.

Ariana folded her hands on the kitchen counter. "Oh my… This is more complicated than I thought."

"Complicated how?" Sasha asked. In her view, there was nothing complicated about the way she and Nik had come together. It was easy and fun.

"You like him," Ari said.

Sasha rinsed their wine glasses. "What's not to like?"

"No…. I mean, you *like* him."

"Sure," she conceded. "Obviously."

"He likes you, too. I can tell."

"I hope so."

"Where do you see things going?" Ari asked.

Sasha dismissed the question with a laugh. "Going? We just met today!"

Ariana jutted her chin, defiant. "I knew how I felt about Xavier the day we met."

"We're not all as brilliant as you," Sasha quipped. "Some of us are a little slow."

"You're the sharpest person I know," Ari said. "You have a plan for everything. I'm sure you've charted the course of this budding relationship."

"There's no course to chart!" Sasha shut the dishwasher door with far more force than the task needed. "I'll be gone in a few weeks."

"Aha!" Ari cried. "I knew it!"

"Knew what?"

"You're doing it again."

"I don't know what you're talking about."

Ari's eyes narrowed. "I think you do."

Suddenly frightened, Sasha left the kitchen for her bedroom. Ariana hounded her all the way. Sasha threw herself onto her bed. Ariana did the same.

"There's no getting rid of you, is there?" Sasha wailed.

"Nope! We're going to have this conversation, like it or not," Ari said. "You made me your accountability partner for a reason."

"When did I do that?" Sasha asked.

"The night you called me—in tears—with the list of your therapist's recommendations."

Damn it! In a rare moment of candor, she'd called her sister and confided about the issues that had pushed her to seek therapy. Her therapist had some ideas as to why Sasha's love life had grown stagnant. If she wasn't in a committed relationship, there was no risk of being looped into marriage. By restricting her dating pool to emotionally unavailable men, she'd eliminated the risk of ever enduring a marriage proposal that she would likely turn down. It was a foolproof plan. Only years and years of this had left her depleted and numb. That night, on the call to her sister, she'd tearfully admitted to feeling lonely.

"Nik is nothing like the guys I've dated," Sasha said.

There was no shortage of tech bros and finance bros in the bay area. Nik had nothing in common with them. He was decent, generous and considerate. He wasn't a "bro" of any kind. He was a man.

"What does it matter what kind of guy he is if you plan to write him off after the wedding."

"He might be okay with it, Ari," Sasha said. "Have you considered that? He's here on business and may not have the time to—"

"You're proving my point," Ari said. "If he's not open to a relationship, and you know this going in, how is this any different from your past relationships? Wasn't the point to break the cycle?"

Sasha sat up and drew her knees to her chest. Ariana was aggravating, irritating, but she was also right. Under normal circumstances, a fling with a handsome stranger at her sister's wedding was no big deal. Her circumstances were far from normal. She'd enrolled in therapy to deal with the aftermath of ending her engagement and being labeled a runaway bride. She had been dealing with her issues in an open and honest way, going so far as to asking her sister to hold her accountable. Once she'd touched ground in Texas, all of that flew out the window. She was willing to toss out the progress she'd made for Nik's easy smile.

Ari tugged on one of her braids. "With all my heart, I want you to be happy, Sasha."

"I *am* happy," Sasha insisted. "You don't have to worry about that. I'm doing great. I love my job. Did you see last month's spread in *New Day*? That was pretty epic."

"It was epic, and I'm proud of you," Ari said. "I'm just as proud of the work you've done to turn your life around. Promise me you won't flush it down the toilet."

Heart sinking, Sasha turned to her brilliant big sister and said, "I promise."

Sasha couldn't sleep that night. She got out of bed and found her therapy journal. She read the first entry.

Dream I

My grandmother's lace veil cascades down the back of my gown. The chapel is full. He waits at the altar. I take a few steps toward him, gripping my bouquet so hard the flower stems crack. Someone bangs out "The Bridal Chorus" on an organ. The groundswell of music carries me along. Step by step, I make it halfway down the aisle, but no further. My feet sink into the red carpet. Panicked, I look around for help. The wedding guests are strangers. I don't recognize a single one. Panicked, I seek the eyes of the man I'm going to marry and devote my life to. His face is a blur.

My instincts tell me to run, and I do.

Organ music, the swish of taffeta and the cries of the assembly combine in one horrible sound. I push past the ushers, out the chapel doors, and stumble down the steps. Outside all is peaceful. The air is fresh and I can breathe freely. I toss the crumbled bouquet and march down the road.

Dream II

It's a scene straight out of a noir film. I'm in a phone booth, the kind that doesn't exist anymore, weeping into the phone. I tell him that I can't go through with it. The life that he wants is nothing like the one I envisioned for myself. I fear that if I marry him, I'll lose me. I apologize over and over again. His voice comes out loud and clear through the phone line. He is angry and hurt. He should've known better than to trust a woman like me.

"What does that mean?" I say.

The line goes dead.

The second dream was closer to the truth.

Sasha was engaged to a hedge fund manager named Terrence Rhodes. Looking back, she barely recognized the girl who'd said yes to a lifetime of sameness. They met in college. He was the clever one, she the moody artist. They went out on a few dates and just kept on dating. After a few months, their circle of friends had labeled them a couple. Sasha didn't mind so much. Although her feelings for Terrance were lukewarm at best, it beat vying for the attention of the frat bros and jocks. She'd never envisioned a future with him and just assumed they'd part ways after graduation. Instead, they stayed together through graduate school. Terrence went on to business school and Sasha earned her MFA. There was nothing wrong with their relationship, but there was nothing right with it, either. They were an image in muted sepia tones, and Sasha craved color. Just when she started to feel restless and mere weeks after sharing her feelings with Terrence, he went ahead and staged a proposal at a party in front of all their friends. What was she to do? Turn him down in front of everyone?

They postponed the wedding for two years to focus on their careers. Terrence's career in finance took off. Hers putted along, which was expected in her field. Soon, Terrence floated the idea that Sasha quit working altogether after. "No one is saying you can't take photos. Set up a blog or whatever. Soon enough we'll have kids and you won't be able to travel as much if at all."

Set up a blog or whatever... Those words lived rent-free in her soul.

It was the beginning of the end. The wedding plans marched forward as Sasha fell back, retreating into a cave of doubts. It wasn't until the day before the wedding—hours before the rehearsal dinner—that she unraveled before her mother, sister and future in-laws. Sasha slumped down to the floor in a pink tulle dress and burst into tears, proving once and for all that Ariana wasn't the only drama queen in the family.

Terrence walked in and took in the scene. The look he gave her continued to haunt Sasha's dreams.

Her mother reassured her that everything would be all right. Her grandmother stroked her back and muttered, "It's like we're cursed."

Sasha put away the journal and checked her phone for the time. There were two texts from Nik, the one with his number and another one she'd missed.

Sorry I couldn't stay. Would love to meet for a drink when you're free.

Sunshine burst through her cloudy thoughts. Nik made everything better and even though a fling was off the table, no law prohibited them from being friends. She had dinner plans with Ari tomorrow night, but could carve out time for a drink or two. She bit back a smile as she typed a reply.

Tomorrow at 7?

It was close to midnight. She didn't expect to hear back until the morning. However, Nik's response came lightning fast. It's a date.

Seven

"It's not a date," she announced, the moment she arrived.

Nik was waiting at the bar of The Silver Saddle, thumbing through messages on his phone while keeping an eye on the door. For a guy who came up in the school of "time is money," sitting idle like this wasn't his style. Yet here he was, and he didn't even mind. He was just so eager to see her again. And here she was, looking exquisite in a black slip dress that skimmed her body and her braids loose on her back.

After spending all of yesterday with Sasha, Nik found the hours apart dragged on. Nik knew her sister would keep her busy and hadn't expected to see her for days. The open invitation for drinks was just to cover his bases. He had finally gotten around to take a shower when her reply came through. His phone got drenched while he typed out his answer. Even if the thing had fizzled and died, it would have been worth it to learn that Sasha was as eager as he was to meet again.

The hostess pointed in his direction and she glided over, eyeliner-rimmed eyes locked on him. Nik rose to attention. He'd seen her in casual clothes and he'd seen her in a bathrobe; this was a different, dangerous woman. And then she said the words: "This is not a date. Got that? We can only be friends."

"Sasha," he said. "Why don't you have a drink before you decide our future."

"Fine."

She eased onto a barstool and perused the cocktail menu, trying and failing to appear calm.

"What's good here?" she asked.

"The Silver Moon," Nik replied. "It's their signature margarita. Fair warning, it's spicy."

She slid him a glance. "I can handle spicy," she said. "I'm not scared."

"Really?" Then what was leaping like a flame in her eyes if not fear?

Nik signaled the bartender and placed the order. "For how long do I have you?"

Her shoulders drooped. "I'm meeting Ariana for dinner at eight."

That sounded about right. He was no expert, but a non-date date had a cap of sixty minutes. "Let's talk."

She crossed her arms and folded within herself. Where was the wild-hearted woman who'd kissed him in a parked car under the pouring rain?

"I like you," she said quietly.

"I like you, too," he said.

"And I know I might've given you mixed signals—"

"Never mind that," he said.

"I'm only here for a few weeks," she said. "Half that time I'll be busy with wedding stuff. What's the point of starting anything?"

The point was to feel the way they'd felt alone in a rental car with the rain crashing around them. Reigniting that flame *was* the point. She had to know that.

"Before you call me flighty, please know that I've given this a lot of thought."

"I wouldn't call you that," he said. "You can change your mind anytime."

Their cocktails arrived. Sasha sought refuge in hers.

Nik watched her and wondered what had changed since last night.

"Hey, Nik!"

A familiar voice called out his name. It was Oliver, and his new girlfriend Jessica. Nik made the introductions. "Jessica, Oliver, this is Sasha Ramos."

The couple exchanged knowing looks. Nik cleared his throat and continued. "Sasha is a talented photojournalist. Her latest work was featured in *New Day*. She's also Ariana Ramos's sister."

"Wait…" Sasha said. "How do you know about the *New Day* feature?"

"It's this thing called Google," Nik replied.

He wasn't going to hide the fact that he'd searched for her work and combed through her online portfolio. She was extremely talented.

"You didn't tell me," she said.

"I didn't have a chance."

"You guys are so cute," Jessica said "How do you two know each other? Are you old friends?"

"New friends," Nik said, as casually as he could. "Sasha is here for the wedding, as you might've guessed. I've offered to show her around, that's all."

Sasha stiffened at his side. Still, she offered Oliver and Jessica a wide smile.

"We met on the plane to Royal."

It was such a deceptively simple explanation, erasing everything they'd been through together.

"Where were you traveling from?" Jessica asked.

"Georgia. I was there on business," Sasha replied. "Oliver, you must be the business partner I've heard so much about."

Oliver let out a stiff laugh. "Depends. What did you hear?"

"Very little," Sasha admitted. "But only good things."

"So, what are you guys up to?" Nik asked in an effort to move things along. He had nothing but love for Oliver, but he didn't have much time with Sasha. The way things were going, who knew if she'd agree to see him again?

"It's date night," Jessica said.

Oliver and Jessica had come a long way, from fake dating (a long story) to established date nights. That was a leap, and yet they'd made it.

"Hey," Oliver said. "Have you heard anything from Mad Dash?"

Mad Dash was a fast-growing store-to-door delivery service seeking to expand in Texas. Their efforts to get a meeting with the CEO were going nowhere.

"Not a word," Nik said.

"God. It's like they're freezing us out."

Jessica stepped between them. "Sasha, these two will talk business all night if we let them."

Sasha laughed. "What should we do? Tackle them?"

It didn't come to that. The hostess arrived and announced their table was ready. Oliver slid an arm around Jessica's waist. "Why don't you two join us? Let's make this a double date."

Nik was quick to answer. "This isn't a date, and Sasha has somewhere to be."

Again, he felt her stiffen.

"Some other time," Jessica said.

They took off to enjoy their date while he and Sasha endured a stretch of silence. "They're nice people," she said, finally.

"They're the best."

A moment later, she checked her phone. "We should go."

Nik settled the tab without argument. "Where are you meeting Ariana?" he said. "I'll take you."

She grabbed him by the arm and steered him out of the restaurant. "I'm not meeting Ariana. She just canceled. A Zoom meeting with her team is running long."

"Want me to take you home?"

She didn't answer, and he took her silence to mean yes. Disappointment drilled through him. Outside it looked like rain yet again. "Wait here," he said. "I'll get my car."

"Stop!"

Nik stopped cold. "Sasha?"

She stood with her arms at her side, palms open. The doorman, the hostess and even a couple who'd exited right after them, tossed quizzical looks her way. She went to him and spoke in a hushed, urgent tone, as fine needles of raindrops wisped past her face.

"I don't want to go home," she said in a hushed voice.

Nik couldn't help it. He cupped her face and brushed a drop of rain off her cheek with the pad of his thumb. "Tell me what you want."

"I'm starving," she said. "I want dinner, and I don't want to be just friends, not really. It's just that things are murky right now."

The ache of disappointment dulled. He took the first deep breath in a while. "Sasha, one thing at a time. If you're hungry and want to stay, we'll stay."

"No," she said, firmly. "Take me somewhere quiet. We still need to talk."

"Okay," he said. "All you had to do was ask."

Eight

Nik brought her to Royal Diner, breakfast for dinner. They sat at a cozy booth with stacks of pancakes and butter melting on toast. For dessert, they had a choice of cherry or apple pie. The aroma of coffee clung to the air. It was the perfect spot. Sasha felt safe, supported and…still a little out of sorts.

Sasha respected Nik and believed she owed him the truth. On the other hand, she worried he'd see her differently, wouldn't like her as much. It wasn't an irrational fear. Years ago, the truth had cost her most of her friends. To this day, she had very few.

"Look," she said. "I know it's a lot to spring on you. We literally met yesterday."

Nik cut into his pancakes. "Sasha, stop thinking so much. Tell me what's bothering you."

The words were right there, stuck in her throat that had gone dry just watching him handle his utensils. He had beautiful hands. Her gaze drifted to his face. His brows were slightly drawn and his jaw was tight. She'd done that to him.

She'd stressed him out with her "Let's be friends" speech, and immediately regretted it.

His eyes cut to her face. "Sasha, just talk to me."

She picked up her fork and twirled it. There was no other way to go about it except to jump right in. "I'm in therapy."

"That's interesting," he said. "I'm in therapy, too."

She dropped the fork. "You are?"

"No, not really," he conceded. "My therapist is my cousin. Most of our therapy sessions occur over margaritas."

Did happy hour with his cousin count as therapy? Wait... "Your cousin Krystal?"

Something moved behind his eyes. "Dr. Krystal Ann Williams," he said. "She provides counseling for athletes."

Sasha's therapist was a licensed professional who specialized in trauma with whom she met biweekly via live chat, and not a bar. But who was she to judge? To each their own.

"What do you talk to her about?"

"Let's focus on you."

It was too late for that. Curiosity was nibbling at her everywhere. He was so self-possessed. She couldn't imagine anything unraveling him. "I need to know, Nik. Tell me your demons."

"Alright," he said. "I'm invited to your sister's wedding."

That explained nothing. "Pretty sure most of Royal is."

"I don't have a date, and that's fine," he said. "Krystal pointed out, over margaritas, that my relationships don't stand the test of time."

"Because you like the *wild* ones."

"*I* like the wild ones."

He looked her dead in the eyes, sending a shiver racing down her spine.

If he thought she fell into that category, he was in for bitter disappointment. She wasn't the wild girl, or the party girl, or the girl who lived off coffee fumes and crept home at 3:00 a.m. Work-related travel aside, she lived a sedentary life...for a witch.

Sasha slathered even more butter on her toast. "Tell me about these wild women."

A hint of a smile lit up his gorgeous face. "I'm not a lion-tamer, Sasha. The last woman I dated worked in luxury retail. She moved to London for a promotion. She now works at the flagship store. She chased her dream. There's nothing outrageous about that."

"You didn't chase after her?"

"No," he said. "I chase my own dreams."

Those words landed with a thump in her gut. Nik wouldn't chase anyone. If she, or anyone, really, it didn't have to be her, ran away, he'd let them go.

"Last summer, I met Tracie, a forensic accountant. She *was* wild, but she was fun."

Sasha reached for the syrup. "I bet."

"Now tell me your demons, Sasha," he whispered. "I need to know."

"I am what they call a runaway bride," she said easily. When he said her name like that, she'd confess to arson.

He stopped and considered her words. She watched the internal debate play out. "You were engaged before?"

"Yes."

"It didn't work out."

"Accurate."

"You...ran out of the chapel or whatever."

"I called off the wedding the night before," she said. "There was no dramatic music."

"You changed your mind."

"Yes, but it's not as simple as that."

He dunked a forkful of pancakes into a shallow puddle of syrup. Sasha couldn't touch her food. Her appetite was gone.

"Did you love him?" he asked.

"Not enough, apparently," she replied. "I was twenty-five, and wanted to chase my own dreams, too."

"Everyone deserves the chance," he said. "Do you feel guilty about that?"

There was plenty to feel guilty about. She'd hurt Terrence, humiliated his family, disappointed her friends, and had a hand in perpetuating a family curse.

"It's not as simple as that, Nik."

"You keep saying that, but I don't see it," he said. "Twenty-five is young. Most people aren't ready for marriage. You're allowed to change your mind, Sasha. I get the timing wasn't ideal."

"I'm not the first person in my family to have changed my mind. I'm not even the second."

He paused at that. "Really?"

"My mother and grandmother both canceled their engagements."

It was a long story, so she dove right in. She told him how her grandmother had quietly ended her engagement to her neighbor's son. It wasn't a great scandal. She returned the ring and it was never spoken of again. Her grandmother called it a "false start."

With her mother, things didn't go so well. She jilted a handsome young doctor, left him standing at the altar, the sin of sins. The community uproar was deafening. She paid a high price for that act of bravery. Sasha's grandmother understood and supported her decision. At the time, her grandfather could not bear the sting of humiliation. He did not yell or threaten. He gave her the silent treatment, instead. He even went so far as cutting her off financially to "make up for the expenses of the wedding." It became too much for her mother to bear. She fled her small town and relocated to San Bernardino.

"It's a pattern," he said. "Is that why you're in therapy? To understand the pattern."

When he put it that way it sounded so logical. She had to set the record straight. "It's not a pattern, Nik. It's a curse, a family curse."

Nik pushed back his plate. "We need coffee."

Sasha took a bite of toast and waited for Nik to return from the counter with their drinks, certain he would never take her seriously again.

"I have questions," he said.

Sasha expected as much. She wrapped her hands around her coffee mug just to warm her hands. "Go ahead."

"If it's a curse we're talking about, do you need a therapist or some other kind of professional?"

"Nik."

"What about Ariana? Will she go through with this wedding, or are you worried about that?"

"My sister will marry Xavier come hell or high water," Sasha said. "She's the exception that proves the rule."

Nik took a sip of coffee as he tried to puzzle it out. Far from clearing things up, she'd muddied the already murky waters. "You're confused. I shouldn't have said anything."

"I am confused," he said slowly. "I'm wondering what, if anything, this has to do with you and me."

"I…uh…my therapist thinks I've developed an avoidant trait when it comes to relationships. I've been doing the 'no strings attached' thing for a while now as a way of avoiding… See, if you're not anyone's girlfriend, odds are you'll never be anyone's fiancée."

"That's one way to go about it," he said.

"It's tiresome in the long run, holding people at arm's length," she said. "It's lonely."

She'd dated some pretty nice guys. Having always to pretend that she was too busy with work to commit to a relationship, always being the one to disappoint the other, it eroded her heart. She wasn't that person.

"I can see how it would be," Nik said.

"You're big on patterns. My therapist recommends I break the pattern."

Sasha stirred sugar in her coffee, folded her napkin, and wondered aloud if it were time to ask for the check, anything to avoid Nik's eyes.

"What about cherry pie?" he said.

"Did we agree to that?" Sasha asked. "I was leaning toward apple."

"We'll get both."

"Good call." Sasha scanned the sleepy diner for the waitress.

"Sasha, look at me."

She shook her head. "I can't."

"Okay, don't." He rested his hand, palm up, on the table. "Put your hand in mine."

It took a while before she placed her trembling hand in his. His fingers folded around hers. Sasha let out a jagged laugh. "You think I'm ridiculous, don't you?"

"I don't."

"I wouldn't blame you if you did."

"Want to know what I think?"

Sasha finally looked at him. She searched his face for judgment and ridicule and was relieved to find no trace of either.

"I think you've been through some things," he said. "I'm no therapist, but I imagine your sister's wedding is wildly triggering. So, how about we split some pie and be friends?"

Sasha welcomed his words with a smile, even though nothing felt quite right.

Nine

Ariana invaded at dawn. She bolted into the bedroom without so much as a courtesy knock. "Wake up!"

Sasha roused from sleep with a start. "Ari! Seriously?"

"Sorry! You have to see this video."

Sasha groaned and buried her face in a pillow. "It's five o'clock in the morning. Unless someone we love is breaking a world's record of some kind I don't want to see it."

"It's ten thirty," Ariana shot back. "I've done Pilates and made scrambled eggs."

Sasha looked up and around in a stunned stupor? "Ten thirty in the *morning*? How?"

Her sister grabbed a remote control off the bedside table. "It's the blackout drapes. I told you, they're amazing."

With a push of a button, the drapes parted to reveal a splendid midmorning sky. Sasha could only peer at it through the web of interlaced fingers. The pristine light was blinding. "I haven't slept so well in years."

"It's this bed. I told you, it's amazing."

Ari went on about the bedding. Sasha doubted the down-filled pillows or Belgian linen sheets had anything to do with it. Her conversation with Nik last night had left her feeling light and unburdened like never before. That feeling had stayed with her. She hadn't slept so soundly or felt this clearheaded in years.

She stretched and yawned. "Okay, I'm up! What's this video about?"

"A wedding crasher."

"Ari, the wedding is weeks away. A wedding crasher doesn't announce itself."

"Well, this one does," she said stubbornly. "Have you heard of Trick MacArthur?"

"Trick who?"

"He's a professional wedding crasher," Ari replied. "He stalks celebrities and finds out as much as he can about their wedding plans and leaks the information on social media. He's been seen poking around Royal and it's driving my wedding planner crazy."

Sasha couldn't believe it. "You mean to tell me there's a grown man out there crashing weddings just for kicks?"

"Not just any wedding!" Ari exclaimed. "*Celebrity* weddings."

Sasha looked up to the vaulted ceiling. "Excuse me. I misspoke."

"He's not doing it for fun, either," Ari said. "He's doing it for money. His videos consistently go viral." Ari climbed onto the bed and thrust her phone in Sasha's face. "Look what he's posted to his stories this morning!"

A video was cued up. Sasha hit play.

A guy with thick brown hair and friendly eyes grinned and waved hello. "Hey, all! Good morning from Texas!"

All told, he looked harmless enough. Handsome, too.

"I'm at this charming little bakery in Royal, Texas," he went on. "My sources say the Noble-Ramos wedding planner has been spotted ducking in and out of this establishment. Should the couple order their wedding cake from here, I have a few suggestions. According to the head baker, Funfetti is the most popular flavor. Can you imagine Ariana Ramos going for anything as *fun* as that? Me, neither! If it were up to me, I'd go with either chocolate raspberry or chocolate cappuccino. Both are excellent flavors, but then again I got a thing for chocolate. Who knows what the actress will pick in the end. So long as they don't go for plain old vanilla! Signing off now. Don't forget to like, subscribe and all the things."

Sasha hit Pause. Silence settled in the sun-filled bedroom. She turned to Ari, curled up beside her. "You're going with plain old vanilla, aren't you?"

"Xavier's grandmother is allergic to chocolate!" Ari wailed. "We went with a Tahitian vanilla laced with bourbon from a local distillery."

Sasha stifled a laugh. "Sounds delicious."

Ariana grabbed a pillow and curled into a fetal position. "I like funfetti just as much as anyone! How dare he suggest I don't?"

"The audacity!" Sasha chimed.

"Our cake will be covered in bluebonnet flowers made of sugar in honor of Texas!"

"See? Shows what he knows."

"Do you think we should add an extra Funfetti cake... for the kids?"

"No, I don't." Sasha rubbed her sister's back. "And you don't have to justify your choices to this trickster."

"He won't stop at the cake," Ari said. "Nothing is off limits. He leaked photos of Chelsea Carlisle's bridesmaid dresses and revealed her song choice for the father-daughter dance."

"How did he know?" Sasha asked. "Did he hack the DJ's computer?"

"How would I know?" Ari wailed. "He's dangerous!"

"Calm down, Ariana. You're overreacting."

"Easy for you to say! I'm freaking out. Rylee is stressed out."

"Who's Rylee?"

"My wedding planner!" Ari snapped. "She's excellent!"

"Oh, right…" Sasha collected her sister in her arms. "Don't freak out. I can see how this is aggravating. I totally understand."

"What should I do?" Ari asked.

It wasn't every day that your older, wiser and more fabulous sister asked for advice. Sasha was at a loss. "What did Chelsea Carlisle do?"

"Nothing."

"That's probably all you can do," Sasha said. "If you go for a restraining order or anything like that, you'll end up generating more publicity for him."

"That's what Xavier said," Ari said quietly.

"Listen to me," Sasha said. "When did we start caring about what random people think of us? We are the Witches of San Bernardino Valley, remember? We're no strangers to a little wedding drama."

"You're right," Ari said with grim determination. "Our grandmother didn't buckle, our mother faced it head-on, and you thrived."

"I wouldn't go that far," Sasha said, interrupting. "I'm barely holding it together."

"False," her sister said. "You're radiant, confident and successful."

"Ari, I'm in therapy for a reason."

"The reason being that you're self-aware enough to analyze your issues instead of burying them."

"When you put it that way, it doesn't sound so bad."

"You're on the right track, Sasha. Believe in yourself." Ari pulled away from her. "Now tell me the truth. Do you think my cake is boring?"

"Are you kidding?" Sasha said. "If I don't get a sugar bluebonnet on my plate I'm going to have a fit. And Trick can choke on it!"

Ari cuddled closer. "I'm so glad you're finally here. You keep me grounded."

"And you keep me sane," Sasha said. "We'll get through this together."

Ari sniffled. "Hug me tighter."

Sasha laughed. "Whatever you need."

Her sister tugged on one of her braids. "Sorry I skipped out on dinner last night."

"Don't worry about it. It's fine."

"I'll make it up to you. Tonight we're going to a cocktail party at the Cattleman's Club."

"That's how you plan on making it up to me? By dragging me to a cocktail party? You know I hate those things."

"Come on, Sasha. It's for a good cause, and I can't get out of it," Ari pleaded. "We won't stay long. I promise. A half hour tops. Then we'll duck out to the club's wine bar and hang out. It'll be fun."

"You mean, Funfetti?"

"Ha ha!" Ari droned. "What will you wear to the party?"

Sasha responded with a lazy one-shoulder shrug. "A little black dress. I packed a few of those."

Ari frowned. "That won't work."

"Don't be ridiculous. A little black dress always works."

"There's a dress code. We're supposed to wear white."

"Now you're just screwing with me!"

"Didn't you pack a little white dress?" she asked sweetly.

"No, Ariana. I didn't," Sasha said. "Do you know why? I was packing for a wedding. I figured I'd let the bride shine."

"That's so considerate of you, but you didn't have to take it that far! I'll shine no matter what."

"I'm sure," Sasha grumbled.

"Don't worry. I have a white sundress you can borrow. It's super sexy."

"Gee, thanks."

Ariana climbed out of the bed. "Now you really have to get up. I made you breakfast and it's getting cold."

She bolted out the door, leaving Sasha to wonder if the wedding was causing her to unravel. Sasha reached for her phone and saw she had two messages from Nik.

Thank you for last night.

Pancakes never tasted so good.

Sasha wiggled her toes under the fine linen sheets. *This* was how she was meant to start her day. She typed a response.

Therapy has never been so effective.

Had she known that a conversation with a friend was all it took to clear the cobwebs of the past, she would have done it ages ago. Sasha felt unburdened as never before. Then again, no one, besides family, had showed the patience and respect that Nik had last night.

Are you warming up to the idea that therapy doesn't have to happen in a clinical setting?

No, that wasn't it. I'm warming up to you.

Three dots popped up and vanished. Sasha's heart skipped with each second his answer was delayed. She couldn't blame him for being cautious. She was all over the place. One minute she was kissing him in a rental car in the rain. The next she was claiming she only wanted to be friends. *And then* she went and told him that she was cursed. What must he think of her? For his own sake, he should run away screaming.

I want to see you again.

I should give you space, but that's what I want.

While she went on a merry-go-round of madness, he'd sent two clear, concise messages expressing his desires and misgivings. God, this man!

I want to see you, too!

Like now! Like right now!

Do you have plans with Ariana for tonight?

She's dragging me to a cocktail party at a country club.

The three dots of purgatory popped up and vanished once again. And finally, a response: I have something like that on my calendar. Do you have to wear white?

That's the one! Please come.

I'll see what I can do.

Ten

So, this is the world-famous Texas Cattleman's Club... Sasha caught her reflection in one of the gilded mirrors in the club's lobby. In a white fitted halter dress and her braids loose down her bare back, she looked...amazing. Yay for her, but really she was on the lookout for Nik. The mirrors allowed her to go about it as discreetly as possible until they were led out to a terrace overlooking the club's sweeping grounds. She scanned the crowd. Nik wasn't among the beautiful people dressed in white.

"This is fancy," she said to Ariana. "What's this event for again?"

"We're raising awareness for melting polar ice caps."

"Really? Is that what we're doing?"

"*Yes.*"

"Can't you do what I do? Just write a check!"

"It's not enough, Sasha. Sometimes, you have to show up and—"

Ari's speech was cut short. A small crowd gathered and swallowed her up. Everyone wanted to meet the Hollywood

actress poised to join Royal's elite. Some wanted her auto-
graph. Others wanted to pitch ideas. Others, still, solicited
charitable contributions.

Sasha stood to the side, ignored and unnoticed. A waiter
approached. "Champagne, miss?"

"Yes, please." She lifted a flute off the server's tray.

Sasha sipped her champagne and enjoyed the spoils of anonymity. The waiter, however, did not move. "Is there something else?" she asked.

"Mr. Williams requests that you meet him at the bottom
of the stairs in ten minutes, if you can."

Sasha brightened. He deserved a tip for that. "Which
stairs? Where?"

The waiter pointed to the winding staircase, which, according to him, led to the tropical gardens.

"Thanks!" She slipped him a twenty.

Sasha didn't wear a watch. She kept track of the time
on her phone. This was considered rude in most settings,
let alone an elegant cocktail party. There was no way to go
about it without looking bored and disengaged. She must
have caught Ariana's attention because she excused herself
from the crowd and shuffled over to Sasha. "Sorry I've abandoned you."

"No worries!" Sasha said lightly. "Do your thing. It's alright."

"It's *not* alright," Ari said. "Come with me."

She gripped Sasha's arm and drew her to the group. "Have
you met my sister? She's a talented photojournalist. You
might be familiar with her work."

Sasha had no choice but to engage in small talk, even as
a countdown clock was ticking off the seconds in her brain.
In just a few minutes, she'd see Nik again. She answered a
few questions about her work and nodded to show interest in

what the others had to say right up until an imaginary alarm went off in her head. *Okay. That's it. Gotta go.*

Ariana was engaged in a discussion with the non-profit organization's treasurer. This was her chance to slip away. She worked her way through the crowd and, heart pounding, heels clicking on the stone tile, raced down the stairs before anyone or anything could stop her. She spotted him at the bottom of the stairs, his back to her, looking stylish in cool tones of gray. Sasha stopped to catch her breath. If she didn't grip the handrail, she'd swoon.

"Hey you!" she called out.

He turned around and took a step back. "Hey gorgeous!"

"You're not observing the dress code. That's a bold move."

He grinned at her. The fading sun tinged his brown skin gold. "Sorry. I don't own white trousers and didn't have time to shop for a pair."

"Is that why you're not coming up?"

"I don't think they'll miss me." He held up a picnic basket. "I tipped a waiter and look what I got. Party of two?"

She rushed down the few remaining steps and into his arms. "Take me away."

He brushed her braids off her shoulder. "I hate to steal you away from your sister. You're here to spend time with her."

But I want to spend time with you.

She slipped her hand in his and tugged him down the brick garden path. "Are you kidding? Ariana has been driving me crazy."

"Is it the wedding?" he asked.

"This time it's a wedding *crasher.*"

"What?"

"I'll send you one of his videos," Sasha said. "He's real funny, actually. Just wish he wasn't targeting my sister."

They came across a fountain surrounded by trees. "This'll do," Nik said.

He spread a blanket on a patch of grass. Sasha stretched out on her side and watched him unpack a chilled bottle of sparkling wine and the assortment of appetizers that the catering staff were offering on trays at the party. "Speaking of my sister," she said.

"Yes?" He uncorked the bottle of sparkling wine and carefully poured her a glass.

"She can't know about us."

Nik looked up at her, his beautifully chiseled face frozen in surprise. "Us?"

"She...disapproves." Sasha took the glass from him and sipped. "Ariana wants me to follow through my therapist's recommendations and wait until I'm ready for something real. We had a long talk about it. I don't want to upset her this close to the wedding. She's stressed out enough as is."

"I don't understand." Nik picked a bright red strawberry from a container and brought it to her lips. Sasha bit into the fruit. It was sweet as summer. "We're just friends. What's to approve of?"

"Friends don't look at their friends like that, Mr. Williams."

"You got me there," he said. "I'll do better."

Nik dipped the half-eaten fruit in cream and returned it to her lips. Sasha had a sudden pang of hunger. Her lips parted slightly. She licked the cream before taking a bite. The gurgle of the fountain, the setting sun, the scent of fresh-cut grass, all of it was going to her head. Being here with Nik was an incredible luxury. She did not take it for granted.

"Here's what worries *me*," Sasha said. "I don't have warm, fuzzy, friendly feelings for you. I think about the way we kissed. The memory doesn't go away. It never fades."

Nik went still. "Then come kiss me."

God, she wanted to! Nothing was holding her back except a thread of defiance. "*You* come *here*."

He set aside the bowl of berries from which he was feeding her and focused on her. "If I kiss you," he said, "I won't want to stop."

Her sharp laugh betrayed her inner turmoil. "There's not much we can do out here in the open. Is it safe?"

"That's not what I mean."

He rested a hand on the rise of her hip. Sasha closed her eyes. The warmth of the sun and the subtler warmth of his hand spread throughout her body.

This put an end to the "let's be friends" debate. Let's *not* be friends, she thought. That was a stupid idea from the start. All she wanted was his body, to know his kiss, and find out what those strong hands could do. These were not warm, fuzzy, friendly thoughts.

Sasha opened her eyes and found him studying her. She drew him to her by the sleeves of his crisp gray shirt. "I know what you mean," she said. "I want you to kiss me anyway."

This was the time for him to press his body on hers and crush her lips with his kiss. He did not do that. He took his time, sliding his hand from her hip to the curve of her breasts. She fit nicely into his palm. His other hand found the tie of the halter dress. "Sasha," he said. "How committed are you to playing it safe?"

She always felt safe with Nik. They had their own special kind of luck, carrying them through near disasters, accidents and freak storms.

"Not very much," she admitted.

With one tug of the tie, the knot came undone. She brought her hand to her chest and inched down the fabric, offering herself to his gaze.

"I've been wondering and wondering and wondering…" Nik whispered.

"What about?"

"This."

He swiped the pad of his thumb against a tender nipple. Sasha tensed with frustration. There was too much space between them. She reached up and pulled him close by the nape of his neck. Their kiss was less urgent than their first. This kiss was deep and slow. It sealed a silent pact between them. They could be lovers. They could be friends. Nothing was off limits.

He pulled away and murmured "strawberries" before his mouth slid down her throat and closed on her other aching nipple. Every flick of his tongue brought agony and pleasure. Sasha raked her fingernails down his back. She wanted to claw off his shirt and feel his skin. She would have, too, if not for the sound of footsteps and laughter in the distance.

Nik pressed his chest to hers and hastily fastened the ties to her halter top. The voices faded and the footsteps veered in the opposite direction, yet Sasha clung to Nik, laughing at the thought of getting caught topless in the well-kept gardens of a country club in Royal.

He kissed her shoulder. "I should take you back to the party."

Sasha had a better idea. "You rescued me. Now it's time to rescue my sister."

They plotted to pull Ariana out of the party. It was for her own good, Sasha reasoned. Her sister was intent on stunning the world with her charm, grace and beauty until her star burned out. Someone had to save her from herself.

Nik recruited his inside man. This time the waiter was less accommodating. Throwing together a picnic basket and passing a message on to Sasha, an unknown, was one thing. Interrupting the famous Ariana Ramos while she held court was quite another.

Sasha slid him a twenty-dollar bill. "Tell her Sasha is asking to speak with her at the lobby. Tell her it's an emergency."

"I can't do that," the young man protested. "I'll lose my job."

"You won't," Sasha said. "I'm her sister. She won't mind."

"With all due respect, ma'am, why not approach her yourself?"

Nik pulled a hundred-dollar bill from his wallet. "With all due respect, will this cover the inconvenience?"

The waiter pocketed the money. "It will. Thanks."

The waiter took off. Sasha inched closer to Nik. Giddy as children, they watched the scene play out from outside the French doors to the terrace. The young man approached the group of six that had tightened around Ariana. He delivered the message. Her eyebrows soared heavenward. Sasha almost felt sorry for her.

Ariana promptly excused herself and exited the terrace. Her white dress had a full skirt and it twirled with each urgent step. Even in a panic, she was graceful and elegant.

"Sasha!" she cried. "Where were you? What's the emergency?" Her gaze cut to Nik. "Hey! You're here, too!"

"Calm down," Sasha said. "We're breaking you out of here."

"This isn't prison, Sasha!"

Sasha threw her hands up. "It might as well be!"

Ari scolded them in her motherly way. "You two are terrible!" she said. "Nik, you're a serious person. Did Sasha put you up to this?"

Nik bore a serious expression that brought out his high cheekbones and sharp jaw. "She did, actually."

"Nik!" Sasha cried.

"Keep your voice down!" Ari hissed. "This is the TCC."

She said it as if it were the Vatican. "Look, are you coming or not?"

"Of course I'm coming," Ari said. "Let's go."

Eleven

Nik was enjoying dinner in the company of the two most beautiful women in Royal, arguably in the world. He had no complaints.

At Ariana's suggestion, they left the party and walked over to the wine bar on-site. Dinner was simple: burgers, fries and a vintage bottle of wine. Nik sat next to Ariana and across from Sasha. It took everything he had inside to keep from staring at her beautiful heart-shaped face. He hung on Ariana's every word just to prove that he found her just as interesting as her sister, but the truth was in the drumbeat of his heart. If Sasha laughed, which she did often, particularly when she showed him snippets of videos of the "wedding crasher" prowling around Royal, his heart gave chase.

"You have to agree, it's hysterical."

"It's stupid," Ariana retorted through uncontrolled laughter. "And stop watching his content! You're encouraging him."

Love him, hate him, the videos were funny. The guy had a workable concept. Nik would sign him on as a client, if it wouldn't cause them to lose Xavier's account.

The waiter set the dessert menu on the table. Ariana immediately protested. "Just coffee for me," she said. "I have to fit into a dress in a few weeks."

"Sasha, how about you?"

It was the first time he'd uttered her name all night. It felt like a caress on his lips. She looked up at him, beaming. That was the only word for it. She beamed.

"I'm up for pie," she said. "Apple or cherry."

"Or both?" he said. "We'll share."

"Why not?"

"I'll tell you why not," Ari said. "I can't be around so much pie!"

"You have to eat it before it does any harm," Nik said.

"Or any good!" Sasha fired back.

Ariana brought her fingers to her temples. Her diamond engagement ring caught the candlelight and flashed. "You two together are a menace," she said. "Nik, I'm sorry to say, you've let my sister corrupt you."

Even if that were the case, Nik wouldn't mind at all. *Corrupt me all you want, Sasha.*

His phone rang. He recognized the number as his contact over at Mad Dash, the start-up company whose business he was chasing. "If you don't mind, I have to take this. It's business."

This time he spoke directly to Sasha. She responded with a hint of a smile. He knew she was thinking about the last time he'd missed a business call and all the things which had followed.

"We don't mind," Ariana said. "Don't worry. We'll order your pie."

Nik stepped outside. The call had gone to voice mail. He phoned back. Tony Collins, an old college buddy and the director of development at Mad Dash, delivered bad news.

"Caroline left for Arizona for three weeks. She's on a wellness retreat and not taking any calls."

Caroline Lewis was the start-up's CEO and founder. Nik needed only a meeting to show her all the ways Nexus could get Mad Dash established in Texas. She'd avoided him at every turn. Nik wasn't one to give up easily, but it was starting to look like he was wasting his time chasing this account. "How many interviews did she take, Tony? Do you know?"

"About three," Tony replied. "I'll tell you the truth. I don't think she's comfortable switching teams right now."

The company had received an influx of cash at its last financing round. Now was the time to expand and grow. "That makes no sense."

"The current head of marketing is her best friend," Tony explained. "That's why she's dragging her feet on this. She might not want to shake things up."

Nik considered this. He wouldn't toss over Oliver for anyone. This was beginning to look like a dead end.

Krystal called just when he got off the call with Tony. "Hey you," she said. "I'm leaving for Italy tomorrow."

"I know. I meant to call you later."

A clinical therapist by day, a self-taught cook by night, Krystal was chasing a lifelong dream. She secured a spot in an art class for the summer. It was expensive and impractical, but she was doing it. He was proud of her.

"Just calling to let you know that I changed my security code in case you want to crash here while I'm gone," she said. "I don't feel comfortable sending it to you in a text message, so here it is." She repeated a five-digit code five times. "Got it?"

"I got it!"

"Good. Write it down somewhere safe."

Krystal lived alone and took her security seriously. He

couldn't even blame her. The world was a scary place. "I got it," Nik said. "Anything else? I've got to get back to dinner."

"Nothing at the moment," she said. "Talk soon."

"Hey Krystal!"

"Yes?"

Nik stepped away from the door, even though no one was around. "I've been thinking a lot about what you said. That thing about the type of woman I'm attracted to."

"I'm listening."

"I don't think it's wrong."

He'd been thinking about this a lot. According to Krystal's theory, he'd have to give up excitement and spontaneity for love, happiness and fulfillment. He wasn't prepared to make that exchange. He wanted what he wanted. For now, it looked very much as if he wanted Sasha Ramos.

"There's no right or wrong," Krystal said. "There's just what is. I want you to be clear-eyed about the choices you make."

He was nodding, aware that Krystal couldn't see him.

"Are you there?" she said.

"Yes," he said. "But I gotta go."

"Call me later this week. We'll talk more."

"Sure," he said, although he didn't need to talk much more. He'd already made his choice.

Sasha was alone at the table when he returned. "Why are you alone?" he asked. "Where's Ariana?"

"She's in the ladies' room, and I'm not alone. I've got pie."

She presented the two plates with the grace of a game show host. Nik grabbed a fork. "Your sister doesn't know what she's missing."

"I had a good time tonight," Sasha said. "Thanks for coming."

Her voice was uncharacteristically subdued. Nik set down his fork and looked at her, took in the lines of her face from the gracious arch of her brows to her sharp cupid's bow. In her white dress, she looked like something from a fairy tale. He could not keep his eyes or his hands off her all night.

"Sasha, all I want is to be around you. I want…more of you, all the time. I know it makes no sense." He used his spoon to drive his point. "Before you say that it's too soon—"

She grinned. "I would never say that."

"Good," he said, and drove his spoon into the golden slice of apple pie. "I know my mind."

"'I know my mind'…" She repeated his words in a whisper. "God, I love it when you talk that way, so self-assured, so sexy."

"You wild thing," he said.

"Should we ditch Ari and work out all this sexual tension in your car?"

As much as he liked the idea, he had to pass. "Your sister doesn't trust me."

"That's not true! She likes you a lot."

"Sure," he said. "But she doesn't trust me around *you*."

Sasha took a bite of cherry pie and considered his words. "You've got it wrong," she said. "She doesn't trust *me* around you."

At that moment, Ariana came rushing back. "Oh God," she said. "That does look good. I'll have to try the cherry pie. We can run it off tomorrow."

"Who's we?" Sasha said, and handed her a spoon.

"You and me," Ariana replied. "Get ready. Tomorrow is a packed day, and we're starting off with a quick run. I've booked facials with the local esthetician at Pure—you know I had to find one. We have to stop by the calligrapher at some point, maybe after lunch. We'll finish the day with a girl's night in. Ex is coming home the following day, so we have to make the most of it."

The waiter poured their coffees. Nik took a spoon of apple

pie to sweeten his bitter disappointment; he was certain he wouldn't see Sasha again for the next couple days.

"Have you tried the trails of North Cove Park?" he asked. "It overlooks a pink granite quarry. It's great for hiking."

"Sounds beautiful," Sasha said. "Do you hike there?"

"When I am in town. It's peaceful."

"Is it far?" Ariana asked.

"It's a quick drive. I'll send you the directions."

"How about you meet us there tomorrow?" Ariana proposed. "Seven thirty a.m. Are you up for it?"

Nik met Sasha's eyes and saw the silent plea there. "Why not? My first meeting isn't until ten."

"Will you join us for facials, too?" Sasha teased.

"I'll pass on that," he said. "Although it does sound good."

"It's settled," Ariana said. "Now that you're meeting us, I won't have any trouble dragging Sasha out of bed."

Twelve

Ari was the early riser. Sasha was the restless sleeper who had to hit the snooze button once or twice before dragging herself out of bed. Not this morning. She was up before her sister and knocking on her door. "Come on! Let's go!"

"You can come in, you know!" Ari hollered back.

Sasha found her sitting at the edge of her bed, fastening her running shoes. "I didn't pack hiking boots," she said.

"Since when do you hike?" Sasha asked.

"Ex and I go on regular hikes back in LA."

"Of course you do," Sasha said. "Let's get moving. I don't want Nik to wait too long."

"Of course not," Ari said with a wry smile. "How's it going between you two?"

"We're friends," she replied far too quickly. "What else can we be?"

"I know you like him, Sasha. But you're doing the right thing. Prioritize your well-being. Don't rush into anything."

Sasha avoided her sister's penetrating glare. "Uh-huh."

Ari hopped to her feet. "Let's go!"

On the ride to the park, Sasha debated whether she should just come clean with Ariana. She had no intention of prioritizing her well-being, of sacrificing passion for inner peace. She had no choice, really. It was as if she and Nik had bought two tickets on an insane roller-coaster ride the minute they boarded that plane in Atlanta. There was no getting off.

He wanted her. When was the last time anyone had said that to her so clearly? There were never any games with him. He was serious and straightforward in all things. She'd never met anyone so in command of himself. If only some of that could rub off on her.

Nik was waiting by his car at the North Cove parking lot. Wearing sunglasses, shorts and a white T-shirt that looked so soft. His short, barely there hair glistened from a shower. As always, his brown skin turned honey in the sun. Sasha wanted to bolt out of Ariana's Mercedes and run to him like a puppy let off her leash.

He greeted her with a knowing smile. "Sasha, good morning."

"Good morning to you," she said. "Ready to hike?"

"We can just walk, you know," he said. "The views are great."

"Thank God," Sasha said. "Tell it to her."

Ariana came around the hood of the car. "Tell me what?"

"Nik says—" Sasha reached out for Nik's hand and stopped herself just in time. The gesture felt so natural, refraining from it was forced.

"Says what?" Ari asked.

"Let's start slow," Nik replied on her behalf. "We can pick up the pace as we go."

"Sounds reasonable." Ari slipped on dark sunglasses for anonymity, no doubt. Only they made her look even more like a movie star. "Let's go."

Ten minutes into the run/hike/walk, Ariana's phone

buzzed in her hand. She glanced at the screen. "Rylee!" she cried. "I have to get this."

She scurried off to the side to talk in private.

"Who's Rylee?" Nik asked.

"The wedding planner," Sasha replied. "The plan is top secret. It's all very hush-hush."

"Because of that wedding crasher dude sneaking around?" Nik asked.

"Yeah, but also because Ariana is taking this to the crazy place."

"Understood," Nik said. "You look beautiful."

Sasha acknowledged the compliment with a shrug. She hadn't worn her most shapely leggings for nothing.

They moved to the shade of an oak tree. A carving on the bark read: A-JACKS 4EVER <3. Sasha traced the letters with her finger. "Cute."

"According to Oliver, this place turns into lovers' lane by sundown," Nik said.

"Should we meet here at midnight?" Sasha said, only partly teasing.

"God, no," he said. "How about dinner? I'll make reservations somewhere nice."

"God, no." Sasha mimicked his tone. "I'm done running around Royal. Could we hang out at your place, order in?"

"How about tomorrow night?"

Tomorrow night. Two words never held so much promise. "It's a date."

Ariana came skipping back. "Guys! I just got off the phone with Ex."

Sasha tore her gaze away from Nik, from that mouth she wanted to kiss, and those strong arms she needed to feel around her waist. "Uh...thought you were on the phone with Rylee."

"Yes, and then I called Ex to update him on the plans,"

Ari explained, as if it should have been obvious to anyone. "I told him we've been hanging out with Nik."

Sasha wanted to correct her. *She* had been hanging out with Nik, and Ari had been chaperoning as if she were a heroine of some regency romance.

"He wants us all to have dinner at Sheen tomorrow night when he gets back," Ariana said. "Nik, what do you say? Are you in?"

Sasha felt as if she might explode, particularly when Nik said he was up for it. But what else could they do but accept? Xavier was one of his top clients and her future brother-in-law.

Ari squealed. "It's settled! Give me a minute to send Ex a quick text."

She wandered off again. Sasha whirled around to confront Nik, in jest. "How could you? We had plans!"

He raised an eyebrow like she knew he would. "Should I have told her I was planning to seduce you tomorrow night? Think that might have gone over better?"

Sasha stepped closer, hands on her hips. "When *do* you plan on seducing me then?"

Nik gave this some thought. "I'll break you out of confinement tonight. Meet me by the service elevators."

"Knowing Ari, she's set up motion detectors."

He slipped off his sunglasses and rubbed his eyes. "I'm fresh out of ideas. We're screwed."

Sasha burst into laughter. Nik laughed, too. Ariana returned to find them both laughing hysterically. "Hey! What's so funny?"

"Never mind!" Sasha squeaked. She was breathless. "It's late. Let's hike!"

Later, at the esthetician's office, Sasha received notification from the hotel where she was meant to stay for the remainder of her trip. She could check in tomorrow as early as noon. She shared the news with Ariana.

"You don't have to leave us," she said. "I made that reservation for you weeks ago. Now that you're with me, I want you to keep you close."

"You and your fiancé deserve some alone time," Sasha said. "And I don't want to be anywhere around you when you get busy...so to speak."

"But Sasha—"

"But nothing, Ari!" She borrowed one of her sister's favorite phrases. "It's settled!"

"What if Ex spends a few extra days at his cousin's place?" Ariana proposed.

"Ari, stop," Sasha said wearily. "You don't have to babysit me."

They were sitting alone in the spa's chic waiting area. Sasha reached for her sister's hand and clasped it between her own. It was slowly dawning on her that Ariana's micromanaging was a symptom of a greater problem, as her therapist would say. "What are you worried about?" she asked.

"This can't be easy," Ari said. "My wedding is triggering all this stuff for you. I want you to know that I'm sensitive to that."

Tears sprung from Sasha's eyes. This was her fault for bringing up "the curse" on her first night. This was a special time for Ariana. She was marrying a wonderful man and deserved to enjoy this time.

"I'm so lucky to have you in my life," Sasha said. "You're my star, and I'd be lost without you."

"And you're my favorite person in the world," Ari said. "I'd do anything for you."

Sasha twisted in the leather armchair to face her. "There *is* something I need."

"Name it. Anything at all."

Sasha met Ari's wide brown eyes. "Anything?"

"Yes. I promise," Ari said. "Do you need money?"

"I need space."

Ariana made a face. "Oh."

"I've been living on my own a long time and enjoying it," Sasha explained. "I want to spread out, set up a mini studio, and work on a few projects while I'm here. That doesn't mean I won't be available for cake tastings and dress fittings. We'll see each other every day. I want to be a part of all of it. Your wedding day is my big special day, too."

"Alright," Ariana said. "I'll give you space."

The technician escorted them into the treatment rooms. As she lay on her back with thick cream slathered on her face, a tingle of excitement rushed through her. She couldn't wait to tell Nik that she was finally free!

Almost immediately, a shiver of fear chased away her excitement. Ariana wasn't unreasonable in urging her to slow down. After she broke off her engagement, things were bleak for a long while. In the months and years that followed, she'd lost a person she loved and the friendship forged through college. Their mutual friends sided with Terrence. Not only that, they took measures to protect him. They did not invite her to events when he was expected to attend; this meant birthday parties, brunches and weekend trips. Sasha found herself alone a lot. She left San Bernardino for San Francisco for a work opportunity, but really to escape the long shadow of her mistake.

Only, it wasn't a mistake. She could not have married Terrence.

When Ariana had called her with the news of her engagement, Sasha asked how she knew Xavier was the "one."

"It's not just *one* thing," she replied. "Let's start with the way he looks at me. People look at me all the time, but never like that. For such a confident, even cocky, person, he's kind of shy around me. It's endearing. He makes me feel protected and loved, like no one else can. So, we were at this crowded rooftop bar, right? Some guy was trying to take a photo of me. Ex wasn't having it. I told him to let it go. I didn't want to make a scene. He went and confronted the guy and had him delete the photo. I didn't have the heart to tell him that nearly everyone at that bar had posted photos of us and we were already trending on social media. And when we're alone together, we never run out of things to talk about. We have our silly jokes. His text messages make me smile. It's everything about him."

Ariana's words freed Sasha of any lingering doubts. Terrence was *not* the one for her. Her only regret was the way she'd gone about things. She should have never said yes to marrying him, should have never worn his ring. That serious lack of judgment troubled her. Her reasoning at the time was: Take a chance! Her motto now was: Take no chances. Which was proving to be just as harmful.

She liked Nik. She *really* liked him. She turned to sugar whenever he was around. The fires that he set in her soul just by looking at her never died down. She was more playful and flirtatious with him than she'd ever known herself to be. Nik wasn't Terrence. He knew her secrets and liked her anyway. He respected her work. He made her feel safe, like no one else could. To her mind, their attraction was worth exploring, even if it went nowhere, even if it meant risking all the progress she'd made.

Thirteen

Xavier returned earlier than expected. Ariana's cries of delight could drill a hole in concrete. Sasha was up and brewing her first cup of coffee when the sound of the key in the lock had her sister bolting to the front door. He lifted her off the ground and spun her around.

Only the most hardened cynic wouldn't be moved by their love.

"Hey Sasha!" Ari cried. "Look who's back!"

Sasha waved hello from the kitchen doorway. "Welcome home, Ex."

Her future brother-in-law beamed. "Welcome to you, Sasha! Ariana is so happy you're here. Did you two have fun?"

"We got into all sorts of trouble," Sasha said.

Xavier Noble flashed his trademark smile. It was similar to the one he flashed at late-night talk show hosts, but with a hint of shyness. "I want to hear all about it."

"Not before you take a shower," Ari said.

Ex made his eyebrows dance. "It's just a little sweat. Fishing is hard work."

"Go on," Ari said. "There are fresh towels in our bathroom. I'll make you coffee."

Ex drew her close and pressed his forehead to Ari's. "Thank you, honey."

Sasha swiveled on her heels and returned to the kitchen. When Ari joined her, she wore a silly little grin.

"Still want me to stay?" Sasha said. "Or could you two use some alone time?"

Ari rummaged through a jar of coffee pods for Xavier's favorite flavor. "You could go for a walk around the block for an hour or so."

"Do you have one of those Do Not Disturb door hangers?"

Ari pulled Ex's preferred mug that she'd brought from California out of the top cabinet. "I'll hang a tie."

Sasha grinned into her coffee cup and mumbled, "I'm outta here."

Ari dropped everything onto the counter and rushed over to give her a hug. "I loved this time with you."

Sasha let her sister hold and cradle and love her, and then she got out of her hair.

After his shower, Xavier took Sasha to the hotel. He waited as she checked in and wheeled her suitcases up to her room himself. "Just want to make sure you're comfortable," he said.

"I will be," Sasha said. "This place is gorgeous. I'm starting to think all of Royal is a movie set."

"It was a great place to grow up," he said.

"Do you think you'll ever return?" Sasha asked.

His answer warmed her heart. "Ariana is my home now. I want to be where she can thrive and that's in LA."

"Speaking of Ariana," Sasha said. "She's a little rattled by this wedding crasher stuff. The guy seems harmless enough, at least to me. She thinks he's the Grim Reaper. Pro tip: whatever you do, don't dismiss her concerns."

"I hear you," Ex said. "Thanks for looking out."

They made it to her room on the tenth floor. Ex waved the key card and unlocked the door to a cozy suite complete with kitchenette. Some studio apartments in New York City weren't so well appointed. Ex brought her luggage into the bedroom. Sasha kicked off her sandals and made herself at home.

"So... Dinner tonight at Sheen?" Ex said on his way out.

"That's right," Sasha replied.

"And Nik is joining us?"

"Yep."

He'd texted earlier to confirm. She hadn't told him she was moving into the hotel. That was a surprise for later.

Ex lingered by the entryway. "You two are friends now?"

"It just happened. We flew in on the same plane."

"He's a great guy," he said. "I like him a lot."

Ex endorsing Nik's bid for her time was not on Sasha's bingo card, but there you had it. "I agree," she said. "He's awesome, and great in an emergency."

"Ari told me all about it."

"I bet she did." Sasha went to him and gently walked him out the door. "See you tonight!"

"We'll swing by and get you at seven."

"I'll be ready," she said. "And thanks again."

Sasha shut the door and leaned against it. She had lots to do. For starters, she had to unpack, then she had to pick a great dress to seduce a great guy.

Sheen was a glass house, all shimmer and shine. Ari pointed out that they could see the celebrity chef at work in the kitchen from the dining room. Sasha pointed out that she could see Nik already at the table, sipping water and looking like a snack in a dark suit. That last part she kept to herself. She brushed past the star couple as they meandered into the dining room, hopping from table to table, schmoozing and shaking hands. They'd catch up eventually, but her heart, her breath, every cell in her body were running ahead.

Nik locked eyes with her and rose to his feet. It took a glass house for her to see him clearly. Handsome, strong, steadfast. She might not walk down an aisle for this man, but she would walk on crushed glass.

His eyes raked over her body. His voice faltered as he said hello.

Sasha's dress was nothing more than wispy black silk held together by spaghetti straps. It was her secret weapon, packed at the last minute "just in case." She had no regrets.

He held out her chair and whispered, "I want to be good tonight. Why are you making it hard?"

"I'm sorry," she said. "The whole point of this dress was to make it hard."

Nik pushed out a laugh. They were giggling like naughty teens when Ari and Ex finally made their way to the table, hand in hand, sporting matching smiles.

"I feel like I'm meeting your parents," Nik said.

"Don't be ridiculous," Sasha said. "My parents are way more laid-back."

"Nikolai Williams," Ex bellowed. "Good seeing you again, man. Ari keeps raving about you."

Nik stood to shake Ex's hand. Ari went in for a full hug. Sasha's stomach did a little flip. She could picture a future in which nights like this were a regular occurrence, she and Nik meeting up with Ari and Ex for lunch, dinner and weekends away.

Ex started things off by asking typical dad questions like "How's work?" Meanwhile Ari nodded her approval at Nik's answers. Sasha had the impression they were vetting him and wished they'd back off.

"I was really impressed by the way Nexus swooped in and bought my publisher's PR firm. It was aggressive. Good work."

Ex was this close to calling Nik "son."

"Oliver gets all the credit on that one," Nik said.

Ex brushed his words aside. "It was a team win."

"I wish it was always that easy," Nik said. "We're trying to swoop in on a company called Mad Dash, and we're not getting very far."

"I used Mad Dash while I was filming in Georgia," Ari said. "Their fees are manageable. I still have the app. Do they service Texas?"

"They don't. That's why we want to work with them. We see their potential for growth, but they won't meet with us."

"Their loss."

Between the appetizers and main course, Ari left the table to take a call from the executive producer of one of her projects. Between the main course and dessert, Nik had to step away to take a call from Oliver. He apologized and promised to turn off his phone for the rest of the night.

"Never mind," Ex said. "Do you think my future wife would ever turn off her phone?"

Ari smiled meekly. "Sorry, guys. I'm plugged in 24/7."

Before he left to take the call, Nik reached under the table for Sasha's hand and looped an index finger around her pinky in a sweetly possessive gesture. A million fireflies swirled around her heart.

As soon as he was out of earshot, Ariana said, "Do you know who's the CFO of Mad Dash?"

"How would I?" Unlike Nik, Sasha didn't read the *Royal Financial Times* for fun.

"Your old friend, Teresa Price!" Ari exclaimed.

"Really?" Sasha asked.

"Why do you think I downloaded the app in the first place?" Ari said. "Forbes posted about it on Instagram and I was curious. Turns out, I love it! Why don't you know about this? Don't you two keep in touch?"

Sasha crumbled inside. She and Teresa were not in touch. Teresa had gone to business school with her ex-fiancé and was "Team Terrence" all the way. Now her "old friend" was on the board of a company Nik was interested in. *Guess it's a small world after all.*

Over flourless chocolate cake, Ari asked Nik if he'd RSVP'd for the wedding.

"I did," he said. "Again, thanks for the invitation."

"Did you request a plus-one?" she asked.

"Ari!" Sasha cried.

"What?" Ari said. "We're just talking among friends."

"No," Nik said gracefully. "I don't have a plus-one."

"Well, you have one now!" With a flourish, Ari offered Sasha up as an all-purpose plus-one. "Sasha doesn't have a date, either. She loves to dance."

"Thanks for the intervention," Sasha said dryly. "We could've figured it out on our own."

"Sorry," Ari said. "Couldn't wait around for you to figure it out. Rylee has to finalize the seating chart."

"Rylee runs our lives," Ex said. "You'll get used to it."

Under the table, safe from view, Nik curled his finger around hers once again. "I'd be more than honored to be Sasha's date."

"Good answer," Ex said, and looked around for the waiter to request the check.

"Don't mind that," Nik said. "It's taken care of."

Ex and Ari thanked him in unison. Sasha took another sip of espresso to hide the fact that she was beaming with pride.

"Next time it's on us," Ari said.

"I'm looking forward to next time," Nik said.

They rose from the table. This time there was less meandering. The four of them filed out of the dining room, chatting all the way, only to come to a full stop and crowd around the maître d' station.

The thing with a glass house, however shimmery, it ultimately left you exposed.

Fourteen

Outside the door, paparazzi swarmed like angry bees. Sasha knew exactly why they were there. Before she could stop herself, she slipped her hand in Nik's. He squeezed it reassuringly.

"There's nothing we can do," the hostess said. "Someone must have tipped them off that you are here tonight."

Ari stepped behind Ex, her love and her shield.

"Don't worry," the hostess said. "We can see them, but they can't see us."

"Okay." Ari squared her shoulders, never one to display her weakness. "We'll just march through."

"No," Ex said firmly. "You're not up for this nonsense tonight, and I won't put you through it."

Nik stepped up. After conferring with the hostess who brought in the restaurant owner, Colin Reynolds, he came up with a plan.

"Sasha stays with me," he said. "Xavier, take Ariana out through the rear exit. Your car will be waiting. When you've made it out, send us a text. We'll wait until you're gone before we walk out."

This was Nik's superpower. He took charge and made sure everyone got home safe.

"You don't have to do that," Ari said, even though she was clearly relieved.

"It's already done," Nik said.

Ari turned to Sasha. "Do you mind?"

"Of course not!" Sasha pulled her into a hug and squeezed her tight. "Go! Run out back before they figure it out and camp out there, too."

Ex draped a protective arm over Ari's shoulders and led her away. They followed the hostess through the state-of-the-art kitchen. Sasha kept her eyes on them until they were out of sight. Then she stared at her phone until Ariana confirmed their safety with a thumbs-up emoji.

She looked up at Nik who was staring out at the mob of photographers. More than anyone, Sasha understood the value of capturing the right image at the right time. Getting photographed with the right people could boost a career. And still, she resented these men with cameras who made her sister's life difficult. She had a new understanding of the high price her sister paid to pursue her passions.

She touched Nik's arm. "They made it out. We can go."

Colin returned with a security guard. He confirmed that Ari and Ex had made it out safely. "Bill will escort you to your car."

"Good," Nik said. "Give us a minute." He slipped off his dinner jacket and draped it over Sasha's shoulders. She was instantly enveloped in his scent. "When they open the door, lower your head and stay close. I'll guide you out. Don't worry."

"I'm not worried," Sasha said. "They're not here for me."

"Even so," Nik said. "You're the maid of honor at one of

the most talked-about weddings in the country. If they can get a piece of you, they will."

Sasha looked past his shoulders at the horde of photographers standing at the ready. She had never been at the receiving end of so much attention. She quivered with trepidation.

Bill opened the door. Nik drew her to him. Sasha nestled close and molded herself against his hard body. Head low, braids like a curtain around her face, Sasha fell in lockstep with Nik and let him guide her to safety, one more time.

Nik mostly kept his eyes on the road. Every now and then, he checked on her, his honey brown eyes flickered her way. "Are you okay?"

"I'm fine," Sasha said. "We've lived through worse."

"True." He reached for her hand. "Do I have to take you back straightaway?"

"I'm afraid so," Sasha replied. "Straightaway."

"Okay," he said flatly.

She let him stew in his disappointment before she revealed her secret. "I'll give you the address."

"I know it," he said, brows drawn in confusion.

"I'm not staying with my sister anymore," she said. "Please take me to Cascades Suites."

"Hold on. You moved out?"

"This morning," Sasha replied lightly. "Three's a crowd, you know what I mean?"

Nik withdrew his hand from hers. "And you waited until now to tell me?"

"No need to sound betrayed," Sasha teased. "It was a busy day. So, if you don't mind, take me straight to my hotel. I'd invite you up but the fridge is bare. I can't offer you a drink."

"I don't need a drink."

"Fine." Sasha slipped a key card in his pocket. "Cascade Suites is on Tenth and Lexington."

* * *

While Nik parked the car, Sasha went up to her suite. She tidied the mess she'd made in her bedroom while getting ready for dinner. Then she tackled the bathroom, freshening up before putting away her cosmetics. Twenty minutes passed and Nik still hadn't made it upstairs. What could be taking so long?

Finally, a knock on her door! She rushed to answer. "That took forever! Did you lose the key?"

Nik held up a bottle of wine and two glasses. Sasha knew exactly how he'd gone about getting it. "Who did you have to bribe to get that?"

"Never mind," he said. "Let me in."

She stepped aside. Before shutting the door behind them, she hung the Do Not Disturb hanger on the knob. Everything about tonight felt illicit and exciting, even though they were consenting adults and free to make their own mistakes.

This isn't a mistake.

Nik was in the kitchen, ripping the foil of the bottle.

"Stop!" she cried, and took the bottle from him. "We don't have time for an elaborate seduction."

"We don't?" Nik said. "Please don't tell me your sister is coming to check on you."

"No." She put the wine in the empty fridge and shut the door. "I don't need any more priming. We've had drinks, we've had pancakes for dinner, we've taken long strolls and picnicked in a garden, and tonight counts as a formal date, that's enough."

"You think this was for me?" Nik said. "This was for *you.* I'm ready."

To demonstrate how ready he was, he started on the buttons on his shirt.

"Let me."

Sasha brushed his hands away. She unfastened the little

white buttons, starting at his collar, only to give up half-way and press her lips to the base of his neck. Nik let out a groan and gathered her into his arms. They kissed hungrily in her empty kitchen, tasting and feeding off each other. He slid his mouth down her neck and murmured, "You always smell so good."

Sasha pushed up against his lean, hard body. "And you always *feel* so good."

Nik gathered the silky fabric of her dress. "Take this off," he whispered hoarsely. "I want to see you."

Sasha stumbled away from him. "Good idea, actually. Everyone is responsible for removing their own clothes. We can do the sexy undressing another time."

Nik stripped off his shirt. "I appreciated your help, but you're too easily distracted."

She laughed and slipped her dress over her head. Could he blame her if she was excited?

Underneath her dress, she wore a simple bandeau bra and undies. The caramel color matched her skin perfectly. Nik fell back against the counter, and quietly took her in. "Oh, Sasha... How did I get so lucky?"

She let the dress fall to the floor and reached for his belt buckle. "If we weren't on that doomed flight, we might not have met. Can you imagine?"

"That would've been the real tragedy." He threaded his fingers through her braids as she struggled with the belt buckle with overly eager fingers. "Kiss me. I'll do the rest."

Sasha stretched onto her tiptoes and kissed him hotly. Nik gripped her behind and deepened their kiss. Why would she need wine if his kisses made her drunk?

"Take me to your bedroom," he whispered against her mouth. "Or I'll take you right here."

There was no time for location scouting. Her need for him was too great. "Take me right here."

He crushed her mouth with a kiss so demanding, her whole body started to pulse. He slipped a hand between her legs. "May I?" he said.

She caught his lower lip between her teeth. "Stop teasing me."

He pushed aside the damp panties and sunk his fingers into her wetness. Sasha tightened around him. Her head fell back as pleasure spread from her core up her spine.

He withdrew and placed both hands on her hips. He held her steady a moment then eased the underwear down and over her thighs. "It's not fair that you're still half-dressed," she said, as she readily stepped out of her underwear.

"It's not fair that I haven't seen my beauties yet. Let's set them free."

Nik walked her back against the refrigerator. He pushed her bra up and hungrily closed his mouth on her nipple. His teeth scraped against the sensitive tip. Sasha gasped and arched against the cold stainless steel. His fingers were inside her and his mouth was sucking her in. She twisted and whimpered, unsure she could take much more. She reached and felt for his erection and quickly withdrew her hand, stunned by what she found. "Oh, God, Nik..." She frantically pushed down at his waistband.

"Wait, wait, honey, wait..." Nik urged. From his pocket, he produced a wrapped condom. "Why do you think it took me so long to get here? I had to make a stop. I didn't expect this night to end this way."

Sasha thanked the heavens that one of them was still thinking straight. She plucked the foil packet and tore it open. "Take your clothes off," she ordered.

The clothes were off and the condom was on in under a minute. Sasha first cut off the overhead light, knowing the image of Nik's long, lean, taut body was forever stored in her imagination.

He grabbed hold of her waist and lifted her onto the cold stone countertop. It didn't feel quite right. "Sorry!" she said. "I've changed my mind."

Nik stepped back. "You want to stop?"

"NO!" Shivering with want, she reached for him and yanked him back between her legs. "I changed my mind about the kitchen. It's not…giving what I thought it would."

He agreed. "We're too sober for this."

"I guess we'll have to do it the old-fashioned way." Sasha sighed, resigned. "To the bedroom!"

"Let's go!"

In one smooth move, Nik picked her up off the counter and hauled her onto one shoulder. Sasha squealed. "You caveman! Put me down!"

"Point the way."

"It's the door to the left!" she cried. "My left!"

The door was ajar. Her caveman kicked it wide open and flopped her onto the bed. Sasha shook with laughter. Nik stood at the foot of the bed, grinning, proud of his prowess. His erection, though, was proudest of all.

She extended her arms. "Come to me."

Nik crawled onto the bed. All laughter subsided when he brushed her braids away from her face and coaxed her to look at him. "This current between us," he said. "I've felt it since the day we met. Say you felt it, too."

Sasha nodded. Her throat was too tight to speak.

Nik brushed his lips to hers. "Say it."

"You know I did," she said, her voice thin.

He dragged his nose down her neck. "Yes, but I want to hear it."

"I felt it the first time you looked at me," Sasha said.

"On the plane?" he murmured against her skin.

She shook her head, her breath shallow. "Not on the plane."

"When?"

"When I found you at the airport coffee shop."

He kissed her. "You found me."

"Yes." Sasha wrapped her legs around his waist. "Now come find me."

He held her still and eased inside her. She couldn't help but tighten around him. "Sasha..." he whispered.

She buried her face in his chest. "Oh my God...please..."

That was the moment Nik lost his fantastic self-control. He entered her fully and they started moving, effortlessly finding a rhythm all their own. She gripped his arms and when that wasn't enough she bit his shoulder. Nik teased and called her his wild one. Pleasure rolled through her, she lost the trail of his voice. She could only feel him inside her, all around her.

Come find me.

She wrapped her legs tighter around his waist. He burrowed deeper and deeper still, nudging her up to the edge of a cliff. Sasha would have happily toppled into an abyss of pleasure, but Nik wouldn't let her. He withdrew and fell onto his back and motioned for her to straddle him.

"Okay, fine!" she said begrudgingly. "I'm in charge."

He laughed softly into the darkness. "No, honey, you're not. I want to watch you, that's all."

"Oh, is that all?" Sasha's laugh was wild and wicked. She was going to ride this man to the ground.

As it turned out, that was wishful thinking on her part. She couldn't stand to be apart from him for too long. She bent low for a quick kiss. His fingers tangled in her braids and, despite his earlier claim, he kept her close. Heat roped them together, ever tightening, until she could barely breathe, until the rope snapped and sent her into free fall.

Fifteen

Out of breath, his body still crackling with desire for her, Nik stared up at the ceiling. "Sasha…why did we wait for so long to do this?"

"We literally waited three days," she replied. "That's not very long by most standards."

"Whose standards are we playing by?" he asked.

"Society?"

"I hate society," he grumbled.

"Me, too. They ruin everything." Sasha curled up to him and pressed the palm of her hand to his sternum. "Did I tell you that I love your body?"

He ran a hand down the curve of her side. "Did I tell you that I'm obsessed with yours?"

She laughed and said, "You're right. We should've done this sooner. We should've joined the Mile High Club as the plane came crashing down."

Nik tried to picture it. "That's a story for our grandchildren."

Her face clouded and he regretted the joke almost immediately.

"I didn't mean it," he said. "It was just a joke."

"I know that!" she said, brightening all too suddenly.

He cupped her face to reassure her, even as an image sharpened in his mind: children, grandchildren, a lifelong road trip of adventures with this woman. It scared him to death. Sasha would never agree to any of that.

Here he was, back where he'd started. He loved the wild ones, and the wild ones had to run free.

Nik had dismissed his cousin's concerns the night they'd discussed his personal life over margaritas. He told her she was way off course.

"It's because of your parents," Krystal said.

"Not everything is because of our parents," he said.

"Maybe, but in this case we can draw a straight line to your dad leaving and your mother—"

"Hold on," he said, interrupting her. "If I follow your logic, my dad was the wild card of my family. He took off and never looked back. Why would I chase after that? My mother was steadfast, steady. I admire her so much. To this day, she's my hero."

"Pardon my saying this, but your mom, who happens to be my beloved godmother and aunt, was tired, overworked, a little cranky and always complaining about money—"

"Come on! How can you blame her for that?"

"I don't blame her," Krystal said. "Don't put words in my mouth."

"Then what?"

"Of course, you admire her strength and appreciate her sacrifices," Krystal went on. "You're not a monster. But your dad got to run free. He got to be a supernova, a rock star. That's the quality that you're chasing after."

Nik tried to make sense of her words. Maybe he'd had too much to drink, but he found it too abstract a concept for him to grasp.

"Sorry," he said. "I don't see it."

"You may not be ready to admit it now," Krystal said. "You're a smart guy. One day, you'll figure it out."

He'd figured it out, all right. Here and now, in Sasha's bed.

He ran a hand over his face. Sasha pulled it away. "What's wrong?"

"Nothing's wrong," he said.

"Why do you look like that?" she asked.

"No reason."

"Listen, I can take a joke."

"I know, honey," he said. "It's not that. I should get going now."

She drummed his chest with her fingertips. "Tomorrow is Saturday. Do you have to work?"

"No, actually. I don't."

"Why leave, then? We have so much lost time to make up for."

She stared up at him with wide, pleading eyes. Nik didn't want to leave her. In all honesty, he didn't think he could. But he didn't want to stay here and dream of their grandchildren, either. It was all moving so fast. It had only been three days…

"Do you want me to stay?" he asked, at a loss.

"I'm practically begging you," Sasha said. "Come on… please."

"Okay, I'll stay," he said. "We'll have to order groceries, though. Your refrigerator has exactly one bottle of wine."

"There's also some icicles in the freezer," she said. "A welcome gift from the hotel."

He propped himself up on an elbow. "This just got real," he said. "Let's compile a grocery list."

Sasha got up and stretched languidly on her way to the bathroom. "Order enough for two days. I don't think I'm going to let you out."

Nik looked up from his phone. "Most women just ask me to spend the night."

"I'm not most women, Nik!" she said, balking.

Standing at the bathroom doorway, naked, veiled only with light, her braids long and loose on her back, Sasha was surreal. Nik had to agree. She was unlike any woman he had ever met in his life.

"Those women have their lives together," she said. "They're way more secure than I am. I'm needy. Right now I need more of your time. Spend the weekend with me."

At this point, rabid dogs couldn't chase him away. She didn't need to know that. "I'm staying," he said. "And I'm ordering ice cream."

"Do what you must!" She moved to shut the bathroom door and stopped. "This weekend is just for us. We can say and do whatever we like. I don't want to see that worried look on your face ever again!"

Nik stared at the closed door. Sasha locking him up in her bedroom for a weekend was sexy as fuck, and here he was analyzing his past and dreaming about grandchildren. He had to get his head back in the game.

Sixteen

There were some things they couldn't order in, like a change of underwear. For that reason alone, Sasha agreed for Nik to return to his place in the morning for the limited purpose of packing a bag. It wasn't like her to be so straightforward and demanding, so *clingy*, but the moment had called for it. She wanted him. Her time at Ariana's place should have been a cooling-off period. Instead, it fueled her desire. He wanted her, too. There was no doubt in her mind he felt the same way. That stupid joke about grandchildren had sent her into a tailspin and he must have misread her reaction.

Sasha knew he was joking. Nik was a reasonable person. He wasn't thinking about grandkids or a future together after their first roll in the sack, but she was. Just like at the restaurant, she caught a glimpse of it, a future for her and Nik that might include a brood of bossy and opinionated children. Far from freaking her out, it had pleased her to her core. *That* was scary.

Nik kissed her goodbye. "I won't be long."

She wrapped her arms around his neck. "Are you sure you're not going to run for your life?"

"No," he said in his serious voice. "I'm running right back to you so we can lock this door and keep it locked for the next forty-eight hours."

"I like the sound of that."

"Not as much as me. I'll be back."

He kissed her again and was gone. Sasha could not sit still. She wanted to do cartwheels. She couldn't believe it. She and Nik had the weekend to themselves. They deserved this, if only for surviving the trip to Royal. She was going to make it wonderful for him. They would talk, cook, make love, watch television shows and just be together. It was going to be glorious.

A knock on her door knocked her back to her senses. Nik? She opened the door. "Did you forget something?"

"What do you mean? Did you leave something behind at the apartment?"

It was Ari, dressed in black linen and sporting her black sunglasses. Sasha blinked, confused. Were they supposed to meet today?

"I left my hairbrush," Sasha said absently.

"Your hair is in braids."

She ran her hair through her tangled braids. "Right."

"Are you busy?" Ari asked.

"Yes."

"Come with me. It won't take long."

"Where are we going? And why are you acting so weird?"

"Never mind," Ari said. "I'll have you back in no time. I promise."

Damn. There was no way out of this! "Okay. Give me a second. I have to put on my sneakers and grab my phone and..."

"Just hurry. I'll use your bathroom."

"No!"

Ari paused. "Why no?"

There was an open box of condoms on the bathroom vanity. That was why.

"I'll take you to the one off the lobby," Sasha said. "It's pink marble and perfect. So lovely! You'll love it."

"It doesn't matter," Ari said. "We don't have time. Let's just go."

Ariana drove them to the center of town, to the chic shopping plaza they'd visited on their last outing. She parked across the street from the florist's boutique.

"Why are we here?" Sasha asked, arms folded across her chest. "Is there some flower emergency? A shortage of bluebonnets in the great state of Texas?"

Ariana ripped off her seat belt and tilted her seatback. "Get low," she said. "We're incognito."

"Are we, though?"

They were driving around in a black Mercedes that she was pretty sure anyone could identify as Xavier's. They weren't fooling anyone.

"What's the point of all this, Ariana?" Sasha demanded. "Aren't we going in?"

"We're on a stakeout."

"Are you kidding me?"

"I'm not," Ari said bluntly. "*He's* in there."

"*Who's* in there?"

"The wedding crasher."

"Jesus Christ!" Sasha reached for the door handle and pushed the door open. "I'm going to talk to him."

Ari grabbed her by the arm and yanked her back in. "Stay here! I'm not even sure he's in there. I got a tip and wanted to see for myself."

Unbelievable!

"So what if he's in there?" Sasha said. "What can you do?

He has every right to be in a public place. Who knows? He might be buying flowers for his girlfriend."

"He's not buying flowers for anyone. I can tell you that!" Ari snapped. "He's trying to get our florist, Corynna, to spill to spill. This is how he operates. He asks innocent questions of the cashier or some unsuspecting employee. They share a silly anecdote and from those bits and pieces he constructs his story."

"Such a man is on the loose and the FBI hasn't recruited him?" Sasha pondered. "This country has lost its edge."

"Joke around all you want," Ari said. "*My* wedding is big business for a guy like him."

"Here's my issue," Sasha said. "You said this wasn't going to take long. In my limited experience, watching movies and TV shows, a stakeout can last for hours. I didn't sign up for that."

"Doubt it," Ari said. "How long can anyone stay in a flower shop?"

"Which brings me to my next issue. What if he's already gone?"

Ari didn't have a quick answer to that.

"What if I go inside just to take a quick look?" she proposed. "I won't approach him. I'll use my superpowers to figure out exactly what he's up to."

"Your superpowers," Ari said, pausing to add air quotes, "won't work in this case. The shop has one of those old-timey bells above the door. As soon as you walk in he'll be alerted of your presence."

Sasha threw her hands up. "Sorry, Ari, I don't see the point of this. And next time we go on a stakeout, buy me an ice coffee first."

"I don't see the point, either," Ari admitted. She slipped off her sunglasses and covered her eyes with her hands. "Rylee said that he was poking around the flower shop and I rushed out in a rage."

"Ex didn't try to talk you out of it?" Sasha seriously questioned her future brother-in-law's judgment. She'd asked him not to dismiss Ari's feelings. That didn't mean he should let her act on those feelings. There was a line that logic didn't cross.

Ari sighed. "Ex doesn't know. He was working when I left the apartment."

"Ah." That made sense.

Ari's shoulders dropped in defeat. "I just want this wedding to be perfect, you know?"

"It can't be perfect," Sasha said. "You'll never have the picture-perfect wedding of your little girl dreams. How could you? Our aunts and uncles will be there. Our tribe of cousins, too. We're not country-club type people. It's gonna get wild. A wedding crasher is the least of your problems."

"Oh, God!" Ari moaned. "You're so right. When the DJ switches to House music it's going to get loud."

"Exactly!"

"Hey!" Ari exclaimed. "Why can't you show yourself that same grace?"

"Excuse me? I don't know what you mean."

"Your life isn't perfect. You had some setbacks. Maybe now it's time to lay it all to rest and move on with someone new, don't you think?" Ari explained. "Have you given any thought to what I said about Nik?"

"Uh… You said to stay away from him."

Ari bristled. "That's what I said, but that's not what I meant."

"What did you mean, then?"

"To wait until you were sure," Ari said. "I thought I made that point clear."

"Oh."

Ari touched her arm. "Nik is into you. That's obvious to everyone. All I asked was for you to take it slow, not to dismiss it as a fling."

This was the time to come clean to her sister and tell her that she and Nik were way past taking it slow. They'd burned through every red light. That wasn't what Ariana wanted to hear. Even though it felt rare and special and real, it pretty much had all the trappings of a fling. They hadn't discussed the future, not even the immediate future beyond this weekend. Ariana would have questions and she had no answers. Her mind was as bare as her refrigerator. So, she kept quiet.

"I guess we should head back now," Ari said. "This was stupid."

"Yeah…" Sasha agreed.

"I won't do it again."

"Good."

"What will I tell Ex? He'll think I lost my mind."

"Don't tell him," Sasha said. "This can be our little secret."

"Yeah, right," Ari said. "In five years you'll tell the whole family the story at Christmas."

Sasha winked. "More like next year. It's a great story."

Nik was home, unpacking groceries, when Sasha got back. "Hey! Where were you?" he said. "I sent you a text."

The sight of him in the tiny kitchen stirred up memories of the night before and all the things they'd been up to since.

"Sasha? Are you okay?"

"I'm not okay! I was kidnapped by my sister!"

"What?"

"She got word that the wedding crasher guy was at the flower shop, and she wanted to stake it out."

"Are you kidding?"

"I wish I were."

Nik put a quart of ice cream in the freezer. "Has he done

anything all that bad? He hasn't revealed anything specific. From what you've shown me, he's dealing in speculation."

"Tell that to Ari," Sasha quipped. "She's convinced he has the power to ruin her wedding."

"She's stressed."

"And she's stressing me out." Sasha slipped off her sneakers and padded barefoot into the sitting room.

"Why don't you pull up those videos," Nik suggested. "Let's see how bad it can get."

"Really?"

Why did this simple request make her so unreasonably happy? She'd been secretly binge-watching Trick MacArthur's YouTube channel, and feeling intense shame about it. It was by definition a guilty pleasure. Ariana would kill her if she found out. Here, Nik presented the opportunity to do so in a guilt-free way. *Let's see how bad it can get.* This was research. Really, they were doing Ariana a favor, looking out for her.

For the next half hour, they sat on the couch, snacking on chips, watching the videos on the wall-mounted TV, pausing now and then to argue a point or break out in laughter. The Carlisle wedding had them rolling with laughter.

Nik hit Pause. "I can't believe she picked that ugly dress. I don't care who designed it or how much it costs."

Sasha wiped tears from her eyes with the back of her hands. "Don't say that! Brides are like babies. They're all beautiful."

"She's lovely. That dress is *not*," Nik said. "Trick was right."

"Trick is always right. Ariana should be taking notes."

Nik stretched out and propped his head on a throw pillow. "That's a lot to go through to get married."

Sasha folded her legs underneath her. "How would you like to get married?"

"Something small with family and only the closest of friends," he said without hesitation.

"Me, too," Sasha said. "When you're rich and famous, a wedding becomes an event. The photos are sold and the public gets to pick apart your choices down to the cake flavor. I'm glad I'm not famous. Although, I wouldn't mind being rich."

"Do you like where you are, career-wise?" he asked.

"It's going well, so far. Obviously, photographers don't make too much money until they win a Pulitzer."

He tilted his head, looked at her through narrowed eyes. "Is that something you aspire to?"

She nodded, unable to say the words. It made sense that Ariana would win an Oscar someday, either as an actor or director. Those same shiny statues were always out of her reach. "I'd like to do something worthwhile with my talent and my tools."

"The work you did for *New Day* magazine was exceptional."

"Thank you."

"I mean it," he said. "It must have been taxing, too."

"It was."

The magazine had sent her to Kansas after a tornado had ravaged a small town. It was heartbreaking work, but necessary. Video was great; however, nothing captured the emotional weight of a moment better than photography.

"I think you're a genius and an artist," he said. "Not only that, I think you'll win that Pulitzer."

"How about you?" she asked. "What does the future look like for you?"

"I'm sort of drifting," he replied. "I sold my Miami Beach condo."

Sasha sat up straighter. "That's right. You mentioned it."

"I didn't care for the place. So when I was offered three times the amount I'd paid for it, I let it go."

"Will you stay in Royal?" she asked.

"I'm not needed in Royal," he said. "Oliver has it covered. It's not where the action is, at least in my mind."

Sasha wondered where that might be. New York, maybe?

Nik set the bag of chips he'd been munching on to the side and wiped his hands on a napkin. "Should you ever consider getting married, how would you go about it?"

"I...um..." Sasha looked down at her hands. "I'd...um..."

"If it makes you uncomfortable, we don't have to talk about it."

She wanted to talk about it. Her past mistakes shouldn't keep her from dreaming of a future. Sasha believed in the power of visualization. It made her good at her job. She had to picture a future in which she was happy and fulfilled or else it would never happen.

"I'd put on a minidress, grab a bouquet of tulips and dash off to San Francisco City Hall on a Friday afternoon. Afterwards I'd host a big family dinner at my airy loft overlooking the Golden Gate Bridge."

Nik went silent for a while. Sasha's heart felt exposed in her chest. She didn't breathe until he extended his arms. "Come to me."

Seventeen

If she believed in curses, then Nik had no reason to doubt that she had cast a spell on him. When she melted in his arms and kissed him slowly, pulled away and tugged off his clothes, traced every line of his body with her fingertips and tongue and finally gave him what he thought he'd wanted the night before but couldn't handle, straddling him, magnificent, head tossed back, braids cascading the length of her spine, until he gripped her by the waist and got her where she wanted to go, then collapsed into his arms, her heart pounded into his chest—when she'd done all that, Nik knew he was under a spell. There was no talisman, no charm, no mantra he could repeat three times to free him from it. Everything in him was now linked to Sasha.

The weekend went by all too fast. One moment, he was holding Sasha while she slept, loving her in the shower, spoon-feeding her ice cream in the kitchen, the next he was back at work.

On Monday morning, bright and early, Nik was discussing the chances of the local tennis champion at Wimbledon with

Mavis, the office building's security guard. That's where Oliver found him, coffee cup in hand, while Mavis mimed the killer backhand that would secure the tennis pro's victory.

"I don't know," Nik said. "I still like Naomi Osaka's chances."

"This is *our* chance to bring the trophy home to Texas!"

Oliver grabbed his elbow and dragged him off to the elevators. "I support Texas!" he called out to Mavis. Once in the car, he hit the button to the sixteenth floor and said, "Nah. It's Naomi for the win."

"Right?" Nik said. "No doubt about it."

Oliver ran a hand through his hair. "How was the weekend? I got some stuff done, but not much. You?"

Nik took a sip of black coffee. He was going to need several cups to make it through the day. "I fell in love with Sasha Ramos this weekend."

Oliver dropped his laptop case. "What did you just say?"

"I didn't get anything done," Nik said. "I'm going to lock myself in my office and double down on—"

"Hold on! Back up! I don't care about work."

Nik blinked at him. "What?"

"You said you fell in love with Sasha Ramos this weekend."

"Oh, shit…"

"Oh, yeah!" Oliver laughed and picked up his laptop case off the elevator floor. "You were going to speed past that?"

Nik let out a groan. "I didn't mean to say that."

"Nice! We're keeping secrets now?"

The elevator opened to their floor. Oliver gripped Nik's arm and steered him into his office. Although the floor was empty at this hour, he shut the door behind them for added privacy. Nik fell onto one of the two armchairs facing the desk.

Oliver paced the floor. "So, like, what? You stared across

a crowded room and fell in love with Ariana Ramos's little sister?"

Nik chafed at his description of Sasha. People weren't willing to let her out of Ariana's shadow. "Let's not call her 'little.' She's a woman."

"I'm sure you know all about that," Oliver quipped.

Yeah, he did, but that was neither here nor there. "I'm just saying there's more to her than that."

"I'm concerned how our *client*, worldwide bestselling author Xavier Noble, will take it, that's all."

"I wouldn't worry," Nik said. "We all had dinner Friday night."

Oliver threw his hands up. "Well, in that case!"

"I know what it looks like," Nik said.

"I don't think you do," Oliver said. "Your head is in the clouds."

Nik didn't deny it. He was a fool in love. "Sasha is amazing."

"Uh-huh," Oliver said. "So long as you keep her happy. We can't piss off one of our most famous clients. If she tells her sister and her sister tells her husband… See where I'm headed? It can get messy. Now, I'm not judging you. I'm no stranger to mess."

Nik lifted the cap off his coffee cup and studied the contents. "It's not like that. Sasha is leaving after the wedding, and that's the end of it."

"Oh." Oliver sat at the corner of his desk. "How do you feel about that?"

He shrugged. "I'll deal with it."

He had no choice but to deal with it. He knew what he'd signed up for. No one had told him to fall in love with a woman who ran from love. That was on him. He would have to climb out of that wholly all on his own. It wasn't going to be easy, and it might take a lifetime. Even so, he didn't care. It was worth it to feel this way.

"When did all this happen?" Oliver asked. "Just the other night we ran into you and you claimed *not* to be on a date. I took your word for it."

"We weren't on a date," Nik said. "Obviously, things steamrolled from there."

Oliver let out a low laugh. "I bet!"

"People write poetry about what I lived through this weekend," Nik said.

"Stop! Spare me!" Oliver cried. "I'm getting goose bumps."

Nik rose to his feet. "Now you know everything. I got to catch up on work."

"Hold on. Not so fast," Oliver said. "Isn't she from the Bay Area?"

Nik shifted his weight from one foot to the other. He had a feeling where Oliver was headed, and he didn't like it. "Uh-huh."

"So, it's not as open-and-shut as you're making it sound," Oliver said. "You're relocating our office from LA to San Francisco by the end of the year."

"About that," Nik said. "I haven't told her, so please don't mention it."

"Uh...why? It's a solution to your problem."

Nik sat back down again. "The window passed. I should've mentioned it when we first met. Now it'll sound like I'm following her to her city. It'll be weird."

For someone as commitment averse as Sasha, it would likely creep her out.

"It'll be weird when you show up at her local coffee shop, one morning out of the blue, without her ever knowing that you were in town."

"San Francisco is a big city. We may never run into each other."

"Don't kid yourself. That's not how it works," Oliver said. "You'll run into her just as soon as you step out of the airport.

You're going to have to tell her. The window isn't closed. I get that it may be a lot to spring on someone, but it may not be as bad as we're making it out to be. Just because you're moving to her city, doesn't mean you're moving into her apartment. San Francisco is big enough for both of you."

Nik took another sip of coffee only to find that the cup was empty.

Oliver was looking at him quizzically. "Oh, shit…" he said. "You don't think she feels the same about you. You're out there drowning in love. Meanwhile, she's safe on the shore."

Every muscle in Nik's body tensed. "It's not like that."

"Okay, buddy," Oliver said. "Tell me how it is."

"I don't want to scare her."

"She doesn't look like the type of person who scares easily," Oliver said. "Then again, I don't know her as well as you do."

Nik slumped in his chair. How did it get so complicated? The move to Silicon Valley was months in the planning. He wanted to be where tech innovation brewed, get on the ground floor of some of the most innovative start-ups. His work was at the core of his life. It thrilled and motivated him. He wanted to share his plans with her without her worrying that he was trying to crowd her.

"Obviously, honesty is the best policy," Oliver said. "You can bend the truth a little. Delay the move by a couple months. There's no rush. That way, if you run into her at her coffee shop, it won't be awkward. It'll be water under the bridge."

Oliver had a point. If he delayed the move, he wouldn't have to tell her anything. A year would have passed. They would be over each other, and he wouldn't owe her an explanation. The idea alone made him sick. A part of him couldn't believe he was second-guessing the plan to accommodate Sasha, yet he was. When you loved someone, you put her needs first. Sasha had been through too much. For all her toughness, she was more fragile than most. Oliver didn't know this, and he wouldn't understand.

He got up and went to the door. "I should get busy. Thanks for giving me 'the talk.' I'll think about what you said."

"Anytime!" Oliver said, grinning. "Hey, Nik?"

"Yeah."

"She's smart. She'll figure out that she's scored big with you."

By midday, Nik could no longer focus on anything. His talk with Oliver had unearthed too much. He shot a text to Krystal. Free to talk?

She promptly responded with a video call. Her grinning face filled the screen. She raised a glass of what looked like an Aperol Spritz. "*Buona sera*, cousin!" she said. "I'm enjoying an *aperitivo! Cin cin!*"

Nik pinched the bridge of his nose. "Is this how it's going to be all summer long?"

"Assolutamente!"

"My God…" Nik groaned.

Krystal excused herself from a group and ventured out to a terrace overlooking a quintessential Roman street, cobblestones and all. She had sent him her itinerary. After a few nights in Rome, she would settle in Milan to study classical drawing techniques.

"How do you like it so far?" Nik asked.

"What? Are you kidding me?" Krystal cried. "I'm living a dream!"

Nik was happy for her. Ever the dutiful daughter, she'd done everything to make her parents proud. She'd gone to college, instead of art school, and pursued a traditional career. It wasn't until her father had passed away that she gave herself permission to pursue the desires of her heart.

"You look radiant, and I'm proud of you."

"Aw!" she cooed. "Thanks, baby cousin! You look a little worn out. What's up?"

"Thought I'd call to tell you that you were right, and I'm an idiot."

"I already knew that," Krystal said. "What else you got?"

I love someone who loves to run. That was as far as the words would go. He didn't want Oliver's hot takes or Krystal's clinical advice. He wanted to talk to Sasha. Whatever her reaction, he would take it.

"That's it," he said. "That's all I got."

"Hey, listen," Krystal said. "I might've been a little harsh on you the last we talked. Who am I to tell you who to love or how to live your life? Of all of us, you've got your act together. Look at me in Italy spending a fortune on art classes, picking up a skill I'll never use in a professional capacity. If I think about it too much, I'll burst into tears."

"Krystal, if you want to pursue art in one way or another, no one can stop you," he said. "Even if the family tried to give you grief, I'd call each one of them up and set them straight."

She dabbed at a tear swelling in the outer corner of her eye. "You'd do that?"

"Damn right I would."

"Thank you," she said. "I needed to hear that today."

He'd called to talk out his issues. Of the two of them, she was the one who was in need of counseling and support. He was here for it. "Is everything alright?"

Krystal took a breath. "I don't think I can go on counseling athletes, encouraging them to pursue their dreams while I ignore my own."

"That makes total sense," he said.

"I don't think I am who I was meant to be," she said. "I ended up with a life that doesn't feel like mine."

Nik ached for her. Krystal was more than a cousin. She was the sibling he'd never had. If she wanted to live her life in Europe, studying art history and drawing ancient statues, then she deserved to try and fail, try again and succeed.

Similarly, if he wanted to chase a wild love, he shouldn't let anything get in his way. His father might have planted the seed in him, but he was his own man now. Nik would take his chances with Sasha. He'd rather chase a shooting star than wait, complacent, for one to fall on his lap.

"I have to join the others now."

"Go on," he said. "We'll talk soon."

"Ciao, bello!"

"Oh, shut up!"

"And good luck with the girl, whoever she is this time around! Go get her!"

Eighteen

Sasha spent Monday afternoon with Ariana. Her sister was more relaxed this time around and Sasha tried her best not to jinx it. She kept the conversation light and bubbly. At Natalie Valentine's Bridal Shop, she tried on her bridesmaid's gown for the first time, twirled in it, posed for photos, toasted with champagne and did not fidget during the fitting. Afterward, they stopped by the florist, approved a last-minute change to the centerpieces, checked out the bluebonnets, and the name "Trick" did not come up once.

"Thanks for hanging out with me today," Ari said.

"I meant what I said. I'm here for all of it," Sasha replied. "What's on the list for tomorrow?"

Ariana flashed a smile. "Tomorrow is a fun day. We meet with the mixologist and sample the signature cocktail. Ex is coming along for that one."

"Sounds like a good time."

They were on the sidewalk outside the shop, in plain sight of everyone, like normal people. Sasha was getting anxious.

"I know what you're thinking," Ari said.

"What's that?"

"You're wondering why I'm not ranting and raging about the wedding crasher."

"I was, actually."

Ari squared her shoulders. "I had a good cry last night and got it out of my system."

"Good for you. Maybe we should have this conversation in the car."

"It's okay, Sasha. I'm not running from paparazzi anymore."

"Why the hell not?"

That didn't seem wise. Sasha looked around just in case a photographer was lurking behind the esthetically pleasing recycle bin.

"Because I'm taking your advice."

That didn't seem wise, either. "Which advice?"

"I'm enjoying this time with its ups and downs," Ari said. "I'm enjoying my crazy circus of a wedding. With any luck, it's the only one I'll ever have."

"That's the spirit!"

"I don't know what I was thinking, dragging you into a stakeout on Saturday. I apologize."

"Don't get me wrong," Sasha said. "I'm all for a stakeout with proper notice. Had you told me what we were up to, I would've grabbed my camera, the one with the super lens. What's the point of a stakeout without incriminating photos?"

"You got a point there." Ari smiled. "Anyway, I wanted you to see for yourself that I'm calmer now. I don't want to worry you."

"Hey! That's my line!" Sasha cried. "I'm the lost soul. You're the bright shiny star. We picked those roles at birth. There's no going back."

"Nonsense!" Ari scoffed. "You're the most beautiful soul I know."

"I have my moments."

Ari checked her watch, a gold Cartier. "I'm meeting Ex for dinner. Want to join us?"

"Not tonight," Sasha said. Although she had no definite plans, she knew whom, if given a choice, she would rather have dinner with. "You two have fun. I'd like to wander around, do some window shopping."

Ariana left and Sasha wandered straight into an ice cream shop and bought a gourmet vanilla Popsicle dipped in Belgian chocolate and smothered in nuts. This could be dinner, she thought. She could catch up on reading or watch a movie... or...she could call Nik.

He'd left early this morning with a kiss goodbye. The question hung in the air long after he was gone: When will I see you again?

Sasha was reluctant to ask because she'd taken so much of his time already. Now she felt a little foolish for not asking. They had so little time to spend together, she didn't want to waste any of it by playing it safe.

She decided to send a feeler in the form of a selfie. She snapped a photo of herself biting into the ice cream bar.

His answer: Cute. Is that from earlier today?

Her response: No. That's from right now. I'm at the shops in Midtown.

Him: I know exactly where you are. Give me 5 minutes.

Sasha would've squealed in delight if she weren't in public. This was what she loved about Nik. He was spontaneous, up for whatever and...coming around the corner, a wide grin on his face.

Sasha ran toward him. They crashed into each other.

Nik circled an arm around her waist. "I need a bite of that!"

Sasha laughed. "Of what, exactly?"

"Give me this."

He took a greedy bite of her Popsicle. Sasha kissed his

cheek while he chewed. "Admit it. You came all this way just for the ice cream."

"Don't tease me with ice cream," he said. "I'll come running."

"Where did you come running from?" she asked.

"My office isn't far, neither is my rental apartment."

"Is that a fact?"

"It is," he said. "I'd invite you up, but I'm all out of champagne and caviar."

"Don't need it," Sasha said. "I had champagne at the bridal shop. I'm good."

"In that case, it's my turn to lock you up."

She slid her arms around his neck. "Please do."

He took another bite of ice cream. Sasha laughed; her eyes squeezed shut. When she opened her eyes again, the first thing she saw was a young man with wavy brown hair duck into the corner store.

"That bastard!" she swore under her breath.

Nik stepped away. "Who, me?"

"No, sweetie." She pressed a hand to his cheek to reassure him. "Not you. *Never* you."

"Who then?" He glanced over his shoulder, scanned around for the bastard.

"Trick! I saw him go into that shop."

"Which one?"

She pointed to the shop with the Popsicle. "That one."

"Christ," he mumbled.

"He's stalking Ariana," Sasha said. "She was here a moment ago. Someone must have tipped him off and now he's poking around."

"Want me to check it out?" he offered.

"No, I'll go," Sasha said. "This job calls for my superpowers. If he's poking around and asking questions, I'll figure out what he's after. That way, Ariana can get one step ahead of him."

"Bad idea," Nik said. "Your superpowers only work when your target is unaware of you. You're a key player in this event. He probably has a picture of you on his pinboard."

"Damn it! You're right."

Nik repeated his offer to spy on her sister's stalker. "He won't notice me. I'm just a guy."

In the suit he'd worn to dinner Friday night, which had hung in her closet all weekend, he was way more than "just a guy." He was one good-looking man. That said, he had a point: he was just another local businessman. There was no reason for Trick to suspect him.

"Alright, go!" She handed him his marching orders. "Keep your ears open. According to Ari, he chats up the locals and gets them talking."

"Will do," he said. "You stay here, under this awning, safe and out of sight."

"What are you worried about?" she asked. "He's not dangerous."

"You don't know that."

"Actually, I do." The guy was a content creator, not a serial killer. "Don't worry. I'll be safe."

Nik took off. Sasha had a camera with her this time around. It was a simple point-and-shoot with a better zoom lens than her phone—still not ideal. She snapped a few photos of Nik crossing the street. His swagger alone made her swoon. She couldn't wait for this mission to be over with. Sasha was dying to see his apartment. She expected a generic space, but did it hold clues to his past life? He would love her place in California. It was small but full of light and plants. She loved its warm wood floors high archways and vintage bath with claw-foot tub. Her bedroom was a loft you couldn't stand upright in. Somehow, she didn't think Nik would mind.

Sticky ice cream dripping down her arm brought her back to reality. It occurred to her how ridiculous this plan was. She'd sent Nik on a fool's errand, and yet he was game. This man had her heart.

Trick exited the shop and strolled off in the opposite direction. Sasha snapped a photo, not sure what, if anything, she'd do with it.

Nik came out a moment later. Sasha snapped a few more photos for which she had very specific designs.

She held out the melting Popsicle. "I saved you the last of the ice cream."

"Thank you, honey." He finished it in one bite. "You won't believe what I found out."

It was too late to tell him that she no longer cared. If Ariana could shake off her obsession with this trickster, so could she. Except, he had her attention now and her curiosity had won out. "Tell me," she said.

Nik draped an arm over her shoulders and together they strolled along the sidewalk. "Trick...has heartburn."

"What?"

"It's a drugstore, Sasha. He bought over-the-counter antacid medication."

"That's it?"

"That's it."

"He didn't ask any questions?"

"Not while I was there."

"Well... Okay then."

"Are we done here?" he asked.

She nudged him in the ribs. "You're such a good sport."

"Anything for you," he said.

The way he said it made her want to believe it was true.

After the grand tour of Nik's one-bedroom apartment, she said, "How can you stand it? It's too generic. Nothing personal. Ari at least brought stuff from home for her rental. I miss my apartment. Don't you miss your place in Miami?"

He was scrolling his phone, about to order dinner. He looked up with a quizzical look on his face.

"Did I say something wrong?" Sasha asked.

He clammed up whenever she mentioned the sale of his condo, or at least he'd done so the one and only time he'd mentioned it. What was going on there?

Nik set his phone down on the coffee table and pulled her onto the oatmeal-colored couch. "We have to talk."

Oh, no. Sasha's stomach dropped. "What is it?"

"I was going to wait until after dinner."

Again, curiosity got the best of her. "Just tell me now!"

Nik folded into himself before her eyes. She reached out to him, grabbed him by the arms, and pulled him back. "Don't do that. Stay here with me."

"Oh, honey," he said. "What do you think I'm going to say?"

"I don't know! Just say it!"

"I plan on moving to California permanently by the end of the year. We're moving our LA office to Silicon Valley and I plan to be there full-time."

She was stunned. "What? Really?"

"Yes, really."

Huh… That was a startling revelation. "Are you familiar with California at all?" she asked.

"I fly in and out of Los Angeles every month, but I don't see more than the office and hotel."

"Okay," she proceeded sheepishly. "Silicon Valley is in the Bay Area, which is where I live."

His beautiful mouth twisted as he suppressed a smile. "I realize that."

"So…like…we'd be in the same geographic area."

"I figured that out, Sasha."

Sasha withdrew from him, dropping her hands onto her lap. "Why didn't you want to tell me?"

Nik swallowed hard. "Because it would be awkward."

"Awkward how?"

She could see his inner turmoil, but Sasha had to have these answers. Given the option, would he prefer not to go on seeing her? Had this already solidified as a temporary thing in his mind? She'd spent so much time wondering if she could commit to Nik, and no thought at all to if he even wanted a committed relationship. After all, he was moving to California for work. Maybe that was his first priority.

"I didn't want it to seem like I was taking over your turf."

Her turf? Seriously? It came down to turf wars?

"Sasha," he said, and took her hands. "I'm fumbling this. Let me start again."

Sasha waited while he collected his thoughts, her heart cracking with each passing second. How was it that she was already so invested in this?

"You made it clear this is just a fling."

"No," she said. "We never defined this, Nik."

His eyes went dark as he considered her words. "I'm just going to ask," he said. "Does it bother you that I'm moving to your city?"

Sasha shook her head. It truly didn't bother her. "I'd love to take you to my favorite restaurants."

Her answer didn't satisfy him. "I want to be clear about this," he said. "I don't need a tour guide around the city. I'd like to keep seeing you."

That was pretty clear! Sasha released all the air trapped in her lungs. "Why didn't you just say that? Were you scared I'd scurry away?"

"Yes," he said, categorically. "I was scared."

In her linen blouse and cutoff shorts, Sasha wasn't dressed for seduction. She was going to attempt it anyway. She slipped off her top. "I'll make a few things clear. I like you, and I like how I feel around you. And no matter what you say, I'm taking you on a tour of my city. If you think you can stop me—"

Nik cupped her face and kissed her hard. She leaned back against the cushions and drew him on top of her. Then she changed her mind and pushed him off. "Not here! We've already done it on a couch," she explained. "We should try something new."

"The shower?" he suggested.

She glared at him. "Did you forget this morning already?"

"Does that really count?"

Arguably, it didn't. They'd kissed until the water ran cold.

"That only leaves the kitchen," Nik said, his voice husky with desire. "And we both think that's overrated."

"True."

"What's the issue?" he asked. "We don't have to tik every box right away We've got time."

They had time. There was no rush, no hard and fast deadline. Nik was coming to San Francisco. He would see her charming apartment, and he'd love it. They'd go for authentic dim sum in Chinatown. They'd get to know each other slowly. She would open her life and make room for him. This was not the beginning, middle and end. She could dim the fire to a slow simmer.

"I've been rushing this because I thought it would be over soon," she said. "I wanted to experience everything, make sure we left nothing on the table."

Nik pressed his forehead to hers. "I can promise you this— we're not leaving anything on the table."

Sasha kissed him, her tongue sweeping and exploring his mouth. When she pulled away, breathless, her gaze slid to the dining table.

"Don't even think about it," Nik said. "That thing is basically particleboard. It'll break."

* * *

Dinner was pizza eaten out of the carton. They sat on scattered pillows and drank wine and talked into the night.

Nik told her about a conversation with his cousin. She'd cashed in her 401K to pay for art classes in Europe. "I want to help her out. I know she won't let me. She's so stubborn."

"Financially, you mean. Otherwise, she has it in hand."

"Yeah." Nik set aside his plate and rested his head on Sasha's lap. "She shouldn't go broke to pursue her dream."

Sasha wiped her hands on the paper-thin napkins and cradled Nik's face between her palms. "You're going to have to get creative. Ariana helped me out those early days. One Christmas, she paid my rent for a year. I made a fuss, but I would've been a fool to turn it down. I wouldn't be where I am now without her help. I was able to leave my hometown at a time that I desperately needed to, and take an unpaid internship in one of the most expensive cities in the country. Six months later, I had a job."

"Why were you desperate to leave your hometown?" he asked.

Sasha shrugged. "You're missing the point of the story."

Nik traced the curve of her jawline with a tip of a finger. "Why were you desperate, Sasha?"

She caught his hand and pressed a kiss to the back of it. They were talking about his cousin and her issues. There was no need to stir up all this.

A crinkle appeared between his brows. "Was this right after the wedding?"

"The canceled wedding, you mean?"

Nik said nothing. Somehow, his silence added weight to her question. She blinked back fresh tears. "It was a difficult year," she said. "I lost friends. Nothing dramatic, obviously, it was an awkward situation all around. Some pitied me. Others picked sides. I was alone a lot. I felt left out. Leaving San Bernardino was the best decision I ever made."

Nik sat up and looked at her a long time. "I don't ever want you to feel that lonely again."

He said it as if he could decide her fate. "One can only hope," she said. "Anyway, I'm in a good place now."

He eased her back onto a bed of pillows and crawled over her. "Here with me, you mean?"

Sasha let out a small laugh. "I meant in life in general, but sure."

"May I make love to you here? Or is it not innovative enough?"

"It's fine." She wrapped her legs around his. "You can make love to me on the rooftop later on."

He kissed the hollow of her neck. "Deal."

Sometime in the night, they made love in Nik's soft bed. He parted her knees, and Sasha lost all sense of time to the stroke of his tongue and the scrape of his scruff on her thighs. When he went away to find a condom, she felt a sense of loss so deep, she had to call out his name. "I'm not going any-where," he tried to reassure her, but words were not enough. She wasn't satisfied until he was deep inside her, his breath fanning her cheek, his voice in her ear coaxing her to sur-render to him.

Sasha didn't need coaxing. She was already in his power.

Nineteen

Back at the hotel the next morning, Sasha poured a cup of coffee and caught up on some editing. Watching Nik whirl around his apartment, prepping for a busy day while taking calls from Oliver, was enough to make her miss work, or at least the sense of purpose that came with every new assignment. She decided to pitch the smokehouse story to the editor of *Table for Two*, a culinary magazine.

Sasha shifted through the images of Donna's kitchen, the old barn and the surrounding fields. She came across the one photo she'd taken of Nik. He sat with his elbows on the table; his golden-brown eyes gleamed in the sun. It was hard to believe that he was practically a stranger then. And yet, she'd snapped that photo only minutes before they'd kissed. In such a short time, he'd done so much to make her life beautiful, to make her feel safe. He was so concerned for her well-being that he was willing to put her interests above his own, rethinking a move to California.

What had she done for him in return? Not much.

It was time to correct that.

This morning, while getting dressed, she overheard Nik on the phone with Oliver, discussing yet another failed attempt at a meeting with the CEO of Mad Dash. She went into the bathroom to gather her braids into a high ponytail when she heard Nik admit that he was ready to give up. That didn't sit well with her.

She exited the photo-editing app and logged into her social media account. She had no trouble finding Teresa Price; they had ten friends in common. Sasha composed a quick direct message, asking if they could talk. In the subject line, she wrote: I need a favor. There was no use playing around. She didn't want to catch up or talk about old times. She wouldn't propose they meet for coffee. A straightforward request would catch Teresa's attention. She would not miss the opportunity to show off.

Sasha was right. Before she'd finished up with her photo edits, Teresa had messaged her back: Video chat?

Sasha's hands fell away from the laptop keyboard. It was ridiculous how a chance encounter with one of her ex-fiancé's many cousins at an airport or the prospect of a video call with an old friend of his could cause so much inner turmoil. She was not going to spend the rest of her life punishing herself for letting Terrence down, for choosing her happiness over his. Underneath the grief, she was thankful to her former self for having the courage to walk away. She loved her life and now she'd found a person who wanted to be in it as it was. That was what this video call was all about.

Even so, she had to look good. Sasha let down her braids and swiped on lipstick. A moment later, she was face-to-face with Teresa, a dark-eyed brunette with a soft round face and the pointy teeth of a predator.

"Sasha!" she cried. "Long time no see!"

Terrence and Teresa were "TNT" to the group. Sasha prepared herself to be detonated.

"I know!" Sasha said. "Wild, right?"

"How have you been?" she asked with a tone that fell just short of condescension.

Sasha held an even smile. "I'm doing great. Thanks."

"I might have come across one of a photo of you in a magazine, but I can't say for sure."

She didn't work for tabloids, so the chances of Teresa coming across her work were slim. "I'm published widely, so it's possible."

"Not one of your photos," she said. "A photograph of you leaving a restaurant in Texas on the arm of a striking man."

Ah...well...one way or the other, she'd landed in the tabloids. "Yup. That was me. I plead guilty."

"There's a lot of talk surrounding your sister's wedding. Can you believe it?"

"It's to be expected. Ari and Ex *are* the power couple of the moment."

"If this wedding even happens."

The knives were out. "Stay tuned!"

Teresa checked her watch. "I'm short on time. You said you needed a favor."

"Yes, I do," Sasha said, eager to get off the call herself. "Ari tells me you're the CFO of Mad Dash."

"Oh my God! She knows about that?"

"She's a customer. She loves the service."

"Wow!" Teresa exclaimed. "Would she be willing to endorse us?"

"No." Sasha was firm on that. She was accustomed to dodging these types of requests. "I'm here on behalf of the striking man in the photo."

Teresa leaned in toward the screen. "Really?"

"His name in Nikolai Williams," Sasha said. "His PR firm, Nexus, wants a meeting with Mad Dash. They handle Xavier Noble's account, and he couldn't be happier."

"Really?"

"Yes, really."

"Hmm… Obviously, I can't say yes or no, right now on the spot."

"I understand," Sasha said. "Look up the firm, and give it some thought. If you're interested, contact the firm directly. I'll stay out of it from here on out."

"Sounds fair," Teresa said. "I'll tell you this. If they're good enough for Xavier Noble, they should be good enough for our little start-up."

"According to Forbes, there's nothing little about your start-up."

Teresa cackled. "Who am I to argue with Forbes?"

It was time to pull the plug. "Thanks for your time. I know you're busy."

"We'll keep in touch, Sasha!" Teresa said, all smiles. "Don't be a stranger."

Sasha exited the video chat and fell back into her chair. The five-minute conversation left her depleted. Who knew name-dropping required so much energy? All in all, it was the right thing to do. Nik worked so hard. He deserved a break.

A calendar alert popped on the computer screen. She had an appointment with her therapist in *five* minutes. Sasha had forgotten all about it. Crap! What was there to report? She was happy and doing well for the first time ever. But it was too late to cancel. She poured herself another cup of coffee and got settled for the half-hour session.

It began in the usual way. After polite greetings, her therapist read from his notes. "The last time we spoke, your sister's wedding was coming up. You had some anxiety about that. It exposed some unhealed trauma. You should be in Texas now. How's it going?"

Her therapist was a middle-aged man named Jonas Bradford. There were times Sasha wished she'd gone with a woman therapist. Dr. Jonas could be quite dry, and she would have preferred a chattier approach to therapy. However, Dr. Jonas came highly recommended and Ariana pointed out that her expectation of a chatty, sassy woman therapist was sexist. "She's not your bestie."

"It's going great," Sasha said.

"Good to hear," Dr. Jonas said. "Tell me more."

"I met someone," she said. "He's perfect."

Dr. Jonas stared back at her from over the rim of his drugstore reading glasses. He'd mentioned he bought them in bulk. "When did you meet this person?"

"On the flight to Royal," Sasha said. "His name is Nik."

Dr. Jonas started scribbling furiously on his digital notepad. Sasha waited patiently. "It's Nik with a K."

He crossed out a word and rewrote it.

"He does business in Texas, but soon he'll be settling down near me to run their West Coast office. Isn't that awesome?"

The look Dr. Jonas gave her made it clear he didn't think it was awesome at all. "Are you comfortable with the pace at which this new relationship is advancing?"

"I am," Sasha said. "When you know, you know."

The Harvard-trained psychologist could hardly hide his skepticism. "Let's analyze this more deeply, shall we?"

Sasha twisted in her seat. "Okay."

"It is worth noting that you are starting something new mere weeks before a triggering event."

She preferred not to think of her only sister's wedding as a triggering event; still, she understood where he was coming from.

"I agree the timing isn't ideal," Sasha said. "But Nik is so wonderful. He put all my fears to rest."

"There is no ideal timing," Dr. Jonas said. "However, there are advantages to taking it slow. You may want to check on how you feel about him when your sister's wedding is over and done, and you're back to your everyday life."

"You think I'm clinging to Nik like a life raft to avoid drowning in my feelings," Sasha said.

"Those are your words," Dr. Jonas said. "Nonetheless, it's a theory worth exploring."

Long after the session was over, Sasha sat staring at her blank computer screen. *Those are your words...* Was she moving this fast with Nik as a way to prove to Ariana and herself that she was over the past? Was she using him? The answer erupted violently inside her.

NO!

Every time he touched her, every look they shared, she had all the confirmation she needed. Yes, she was going through some things. *Nonetheless*, Nik was worth holding onto, particularly in times of great turbulence. She had no intention of letting him go or slowing things down or anything else. If this plane was crashing down, she was going down with it.

Twenty

After an exceptional lunch meeting with a client, Oliver and Nik stayed behind at the restaurant to toast their accomplishment.

"I'll have a whisky neat," Nik said to the waiter.

"Me, too," Oliver said. "It's five o'clock somewhere."

"This is Texas," the waiter replied. "You don't have to rationalize it."

When the whiskies arrived, they toasted to Nexus and Texas.

"It's been twenty-four hours," Oliver said. "It's time for a status report. Are you still in love or was that a passing feeling?"

Nik swirled his glass. "Still in love. Can't shake it."

"Does Sasha know how you feel?" Oliver asked.

"Not yet."

"I know how you feel before she does?" Oliver folded over with laughter. "Man! We're close, but you're taking this too far!"

"I've made some progress. I told her about the move to California."

"And? How did she take it?"

Nik relived the moment. Either he'd done a poor job expressing himself or she'd misread him completely. Either way, he saw the pain and confusion in her eyes. He felt like the biggest jerk then. She deserved honesty. In the end, his fears were unfounded.

"She was amazing about it. She wants to show me around."

"See?" Oliver grinned like the know-it-all he was. "It was all in your head. Now go tell her that you love her."

"We're not there yet."

"How do you know?" Oliver asked. "If you feel so strongly, there's a good chance she feels the same."

Nik doubted it. Sasha had his head spinning at hello. "There's no rush," he said. "We have time."

Right then, both their phones buzzed with messages. Their accounts manager, Daria, had messaged them both in all caps: TERESA PRICE, CFO OF MAD DASH, HAS REQUESTED A MEETING. WHAT SAY YOU GUYS?

Oliver barked out a laugh and started typing right away. WE SAY: HELL YEAH! ANYTIME.

Nik couldn't wrap his mind around it. His every lead had gone stale. "I don't get it," he said. "Why now?"

"I get it," Oliver said. "You did the work. You wore them down. And now we have one more thing to toast to." He raised his glass. "Good job, man! Here's to you!"

Although the victory didn't feel earned, Nik raised his glass. "To us!"

They met at the TCC. After much fawning over Ari and Ex, the mixologist got to the point and proposed a signature mocktail. "It is thoughtful to accommodate everyone."

Ariana agreed. "Of course."

Sasha nodded and kept on sipping the pineapple-based beverage.

When the mixologist offered a tour of the wine cellar where the TCC allowed them storage space for the wedding, Xavier leaped at the chance. Ari rested a hand on Sasha's shoulder and pinned her down on the barstool. "We'll stay here."

Her tone made it clear that Sasha did not have a choice.

Sasha mumbled into her glass, "Fine with me."

Once the men were out of earshot, Ariana's grip turned tighter. "What's wrong?"

Sasha winced. "What do you mean?"

"You've been sulking all afternoon," she said. "This is the fun errand! You had more fun at the dress shop yesterday and you hate shopping."

"I'm sorry." Sasha slumped over the polished mahogany bar.

"Don't be sorry. Tell me what's wrong. Is it…" Ari hesitated. "Is it Nik? Did you two have a falling-out?"

Sasha could have drowned in her mocktail at the mention of his name. "Can I get something stronger?"

Ariana reached for a bottle of gin left on the bar and topped off her glass. "Talk. What did he do?"

"He did nothing!"

"He did *something*."

Sasha swiveled in her seat to face her sister. It was time to come clean. "I have something to confess. Nik and I have grown closer these past few days."

Ari topped off her own glass. "Who are you telling? I've witnessed this *closeness*."

"He plans to move to the Bay Area in a few months for its proximity to Silicon Valley. That's the next frontier for Nexus."

"How exciting!" Ari cried. "Is that why you're freaking out?"

"Not at all." It was the opposite: she was elated. This was the best thing that could happen. She and Nik had time on their side now. "I spoke to my therapist today."

"And you told him you're making healthy choices," Ari supplied.

Well, not quite. "He thinks the timing of this blossoming friendship is suspect. He thinks that I may be using Nik as a distraction to avoid dealing with the issues your wedding brought up."

"What do you think?" Ari asked.

"I think he thinks the same thing *you* thought," Sasha retorted.

"I have no reason to think that way now that he's moving to the Bay Area," Ari said. "There's a path forward. Whatever is *blossoming* can take root."

Sasha rolled her eyes. So many metaphors to skirt the truth! "I have to wonder if he's right. I was nervous about this trip and what did I do? I latched on to the first man I locked eyes with even before the plane landed."

"In this case, the plane didn't land as much as it skidded to a stop," Ari said. "What choice did you have?"

"None, really."

"It's serendipity or whatever."

"Is that even a real thing?" Sasha said, skeptical.

Ari was having none of it. "That's rich coming from a woman who believes in curses."

She had a point there.

"If it weren't for my wedding, you likely wouldn't have started therapy. If it weren't for my wedding, you wouldn't have traveled to Royal at all. And, lastly, if it weren't for my wedding, you might have never met Nik."

"Right! This is all *your* fault."

"Ha ha!" she said dryly. "I'm serious, Sasha."

"So am I!" Sasha wailed. "That's what I'm trying to tell you. I'm serious about Nik. He's stirred up so many feelings..."

Ari was at the edge of her seat. "You have feelings?"

Sasha let out a breath. "Yes," she said. "I have feelings for Nik."

"Whew!" Ari mimed wiping sweat off her brow. "I had to work for that one."

"What are you talking about?"

"It was obvious to me from the start that you liked him," Ari said. "You lit up when he walked through the door. I didn't want you to mess it up. So you can report back to your therapist that I took the necessary steps to force you to examine your feelings."

"Thank you, Dr. Ramos."

Ari flashed a cocky little smile. "You're welcome."

"So...you don't think we're moving too fast?" Sasha asked sheepishly.

"Not unless you think so," Ari said.

"I do, absolutely," Sasha said. "But I like where things are headed."

"Well then, this calls for a toast." Ari raised her glass. "To new beginnings!"

Sasha didn't have it in her to say that she and Nik had sprinted far past the starting line. She fixed a smile on her face and raised her glass. "To new beginnings!"

Twenty-One

Good luck with your meeting!

Nik received the text message five minutes before they were scheduled to start. A smile crept on his face as he typed a response: Why do I need luck? I have you.

He hadn't seen her in two days. Ever since Teresa Price of Mad Dash had requested a meeting, it was all hands on deck for the team. Long days spent at the office, no time for lunch breaks, eating dinner out of takeout containers—that was their standard operational procedure. Signing Mad Dash wouldn't make or break Nexus; they'd had a banner year. However, this was the sort of energy they brought to any deal. They went in hot.

He and Sasha still managed to talk every night. When he explained the situation to her, she was supportive. She was gleeful, even. He felt more than lucky to have her in his life.

Presently, they were all in the conference room. With a few clicks, they initiated the video call. Teresa Price appeared on the wall-mounted monitor.

"Good evening!" she said brightly. "Or good afternoon! Forgive me. I don't know what time it is over there."

They exchanged pleasantries, discussed the weather and finally got down to business. Nik started with their usual opening: "Today we want to persuade you to switch teams and take a chance with us."

"It wouldn't be a risk," Teresa said. "Isn't it true you handle Xavier Noble's PR?"

Considering that Xavier was trending on all social media platforms at the moment, Nik didn't consider this answer odd.

"Xavier Noble is one of our newest clients," Oliver said. "He's a novelist with specific goals for his career."

"Mad Dash is shaping how commerce is done in the United States and we want to help you make an impact," Nik added.

"I'm listening," Teresa said.

Nik went on to present a brief overview of Mad Dash's current state of affairs and the markets in which it could potentially grow. "You fare better in sprawling suburban areas with aging populations, places where quick trips to a convenience store or the shoe repair shop becomes a hassle for the elderly or the disabled. Texas has its big cities, of course, but there are a great many communities, such as Royal, where your services could benefit the population. It's about micro-targeting."

"Micro-targeting, that sounds smart," Teresa said. "May I ask you a question?"

"Of course," Nik replied. "Interrupt me at any time."

"Are you Sasha Ramos's new boyfriend?"

Was he...what?

Nik didn't know what to say. Aside from the fact that his relationship status wasn't this woman's business, he wasn't comfortable presenting himself as Sasha's boyfriend. They hadn't had that talk yet.

"You're the man in the photo, right? The one in all the magazines?"

Nik was aware that the photo of him and Sasha leaving Sheen had made the tabloid rounds. He didn't expect it to come up five minutes into his presentation.

Oliver tossed him a glance, letting him know that he could handle Teresa's questions any way he liked.

"That was me," he said. "Sasha is a friend."

Teresa's smile exposed a row of pointy teeth. "That was rude of me," she said. "I didn't mean to interrupt your presentation. Continue."

Thick silence weaved through the room. Oliver cut through it by clearing his throat. He went on to point out the various markets in which Mad Dash had the most potential for growth in Texas. "Once you've covered these areas, it'll only be a matter of time before the city dwellers start clamoring for your services," Oliver concluded. "You know how much they hate to be left out."

They all laughed. The mood lightened somewhat until Teresa brought it crashing down.

"Sasha—"

"What?" Nik interrupted. If they could conclude this meeting without bringing up Sasha, he would be grateful.

"*Sasha,*" she repeated with bloody satisfaction, "highly recommended you."

"You spoke to Sasha about us?"

"Yes," Teresa said with a rolling laugh. "I should have mentioned it at the top. She's an old friend. She recommended I take this meeting. I like what I'm hearing so far. It all sounds great. It just doesn't sound great *enough*. What else do you bring to the table?"

At this point, Oliver had to take over the meeting. Nik was too astonished to behave professionally. He was furious with this woman who was clearly here to toy with them. To a degree less, he was angry with Sasha for putting them in this situation. She had never shown any interest in his business beyond offering general support and encouragement, and here she was reaching out to old friends and setting up meetings. He thought of her text. Good luck with the meeting. It blew his mind. Good luck with the meeting that she'd arranged?

"With Nexus you get a team dedicated to building sustainable growth," Oliver said.

"That's what they all say," Teresa said with a slight roll of her eyes.

"We know you're interested in Texas," Nik cut in. "But Texas is not a monolith. We see the potential of Mad Dash becoming an essential resource in communities with the most need. It's a smarter and more cost-effective approach than blanketing the state of Texas in a hit-or-miss fashion. But if you'd rather talk about my girlfriend—"

"Don't get testy!" Teresa said. "I'm a businesswoman first—I had to push your buttons. I heard what you had to say and I'll take it back to the team. They'll probably want to meet with you, too. For the moment, our CEO is out of town and can't be reached so it'll have to wait."

"That's all we ask," Oliver said. "Thanks for meeting with us."

"You're welcome," Teresa said. "I'll be honest. I only agreed to this in the hopes of scoring a last-minute invite to the *royal wedding* of our times. I'm obsessed with the story! I knew Ariana before she was famous. We're all from San Bernardino. That said, you made some valid points. If we want to conquer Texas, so to speak, it would be wise to partner with a company with boots on the ground. We'll be in touch."

The monitor screen went dark. Oliver gave Nik a blank stare. "What the hell was that?"

Nik snapped shut his notebook. "I have no idea," he said through clenched teeth.

"Did Sasha mention—"

"No, she did *not*."

"Hold on," Oliver said. "She had to have done it in good faith. Anyway, we killed it. So, kudos to her! We probably wouldn't have gotten a meeting otherwise."

Nik wasn't willing to go that far. "Yes, but—"

"I know," Oliver said. "You were blindsided, and it's not cool."

"It's not cool!" Nik repeated hotly. After all the work he'd put into preparing, to be thrown off like that, unnecessarily. They'd talked every night. She'd had ample opportunity to clue him in.

"No argument here," Oliver said.

Nik rose from the table and collected his things. He had to talk to her.

"Where are you going?" Oliver asked.

"Where do you think?"

"I think you should go home, go on a run, whatever, just cool off before you speak with her. Turn off your phone, if that helps," Oliver said. "That's my advice. Take it for what it's worth."

Nik turned off his phone. "Going dark."

Oliver called out to him just when he reached the conference room door. "Hey! One last thing."

"What's that?"

"You called Sasha your girlfriend earlier."

"I did?"

Oliver grinned. "Yep, it's official!"

For once, they were staying in. Sasha was spending the evening at her sister's place. Ari was puttering about in her favorite faded jeans. She'd lit a fragrant candle and put on a jazz record. Ex was in the other room, revising an article he'd written for a popular men's magazine. Sasha sat at the marble dinner table, sifting through a collection of ribbons for the perfect shade of bluebonnet blue.

She held up a short ribbon for Ari to inspect. "How about this?"

"Mmm... Too light."

She held up another. "And this?"

"Too dark."

"Oh, God!" Sasha muttered.

"Just keep looking!" Ari insisted. "Bluebonnet blue is a specific color. That first one was more turquoise than anything else."

"Bluebonnets come in pink, purple and white. Look it up."

Ari switched the record. "That's not helpful."

Sasha went on sifting.

In the best of times, her heart wouldn't be in the task, but she hadn't heard from Nik, not since his last and very sweet text message: Why do I need luck? I have you.

She'd been all day waiting for an update. Her calls went straight to voice mail. Either he'd turned off his phone in preparation for the meeting and forgot to turn it back on, or he was too busy with follow-up work. That didn't change the fact that she hadn't seen him in two days, and was starting to forget the taste of his kiss.

It took a half hour, but she finally sold Ari on ribbon the color of cornflower.

After a quiet dinner, Sasha turned down Ex's offer for a ride. It was a crisp night and she preferred to walk to her hotel. "It's only a few blocks," she assured them, adding a hug for good measure. "I could use the fresh air."

It had been a struggle keeping her mood even at her sister's place. Sasha was not one to hide her feelings; they were always projected onto her face. She didn't want Ari to suspect anything was amiss with Nik, not that anything was amiss. He was busy with work, work generated from a meeting that she'd arranged. It was her damn fault, and now she was paying for it.

Back at the hotel, while waiting for an elevator, she checked her phone one last time. Nothing. She dropped the phone into her wicker tote. An elevator car opened and a sea of people poured out, Nik among them. Just like that, the gloomy clouds that had followed her around all afternoon dissipated.

Sasha rushed to him and with a hand to his chest, guided him back into the elevator. The doors closed and they were alone. "Where have you been? Why didn't you call?"

"I wanted to talk to you in person," he said.

"Well, here I am," she said. "I've missed you!"

She grabbed his tie and pulled him into a kiss. Hand to her heart, she swore Nik hesitated before he kissed her back. She then promptly forgot all about it when his hands gripped her bottom and pulled her into him.

Two days of separation was too much. They tore at each other, their hands roaming freely, and violently pulled apart when the elevator stopped on a random floor. She swiveled around and smoothed down her minidress. Nik leaned against the handrail and held her close with a hand on her hip. She could feel him hard against her lower back.

The doors slid open, achingly slow. An elderly woman asked, "Going down?"

"No," Sasha answered. "Definitely going up."

"Thanks," the woman said. "Have a good night."

"You, too."

The doors inched shut. Sasha fell onto Nik's chest. He swept her braids aside and slid a hot kiss down her neck. She moaned and reached out blindly for his free hand and placed it over her breast. Nik had other designs. He gathered the hem of her dress and—

They'd reached her floor. The doors slid opened, and they

stumbled out. Sasha grabbed his arm and tugged him in the direction of her suite. In a gesture that she found sexy, he slipped out her key card and waved them in.

The door hadn't clicked shut and she was out of her dress. The white linen shift lay crumpled on the floor. Nik tore off his clothes, scooped her up and carried her into...the kitchen.

So, they were doing this.

He lifted her onto the counter and took care of the condom. The wait was making her mad. *"Hurry!"*

Nik looked up at her, his eyes dark. "You're going to be the end of me."

She wrapped her legs around his waist. "Let's find out."

He sunk inside her. Sasha closed her eyes. The commotion inside her quieted, and roared back up again. Nik controlled the pace, ignoring her pleas. He would not let her rush their pleasure. It was worth the exquisite torture when they unraveled together.

Moments later, they were on the kitchen floor drinking from the bottle of wine that Nik had brought that first night. Sasha pressed the back of her hand to his cheek. "How did the meeting go?"

He met her eyes, and did not answer.

It dawned on her then that Nik hadn't uttered more than a few words to her all day. "Is something wrong?" she asked.

"Why didn't you tell me you set up the meeting?" he said.

"Oh..." Sasha's stomach turned. "That..."

She pulled herself up off the floor. "Let's go to the couch. It's more comfortable over there."

She was stalling for time. Why *hadn't* she told him? When he framed it that way, it seemed deceitful. It wasn't her intention to mislead him. She'd wanted to do something nice for him, and that was what she came up with.

Nik rolled onto his feet. It stung her when he stopped to pull on his pants before joining her on the couch. Feeling exposed, she went into her bathroom and slipped on a robe. When she got back, he had his shirt on. It was unbuttoned and loose over his sculpted chest, but still. Was he planning on leaving?

Sasha knew she'd better clear the air. She stood before him, her hands in her pockets. "It was meant to be a surprise. I wanted to do something nice to make up for everything that I'd put you through. When you brought up Mad Dash over dinner, Ariana pointed out that an old friend of mine was the company's CFO. I got the idea that maybe I could put in a good word for you."

Nik's face remained stone hard. Sasha eased onto the couch next to him. "Did the meeting not go well?"

"It started with Teresa Price asking if I was your boyfriend and ended with her angling for a wedding invitation," Nik said. "It didn't go great."

Sasha was shocked. "I'm sorry. I thought she'd be more professional than that."

"She wasn't professional at all," Nik said. "I don't see how you two could have ever been friends."

"She was Terrence's friend, to be honest."

He scrunched his brows. "Terrence?"

"My ex-fiancé," Sasha said with a sigh. "Teresa and Terrence went to business school together. They were TNT."

Nik blinked at her, unmoved, leading Sasha to think that in life, like in sitcoms, a laugh track was useful. She threw her hands up in exasperation. "That was a joke, by the way!"

"I get the joke," he said evenly. "Here's what I don't understand. You reached out to your ex-fiancé's college buddy to help me out?"

"Yes!"

"And you did it to 'make up for everything' you'd put me through?"

"Exactly!"

"What exactly did you put me through?"

"All of it!" she cried, although she was hard pressed to come up with a single example. "The ride from the airport, for one thing."

"That was my pleasure, Sasha," he said. "I was more than happy to do it."

"Even so, you could have had a quiet, pleasant ride without me there talking up a storm and driving you to distraction."

"Do you think I wanted quiet and pleasant?" he asked.

This discussion was going off the rails. "Nik, can't a person do one nice thing for you? I'm sorry the meeting didn't go well, but you have to believe it wasn't my intention. I wasn't trying to set you up."

Nik wasn't listening to her. "You said your fiancé's friends shunned you after the breakup."

"They did," she said, wearily. "Teresa chief among them."

"And you reached out to her anyway?" Nik dropped his elbows onto his knees. "Why would you think I'd want that?"

"To sign the company!" Sasha was beyond exasperated now. "Isn't that what you business people do?"

"God, Sasha!" Nik was clearly beyond exasperated, as well. "I'd rather walk away from any deal than have you put yourself in that position."

Deep inside, Sasha understood why he was upset. Reaching out to Teresa had left a bad taste in her mouth. It was icky, to say the least. That was probably why she hadn't told him.

"You put yourself though that, meanwhile I'm not sure I want to do business with them," he said. "As much as I think this company has potential, I don't know that the people running it are serious. I've been chasing after them for weeks. It took you pulling strings to get in touch with them at all. The CEO is MIA and the CFO is more interested in a wedding invite than a business plan."

Sasha listened and nodded. "I understand. You're under no obligation to move forward, not on my account."

"Don't reach out to her again," he said. "She's not a good person."

"I know that now," Sasha said. "Please don't scold me."

"I'm not—"

Nik stopped and let out a breath. Next thing, he was on his feet and working on the buttons of his shirt. Sasha watched him wordlessly. Anger and annoyance shot through her. "Are you leaving?"

His hands dropped to his side. "I don't want to fight. It's been a long day, and I'm fried. It's best we cool off tonight."

If Nik Williams thought he'd come by, make love to her on her kitchen counter, drink her wine, accuse her of meddling in his career and take off, well…fine! She wasn't going to stop him. In fact, she would escort him to the door.

"I spoke to Jonas about us. He thinks we're rushing it."

Nik took a step back. "Who is Jonas?"

"My therapist!" she spat. Why she'd weaponized the word was anyone's guess.

"You told your therapist about me?" he asked.

"I did, and he thinks we're taking this too far," Sasha said. "I'm starting to think he's right."

Nik ran a hand through his hair. "Because we're having a disagreement?"

"Because you don't know me!" she shouted. "This is just who I am. I rush into things, realize my mistake way too late, and back out at the last second."

"What are we even talking about?" Nik asked. "Are we still talking about Teresa Price?"

"We're talking about everything!" she kept on shouting. A small voice in her back of her mind was saying: *Don't do this! Settle down, calm down, come back to this with a cool head.* She muted that voice. "And for the record, this is not a *disagreement.* This is a fight, and you're not going to win."

Shock, hurt and anger projected onto his face. To her horror, Sasha realized that she was the villain here. She'd created the problem, aggravated the problem, and now she was going to compound it by theatrically pointing to the door and ordering him to leave. "Good night, Nik."

He walked past her. She sank deeper into the couch, arms folded, listening while he looked around for his shoes and belt. After ordering him to go, she couldn't beg him to stay. That was a bit much, even for her. Yet she didn't want him to walk out like this. If they could keep talking, they could resolve this.

"I have a question," he said.

Sasha was immediately on her feet. "What is it?"

He was wrapping his tie around his fist. Nik didn't usually wear ties. He'd likely pulled all the stops for the train wreck of a meeting she'd set up.

"First it was your sister who didn't want us to jump into anything, now it's your therapist," he said. "When are you going to admit that it's you?"

Sasha took a step back as the chances of her winning this fight were waning.

"You don't think we should be together," he continued. "You think we're moving too fast, and you don't have to hide behind the opinions of others. You can just say what you're thinking yourself."

"I'm perfectly capable of speaking up for myself, Nik," she retorted. "You should know that by now."

"Here's what I know," he said. "You're a spontaneous person. I love that about you. What you did this week was far from spontaneous. You planned this. You placed the call to your former fiancé's friend. You held your tongue for two days while I was busy prepping for the meeting you set up.

This was not a spontaneous gesture. It was a decision on your part."

Sasha charged forward. "Are you done?"

"No, I have one last thing to get off my chest."

"What is it?"

"I'm not convinced you went through this trouble for me."

"Why else would I have done this?"

Sasha was shouting again. She couldn't help it. He had pushed every button there was to push. Maybe he did know her, after all.

"To get back in touch with your fiancé, or at least his friends." He shoved his tie in his pocket. "I never considered the fact that maybe you're not over him. Maybe the reason you can't move on is because you love him."

"If I loved him, I would have married him, don't you think?"

"Not if you believe you're cursed."

"Get out!" she hollered. "GET OUT!"

Nik's eyes clouded with sorrow, but he did what he was told. He set his key card on the console table on his way out the door.

Twenty-Two

Of all the ways to crash down to earth…

Sasha took another swig from the warm wine bottle. It was one in the morning and she still had a lot of fight in her. If anyone were spying on her through the hotel window, they'd catch a glimpse of a disheveled woman, pacing around in circles, drinking from a bottle and talking gibberish to herself.

Nik, her protector, her knight in shining armor, had betrayed her. That was the only way to put it. He'd *betrayed* her trust. She couldn't wrap her mind around it. How could she have so misjudged the man? He thought he wasn't over Terrence? Ha! Just wait until she showed him how fast she could get over him! She snapped her fingers. "Like that!" So fast, his head would spin.

Why is the room spinning?

If anything, this was confirmation that they'd jumped into something prematurely. What was she thinking? She'd meet a handsome stranger on a plane, fall in love and live happily ever after like in a freaking fairy tale?

Why is my head is splitting in two?

Seriously, though, what was she thinking? She and Nik

were strangers swept up by adventure. There was no other explanation. It was all fun and games until things got real.

Sasha wandered into the bedroom and plopped onto the bed. The wine bottle landed with a thump on the rug.

Why is my heart breaking?

The next day, those questions plagued her still. She'd nursed the dull ache in her chest with antacid chewables with no success. At least she was out of bed, on her couch with a cup of coffee, binge-watching videos, her phone clutched in one hand—just in case.

Who knew how long she'd carry on like this if it weren't for Ariana's timely intervention. She banged on her door so forcefully, for a second there Sasha thought it was the local SWAT team. Ironic, considering that *she* was the real victim here.

"Hold on!" she cried.

Sasha wrapped the robe tighter around her body and puttered to the door. She opened without hesitation. It could only be one person.

Ariana jumped back, recoiling at her appearance. "My God, Sasha! What happened to you?"

"Come in, and keep quiet."

It was silly of her to think Ari could ever keep quiet. She stormed in, assessed the mess, and tossed her designer purse onto the one clear surface.

"Why haven't you answered my texts? We're going to the stationery store to pick out thank-you cards."

"Sorry, I'm falling to pieces at the moment," Sasha said. "I'll pass today."

"What's going on?"

"It's over between Nik and me," she said. "And I'm a mess."

As soon as she said the words, the dull ache in her chest lifted. It was as if the truth had been clawing to come out all this time. *It's over. I'm a mess.*

"When did this happen?" Ari asked. "You were fine yesterday."

Sasha plopped onto the couch. "What a difference a day makes."

Ari sat next to her. "Start from the beginning."

She couldn't if she tried. There was no beginning, middle or end. It was as if a bomb had detonated and blew her heart into smithereens. If she had to start somewhere, she might as well start with Teresa Price.

Ariana listened, and grimaced.

"Is it really that bad?" Sasha asked. "I had the best intentions."

"Ex and I have an agreement—we don't meddle or interfere in each other's careers. We don't offer unsolicited advice. How would you like it if I called in favors to get you jobs?"

Sasha wouldn't like it one bit.

"Still, that doesn't excuse Teresa," Ari said. "Who knew she could be such a bitch?"

Sasha raised a hand. "I did."

Ari whipped out her phone. "You know what? I'm deleting her app."

"No, don't do that!"

"It's done," she said, and pocketed the phone. "Is that all, or is there more to this?"

They hadn't even scratched the surface. "Nik thinks I'm not over Terrence."

"That's ridiculous," Ari said. "The whole family is over Terrence. We've moved on. What gave him that idea?"

"The way I keep strumming my pain and guilt over the way things ended," Sasha said. "That might have something to do with it."

Ari pondered this a while. "He may have a point there."

"Ari!" Sasha cried with indignation. "Don't you dare take his side!"

"Calm down," Ari said. "He's not here, so we can talk about it. He has a point. It's past time you move on. The man is engaged, for Christ's sake."

"What?"

It was a good thing Sasha was sitting down, because her ass would have hit the floor. "Are you kidding me?"

Ari blinked at her. "Why would I kid? And why don't you know these things? Don't you keep in touch with anyone?"

"I don't."

After she left San Bernardino, she'd deleted and blocked old contacts. She'd wanted a fresh start.

"Why not?" Ari asked. "I would be nowhere without Dee and—"

"You forget my friends were Terrence's friends, too," Sasha said. "We didn't part ways in the best of terms."

"Oh, sweetie…" Ari swept Sasha's knotted braids away from her face. "Were they mean to you?"

"What are you going to do about it? Bully them for making me feel bad?"

"I am your big sister," Ari said. "It would be well within my rights."

"Never mind," Sasha said. "It's in the past." Except she'd gone through the trouble of digging up the past, like an old smelly bone, for Nik who didn't even appreciate it. "So, Terrence is engaged…wow."

"He proposed to some woman in Hawaii. The photos were all over social media."

Sasha scoffed. "You mean he didn't ambush her at a party in front of all of their friends?"

"Maybe he's learned his lesson?" Ari proposed.

"Maybe…"

"Now that you know he's moved on, does that loosen the burden some?"

Sasha nodded. She wished him well.

"Good. It's time you stopped punishing yourself and cast off this curse."

She may not be cursed, but there was something wrong with her. Nik figured it out last night. What she cleverly packaged as "spontaneity" was in fact a toxic trait. She leaped into things without forethought and hoped for the best. When it turned out to be the worst, she bailed. That was something she'd have to work out on her own. Big sis couldn't come to the rescue.

Sasha slumped even deeper into the couch. "Thanks for putting up with me."

"I'm not putting up with you. I love you."

Ari slipped off her sandals and crossed her ankles on the coffee table next to the open laptop. She narrowed her eyes at it. Trick MacArthur's handsome face was frozen on the screen. "Stop giving this man views! You're only encouraging him."

"I thought you were over it," Sasha said.

"I was over it for like two days," Ari said. "Now I'm back to being petty. I wish he'd go away."

"It's good to have you back," Sasha said with a chuckle. "We're the petty Witches of San Bernardino Valley."

"I can't stand to look at him."

Ari reached for the laptop and minimized the window of the website, only to reveal the expanded photo of Nik looking handsome and serious at Hillside Smokehouse displayed underneath. Sasha closed her eyes and could see him still, honey eyes, skin like molasses, glowing in the sun.

Ari gasped. "Where was this taken?"

"After the accident."

"Wait! You two were in an accident? When?"

"On the ride from the airport."

"Why didn't you mention it?"

"You would've freaked out, Mother Hen."

Already, Ari had gone pale underneath her peachy blush.

"It sounds like the trip from hell. First the plane goes down. Then you're in a car accident."

"It was wild," Sasha said. "We survived it, though."

"Maybe you can survive this, too."

The last embers of hope flamed hot in Sasha's heart. She quickly stomped them out.

"Go take a shower," Ari said.

"You're obsessed with showers," Sasha observed. "Have you noticed that?"

"A hot shower can do wonders for your mental hygiene," she explained. "Now go. I'll clean up around here and make us lunch."

"Good luck with that. I don't have any food."

"Thank God for room service."

After a shower and lunch, Sasha sat at the table with her laptop, only this time she wasn't binge-watching the trickster's channel. She'd called for an emergency meeting with her therapist.

"Hello, Sasha," Dr. Jonas said in his usual reserved way. "Are things going well?"

"If they were, I wouldn't be calling, would I?"

"Therapy isn't solely for crisis management, you know."

"I'll keep that in mind."

"What's troubling you?"

"A lot has changed since we talked last." Sasha blinked fast to keep the tears at bay. "Nik and I are through."

Dr. Jonas nodded, absorbing the information. "I'm sorry to hear that."

"You said we were going too fast and—"

"I'm sorry to interrupt you, but I didn't say that."

"Yes, you did," she said sourly. She didn't think he was the type of person to backtrack on his clinical advice.

Dr. Jonas flipped open his notebook and checked his notes.

"I asked if you were comfortable with pace and whether you questioned the timing. I pointed out that there were advantages to taking it slow."

Of course he had receipts.

"Here are some of the words you used to describe Nik." He slid his glasses further up his nose and started reading. "'He's perfect... He's wonderful'." Dr. Jonas shut the notebook. "Generally, when we use those types of words to describe a person or a situation, it's because we're not digging deep enough. No one and nothing is perfect, as you well know. You've chosen to perceive Nik as such. Call it a mirage. You're only seeing what you want to see."

"Well, he's not perfect, I can tell you that."

"Want to tell me what happened?"

She did her best recount the events. "I was trying to help, and he was so unappreciative."

"In trying to help," Dr. Jonas said tentatively, "you inadvertently put him in a difficult position at his workplace, which likely involved other colleagues."

Oliver was at that meeting, too. Sasha massaged her temples. "I understand that now."

"Where do you want to go from here?" Dr. Jonas asked.

"There's nowhere to go," Sasha said. "We're at an impasse. I kicked him out."

"I see."

"He accused me of hiding behind you and my sister, using you as a shield."

"Is that what you're doing?" Dr. Jonas asked.

"It feels that way..." Sasha admitted. "I don't want to rush into anything if it isn't right. Maybe this is a red flag that I was missing."

"He had a legitimate grievance," Dr. Jonas said. "Did he remain calm and respectful during the argument?"

Sasha looked down at her hands. There wouldn't have

been an argument if it weren't for her. He'd wanted to walk away and cool down. She wouldn't allow it. She was the one-woman red flag marching band.

"Do you have your journal?" Dr. Jonas asked.

She held up the leather-bound notebook.

"I want you to write a letter to your ex-fiancé to let him know how these last years have been, the ups and downs, all of it. Then ask him how he's doing."

She didn't have to ask. "I know how he's doing. I heard he—"

"No matter what you heard, you still don't know," Dr. Jonas said. "None of us knows what the other is going through."

Damn! He was good.

"Write the letter," he said. "See what comes up. Next time we'll talk about it."

Dear Terrence:

Did I ever say that I was sorry for what I'd done?

   Not ending our engagement. I'm not sorry about that.

   I'm sorry for entering the engagement, in the first place. I'm sorry for saying yes, for taking your ring. You were not the one for me. You didn't make me feel safe and respected. You didn't make me feel loved.

   For years I lived under the shadow of your disappointment, your parents' disapproval and our mutual friends' rejection. I lived with the shame. I went so far as believing that something was inherently wrong with me, that I was cursed.

   I'm done with all that, and I'm done with you.

   Nonetheless, I send you love.

Your forever ex,
Sasha

Twenty-Three

Meet me at the trails at dawn.

Okay. That's just wishful thinking. Make that 7 AM.

Nik was at the diner where he'd ended up after a long, trying day at work. He'd told Oliver that he was no longer interested in pursuing Mad Dash, and was grateful when his friend had agreed.

"I didn't want to be the one to say it," he said. "But, yeah, let's ditch them. I'm more than happy to walk away—if there's even a deal to walk away from. We've heard nothing."

Once the decision was made, Nik put it out of his mind.

"Anyway, it's time you pivoted to Silicon Valley, don't you think?" Oliver asked. "That's the future."

"I'm not thinking about anything right now," he admitted. "It's all a freaking mess."

"Why are you even here?" Oliver asked. "Take the week off. Go work on things that matter to you."

That was code for Sasha; he knew it. She was the only

thing that mattered to him at the moment. There was no deal he wanted to close, no future he wanted to imagine without her. They were running on four days without speaking, and Nik wasn't ashamed to admit that his life was crumbling.

The diner was the place he went to think. Ever since he brought Sasha there, it was filled with memories of her. He swore her laugh echoed off the walls. He was sitting at the same booth they had, eating pretty much the same meal, when the text messages popped up in quick succession. He stared at the phone in disbelief. Then he pushed back the stack of pancakes and called for the check.

He had somewhere to be bright and early in the early morning.

Nik was out of bed, dressed for a hike, and on his way to North Cove Park by dawn. He was antsy throughout the half-hour drive, his heart slamming in his chest. When he got there the parking lot was empty for a Friday morning. He welcomed the peace and the stillness. He hadn't yet worked out what he was going to say.

Then he saw the black SUV wind up the road. A moment later, it slid into the space next to the compact company car he drove while in Royal, and she stepped out.

Ariana shielded her eyes from the sun with a hand. The gesture brought back the image of Sasha standing to the side of the road after the accident. Sometimes, he didn't see the resemblance between them. Other times, like this, it was stunningly obvious.

"Good morning, Ariana."

He didn't dare call her "Ari" as she'd asked him to do on several occasions.

"Hello, Nik," she replied. "Let's walk."

They followed the same trail the three of them had taken in happier times. Ariana didn't say much. She walked with her head down, foregoing the large sunglasses she'd sported last time. Nik struggled with what to say, and the silence was as thin as the mountain air. Finally, he couldn't take it anymore.

"How is she?" he asked.

Ariana glared up at him. "She's a mess," she said. "Those are her words, not mine."

Nik's stomach flopped. The idea of her alone and unwell made him physically ill. "When was the last time you saw her?"

"Never mind that," Ariana said. "Have *you* tried to see her?"

"I don't think I'm welcome," he said. "She kicked me out."

Ariana nearly tripped. Nik caught her by the elbow just in time. She regained her balance and pushed forward. "I didn't know that."

"I was sure she was done with me," he said, after a while.

"Nah... She could've done worse."

"Like what?"

"Ask Ex what I put him through," Ariana said with a nervous laugh. "Better yet, don't! Let's focus on you."

"Here's the truth," Nik said. "I'd camp outside her door if I thought it made a difference. The thing is, I don't think she's sure about us."

"It hasn't been that long, you know," Ariana said. "Give her a chance to work up to that."

"We had one argument, and she stole the opportunity to blow us up."

"It's a defense mechanism. Sasha is more tenderhearted than most people realize. Honestly, you two met at the wrong time. She was still going through so much."

Nik refused to believe that. The circumstances that brought them together were unique and special, and could not be recreated. It wasn't as if he'd walked into a bar and picked her up. They'd crashed into each other's life.

"If you're worried she isn't over Terrence, don't be," Ariana said.

"She told you that?"

"She told me some of it. I can see where you're coming from, but I'm here today to tell you that you're wrong. Sasha was never into Terrence—that was the problem. That relationship should have died a natural death. Instead, Terrence resurrected it with a proposal. The breakup was messy. To this day, her sensitive heart couldn't handle the pain she'd caused. She's guilt-ridden. Rather than cling to myths like a family curse, she's come to terms that she's caused someone harm."

They arrived at the edge of a cliff overlooking the quarry. Ariana turned her back to the view. "Are you willing to fight for her?" she asked. "If you're not, let me know now. We'll never speak of this again."

Nik stared at the pink stone gleaming in the morning light. "All this time, I thought you didn't want us to be together."

"Come on, Nik. I saw the way she looked at you that first night, and I knew she was gone. All I wanted was for her to take her time and to see it, live it and believe in it. So, now I'm asking you, how do you feel about her?"

"I love her." This felt like the most natural thing in the world. It was a crime he still hadn't told her.

"Woah!" Ariana cried. "I wasn't expecting that!"

"I don't know what you were expecting," Nik said. "But I'm in love with her, and I'm a mess, too."

She grinned. "I don't have time to clean up these messes! In case you've forgotten, I've got a wedding to plan. So I have no choice but to get you two back together." She looped an arm around his and steered him back toward the trail. "Let's think of a plan."

Nik had been thinking of nothing else for days. "I'm way ahead of you, and I already have a plan."

"Good," Ariana said. "Now let's think of ways to make that plan even grander."

"You don't have to do that," Nik said.

"If this works out, I'm going to be your big sister, too," Ariana said.

"I believe I'm older than you."

"I don't care," Ariana said. "Get used to me bossing you around."

Twenty-Four

"We love the smokehouse submission!" Roxanne from *Table for Two* magazine exclaimed over the phone. "So much, we'd like to feature it in our July issue, rather than post it on our blog."

"That's exciting news!"

Sasha had stepped out of the stationery store to take the call. Ariana stayed behind assessing card stock and analyzing font sizes.

"We need to broaden our focus, step away from Michelin stars and celebrity chefs. Hillside Smokehouse has such a down-home quality, and your photos are incredible. One, in particular, would make an excellent cover."

"I'm on board, absolutely."

"Great. We've reached out to the owner and she's on board, as well."

Sasha loved a cover story as much as any journalist. For the moment, though, she'd take any assignment to keep busy. She hadn't heard from Nik since he'd walked out. The days without him were long and empty. The nights were wearing her down.

"We'll need additional photos," Roxanne said. "The barn is lovely, but it's not enough. We need to see the food, as well. We'll need a photo of Donna if she agrees to it, a few shots of tableware, the overall vibe of the restaurant and maybe a shot of your sister and her future husband enjoying the food."

"No."

It never failed. Everyone wanted a piece of Ari and Ex. If this were just a ploy to get the couple on the cover of the magazine, Sasha would turn it down.

"That's okay!" Roxanne said quickly.

"Are you still interested in running the story?" Sasha asked.

"Yes, of course! I had to ask. What kind of editor would I be if I hadn't?"

"Just so we're clear. The feature should be about Donna, not a celebrity couple."

"I agree. However, you of all people should understand the value of celebrity endorsement. Your sister could put Hillside Smokehouse on the map."

"The answer is still no," Sasha said. She refused to exploit family.

"Very well," Roxanne said. "Let's discuss deadlines. It's a short turnaround, so we'd have to move fast."

"That works for me. I'm in Texas for a limited time."

The sooner they got to work the better. As the wedding approached, she would have very little free time.

After she got off the phone with Roxanne, Sasha entered the boutique through a back door. They were no longer taking chances. The wedding planner arranged for private meetings for Ari with local shop owners. Ari was as paranoid as before. The less information Trick MacArthur could get his hands on, the better.

Ari was wrapping up her meeting with the calligrapher, a

middle-aged man named Gerry with knotty fingers. Sasha browsed a display of stationery sets while she waited.

Late last night, it occurred to her that she ought to write Nik a letter and apologize. She regretted the fight, and paid a high price for winning. She wasn't herself that night. Rather, she was a version of herself that she'd outgrown and was doing her best to leave behind. She wanted him to know that.

Nik was wonderful, but he wasn't perfect, and neither was she. Even so, he was the perfect partner for her.

Ari rose from the table. "We're done here. I'm pleased with my choice."

"That's good to hear," Dennis said. "We're grateful you chose us to fulfill your stationery needs, Ms. Ramos. It means a lot."

"You're welcome!" Ari said. "I'll make sure to post photos of my finished cards on social media and tag your shop."

Sasha couldn't help but think of Donna, and felt a twinge of guilt. She'd helped them out at a moment of need. Most people would not have stopped for total strangers.

"Ready to go?" Ari said.

"Hold on," she said. "I'd like to make a purchase."

Next, Ari had a meeting with Rylee, from which Sasha was blessedly excused. On the ride to the hotel to drop off Sasha, Ari asked about the work call. "How'd it go?"

"Great, actually," Sasha said. "I'd pitched a story to a culinary magazine. My photo might make the cover."

Ari squealed. "Another cover? Sasha, how awesome!"

"They need more photographs," Sasha said. "I'd have to get to work on it right away. I'll reach out to Donna and see when it's convenient to come out."

Ari went silent for a beat. "Is it the restaurant where you took that photo of Nik?"

Sasha stared out the window. It was a bright spring day in Royal. "The same."

"Interesting…"

"Why's that?" Sasha asked.

"No reason."

Ari pulled up to the hotel. The mirrored façade glistened in the sun. Sasha figured if she were going to ask, the time was now. "I wondered if you and Ex would like to help out?"

"What do you have in mind?"

"A photo of you and Ex having a romantic picnic on the grounds would break the internet and do wonders for a small business."

"You'd take the photos?"

"Of course. Who else?"

Ari nodded, as she tended to do when she was puzzling something out. "It would have to be soon. Ex's schedule is packed next week."

"That's fine with me," Sasha said. "I'll see what I can work out with Donna."

"Do that, and get in touch."

That went easier than Sasha had hoped. "Will do! Thanks for doing this."

"Are you kidding me?" Ari said. "A romantic photo shoot at a charming barn with my sister behind the camera? I wouldn't pass on that."

Sasha was glad she'd taken the chance and asked for the favor. Once alone in her suite, she took another chance. She sat at the table and wrote a note on the newly purchased stationery.

Nik,

You've tamed this wild heart. All I want is to come home. I'm knocking. Let me in.

Sasha.

Twenty-Five

That bastard!

No sooner than Sasha left the note with Nik's doorman than she spotted him strolling home, looking smart in his usual suit, shirt collar open, no tie, phone pressed to one ear, and his free hand in his pocket. Chatting animatedly, laughing at times, the bastard didn't seem to have a care in the world.

Sasha's heart popped into a soggy mess, like a water balloon.

She flattened herself against the building across the street from his, hoping the wide-spreading branches of an oak tree would shield her from view. She checked the time. It was 6:30 p.m. on a Friday night. In all likelihood, he was returning home from the office. Maybe he'd stopped for drinks. Maybe he was on his way home to change and meet with whomever he was chatting with. Maybe he was on his way to dinner with someone new and exciting, another wild one caught in his net. Either way, he would get her note, read it and what...laugh?

Sasha broke into a cold sweat. What had possessed her to write those words, commit them to paper? *All I want is to come home? I'm knocking. Let me in.* Maybe she had hit her head in the accident. First thing, she would schedule a CAT scan.

It was too late to get the note back. Sasha had no choice but to stand there, helpless, and watch as he entered the building through the heavy glass doors. He paused midconversation to take the envelope from the doorman. Without a glance, he slid it in the inner pocket of his blazer and walked off.

The small voice of reason, which increasingly sounded like the voice of Dr. Jonas, whispered to her: *You're overreacting. This means nothing. He could be on the phone with his chiropractor or, more realistically, his cousin in Italy, for all you know.*

A sob cracked free from Sasha's throat. Soon a torrent of tears drowned out the voice of reason. Someone asked if she was okay. Clearly, she wasn't.

Sasha's feelings were validated the next morning. Nik hadn't reached out. He hadn't called or texted. He hadn't showed up at her door with flowers or written her a heartfelt note of his own. Her note was likely still in his jacket pocket, and the jacket on its way to the cleaners. Come to think of it, that was the best-case scenario.

Sasha sat up in bed and tossed aside her tear-stained pillow. Enough of this nonsense. She was the witch of San Bernardino Valley. The day she cried a man a river, he better drown in it.

She went into the bathroom, splashed cold water on her face and brushed her teeth with more aggression than any dentist would recommend. Then she ripped the silk scrunchie out of her hair and set her braids free. She was feeling like herself again.

First thing, she contacted Donna and scheduled the photo shoot. The only available date was Monday. "We're closed for business. It'll be easier that way."

"I agree."

With Ari and Ex making an appearance, it would be more discreet as well. They'd be able to roam around the property, unencumbered, like free-range chickens.

"Who knew that stopping to help you two lovebirds would get us featured in *Table for Two*?" Donna said in wonder. "Funny how life works."

Sasha did not have much to say. "Funny. Right?"

She'd obviously picked the wrong project to take her mind off Nik. That old barn was haunted with ghosts: their first meal together, their first real conversation, their first kiss in the parking lot... Everything was there. Donna called them lovebirds. It had felt that way to Sasha at the time. They'd had something. Where had it gone?

Thinking back, there were signs that things were waning. She'd attributed their falling-out to their blowout fight. Yet, he'd been avoiding her for days. He said he was preparing for the meeting, but who knew at this point? The way he'd bolted, eager to get away from her, after they'd had sex in her *kitchen,* of all places. Oh God! There had been so many red flags that she'd simply chosen to ignore. Why was that? Because the man had helped her keep her cool during a flight? That made him a Good Samaritan or a good citizen, not a good boyfriend or life partner. There was a difference. He may deserve a medal, but he hadn't earned her heart.

Sasha closed her eyes and relived the scene:

Nik had reached over the middle passenger to tighten her seat belt and secure the oxygen mask over her nose. There was too much chaos for him to say anything. A child in the row behind them was wailing. He looked her in the eyes and let her know without a word that they were going to be okay, and she believed him. In that moment, she put all her trust in him. He was her hero.

It was time to move on from that fantasy.

After confirming the date and time with Ariana, Sasha sent an email to Roxanne to inform her that Hillside Smokehouse would indeed have the celebrity endorsement of Ariana Ramos and Xavier Noble. Her sister's only request was to not appear on the cover. "We don't want to grab the spotlight."

She spent the afternoon packing her gear. And then it was back to feeling despondent and depressed, as Nik did not call, text, show up with flowers or send a heartfelt note the entire weekend.

On Monday morning, they drove out to Hillside Smokehouse with Ex at the wheel. Three hours later, the navigation system instructed them to turn left onto a narrow road that Sasha knew well. Ari flipped up the car visor and gasped. "It's beautiful!"

The old barn arose in the distance, its faded red paint bleeding into the ochre field. The beauty of the site hadn't escaped her the first time around, which had prompted her to take those initial photos. This time, the sole purpose of her visit was to capture its silent grace, and her heart soared.

"I can't believe I've never heard of this place," Ex said. "Is the food any good, Sasha? Or is it all vibes?"

"Xavier!" Ari scolded.

"I'm just asking!" he said.

"The food is excellent," Sasha assured him. "You won't regret the drive."

"We won't regret it either way," Ari said. "I want our wedding to draw attention to the beauty of the local community. This spot is darling."

They pulled up to the front, bypassing the parking lot altogether. Donna came out to greet them. She looked fresh in a white eyelet dress. Her brown hair was pulled into a low ponytail to better reveal her startling blue eyes.

"You look beautiful!" Sasha cried.

"Sure," she said, "but no one's going to believe I cook in a fancy dress."

She had a point. "How about we start with shots of you in this dress out in the sunshine with the barn in the background. Then you can change into something else when we're in the kitchen."

Donna sighed in relief. "I'm so glad we're doing this with you."

"Thank you," Sasha said. "Allow me to introduce you to my sister, Ariana, and her fiancé, Xavier."

Donna welcomed them with warm hugs. "We're honored to have you here."

"Thanks for having us," Ari said.

"We've prepared a spread for you. Just a few snacks to get you through the day."

"You shouldn't have gone through the trouble," Ex said, in a tone that wasn't fooling anyone.

"It was no trouble at all."

"I'm going inside to set up," Sasha said. "I'll leave you two to get ready."

"Fine with us," Ex said, and made a beeline for the refreshments.

Sasha went into the kitchen, which looked nothing like the last time she was there. Donna's teenaged nephew, her appointed assistant for the day, asked if anything was wrong.

"It's too orderly," she replied. "Let's get some of the copper pots off the shelves and onto the counter."

"Yes, ma'am."

When they were done, she asked him to open some windows and shut others to better control the light. "This looks good," she said. "Let's see what the others are up to."

Ari and Ex were in the main dining hall, chatting with Donna. They'd changed into their first outfits. Ari looked stunning in a paisley dress and espadrilles. Her friend, Dee, had styled her for the occasion and she'd packed several outfit changes, even though the magazine had offered to supply a stylist.

Xavier looked striking in a fitted earthy brown suit, matching Stetson hat and boots. Sasha had no doubt the photo shoot was going to be epic. They may not want to steal the spotlight, but there was no chance they wouldn't.

Donna left them to check in with her aging parents, the restaurant's original founders, who would also be featured in the shoot. Ex grabbed the chance to feed Ari a corn chip loaded with fresh guacamole. Sasha blindly grabbed her camera and took the shot.

The sound of the shutter startled Ari. "Hey! No fair! You didn't give us notice."

"Never mind me," Sasha said. "Just taking some candid shots, getting everyone used to the camera."

"Sure," Ari said. "Don't mind the woman with the telescopic lens."

The couple laughed, and Sasha kept right on snapping photos.

Moments later, Sasha asked her young assistant to take her to the site of the picnic.

"Actually," Ari said. "We changed our minds. No picnic."

"What?" Sasha cried. "I thought you liked the idea!"

"I *love* the idea," Ari said. "But I've been thinking: it's too similar to our engagement photo shoot in Italy. Also, it's too on the nose. Like we're trying to stage our love, and we're not. We'd like the photos to be more low-key and organic."

Says the woman throwing one of the most extravagant weddings ever, Sasha thought.

"Uh-oh," Ex said, still munching on chips and guacamole. "Sasha looks stressed."

"What do you expect? You're throwing me for a loop!"

"Settle down," Ari said. "Here's an idea. Ex and I will join Donna in the kitchen. She'll teach us a few recipes so we don't starve our first year of marriage. I don't know if you know this, but neither of us can cook."

"We're surviving on takeout," Ex added.

"Oh, I know," Sasha said.

"What do you think?" Ari asked.

Truthfully, the more she thought about it, the more she liked it. "It's not a bad idea."

"I'm a storyteller, Sasha!" Ari retorted. "I have good ideas."

"Does that mean I get to lose the hat?" Ex asked.

He was a Texan through and through, but cowboy hats and boots were not the author's style.

"Keep it for now," Sasha said. "You look good in it."

They started with a few photos of Donna and her family then Ex and Ari on the porch. Before they lost the light, they moved into the kitchen at which point Donna changed into her uniform and Ex ditched the hat, shrugged off the blazer and rolled up his sleeves.

Joining Donna in the kitchen turned out to be the absolute best idea Ari had ever had in her life. There was nothing staged about the shoot. Donna was at ease. She was happiest bossing people around in her kitchen and it showed. She walked Ari and Ex through the steps of a family recipe for chicken fried steak and several easy sides including the house favorite potato salad. They even whipped up dessert.

Sasha cleared her mind and got busy. If there were any ghosts lingering about, they'd left her alone for the day. She worked in peace, capturing all the fun, laughter and joy of cooking. Afterwards, they sat at a large wooden table to enjoy the meal. Sasha would never forget this day. Wasn't this the point of coming to Royal in the first place, to bond and make memories with her sister and her future husband?

Ari stepped out to take a call. When she returned, she nodded at Xavier. Sasha helped herself to a second serving of peach cobbler and pretended not to notice.

"Are we done for the day?" Donna asked. "Should I have the boys clear out the picnic setup?"

"Wait. There's a setup?" Sasha asked.

"Oh, yes," Donna replied. "A nice one, too, in the gazebo, using our fine china...collected at the local flea market, but still very fine."

Sasha set down her plate. "There's a gazebo on this property?"

"At the far end, near the orchard," she said. "It's a bit of a walk."

"I'd like to see it." Sasha got up from the table. "Anyone else?"

"Sorry. I'm stuffed," Ex said. "Take a photo."

Ari shook her head. "I'm exhausted. Cooking is hard work."

"I'd take you, but I need to clean up," Donna said.

"Just point the way. I'll find it."

"Follow me." Donna took her out the back door and pointed to a trail that curved around a bend. "You can't miss it."

"Would you be up to posing for photos at the gazebo later?" Sasha asked.

"We'll see how it goes." Donna pulled a cloth napkin from her apron pocket and dabbed at Sasha's chin. "Pardon me. You have a few crumbs."

"Thanks, Donna!"

"You're welcome."

Sasha switched her camera from one shoulder to the next, and slowly made her way down the path, kicking a stone along the way.

Watching Ari and Ex today made her realize that she wanted a love like theirs. It was inspiring to see them work together as a team, respectful of each other, yet always tender and attentive. She wanted a relationship like that, a true partnership with someone who would enhance her life. Sasha had thought that person might be Nik. Even though it hurt her heart to accept this, it was clear he wasn't the one for her. Yet she had hope. Her mother and grandmother had gotten over their pasts and found love and happiness. So could she.

The gazebo came into view in the distance. The white iron structure was softened with green vines. Sasha had to snap a photo. It was too beautiful. Not just the gazebo itself, but the path leading up to it and the cluster of trees beyond. She raised the camera to her eye and adjusted the lens. She framed the image and there he was.

Nik was on the step, looking incredible in jeans and a black T-shirt, a bouquet of white tulips in his hand.

Sasha dropped the camera. Considering that it cost over two thousand dollars, she was thankful that it was secure with a strap. She took a few steps forward, shrinking the distance between them. He was looking at her with those soft honey eyes. She steeled herself against their charms.

"What are you doing here?" she asked.

"Waiting for you."

"Is that right?"

He took a step down. "Can we talk, please?"

"What is there to talk about?" she demanded. "You think you can just show up, looking incredible, and sweep me off my feet?"

"That was the plan," Nik admitted. "Not the looking incredible part. I'm hoping to look lost and sorry."

"Ha!" Sasha spat. "You're not lost. I saw you the other night. You looked as happy as ever."

Nik lowered the flowers onto the step and took a few careful steps toward her.

"You don't have to tiptoe," she said. "I'm not a wild cat. I won't run away."

"Fair enough," he said, and closed the distance between them. The fresh scent of his cologne instantly enveloped her. "I don't understand what you're saying. Where did you see me? I haven't been anywhere."

"The night I dropped off the note," she said.

"Friday?"

"Yes, Friday." This only confirmed that he'd read it. Not responding in any way was a choice.

"I'm confused, Sasha. I worked late, went straight home and ordered in. Where could you have possibly seen me?"

"On your street," she replied. "I'd just left the note with your doorman and saw you walking home. You were on the phone, laughing, as if you didn't have a care in the world. Meanwhile I..."

Sasha could not continue. She'd sooner die than admit that she stood on the sidewalk bawling her eyes out for a good quarter hour.

"Oh, Sasha..." His desire to reach out to her was plain in his eyes. She would not let him. Sasha wanted answers. If he'd showed up at her door on Friday night with those same tulips, she would have thrown herself at him, but she was not that person anymore. With each passing day, she was growing into a stronger version of herself.

Nik pulled out his phone and started scrolling. When he found what he was looking for, he smiled. "Would you say it was around six thirty Friday evening?"

She shrugged. It was six thirty on the dot, but she was keeping her cards close to her chest.

He handed her the phone, opened to a call log.

Friday 4:10 PM UNKNOWN NUMBER SCAM LIKELY
[MISSED CALL]

Friday 6:23 PM ARIANA RAMOS

"Ari called you?"

It made perfect sense. Someone had tipped him off and told him where to find her today. They were all in on this, even Donna! This picnic at the gazebo was a trap.

"We went hiking Friday morning, just the two of us."

Now Sasha was dumbfounded. "Are you like friends now?"

"We're co-conspirators," he said. "I wasn't sure you ever wanted to see me again. Your sister reached out and gave me hope."

Wait one second!

"*I* gave you hope, Nik!" She sounded unhinged, but couldn't stop herself. "Every word of that note was to give you hope. Didn't you read it?"

"Of course I read it."

"And you thought showing up with flowers three days later was the appropriate response?"

"If you think it was easy for me to sit back and wait, then you don't know me very well."

Sasha handed him his phone. "Make me understand."

The voice of reason was back, questioning why she was pushing it? This was literally everything she'd wanted. She ought to rush into his arms and be done with it. Yet she couldn't.

"I was on the phone when the doorman gave me your note," Nik said. "He didn't say who it was from, and frankly I didn't bother to ask. Your sister and I were plotting and scheming, figuring out a way to get you to this very gazebo.

I only read it last night, and by then it was too late. I thought it was best to wait."

Nik hesitated and reached for her hand. "It was my plan to bring you out here all along. I had no idea how to go about it, outside hiring someone to kidnap you. On Friday night, your sister called with news about the photo shoot. I was so proud of you for getting that job, by the way. You're so talented. I would've loved to see you at work."

Sasha could've kissed him then, but held strong. "Thanks," she said. "Go on."

"If I was laughing that night, if I seemed happy at all, it's because everything was falling into place. I was grateful for the chance to tell you how I feel at the very place where I fell in love with you."

That did it. Sasha bolted into his arms. He caught her, and they stumbled together into a bed of grass.

"I love you." Sasha cupped his face and spoke the words into his kiss.

Nik rolled her onto her back and pinned her down. "My wild one..." he said. "I'm the one who desperately wants to come home. I'm sorry I got upset over something so trivial. I could've lost you."

"That's impossible," Sasha said. "I caught you that first day, and you're mine."

"What a lucky day that was!"

She laughed. "That's a bit of revisionist history."

"Honey, I want a future with you," he said. "A life full of adventure."

"So do I," Sasha whispered. She wanted it with all her heart.

"This conversation may be premature, but I promise never to ask you to marry me," he said. "I won't put you in that position again."

Sasha raised her chin, defiant. "What if I asked you?"

Nik pulled away and spoiled her with the most devil-ish grin. "What if you asked for my hand in marriage, you mean?"

"Yes, Nik. Could you handle that?"

"Sasha, you've cursed me to a life of loving you. How could I ever say no?"

* * * * *

THE MAN SHE LOVES
TO HATE

JESSICA LEMMON

To Dr. Shelley—

Thanks for dusting off your MoMA catalog and helping
me navigate the modern art references for this book.
I never would've found those pieces on my own. I also
never expected to find myself watching a YouTube video
of naked women in blue paint pressing against a canvas
while a string quartet played. Your suggestions were
perfect for the book! Thank you!

One

For the last three years, Rylee Meadows had been planning weddings for high profile, wealthy clients. Those clients had ranged from celebrities to regular old rich folks. Special requests were not outside of the norm, nor were last-minute changes. But this was the first time she'd ever had to contend with a wedding *crasher*.

The wedding of Xavier Noble and Ariana Ramos was coming up in a few days. Reaching this point had required Herculean effort. Not only on Rylee's part, but on the parts of the vendors who had been tasked with pulling off nothing short of perfection while navigating a sea of difficulties—including the blackout that had affected half of the town of Royal, Texas.

As a professional used to high-pressure situations, Rylee could have rolled with the blackout alone and not broken a sweat, save for that *other* anomaly keeping everyone involved in this wedding on their toes.

His name? Patrick "Trick" MacArthur.

Trick—oh, how appropriate—was a social media star who'd grown famous for crashing events which he had not been invited to. Right now, his sights were set on the Noble-Ramos wedding.

After all Rylee and the hardworking, talented vendors had been through with planning this wedding, a trouble-maker in town was the last thing any of them needed.

Xavier and Ariana had entrusted her with facilitating the perfect day for them, and Rylee wouldn't let them down. However, it had become apparent that Trick, who had taken up residence close by, wasn't going anywhere. The man had made a living showing up where he wasn't invited, which had pushed more than one of her buttons.

In the past, Rylee had been accused of being a bit of a perfectionist. She understood why. She was used to hav-ing complete control of her environment. Trick's presence at the wedding, and reception, could ruin the day for ev-eryone. She could not, and would not allow it.

She'd done her research, and while she could objec-tively understand Patrick's appeal, she couldn't support his antics. One look at any of his online videos revealed an engaging, smiling man one might describe as the life of the party. He was great-looking, with thick black hair that beckoned a woman's fingers, hazel eyes that held enough mischief to be intriguing, and a seemingly per-manent smirk surrounded by sexy stubble.

Rylee grunted as she parked her car on the curb. She'd never been drawn in by a bad boy type, and had no plans on starting now. She'd tracked down Trick to this very tailor in order to corner him and make him a proposi-tion. If he wouldn't willingly leave Royal, then he would have to agree to stay within the boundary lines she drew. Once she'd convinced him to behave himself, she would approach the bride and groom and explain how this was the way—the only way—to move forward.

She stepped onto the curb, wincing as she walked toward the crosswalk. *These damn shoes.* Gingerly, she slipped the strap from her foot to find a blister forming. She sat on a nearby park bench and pulled the emergency bridal kit from her bag.

She'd learned a long time ago not to show up at a wedding, or anywhere, really, *without* bandages or bobby pins. As she planned weddings and similar "emergencies" arose, she'd added to the kit. Now she carried acid reducers, aspirin and a miniature sewing kit, among other items a panicky bride might need. Or in this case, the bride's harried wedding planner.

Band-Aid in place, she rolled her shoulders, and tucked a strand of hair back into her coiffed chignon. The day had been a long one, and she'd skipped dinner to iron out an issue with the outdoor seating plan. Thankfully this was her last stop for the day, and bonus, Trick wasn't expecting her. She'd crash *his* appointment and see how he liked it.

With a satisfied smile on her face—she loved it when a plan came together—she entered the shop packed with designer suits, ties, shirts and shoes. Glass cases containing cufflinks, watches and jewelry lined the back wall, a familiar sight. She'd been in this shop countless times to help the groom choose the proper wardrobe for his big day.

At the counter, she waved hello to Harold, who was shining the glass with a cloth.

"Rylee." He smiled and offered his hand, which she took and shook cordially. "You're working late."

"I'm here to see one of your customers, actually. I

assume Shayla is with him?" Shayla was a tailor and a damn good one. She had an eye for detail. It wasn't a typical career choice for a gorgeous thirty-two-year-old woman, but Royal was a unique place with unique residents.

"In the back," Harold answered. "Help yourself."

"Thanks, I will." Rylee adjusted her purse on her shoulder and strode into the back room where she encountered Shayla and Patrick. Shayla, dressed in her usual button-down pale blue shirt and trousers, a pin cushion strapped to her wrist, was focused on his suit jacket. Patrick, who caught sight of Rylee in the mirror he faced, was wearing a lot less.

A slow grin spread his lips. The eye contact was intense, sending a drove of gooseflesh to crop up on Rylee's bare arms. The flush on her neck and cheeks had come thanks to what was so obviously missing.

His pants.

"Well, well, if it isn't Rylee Meadows," Patrick said, his gaze unerringly on her reflection.

Shayla lifted her head to offer a casual, "Oh, hey, Rye. We're almost done here and then I can help you with whatever you need."

Rylee snapped her attention from Patrick's bare legs and slouched black socks, accidentally admiring his calf muscles and the scant dark, wiry hair on his strong thighs that disappeared beneath his currently-being-pinned suit jacket. Some part of her she'd rather not acknowledge was disappointed at not having a view of his butt. She shut her eyes to reset her very tired brain.

"I'm, uh, I'm here to talk to Trick. Patrick. Mr. MacArthur."

He looked over his shoulder at her, one dark eyebrow

winging upward. "Please don't call me Mr. MacArthur. It makes me feel geriatric."

Shayla laughed as she gave him a once-over. "You're looking good to me. Ready to lose the jacket?" Shayla sent a rogue look over at Rylee. "And put on some pants so you don't fluster Ms. Meadows any more than you already have?"

"I'm fairly certain Ms. Meadows is un-fluster-able."

"I'm fairly certain you are right." Shayla collected the suit pants set aside on a chair and then waited for him to slip off the suit jacket. She palmed Rylee's shoulder on her way out of the room. "Take your time."

Patrick pulled on a pair of trousers. Rylee watched long enough to discern that he was a boxer-briefs guy with a decent-looking butt, before turning her back and granting him the privacy he hadn't bothered asking for.

"Did you come in to check me out, or is this a professional visit?" he asked, reminding her that wherever he was involved, it was destined to be an uphill climb.

"I have a proposition for you, Mr.—uh, Patrick."

"Trick is fine, Rye."

"It's Rylee to you." She spun around to find him cinching his belt. He wore a white button-down shirt, the collar open to reveal an attractive neck. He stood tall, confident despite not wearing any shoes, as confident as he'd been previously while not wearing any pants. Even so, he struck her as trustworthy and safe, a bizarre assessment given her reason for being here tonight. The infamous Trick MacArthur was known for being disingenuous and opportunistic. The thought caused her eyebrows to meet over her nose.

"Okay. Rylee." He sat on a footstool and slipped on a pair of leather loafers, Italian leather if she wasn't mistaken, and then stood again. As you say in Texas, "What can I do ya for?"

"I'm not sure that saying derived from Texas."

He frowned. "No?"

"No." She straightened her back. "But I am fairly certain that *This ain't my first rodeo* did. Which brings me to the reason for my visit."

"Are you asking me to go to a rodeo with you?"

She ignored the question. "I'm here to make a bargain with you before you cause a ruckus at Xavier and Ariana's wedding."

"A ruckus?" He approached, enveloping her in a bouquet of familiar scents. Bergamot, mandarin and fruity but also peppery.

"Dior Sauvage?" she blurted. Startled by her own outburst, she blinked. "Your cologne. I have a weird talent for guessing men's colognes. A talent I've fostered for the grooms in the weddings I plan," she continued blathering. "Most of the time they don't know what they like, and want something special but not overpowering for the big day. Anyway, never mind."

"I'm impressed. Dior is my go-to."

It suited him. The fragrance was complex. One part bad-boy, one part sophistication. Trick managed to pull off both. The scent was subtle, as if he'd sprayed it on this morning and the fragrance had lessoned as the hours had ticked by. A vision of him stepping out of the shower, water rivulets trickling off his bare chest and over the curve of his round butt invaded her imagination. By the time he was pushing a hand through wet hair and wiping the steam off a mirror, she'd completely lost her place.

"Your proposition?" he prompted.

Right. That.

"I assume you'd like to attend the Noble-Ramos wedding."

His head jerked on his neck. "Are you offering me an invitation?"

"Sort of. As you know Xavier and Ariana are America's favorite couple at the moment."

"Hence my presence here in the great state of Texas." He spread his arms, his toothy grin sharklike, but no less attractive. What must it be like not to worry about anyone but yourself? Rylee worried about everyone else most of the time. Then again, she was in the service industry and Trick…was not.

"If I give you ample access to the final preparations for the wedding, you will be able to film, at your discretion, all of what happens up and until the actual wedding and reception." She hoped that his pursed lips and narrowed eyes were signs he was considering her offer.

"What's the catch?"

"You are prohibited from filming the wedding or reception, though you are welcome to attend as an *invited* guest."

"And…?" he asked as if he'd sensed there was more. He was right.

"*And* you will be asked to donate the revenue for any monetized videos to a charity of Xavier's and Ariana's choosing."

"Done."

"Hear me out before you…" Her tired brain belatedly processed his easy acquiescence. "Excuse me?"

"It's a deal." He held out his hand for her to shake. She regarded it skeptically. "Come on, Rylee. This is why you're here. What are you waiting for?" He flipped his hand so that it was palm up. "Seal the deal."

"Now I'm waiting for the catch."

"You think there's a catch?" His smile hinted at that very probability.

She had five days to pull off this wedding and he was being ten times more agreeable than she could have hoped. She'd ambushed him. She had expected, and was ready for, a fight. He'd been planning to disrupt this wedding for months, and instead of fighting with her, he was in agreement with her.

She wasn't sure she could trust him, but what choice did she have? She placed her hand in his.

He gripped her firmly. "If—"

"Oh, come on."

"—you have dinner with me tonight. I'm starving."

She opened her mouth to refuse him, but before a single word exited her lips, her stomach growled audibly.

Trick chuckled, the warmth of his touch sliding up her arm and curling around her in an entirely comfortable way. He leaned in closer. So close, she could make out each individual hair on his jawline, and the gold flecks dancing in his hazel eyes. His lips parted, his gaze locked with hers...

"That sounds like a yes to me, Rylee Meadows," he murmured before letting go of her. Then he clapped his hands and rubbed them together. "Where's the best sloppy cheeseburger in town?"

Two

The obvious choice for a burger was the Royal diner, but Rylee didn't trust Trick in such a casual atmosphere. The mere thought of him bantering with the waitress and lounging in the red faux leather booths set her teeth on edge. She didn't need a challenge tonight. She needed a cocktail.

She handed off the key fob for her borrowed Mercedes to the valet. As she accepted her ticket, Patrick came around to stand behind her.

"Thanks for driving." He took in the brick exterior and the traditional signage of the restaurant.

"No problem." Her manners had insisted.

"Shall we?" He offered an arm, which was far more gentlemanly than she would have expected from him. Rather than argue, as dinner was a condition of their freshly minted agreement, she rested her hand on his forearm and allowed him to lead her inside.

Despite the late hour, the restaurant was fairly busy.

Not surprising considering the amount of business and pleasure being conducted in town. She would bet there were plenty of opportunists—in addition to Trick—who'd traveled to town to report on the Noble-Ramos wedding.

"The RCW Steakhouse is owned by Rafe Cortez-Williams," she told Trick as the hostess led them to a table. "The beef they serve comes straight from the family's cattle ranch."

"Impressive."

Once they were seated and large leather-bound menus were handed to each of them, he looked around. She joined him. The table and chairs were made of rich, dark wood, the windows framed by heavy drapes. The style was traditional, but she found the decor soothing rather than stodgy. She'd been born into affluent wealth and was accustomed to country-club chic, in its varying forms.

"This is cozy. I thought you'd opt for a brightly lit diner, but instead you've tucked me into a sensual, shadowed corner." His lips flinched, the smirk at home on his face.

"You said sloppy burger." She casually scanned the menu. "No one does it better than RCW. Not even the diner."

"Unpopular opinion?"

"Completely. But I'm an uppity rich girl, so you get what you get." She slapped the menu closed. She didn't consider herself "uppity," but she knew plenty of people who described her family that way. She'd been accused of being particular, a perfectionist and rigid. Her ex-fiancé had labeled her as "too ambitious" before he ended their engagement.

Their waiter arrived and Rylee and Trick put in their food order. He chose a burger with fried onions, pickles and American cheese and she opted for the same, only she added bacon to hers.

"You're brave," he said when the waiter left.

"Not used to a woman ordering a cheeseburger?"

"Not one dressed in a buttercream silk dress. You look beautiful in that color, by the way."

Taken aback by the compliment, she tucked a stray lock of pale blond hair behind her ear. "I'm probably wilting at this point. My hair is falling, my dress is wrinkled. These shoes are well past their expiration date."

He bent to look beneath the table at her feet. "Those straps seem painful."

"They are."

"Why do you wear them?"

She laughed. "Because Converse sneakers would be inappropriate with this dress?"

He nodded, but appeared thoughtful. She didn't know much about Patrick beyond the rumors that had preceded his visit to town. Now that they were here, as he'd said in this "shadowed" corner, the setting *did* feel intimate. Her polite upbringing required cordiality, and so she dipped her toe into well-worn territory: small talk.

"Why weddings?"

"Why...weddings?" he repeated.

"Yes. Why do you crash weddings and film them?" She sipped from her water glass.

"It's not always weddings. I've crashed a few private concerts, birthday parties in Beverly Hills. At least one awards show."

"I saw that one. You were escorted out by security and ended up running from the cops. Classy."

"That was a long time ago." He averted his eyes like he wasn't proud of his past.

"Yes, but you're here *now*. Planning hijinks for the Noble-Ramos wedding. Clearly, you're not reformed."

"Hijinks? That's quite the Scooby-Doo description of my career."

"A career made of showing up where no one wants you?"

He didn't crumble beneath the veiled insult, but smiled and leaned back in his chair instead. He tapped the end of his salad fork on the table lightly as he spoke. "When I was younger, my college friends and I pulled a lot of dumb shit on unsuspecting people. Nothing malicious."

"I've seen a few of those older videos. In one of them, you replaced the speaker at a fast-food restaurant with your own and whenever someone pulled up, you sang a popular song and goaded them into joining you." Watching the unsuspecting person in the car laugh as they eventually sang along *was* entertaining, and had the surprising biproduct of making her feel light and happy.

"You've done your research."

"You didn't give me much of a choice. It's good to know one's adversary."

"Is that what we are? I thought we just became partners."

The waiter delivered their burgers and asked if they needed anything else. Trick waited for Rylee to answer, and when she said *no, thank you*, he followed suit. Charming and polite. How totally unexpected.

They each lifted their burgers, their gazes locking for one charged second before she took her first bite. Juicy, flavorful, tender meat and a butter-brushed Brioche bun was offset by the crunch of lettuce, onions, bacon and pickles in between. The burger was heaven, and drew a low groan of approval from her throat.

He set down his burger and swiped his mouth with the black cloth napkin, nodding as he chewed.

"Damn," he said as soon as his mouth wasn't full. *"Damn."*

"Good, right?" Holding her burger in one hand, Rylee dabbed her lips with her own napkin before taking another bite.

One "damn" had been for how good the burger tasted, the other reserved for Rylee. Her fair blond hair was pulled back, revealing the creamy expanse of her neck. One thin strap of her dress had slipped ever so slightly off her shoulder, and then she'd buried her face into her burger and had taken a hearty bite.

She was exquisite.

He couldn't remember being as enamored by anyone as much as he was by her right now—and he was a guy who noticed the little things. Who noticed nearly everything.

He'd seen her around since he'd arrived in town. The second he'd laid eyes on the take-charge, in-charge, unflappable wedding planner, he'd been smitten. He liked her sass and her professional attitude as much as he liked the way she looked. He liked how tall she was, the way her curves tested the seams of the classy dresses she wore. The way her blue eyes sought him out in earnest, like she was trying to figure him out...

Especially that last part.

When she'd caught him with his pants literally down tonight, he'd been instantly glad to see her.

The friends he used to film videos with had graduated and gone on to lucrative careers. Trick had built an empire without meaning to, and in three short years. He'd landed sponsorships when his social channel's numbers began hitting six digits, and now he was well into the sevens. It wasn't a traditional career path, that was for damn sure. He'd attended film school and had been certain he'd be an intern on a movie set by now, begging for ten seconds with the director so he could pitch his own movie ideas.

"Partners, huh?" she asked out of the blue. Funny, he'd assumed she'd been anxious to change the subject.

"You need me to film the pre-show. I agreed."

"First of all, I don't *need* you to film anything. I'm trying to corral you."

"Many women have tried that tack before, Rylee." He grinned.

"How many?" She raised her fair eyebrows in challenge.

"Not *that* many." He didn't want her thinking he was some social media Lothario. He wasn't trying to impress her, but he definitely didn't want to turn her off. He was having too much fun. They ate their next several bites in amiable silence before setting aside the giant burgers and turning their attention to their fries.

Trick raised his hand to flag the waiter. "I'm going to need a beer with this. You?"

"Oh, I'd love a cocktail."

She'd surprised him again. He'd expected her to stick with water. "Then a cocktail you shall have."

He ordered a beer, and she ordered a peach Bellini. Trick shelved his many questions until their drinks arrived. Rylee lifted her peach fizzy drink to her lips and sipped. She emitted a delicate hum rather than a ravenous groan this time around, and he honestly didn't know which sound he preferred.

"One rarely finds a peach Bellini outside of brunch."

She took another swallow and nodded her agreement.

"Don't I know it. I'm usually working on Saturday and Sunday mornings. I don't often see my favorite weekend meal. Ah, brunch." She'd said it so wistfully he had to smile. She lifted a fry and smiled back at him. Her lips were full, the shimmer of gloss still clinging to the edges of her mouth.

"So, let me get this straight. You hate your shoes, drink brunch drinks in the evening, and even though you're trying not to, you find me disturbingly attractive."

Her light skin slowly gained color, the pink tinge starting at her collarbone and creeping up her neck. She didn't falter, volleying back at him with a, "You're half right. I do find you disturbing."

He couldn't help laughing at her quick wit. She appeared pleased with herself as she lifted her burger and took another hearty bite.

"It's cool that you agreed to donating the money for your views for this event, though," she conceded a moment later. "I thought I'd have to fight you on that point."

"What I do isn't about the money."

She pursed her lips, her gaze softening. She was curious to know more, but he could feel her holding back. He had the idea that she held back often. In life. With other people. He was curious to know more about that as well. Maybe they'd spend more time together in the coming days and he could pry a few answers out of her.

"I may seem like a prankster who has nothing better to do than wedge my way into the spotlight, but that's the public's perception, not reality. You've worked with celebrity clients before, I assume?"

"Many."

"You know there are two sides to us. The public side and the private side."

"Isn't that true of everyone? I am wearing shoes I hate."

"You have a point."

She polished off the peach Bellini and then dug into her purse for her wallet.

"I've got it." He brandished a black metal credit card. "Don't argue with me, either."

She showed empty hands to him. "If you insist. Thank you."

"You're welcome."

"I should give you my number." She reached for her cellphone.

His heart galloped. Hell yes, she should. He hadn't been expecting them to hit it off at this dinner, but there was no doubt they had both enjoyed the company. He looked forward to seeing her again. More of her. A *lot* more of her.

"We are in agreement." He rattled off his phone number and his cellphone chimed a second later. Her incoming text read Hi.

She dropped her phone into her purse and stood. "You're going to need to reach me before you try to set foot in the Texas Cattleman's Club. Security is on alert to look out for riffraff."

Riffraff. He swallowed a chuckle. The word was tame enough to make him wonder if she had given him her number under the guise of business, when in actuality she'd wanted him to have it for pleasurable reasons.

"I'll be leaving for the TCC at 6 a.m. sharp tomorrow morning. I should go to bed."

"I'll see you there." Brighter and earlier than he'd intended, but he was already looking forward to going another round with her.

Three

Rylee's morning started at 5 a.m. She drank a coffee while she readied herself for the day. She chose a mauve dress with ruching on one side, where a tie fashioned into a loose bow hung. She paired the neutral garment with a pair of nude heels—no straps. Her hair was in its usual updo, pinned to resist the Texas winds should they kick up today.

An hour later—she had promised 6 a.m. sharp—she stepped out of the elevator to find Trick walking out of another elevator directly across from hers. They met in the middle, leaving about a foot of space between them. His gray trousers and short-sleeved pale blue crew-neck shirt managed to look dressy rather than casual. The color offset his dark hair and stubble nicely. He gave her a lazy blink, but didn't bother to conceal his surprise.

"Rylee." Hazel eyes perused her outfit before he gave her a grin. "You are stunning. Beautiful."

Unused to being complimented so thoroughly, she was

suddenly bashful. She'd made it a habit to dress so that she blended into the background. The bride and groom were the stars. She was simply the woman behind the curtain.

"Let me." He adjusted the camera bag on his shoulder and reached for her tote. She relinquished the weighty bag, filled with everything she would need for the day—and more. He wrapped one fist around the straps and gave her an *I'm impressed* eyebrow lift when he tested its heft. "You didn't have to track me down at the hotel. I called a car."

"I'm staying in this hotel."

"You're staying *here*? I thought you lived in Royal."

"I grew up in Texas. I moved to LA after I started my business."

"You live in LA." *Like me*, his tone implied.

"Yes. My parents live in Royal. I've been staying with them since March, overseeing every detail of the wedding. The week of the wedding I like to be near the venue. I can't risk being unavailable because of traffic or weather or an unexpected incident."

"Like a blackout."

She tilted her head. "Or a wedding crasher."

His tired smile faded into a yawn, one he was unable to conceal since his hands were full. "Sorry. I'm never up this early. I'm exhausted."

"You get used to it."

They stepped outside into a wall of warmth. Even this early, Mother Nature had cranked up the heat. A car rolled to a stop at the curb.

"That's me. Want to carpool?"

"Uh…" She thought about what he'd said last night

about them being partners. About how odd it'd sounded after months of viewing him as an adversary.

"Don't you want to reduce your carbon footprint?" Trick handed his own bag to the driver and held Rylee's bag in limbo while waiting for her answer.

"Sure. Why not?" No sense in driving separately when they were heading to the same place. He stowed her bag with his and then opened the door for her. She slid into the back seat, and he rounded the car and slid in next to her. The tight confines of their ride put them in close proximity again, and sooner than she'd expected. She inhaled the spicy notes of his cologne, her head spinning. Why did he have to look *and* smell so good?

Once the driver deposited them at the side entrance of the Texas Cattleman's Club and they had their bags, Rylee used her keycard to let herself into the private office she'd arranged for the week.

"Command central," Trick commented as they stepped inside.

She was already unpacking her laptop and a large binder onto the desk, preparing for the many possibilities the day would bring. "You're welcome to leave any equipment you don't need in here. I'm the only one with a key to this room, so your belongings will be safe."

He took a video camera and a handheld tripod with a rubber grip from his bag and then slid his cellphone into his pocket. "I'm all set. Where to first?"

"Wherever you'd like." She waved him off, wary at the idea of him following her. "I'm going to be buzzing around."

"Consider me your shadow. I have nowhere else to be."

They started at the location of the ceremony, an open grassy area with a view of the mountains in the distance.

The chairs, flowers and the arch wouldn't arrive until the morning of, but she liked to have a feel for what to expect. As she walked, she pecked notes into her phone. Number one on her to-do list was to contact the groundskeeper to make sure they had mowing on their schedule for Friday.

As she walked, she kicked a crushed soda can. She picked it up, along with a piece of plastic wrapping that had come from who knew what. She *tsked*. This wouldn't do at all.

"You pick up litter too? Full-service wedding planner."

She turned to find him filming her. "What are you doing?"

"Documenting." He kept the camera pointing in her direction.

"Not *me*. The venue."

"You said I could record at my discretion. Besides, you're the planner, Rylee. Everything and everyone goes through you. You're the star of the pre-show." He lowered the camera and checked the footage. "How did I not notice your dimples yesterday?"

"I don't know. They're a bit much."

"I must've been dazzled." He glanced up from the camera screen. "I can't think when you smile."

She shook her head, still trying to weigh the Trick who, well, *tricked* everyone for views online, and the man she'd gone to dinner with who had been both polite and kind.

"There's no need to lay it on this thick," she said as she walked to a refuse bin. "I get it. You're charming, engaging. The life of the party."

"You think I'm buttering you up?"

"Aren't you?"

He seesawed his head as if he was considering. "I guess that depends. Is it working?"

She didn't deign him with an answer. "Speaking of work, I have a lot of it to do. Stay out of any room marked private. The TCC has added extra security so you'll need this to walk around." She reached into her purse and pulled out a guest pass. "Everywhere else is open. I work better alone."

He accepted the pass and nodded. "Meet up with you in a few hours?"

"Text me if you can't find me."

He lifted the camera, pointing it at her again. "I'll look for the dimples. Can't miss 'em now."

He walked off, and she admired his tight backside for a beat before recovering her professionalism. She had a job to do and not a single item on her itinerary read *be charmed by Trick MacArthur.*

The fans were blowing on high on the covered porch at the rear of the club. Rylee sat in a rocker, leaned her head back and shut her eyes. She had been outside in the heat for most of the morning, walking the property as she made phone calls. She'd double-checked that the Chiavari chairs for the ceremony had arrived, which was important as they couldn't ask the guests to sit in the grass. Gold chairs had been harder to track down than white, as were many of the items required to match with Xavier and Ariana's theme. The old Hollywood glamor theme had been augmented, as had many other details over the last few months, to incorporate the state flower, the blue bonnet. A rich blue-purple shade had been added to the gold, black and cream color scheme.

Rylee had also called to the officiant to quadruple-check he'd be on time and that he'd received his payment. His assistant assured her that he'd arrive ready for the midmorning ceremony. An outdoor venue in Texas in June required an early ceremony, or else the guests would melt. Kind of like she was doing right now.

"There you are. I was about to give up." Trick stepped onto the porch from inside the club, a plastic bag in one hand and a pair of crystal flutes in the other. "This place is enormous." His tripod was tucked under his arm. He carefully set it aside as he placed the bag onto a side table next to her. He handed her a flute. "Peach Bellini."

She accepted the sweating glass, her mouth watering. "Seriously?"

"I figured one wouldn't hurt." He set his own glass down and extracted a Styrofoam container from the plastic bag. He cracked the lid and showed her the contents. "Crab and avocado eggs Benedict. The other box is full of pancakes."

"You brought me brunch?" She was touched. Had anyone *ever* delivered her brunch?

She hadn't had much male attention since she'd split up with Louis—the other reason for her fleeing Texas to live in LA—and that'd been over two years ago. She knew she should resist Trick's advances, but a bigger part of her said *go for it*. It was just brunch. What was the harm? Then she heard herself resist anyway.

"This is so nice, but—"

"C'mon, Peaches. I brought you your favorite drink and the meal you are typically unable to enjoy before nine o'clock at night. Indulge."

Well. Who could say no to that? Besides, she *was* thirsty.

She took a dainty sip of her drink, the bubbles tickling her throat. It was sweet and delicious and perfect. Trick pulled his shoulders back like he was proud of himself.

He should be. No one had successfully wooed her away from her self-enforced work rules.

"That's more like it." He unrolled a set of silverware, sliced off a bite of the eggs Benedict, and offered it to her. She accepted the fork and fed herself, aware of him watching her closely.

"This is good."

"I'm glad you approve." He carved off another bite for her.

"Peaches, huh? Are you married to that nickname?"

"What an appropriate choice of words. And yes." He nodded. "I'm afraid it's going to stick. From the hue of your cheeks to the choice of your drinks. Peaches."

He was too much. Kind of like brunch and a Bellini at ten o'clock on a work day.

Trick opened the other box. The tantalizing smell of fresh pancakes wafted into the air. He poured maple syrup from the packet as Rylee moaned around her breakfast. He liked the sounds she made when she ate. It was the dominating reason he'd bought her brunch in the first place. Plus, it was nice to see her take a minute to enjoy something she clearly loved. He'd bet she didn't do that often enough. Meanwhile, he'd made a lifestyle out of it.

"How long have you been planning weddings?" He offered her a bite of pancake, dripping with sweet, sticky syrup. She reached for the fork, but he shook his head. "Better let me do it. This syrup has a mind of its own."

She admonished him with a look, but opened her mouth and allowed him to feed her. When a drop of maple syrup lingered at the corner of her mouth, he wiped it away with his thumb. His gaze locked with hers, he sucked the sugar off his thumb. Her blue eyes were un-erring in their target—his mouth had piqued her interest.

He hadn't come to Texas to seduce Rylee. Or any woman, for that matter. But the more he'd watched her from afar, the more intrigued he'd become. She was stub-born and strong, poised and confident. He'd begun to wonder if she ever undid that knot from her hair, or wore a pair of short, frayed denim shorts. Last night when she'd left him sitting at the steakhouse alone, he'd wondered what she wore to bed. Then this morning he'd found out that she was staying in the same damn hotel he was staying in.

Intrigued didn't begin to describe how he felt whenever he was with her. He wanted to know more about her. He wanted to experience more *of* her. With the wedding a few days away, he was aware he was running out of time to impress her. Hence, the brunch delivery.

She gathered the perfect bite of avocado and crab, egg and English muffin and offered it to him. He took the fork as she answered his earlier question.

"Almost three years." Her eyebrows knit. "Has it al-ready been three years? It simultaneously feels like I've been doing this forever and like I just started."

"Time's funny like that. I feel like I've been doing what I do for so long I should be eighty years old by now."

"How long have you been a social media influencer?"

His mouth screwed to the side. He didn't care for that title. "I didn't set out to influence anyone. I wanted to entertain them. My focus has changed in the last year."

"How so?" She leaned in the slightest bit, her rocker inching forward. Her pretty blue eyes settled on him, giving off serious all-American girl vibes.

Until today he would have claimed not to have a type,

but this curvy blonde was currently occupying the number one spot at the top of that list. He'd never wanted to film someone so badly in his life, but he didn't want to lose the momentum of their friendly conversation.

"I'm serving up what the world needs most," he answered. "Joy can be in short supply when something scary is happening. Lately the world is full of scary shit."

"No kidding." Her eyebrows bent, suggesting that her world was more than hearts and roses. At first blush, she came off like a perfectionist romantic. But he knew people. Everyone had hidden layers—she was no exception.

"We deserve to laugh. Deserve to be happy. And it's far simpler than most people think. Look how happy you are right now, Peaches. Takeout and a Bellini. Simple."

Her dimples indented her cheeks when she smiled. He still had no idea how in the hell he'd overlooked those. He leaned in, eager to hear what she would say next. Had she changed her mind about him? Or did she still view him as the bad boy with the bad reputation?

"Nothing is ever simple," she said, answering the question in his head.

Four

What was Trick's angle? Rylee couldn't figure him out. Obviously, it was wise for him to stay on her good side. She had given him the offer of a lifetime, after all. Which reminded her, she needed to let Xavier and Ariana know about this arrangement. Ari had been worried about Trick's antics, and Rylee had managed to come up with a palatable solution. It wasn't like her to ask for forgiveness rather than permission, but she had run out of time.

He lifted his own Bellini and took a sip. "Damn. That is good."

"Well, yeah." She polished off the rest of her glass, already feeling better. She would call Ari today and straighten this out. No worries.

"Have you always been detail-oriented? Not much slides by you," he said.

"Are you referring to yourself?"

His boyish, wicked grin was utterly charming. She'd

bet he could've gone everywhere he pleased inside the Texas Cattleman's Club, pass or no.

"Not always," she told him. "Not until I found myself planning a wedding."

Her own wedding, to be precise, but it was way too early for that conversation. If she were two Bellinis in, maybe.

"I have trouble focusing. ADHD." He pointed to himself, seemingly unashamed to admit it. Not that he should be, but Louis hadn't liked admitting to his flaws. "Thank goodness for short-form videos trending right now or I'd be up to my eyeballs in editing."

"You don't edit the videos yourself?"

"That's a job for my editing team."

"You have an editing *team*?" She had assumed Trick was running a one-man show; filming, editing and posting on his own.

"Hell yes. And a few people who do nothing but research hashtags and reply to comments on my behalf. There are a lot of moving parts in the life of a wedding crasher." He leaned back on the rocker, his elbow propped on the arm, looking casual and, okay, she'd admit it. *Fun.*

For all the fun Rylee planned, she hadn't reserved much for herself. Which was probably what rankled her most about Trick. He had fun constantly, and at the expense of everyone who'd worked hard to plan the events he crashed. "Do you ever feel badly for showing up to drink the drinks and eat the food and party with the guests at an event where you contributed nothing?"

His eyebrows lifted.

She didn't blink. It was a fair question.

"You don't think I contribute?"

She held up her cellphone. "When was the last time

you called vendors to ensure there are enough chairs for the ceremony? Have you ever made a last-minute trip to the dollar store in search of votive cups? What about a champagne shortage, which required you to phone a friend and ask if they have a spare bottle or two tucked away for a special occasion?"

He didn't take offense to her line of questioning, and neither did he sit up straight. He stayed in that same lounging position, taking care to finish his drink before answering. "Have *you* ever started a conga line at a wedding reception to liven up a stale dance floor? Or fast-danced with a four-year-old flower girl when her family was too tired to indulge her? How many times have you threatened a guest with bodily harm when he is sniffing around the gift table looking for envelopes filled with cash?" He set his glass on the table and dropped his elbows to his knees, peering up at her with such earnestness that she squirmed in her seat.

She hadn't done any of those things, which he must have assumed.

"Do you enjoy the receptions of the weddings you plan? Or are you on the clock until the last guest leaves?"

"There is always the possibility something could go wrong." She elevated her chin defensively.

"True. But who said *you* have to prevent every possible accident?"

"And who put *you* in charge of being the life of the party and/or temporary security guard?"

He sat back and pulled in a deep breath. "So, we agree. We've assigned ourselves our roles."

"At least I'm invited to the events."

"And paid. I shell out a lot of money to be there."

She assumed he was referring to the cost of traveling

to the event, or buying a new suit. Camera equipment was expensive.

"As far as invitations," he continued, "those come later for me. Baby showers. Birthday parties. One second wedding for a groom."

"You keep in touch with them?" That surprised her.

"I don't seek it, but some of them reach out. It's not uncommon for the bride and groom to thank me for being there, or send me photos that I'm in."

She had to laugh. *What in the Owen Wilson...?* Was Trick serious?

"So because of your history," she said, "you thought you'd win over Ari and Ex the same way? By crashing their high-profile wedding and, what, *wooing* grandmothers or bridesmaids, or, or..."

"Wedding planners?"

She pursed her lips.

"I didn't plan on *wooing* anyone. Just like I didn't plan on becoming a professional wedding crasher. I happen to excel at it, so that's what I do."

"Are you talking about the wooing or the crashing?"

"You tell me." He let that comment dangle. "I fell into this business, but I don't regret it."

Rylee had fallen into her career as well. It was odd learning all that they had in common. She'd relegated Trick to *The Enemy* and frankly, was more comfortable with that dynamic than the idea of them on the same side.

"I should go to the office. I have a handful of emails to return I've been putting off." She reached down and massaged her heel. At least she'd be sitting behind a desk for a few hours and could stop walking around in these stupid shoes.

"They have a spa in our hotel. You should book a massage and a foot soak. You deserve it, considering the hell you put your feet through."

"I paid a lot of money for these shoes." She stood, wincing as one of those very expensive shoes pinched her pinky toe.

"You're worth the pampering, Peaches. Want me to schedule it for you?"

"No." But she spoke the word around a small smile. What was it with this guy? Did he cast a spell on everyone he met? She'd been determined to dislike him before they'd struck this bargain and was losing that battle gradually. *One Bellini at a time.*

He gathered up their trash and the flutes and followed her inside.

"Are you coming to the office with me?"

"Only temporarily. I have a drone to unpack."

She stopped short of unlocking the door. "You have a drone?"

"Yeah. For overhead shots. It's fun. You want to drive?"

"No."

"You are way too comfortable with that word, Peaches. When's the last time you said yes?"

Door open, she turned to face him. He was close, within kissing distance if one was considering kissing him…which she was *not*. She propped a hand on the doorknob effectively blocking his path into the office.

"Mr. MacArthur, the most effective way to persuade me to say yes would be if you asked if you can leave early, stay out of the way, or be a no-show to the wedding and reception."

He shook his head slowly. "You're wrong about that, Ms. Meadows. The most effective way to persuade you to say yes is to stay in your space as much as possible.

You've already said yes to dinner, yes to sharing a car, and yes to brunch."

She had. She didn't like the reminder that she was losing her willpower where he was concerned. "Only because you said yes to me first."

"Know what else?" he continued as if she hadn't spoken. "I don't think you mind me in your space. I think you might *like* me in your space. I think—"

She lifted her hand and pressed her fingertips against his lips. Her heart raced at the touch, more intimate than she'd anticipated. His lips flinched into a half-smile.

"Are you through?" she whispered.

"Nope." He moved her hand aside. "Just getting started."

Ariana Ramos had a great laugh. It was nearly impossible not to join in, or at least smile with her. Especially over video call, which was how Rylee had reached out. "Rye, this is why I pay you. I trust you."

Rylee released the tension from her shoulders, relieved to have finally confessed about the arrangement with Trick. "I'm glad to hear that you aren't upset. I sort of proceeded without you."

Ari had stayed resolutely silent while Rylee had explained the situation, and when Ari's facial expression remained neutral, Rylee had felt the need to explain *more*. When she'd finally stopped explaining, Ari fingered her short hair and let out another laugh that lifted her cheeks.

"I'll be honest with you, I was paranoid for a while that he was going to swoop in and ruin everything. Now that I know you have him under control, I am almost excited to meet this man." Ari lowered herself onto a tuffet in what Rylee recognized as Natalie Valentine's bridal shop.

Rylee wouldn't say that she had Trick "under control" but she wasn't going to volunteer that information.

"He's won over my unflappable wedding planner? Unheard of!"

Since Rylee and Ariana had become friends over the course of planning this wedding, Rylee knew to take that as a compliment. She kept her polite smile, but an old wound that lived within her had opened up at the mention of the word "unflappable." It inferred a rigidity that Louis had pointed out often in their relationship. In a way, Trick had pointed that out as well.

"It's less about winning me, or you and Xavier, over and more about him agreeing to behave and share only the footage of the wedding plans rather than the wedding itself."

"I trust you implicitly." Ari adjusted the bodice of a black dress adorned with bright pink and purple flower embroidery. "You've rolled with a blackout, vendor issues, *and* a wedding crasher and you didn't flinch."

Oh, Rylee had flinched plenty, but she was more of a crying-on-the-inside kind of girl. She'd had her minor meltdown moments over the last few months, but hopefully she'd concealed the majority of her true feelings. As much as she treasured both Ariana and Xavier, this wedding had been the most trying in her professional experience.

"You're the priority, Ari. Ex is *just* the groom."

Ari's chiming laughter rang out again.

"I can see that you're at the bridal shop. How did the final fitting go?"

"Wonderful!" The future bride's face lit up, her wide, pink-lipped smile causing her brown eyes to crinkle at the edges. "Keely is a true artist. And she integrated blue bonnets into the design in a subtle, beautiful way."

"She's amazing. I'm not surprised." Even though they weren't from the same part of the country, Rylee could relate to the born-and-raised-in-New-York designer. Keely had been focused on each and every detail of the dress, and not only because she knew that photographs of Ari in it would boost her career in a big way. Keely cared about details because she was committed to excellence.

Rylee wrinkled her nose. She wished she would have mentioned to Trick that excellence was the reason she appeared rigid. If that's what he thought of her. He seemed to delight in talking her into doing things she shouldn't be doing while on the clock. Like drinking Bellinis.

"I have to run, but keep me posted on the gift bags, okay?" Ari had her own lifestyle brand and had been selective about the gifts for each and every guest to take home. "Look for a gift from me to you, too. It should arrive this evening."

"You didn't have to do that," Rylee said, meaning it. Ari had already been so generous.

"Rye, I didn't do it because I had to. I did it because we're friends. I recognize a hardworking woman who doesn't take enough time for herself when I see one." Ari gave the screen an air kiss. "See you soon, doll."

"Definitely," Rylee said around a lump in her throat. She ended the video call. She had known she and Ari were friendly, but hearing the other woman verify that they were "friends" had touched her. Also, Ari gave great gifts. Rylee was looking forward to opening the care package as soon as it arrived.

Five

Rylee, sitting at the desk in her private office at the TCC, heard her cellphone ping and regarded it with one eye open. She was afraid of what else might potentially go wrong now that they were within spitting distance of the wedding.

So far she'd been contacted about a transportation issue with the vintage cars the best man had lined up for wedding, as well as the fact that some of the accessories for the reception had been shipped to the wrong address. Thankfully, that address belonged to a nearby hotel where Ariana's sister, Sasha Ramos, was staying. Rylee had arranged for a courier to pick up the boxes from Sasha and bring them to the TCC.

She needed to ensure the packages arrived safely and were stored in the correct ballroom, as well as follow up with Tripp about the car situation. A wedding planner's work was truly never done.

Then the call had come from Keely, who was hand-delivering the wedding gown to Rylee at Ari's request. They'd agreed to conceal it in a black dress bag and for it to be locked in Rylee's temporary private office here at the TCC. Rylee couldn't very well stash it in her hotel room, in case there was a sneaky paparazzo who paid off a member of the hotel staff to snap a pic or two. Ironically, she trusted Trick more than a random photographer.

Speaking of, the text message on her phone's screen was from Trick. He hadn't contacted her with an emergency, but a request: Lunch?

"All he does is eat." Was it noon already? She checked the clock on the wall. It read ten after three. "*Three?* It's three o'clock?"

"My point exactly." Trick entered through her open office door holding a charcuterie plate overflowing with cheeses, various meats, plump green grapes, nuts and honeycomb.

"Do I want to know where you stole that from?"

"I did not steal it. I requested it from the kitchen. Pamela is really nice."

Rylee didn't know Pamela, but the idea of him charming charcuterie out of another woman was an unpleasant thought.

"These, though"—from behind his back, he brandished two cans of Perrier—"I stole off a cart by the bar."

"Are you serious?"

"No. God. What do you take me for? Ricardo was restocking, and I asked if I could buy a few cans. He wouldn't let me pay, but I did ask."

She didn't know Ricardo either. How was it that Trick was already on a first-name basis with people at an exclusive club he didn't belong at or belong to? Incredible.

He set down the tray of finger foods and she didn't

hesitate. She stacked a chunk of Gouda on top of a Genoa salami slice and ate it. She'd had no idea how hungry she was until that first bite. He cracked open a can of Perrier and set it in front of her.

"I considered bringing you chardonnay, but I didn't want to push the boundaries of your work rules. Especially since you're finishing up for the day."

The water was lime-flavored and refreshing. "I'm far from finishing up. The dress designer is delivering Ari's dress, and I need to call Tripp about the vintage cars. Plus, there is a courier on the way with some items for the reception hall. I need to check the deliveries that were already stacked in that room and ensure they are for Ari and Ex and not like, a box of toilet paper rolls meant for maintenance instead."

Trick laughed, sobering when she didn't laugh with him. "Wait. For real? That has happened before?"

"Yes. Maintenance received the candles for the candelabras and left them in the warehouse on a day when it was 105 degrees outside."

He winced.

"That's something I'll never allow to happen again." One of many mistakes she'd learned from since starting this business.

"I've been to a lot of weddings, and I've met a handful of wedding planners, but I never bothered finding out what was involved. Much more than I thought."

"Were you too busy trying to take off their shoes or their skirts?" It wasn't hard to imagine Trick with a besotted woman dangling off his arm.

"I was avoiding them. They didn't approach me with an offer like you did. I knew that they would spot me from a mile away. Being friendly with the planner would make it harder to blend in. That's why I crash weddings in the middle and not at the start. After everyone has eaten and downed a few drinks."

"So this is a whole new adventure for you."

"Completely." He ate a cracker topped with prosciutto. "So, do you want me to hang out here and wait for Keely or head to the reception hall to meet the courier?"

Rylee blinked, surprised by the offer. She'd relegated herself to doing everything. "I've got it."

He unpacked a tripod from his bag. "I want to shoot some footage of the reception hall anyway. I'm going to film the progress each day and then show a big reveal of the end result."

"In a time-lapse?" she guessed.

"Maybe. I haven't decided how to handle the footage yet. But people are begging for a livestream, so maybe I'll pop open some of the boxes with you and we'll find out if we have candles or Cottonelle."

She laughed.

"So? Reception hall?" He pointed one thumb over his shoulder and waited for her answer. Part of her wanted to argue that it wasn't his responsibility to meet the courier, but she couldn't be two places at once. She didn't want to miss Keely.

"Sure."

He dipped his head in a nod. Before he was out the door, she called out her thanks. He didn't turn around when he answered, "No problem, Peaches."

On his way to the reception area, Trick encountered the courier. The girl was around his younger sister's age, twenty or so, and wearing boots and a uniform of shorts and a shirt with her name stitched above the left pocket. She looked worried, and he'd bet a hundred bucks that her quivering chin would lead to tears if someone didn't intervene.

The big brother in him went on high alert. He angled toward her, intercepting her as she checked the clipboard in her hands for the third time.

"Mackenzie. Are you the courier I'm searching for?" He gave her a smile to set her at ease.

"Y-yes. Are you Rylee?" There was a hint of doubt in her voice as she looked him up and down.

"Rylee sent me. I'm Patrick." He grinned. "I'm happy to help carry the boxes if that's the issue. The reception hall is right around the corner." As he spoke, he watched the girl's face go slack and mouth drop open.

"Oh, my god. You're—you're Trick MacArthur. The wedding crasher. Oh, my god!"

"Ah, yeah." He sent a nervous look around the empty corridor. "I'm here on official business though, no crashing."

"You have a camera." The girl's smile was unstoppable, her earlier turmoil forgotten. "What are you filming?"

"It's a surprise."

"Can I have a photo of you? Please?"

"Sure." He acquiesced, leaning in and smiling as she took a selfie of them and checked the screen of her phone.

"Thank you! Thank you. Wow. Trick MacArthur." Then her face fell as her earlier worries flooded in and washed away her smile. "Shit. I mean, shoot. I'm, uh, I have a problem."

"Need a dolly for the delivery? Is it too heavy to carry?"

She gave him a dubious look. "Not at all. I left the box in the car until I found out where I was going. I can carry it. But I'm running late for my next delivery."

"Oh-kay." He was lost. If she was in a hurry, why was

she standing here talking to him instead of sprinting back to her car? "How about I bring the box in myself, and then you can leave for your next delivery."

"I can't ask you to do that." Awe slipped into her gaze before she frowned. "I can't leave for my next delivery. I have a flat tire." There was the chin quiver again. "I cancelled triple-A because I never used it, and I'm new at this stupid job and now I'm going to be fired."

Ah-ha. Now he was caught up. "We won't let that happen, Mackenzie. First off, I can change a tire. And secondly, you have a cellphone. Film me changing the tire and you will have proof to show your boss that you weren't lying about the delay."

"Really?" He knew a look of hero worship when he saw it. The one Mackenzie wore now was reminiscent of the way his sister, Cassie, looked at him when he'd picked her up from a party at 2 a.m. and didn't tell their parents she'd sneaked out.

"Lead the way." He held out an arm and the courier bounced toward the exit, checking over her shoulder on the way like she was making sure he hadn't vanished into thin air.

Walking outside was like walking into one of the circles of hell. The heat was stifling, taking his breath and causing sweat to bead above his upper lip. If Texas heat was hell, then air-conditioning must be heaven.

Heaven, kind of like Rylee's pale pink lip gloss and dimples whenever she smiled at him. She'd smiled at him when he brought her lunch today. He was already trying to think of more ways to beckon those dimples forth.

"This is me," Mackenzie gestured to the hatchback parked on the curb.

It'd been a while since he had changed a tire. He silently hoped it was like riding a bike. The box destined for Ariana and Xavier's reception area was awkwardly shaped but weighed next to nothing. He helped unpack the shipment beneath it next. The boxes were considerably heavy by his definition and yet the young female courier lifted them without issue.

Once the boxes were out of the way, and he had the donut spare tire and jack in hand, he ratcheted up the car and got to work.

"I had a bit of trouble at the job today," Mackenzie was saying. "And you will never believe who I ran into. A knight in wedding-crashing armor!"

He recognized the cadence of someone narrating a video. No stranger to being on camera, he raised a hand to wave before returning his attention to the tire.

"Trick MacArthur is at the Texas Cattleman's Club!" Mackenzie whisper-screamed as she videoed herself. "What are the odds? I'm literally *dead*!"

He had to smile, even while sweating his ass off and simultaneously ruining his favorite shirt with a grease stain. And while trying to remember how to loosen and tighten a lug nut so that Mackenzie didn't suffer a fiery car crash on the way to her next delivery.

Her being starstruck over their chance encounter had done more than boost his ego. It had reminded him the reason behind everything he did. The *people*.

He'd always been about more than clicks, follows or beating the pesky algorithm. Sure, he'd been guilty of being caught up in the numbers in the past, but he'd grown up a lot since then.

Mackenzie, still filming and likely assuming he couldn't hear her, whispered loudly into her phone's speaker. "Isn't he hot?"

Six

"Thanks so much, Keely." Rylee accepted the hug from the dress designer, who was taller than her and then some with the added help of three-inch pumps.

"You know I have to see this all the way through." The other woman's smile could light an entire room, but the way she held herself kept anyone from thinking she was only here for the party. Keely was fastidious about her work, which Rylee related to, and respected.

"I'll be seeing you at the wedding, I assume?" Rylee knew that Keely was romantically linked to Jay Chatman, a close friend of the groom.

"Yes," Keely lifted a finger to smooth her eyebrow. "We will be there. I'll also be in Royal a lot more. I have my own space at Jay's, so I'll be working in Texas whenever I can."

A man in a cowboy hat opened the side door and held it for them. Keely's flowy sleeves blew in the warm breeze that swirled around them as they exited.

"I'm sure our paths will cross again. You're at the top of my list for a designer whenever a bride needs a recommendation. If you are able to carve out time in your soon-to-be exploding schedule and in between jet-setting across the globe as a famous designer."

"Stop." Keely gave Rylee's arm a playful tap. "I'll be jet-setting, but I'll always make time for the people I care about. You're one of the good ones, Rylee Meadows."

Rylee was warmed by the compliment. She thought of Keely as a friend, and liked hearing that the feeling was mutual.

"Hey, isn't that your wedding crasher?"

Rylee turned in the direction Keely pointed. Trick was grinning for the camera and chatting with a young woman standing next to her car. By her uniform, Rylee assumed this was the courier she'd sent for. A small crowd had gathered, and Rylee quickly deduced why. Trick held a jack in one hand and there was a grease stain on his shirt.

"He's not technically *mine*," she grumbled.

"I'll let you tend to that...situation." Keely let out a chuckle. "He is cute, though."

Cute? Trick was far from "cute." With his powerful forearm muscles on display, his dark, wavy hair blowing in the hot Texas air and the grin on his face, he was nothing short of gorgeous.

As if drawn in by his sheer magnetism, Rylee approached the car where a handful of people had gathered. Because Trick had put on a show and changed a tire, or because they'd recognized him?

The latter, she soon gathered. The girl wasn't snapping photos, she was filming. He took his eyes off the girl's front-facing camera screen when he saw Rylee coming their way.

"There she is." His grin seemed more real for her. "Mackenzie, this is Rylee Meadows."

The camera swung around to face Rylee and her steps faltered.

"She's pretty," Mackenzie said. "Your girlfriend?"

Trick took the question in stride, but his answer shocked Rylee all the way down to her uncomfortable shoes. "Not yet."

Mackenzie ended the video after promising her audience she would post more later, and then she pocketed her phone. "Ms. Meadows. Can you sign for this?" She handed off a clipboard that had been tucked under her arm. "I brought the package you requested."

Trick hefted a sizable box, showing her. "Weighs next to nothing."

"No, it shouldn't." Rylee scribbled her name on the form.

"I was running late because of a flat tire. Trick saved me." The younger woman's face glowed with admiration as she turned to face him. "Thanks again. I'll see you online?"

"You sure will."

With a delighted little squeal, Mackenzie climbed into her car, waved goodbye and drove out of the club's driveway.

"I couldn't say no," Trick explained as he adjusted the large box in his arms. "She was almost in tears. Reminded me so much of my younger sister, Cassie, my heart broke a little."

That was sweet, actually.

"She recognized me." He elbowed the accessibility button to open the automatic door for the side entrance. "Didn't expect that."

"I noticed you let her film you." At the reception hall, Rylee extracted her keycard and opened the door for him. "Are you always so magnanimous?"

"Nothing new about being on camera for me." He stepped into the darkened room. Rylee flipped on the lights. The venue wasn't much to look at in the moment, but come Saturday, this room would be transformed into old Hollywood utopia. Right now there were boxes upon boxes, several long tables set up in rows and a fully stocked bar in the corner. "Whoa."

"Not what you expected?" she asked as he set the large box onto one of the naked tables.

"I'm not used to seeing this stage. My followers are always begging me for behind-the-scenes stuff. They're going to love this, and it's all thanks to you." He set up his tripod and then ran back and forth from light switches to screen in search the perfect lighting.

Rylee was double-checking the other boxes to ensure that they did, in fact, belong here, when one of the sconces in the center of the room flickered and buzzed.

That was no good.

"I'll be right back," she called out. Trick gave her the thumbs-up signal. Before she left the room she couldn't help adding, "And then we'll talk about that not-yet comment."

He'd wondered if she was going to mention that. Now he knew. Rylee Meadows was not a woman who would take a comment about her being his girlfriend in stride. Even if she thought he'd said it simply for the public. Which he had, but that didn't mean there wasn't a nugget of truth to it.

He intended to win her over in the days ahead. By his

estimations, and by the way she was checking him out a minute ago, he was closer to kissing those lips than before.

Once he had the lighting right, he swapped the camera out for his cellphone and fired up a live video. He typed the title into the keyboard, which read *Early peek at the Noble-Ramos wedding in Royal!* And then hit the record button.

Talking to the camera came naturally to him, so when he addressed his invisible audience, he did so with ease. No longer did he have to practice what he was going to say in the mirror five times before he started. No longer did he suffer heart palpitations before tapping the big red button.

He moved the tripod to the bar and positioned himself behind it. Both hands on the bar top, he announced, "And this is where Ariana and Xavier's guests will be served, among other libations, the signature cocktail for their wedding. If you want to know what it is, you'll have to stick around for my interview with them on Friday night."

He glanced up when Rylee reentered the room, and then did a second take. She was hauling a ladder and a plastic bag. Not a stepladder, either. A full, six-foot-tall *ladder* ladder. She was about a mile away from him, so Trick thought fast, grabbed the tripod and continued the tour while moving closer to her.

"Tables are set up but not decked out," he narrated. "The chairs, stacked against the walls." He panned over to the chairs lining one wall and sent Rylee a glare communicating that she could have—*should* have—asked for his help with the ladder. It looked heavy, and she was hardly dressed for manual labor.

"All of these boxes are filled with accessories, including this one…" He stopped where he'd set the box on the table and drummed his fingers on the top. Then he rested the tripod on the ground and angled the camera on his phone at Rylee who was currently climbing the ladder in front of him. Facing the camera, he mugged for his audience—1,890 watching, not bad—and then he said in a low voice, "Now if you'll excuse me, I'm going to aid the wedding planner with this highly dangerous task she's attempting to complete without my help." He turned away before quickly turning back to say, "I know this is the age of equal rights and she is capable of doing anything she damn well pleases, but ladies, hear me." He paused for effect before continuing, "Take advantage of the men who are struck stupid by your beauty. *Use us*. We'll do whatever you want."

With that, he turned and walked to the ladder, careful not to startle Rylee, who either hadn't noticed or didn't care what or whom he was filming. He reached out to steady the ladder at the same instant the heel of one of her shoes snapped clean off.

She let out a dainty "Ahh!" as she lost her balance. Then she practically sat on his chest. He held tight to the sides of the ladder as she jerked away from him. Wobbling slightly, her wide eyes snapped to his.

"You okay?"

"Of cour—ahh!" Another wobble set her off balance, and he reacted without thinking, letting go of the ladder to wrap his arms around her. They fell to the ground, him padding the blow and landing hard on his ass.

He let out an "oof", but a low groan followed. That was because each and every one of Rylee's soft, supple curves was pressed against him. She was splayed awkwardly over top of him, her hair coming loose from her updo, her blue eyes burning into his. When her mouth dropped open invitingly, he decided to RSVP with a kiss.

He lifted his head to bring his lips closer to hers, when he noticed her raised hand. A hand that was delicately gripping a…light bulb? Both their gazes rerouted to that single, unbroken bulb and then back to each other.

"What the hell are you doing?" she snapped.

"Breaking your fall."

"I could have broken *you*. I'm not a petite woman, you know."

"You're perfect." His hands were resting innocuously on her waist, one of his legs nestled between hers. Every inch of her that was touching him was divine.

She appeared more inconvenienced than embarrassed as she rolled off him and straightened the skirt of her dress. She took off the shoe with the broken heel, and that's when she noticed the camera. He watched as her expression slowly morphed from inconvenienced to pissed off.

He stood to explain, but she swiveled his body so that his head blocked the camera. Her whisper even sounded angry. "What the hell, Trick?"

"We're live. Let's play it up. For Ari and Ex's sake." He nodded subtly, not giving her a chance to react before he knelt and slipped her other shoe off. He felt her hand on his shoulder and then he stood to introduce her.

"Ladies and gentleman, the lovely Rylee making a grand entrance. She's the wedding planner, and apparently is owed a new pair of…"—he turned his head to the side to read the inner sole of the shoe in his hand—"Sergio Rossi pumps."

Rylee futzed with her dress, clearly trying to rein in

her temper. "You shouldn't sneak up on a girl while she's doing her own dirty work."

"You should have asked for my help."

"I don't need your help." Her cheeks grew pink.

"I didn't say you *needed* it. I said you should have asked for it. Hasn't it become apparent that I am willing to chase you around with Bellinis and brunch or charcuterie boards? I can change a light bulb." He snatched the bulb from her hand and started for the ladder.

"It's the last one!" she said when he set one foot on the bottom rung. "Be careful."

He cradled the bulb in his hand, more carefully now that he knew it was a rare commodity. "Okay, okay."

At the top of the ladder, that she was steadying, he noticed, he replaced the flickering bulb for the one in his hand. He came down without incident, but then he didn't have spikes on the heels of his shoes.

Once he was safely on the ground, he waggled the dead bulb at the screen of his phone, coming close to sign off. Now there were—*holy shit*—4,732 viewers on the live video.

"How many wedding crashers does it take to screw in a light bulb?" he asked, but the comments moving up the screen didn't attempt to answer his corny joke. Instead they were painting him as a hero, and Rylee as his "girlfriend."

The last comment he read followed that word with several crying emoji faces. He tried not to laugh. Clearly, they were interested in what was happening between him and the wedding planner. Who was he to sign off when his fans were begging for more?

Seven

Rather than stop the video, Trick turned toward Rylee. With a wink and a smile to let her know he was going to be teasing her, he held up the bulb between the fingers of one hand. "Where did you get this? And the ladder?"

"The maintenance closet." She shifted on her bare feet, never breaking eye contact with him. He wasn't sure when, but he'd won her over to the idea of playing it up for the camera. She was willing, which made this *fun*.

"The maintenance closet." He set down the spent bulb and circled her like a detective on a TV show questioning a suspect. "And was there a maintenance person there when you were in this closet, Ms. Meadows?"

She pressed her lips together, he assumed to hide a laugh at his over-the-top theatrics, but maintained her serious facade. He would have guessed that she'd be annoyed with his antics by now, but for whatever reason—his mentioning Ari and Ex might have helped—she'd decided to play it up as he'd requested.

"There was no maintenance person available, Mr. MacArthur."

"Am I to believe that the staff at the highly acclaimed Texas Cattleman's Club leaves their maintenance closet unattended *and* unlocked?" he asked with a flourish.

She shot out her chin and said the very last thing he'd expected her to say. "I can pick a lock."

Trick dropped character to grin. His audience had to be going crazy for this content. How could they not? She was gorgeous and stubborn and had confessed to a minor B&E.

Hands propped on his hips, he sort of repeated, "You picked the lock?"

Apparently she wasn't the least bit sorry. She doubled down, stating, "It comes in handy more often than you think."

"Remind me to call you if I need to plan a heist, Peaches. Lock-picking would come in handy for a jewelry store. Or a bank. You could do better than light bulbs." He swept a stray blond hair behind her ear, his eyes roaming over her face. She leaned her cheek into the hand he'd raised. Realizing he didn't have full control of his faculties and even less of his hammering heart, he blinked and stepped away from her to address the camera.

"You heard it here, folks. If a bank gets robbed in Royal..." He pointed at the beautiful amateur thief. "Rylee Meadows. More to come. *Crash you later.*" He tapped the red button to stop recording. The comments that scrolled by read, "*Go for it, Trick!* And *Kiss her, Trick!*" Not that he blamed his fans. Kissing Rylee had certainly crossed his mind. Which was why he'd stopped the live video.

"You called me Peaches in front of a million online viewers."

"Just under five thousand," he said. "I didn't even mean to say it. It's just—"

"Just what?" She cocked her head as he approached. When he was standing in front of her, slightly taller than she was since she'd lost the heels, he answered her.

"It's just that I've imagined kissing you at least a hundred times since you took that first sip of a peach Bellini at the steakhouse. Whenever I look at your lips, I wonder if they taste like peaches."

He realized, perhaps belatedly, that he was within slapping distance. Not only had he filmed her *and* outed her as a thief on a live social media feed, but now he'd admitted he wanted to kiss her. But Rylee didn't slap him.

Her expression took on an almost angelic quality, even as challenge straightened her shoulders. "Well? What are you waiting for?"

He slid his palm from her cheek to the back of her neck. "Not a single fucking thing."

He pressed his lips against hers, answering their prayers. Her mouth was plush and warm. *God*—perfect. She didn't taste like peaches, but she did taste like a woman he'd like to taste a hell of a lot more *of.*

His other arm locked around her back, he hugged her curvy body as he slid his tongue over hers. She stroked his back with her short nails, the friction causing a stir behind the fly of his pants.

Electricity skittered along his scalp and jettisoned down his spine. He was on fire for this woman, and over what? A single kiss? A kiss that came to an abrupt end when it became clear they were not alone.

"Are we...interrupting?" came an amused-sounding voice from behind them. Before he turned to look, he soaked up Rylee's dazed expression. Definitely, they were continuing this later.

He released her neck, but kept his other hand on her back to steady her—or himself. Hard to tell.

He didn't recognize the couple in the doorway, but as soon as the woman spoke he knew she recognized him.

"Rylee. Hi." The woman flipped her shoulder-length, sable-colored hair and addressed Trick next. "You must be the 'juvenile, fame-seeking prankster who crashes high-profile weddings.' I'm paraphrasing Rylee, but that is close, isn't it?"

"Um..." Rylee was at a loss for words, a novel concept. He didn't take offense to the insult, but instead extended a hand to the other woman.

"Trick MacArthur."

"Dionna Reed." She gestured at the man who stood at her side. "This is Tripp Noble."

"Maid of honor, and best man, respectively," Rylee supplemented.

"Of course." Trick had heard Rylee mention their names before. "Nice to meet you, Dionna, Tripp."

"You can call me Dee. Apparently you are no longer the enemy." To Rylee, she said, "Ari told me about your agreement with Trick. And then she dispatched us to check on the 'state of affairs.' Her words."

"Our reporting back to Ari and Ex has no bounds." Tripp sounded less inconvenienced than amused. He surveyed the stacks of boxes in the room. "What are we missing?"

"Nothing now." Rylee rushed to the box that Trick had

carried in. She unfolded the top to reveal...feathers? "The pens were delivered to Sasha's hotel by mistake, but here they are. And it looks like they're all here."

Trick extracted a chunky gold pedestal with multiple holes in it and then lifted one of the feather-tipped pens. They were ornate, with gold nibs and bands, the black faux feathers full and silky. He set the pedestal upright on the table and stuck a pen in it. Rylee and Dee began helping. Once every pen was in place, the pedestal looked more like a vase with a waterfall of feathers sprouting out of it.

"For the guest book," Rylee explained.

"It's gorgeous," Dee said approvingly. "What a find!"

"Thank you. Of course I'll ensure each of the pens work and I'll find some backup pens that are attractive in case one of the decorative pens run out of ink."

Trick swallowed a smile. That was his Rylee, planning for every unlikely hiccup. While that trait was admirable, he suspected her over-attention to detail caused more problems in her life than it solved.

"Keely brought the dress by already. I have it locked safe and sound in my private office here in the TCC. You never know who could be lurking around."

"Yeah, I see that." Dee slid Trick a look, but to him it felt approving.

"Now that you're both here, how about drinks?" Trick offered. "I'm buying."

Dee exchanged glances with Tripp and then Rylee.

"I was actually going to call about the vintage car situation, anyway," Rylee said. "Drinks would give us a chance to chat."

"In that case"—Tripp extended an arm toward the exit—"Lead the way."

* * *

Rylee had worked with Dee closely over the last few months. Dee had been making decisions for the bride whenever Ari couldn't be here. Not to mention Tripp had practically mind-read Rylee's plans for an Old Hollywood glamor wedding theme.

They relocated to the Silver Saddle, a tapas bar within the Bellamy, the same hotel where Trick and Rylee were staying. The bar was luxurious yet comfortable. Tripp chose a stand-up table with four high stools, one of which he pulled out for Dee.

"I'm going to grab drinks," Trick said after doing the same for Rylee. "Bellini?"

"White wine."

"No peaches for you, Peaches? What gives?"

The nickname prompted a raised eyebrow from Tripp. Dee gave him her order and the two men walked to the bar to collect the drinks.

"Sorry, I dove right in to asking Tripp about the cars before we sat down. I have no social graces when I'm off the clock."

"Are you ever off the clock?" Dee chuckled.

"Not really." Rylee shook her head abashedly. "I tend to quadruple check every item on my list. And then check once more."

"Hey, you're under a lot of pressure. This wedding is a big deal. Which begs the question, why don't you have, like five assistants?"

"I'm beginning to see the need for them," Rylee admitted. "In the past I've hired remote assistants to place orders and double-check stock and available dates, but with Ari and Ex being so famous, I didn't trust anyone to have their hands on this besides me, you and Tripp.

And the other vendors, of course. They've been wonderful. Ex and Ari's wedding is by far the most extravagant wedding I've planned."

Which had had the added bonus of completely overwhelming Rylee. Maybe that was the real reason behind why she kissed Trick. She'd never behaved so out of character in her life—and while at work.

Dee must have noticed the worry tugging at the corner of Rylee's mouth. The other woman patted her hand. "Ari hired you because she knows your work ethic is unmatched. You have a gift for turning the ordinary into magical. And she trusts you because you have done everything in your power to make this event crease-free."

"I thought she hired me because I'm from Texas," Rylee sort of joked.

"Xavier loves that you're a Texan, but it's not mere geography that landed you this gig, sweetheart. Tripp and I see it too. You are a professional through and through. Everything is going to be perfect. You wouldn't allow it to be anything less."

"Thank you." Rylee meant it. A compliment from Dee went a long way.

"You're welcome." A smile tickled the corner of Dee's mouth as she checked the bar for the guys. "What's up with you making out with the enemy?"

Rylee turned her eyes to the ceiling before closing them and scrunching up her face. "I don't know how that happened. Trick is so different than I thought he was. He's kind, and thoughtful. He changed a tire today for a courier, and then filmed a video with her because she was a fan."

"That's sweet."

"Since he's agreed to film pre-wedding festivities,

he's been around a lot. He continues to surprise me with brunch or snacks or offering to pick up a delivery. I didn't expect him to be this helpful. On his channel, he seemed, I don't know. *Different*."

"He's an entertainer. Not unlike Ari when she's in actress-mode. Or Xavier when he's touring for his latest book. Trust me, I understand what it's like to expect someone to be a certain way and having them surprise you."

Dee's smile warmed when she met eyes with Tripp across the room. "At first, I thought Tripp wasn't taking our assigned task as seriously as he should, but then I learned that he approaches problems from a different vantage point then me."

Rylee thought of Patrick mentioning his ADHD, and considered her own assumptions. He gleefully followed his impulses whereas she tended to plan everything out before attempting.

"Opposites attract," Dee said with a twinkle in her eye. "Don't underestimate how hot it can be between the sheets." Dee whispered that last part at the same time a glass of white wine was placed in front of Rylee.

Busted, she straightened her spine as Trick sat next to her with a beer. He started talking to Tripp about the ranch, and soon enough Dee was pulled into the conversation as well.

Rylee admired Patrick's ability to win over everyone he met. Even her, and she would have thought herself immune to a guy like him. In the end, it hadn't taken much for him to win her over to his side.

She thought about their explosive kiss and considered what Dee had said about how good their differences might play out in the bedroom. For the first time, Rylee considered taking a page from Trick's playbook and not planning ahead for a change. She sipped her wine and watched him through her lashes.

Tonight, she'd see where the evening took her. Or, more aptly, where it took *them*.

Eight

Rylee waved goodbye to Tripp and Dee as they made their way to the exit. She was feeling more relaxed than she had earlier, which was typically a warning sign. Staying vigilant was the only way to keep from overlooking pertinent details.

A quick glance at her watch showed that it was after six o'clock, well past quitting time for the average nine-to-five American, but for a wedding planner of a famous couple whose wedding was three days away...

"Whoa, whoa." Patrick gripped her shoulder. "You were loose and happy a second ago, but now you look as if a ghost walked over your grave."

"One very well might have. I never take this much time off so close to the wedding day." She looked around the bar, as nervous as if Ari and Ex were standing in the corner, ready to scold her. "It's criminal."

"Stealing light bulbs from the Cattleman's Club is

criminal," Trick corrected. "Having a drink after a long day is merely human."

"You're in your own world. Has anyone ever told you that?"

"Almost everyone has told me that." His easy smile suggested he'd taken criticism lightly in the past. Not that she'd meant it that way. His lifestyle was enviable at times. "Lucky for you, you're in my world now."

"I thought you were in mine."

"Oh, I am. But afterhours? That's squarely in my realm." He lifted her wineglass by the stem. A scant amount of warm liquid sat in the bottom of the glass. "You've been nursing this for an hour. Let me freshen it up for you. One more?"

She opened her mouth to say she couldn't. That she had to go back to the TCC office and gather her laptop, and then go up to her room and work in bed until two in the morning. She wasn't sure what changed her mind, but thought it might have something to do with the eager anticipation in Trick's eyes. She wanted to tell him yes, as she'd told him yes several times before.

"I'm concerned by how easily you talk me into things," she said.

"Happens to the best of them, Rylee. No sense fighting enjoying yourself." His grabbed his empty mug as well. "Enjoyment is what life's about."

He was back from the bar in a blink with a fresh, chilled glass of chardonnay for her and another beer for him. She held the wine in her mouth for a second, savoring its oaky, buttery flavor.

"I do need to collect my things from the office tonight," she said, unable to let go of the idea completely.

"Why?" He appeared sincerely perplexed, which made her laugh out loud.

"Because the wedding—"

"Is Saturday. I know. For argument's sake, let's say none of those feathery pens work."

Her blood went as cold as her wine.

"Yep, you heard me. The guests show up, pluck the pens out and set them to the guest book to write their autographs." His eyes widened in faux horror. "And then *nothing* comes out. Not a single drop of ink. Now what?"

"I—I don't know." Worry rippled through her.

"I *do* know. You will break into the maintenance closet—definitely in your wheelhouse—and pilfer a box of Bic stick pens. Black, red, blue. Whatever you can find."

"*Red*?" Unacceptable. The panic must have shown on her face. He reached up and smoothed the wrinkle from her brow with his thumb.

"No one will care. Not Ari. Not Ex. Not the guests. Roll with what life throws you sometime, and watch what happens. You heading off every potential problem isn't what keeps the world spinning, Peaches. It does that on its own."

"I wish I could be spontaneous." She swallowed a gulp of her wine and tried to shake off the idea of red ink on the crisp white pages of the gold guest book. *Appalling*.

"Planner through and through, huh?"

"And back around and through again."

He laughed. She liked hearing him laugh. Liked the way it crinkled the corners of his eyes and loosened his posture. She noticed she was sitting ramrod straight and purposely tried to relax her own posture. It was easier to do while wearing the flat sandals she'd changed into after the high heel snapped off one of her pumps. She'd stashed the spare pair of shoes in her bag in case of emergency this morning. One point for her for planning ahead.

"How'd you start wedding planning, anyway? And don't give me a phone-it-in 'It's what I'm good at' answer. I want the real story."

"That's going to require a lot more wine."

"I can arrange for that." He moved to stand and she put her hand on his arm to stop him. Warmth from his skin transferred to her palm. He was so much more attractive than when she'd first spotted him in Royal. Maybe because she knew him better now.

He folded his arms on the table in front of his beer. "C'mon, Peaches. No one is here but us. It's completely off the record. Unless you still don't trust me."

"It's not that," she blurted out before she thought about it. Oddly enough, she *did* trust him. He'd been nothing but accommodating and agreeable. Plus, she liked finding out more about him. He operated so differently from her. He was sort of fascinating. "But if I tell you, you have to tell me something juicy about yourself."

"You mean like my wedding conquests past?"

"Ew."

"I'm joking." He gave her another of those broad, crinkly smiles that made her belly clench and her face heat. His sincere expression towed her in when he amended, "I'll tell you something I've never told anyone. How about that?"

As stoic as Rylee appeared on the outside, she *loved* secrets. Intrigued, she pursed her lips. Trick's gaze zoomed in on her mouth. She licked her bottom lip, watching as he shifted in his seat. A zing of awareness flitted through her veins.

While her past wasn't a topic she typically discussed, she was aware that the situation with Trick was far from typical. Tucking a strand of hair behind her ear, she warned him with three words. "Are you ready?"

"Born that way." He grinned. "Hit me."

"Okay. Here goes."

Trick leaned in, expecting to hear a tale of a young, spunky, headstrong Rylee Meadows. Picturing her diving into the unknown excited him in a way that felt almost foreign. While he generally lived life flying by the seat of his pants, the women in his life rarely "excited" him in a way other than the physical. Rylee was a bold-faced exception to that rule. Not that he wasn't physically attracted to her—he could hardly keep his mind off kissing her again—but he was also insatiably curious about her.

"I grew up in a country club, don't-lift-a-finger household, I was taught that becoming a wife was the penultimate goal. I'd been dating a man two years older than my twenty-two, but Louis seemed older. He'd graduated with a degree in business, and had lined up a lucrative spot at my family's company. President was in his future."

"A professional." Trick wasn't surprised. Everything about Rylee screamed that she should be married to a doctor or a lawyer. Or the president of a company. "Does he still work for your family's company?"

She nodded. That must suck.

"Anyway, my future was laid out for me. It wasn't one I chose. My parents were thrilled that their daughter was engaged to a man who could provide, and had come from good stock."

"Sounds sexy," he said with a dab of jealousy. He couldn't imagine referring to a significant other as "stock" but then he wasn't from her world, was he? No one had expected too much from him after he'd been diagnosed with ADHD.

He'd been raised in an upper middle-class neighborhood in LA. His mom and dad worked hard every day. While his younger sister had been encouraged to pursue college, their parents hadn't pressed Patrick in the same way. Cassie had gone from a high school student to a college student in a blink. Trick had attended film school, but had found a career adjacent to movies. He'd always done his own thing, made his own choices.

"I didn't feel butterflies or sparks for Louis," Rylee continued, "but I remember how well he was liked. I'd known him for years. He was a country-club kid, too. Nearly everyone in our families' circles gushed over how "perfect" we were together, and how "beautiful" our future babies would be."

Trick swallowed a mouth full of beer to keep from offering criticism. This Louis guy sounded bland. Tepid. Unforgivably boring. He didn't know Rylee, but what he knew of her suggested that a cardboard cutout of a husband was the last thing she needed in her life. She deserved someone who would take care of her, not someone who expected *her* to take care of *him*.

"I took a few college classes, but didn't fully commit to a full-time curriculum. Just generals while I decided what I wanted to be when I grew up. By the time Louis proposed that summer, his mind was made up. I wouldn't work. He was making great money. I was going to be a wife, a mom and live out the rest of my days in wedded bliss.

"I threw myself into planning our wedding. I consulted with multiple florists and reception sites, dance instructors, caterers, bakers. You name it. I loved the organization of it, and the lists." Her smile revealed both dimples. "Ah, the lists."

"Some things didn't change, I see."

"The lists stayed." She took another drink from her glass before she continued. "About eight months into our engagement, I'd started talking about wanting to go into event planning as a career. I had recently offered my services for a friend's baby shower, and another friend's birthday party. I had been bitten by the entrepreneur bug. Louis saw my working as beneath us. He wanted to be seen as the husband who provided for his wife, and he found it embarrassing that I would stoop to, as he put it, 'serve others'. Shortly after, he called off the engagement.

"That's the stupidest thing I've ever heard," Trick grumbled, disliking this Louis guy more and more by the second.

"I was sheltered. Everyone else thought Louis was right for me, so why shouldn't I? I didn't know any better than to blindly accept the life presented to me on a silver platter."

He reached for her hand and stroked her fingers with his. "Your ex sounds like a complete troglodyte."

She surprised him by laughing. "He was more taciturn than caveman. I'm not sure he'd ever been passionate about anything before he was passionate about me *not* going into business for myself."

"I'm sorry." Trick meant it. It was a shitty reason to end a relationship.

"I was sad that it ended, but mostly I was angry. Do you know how many non-refundable deposits I'd paid? Which, yes, was Louis's money, but it felt so wasteful. I'd carefully vetted everyone from the band members to the sommelier. And now, because I was damn good at what I did, I was supposed to let it go to waste?"

Damn, Trick liked hearing her talk like this. With enough passion to blaze a fiery trail through the center of town. When she described her abilities and talents, she came alive. She gestured with her hands, pulled her shoulders back and elevated her chin. Rylee was proud of what she'd accomplished—then and now. She should be. No way in hell would Trick attempt to plan anything as complex as a celebrity wedding—no matter how much help he had doing it.

"A friend of mine ended up pregnant, and was in a rush to be married before our entire community was *scandalized.* Can you believe that? In our modern society?" Rylee rolled her eyes.

He could believe it. Modern society could, at times, be downright ancient when it came to traditions.

"I asked her if it would be strange for her to take my entire wedding package, since the arrangements were already made. Free of charge, of course. I offered to help her with the details. The only thing she had to do was show up in a white dress."

"And she said yes," he concluded.

Rylee held up a finger. "Not at first. She'd voiced concerns that I was heartbroken and would regret handing over my wedding plans. I assured her that while I wasn't happy about being dumped, I had known deep down that Louis wasn't right for me. Eventually she said yes. If she hadn't, she would have run out of time to conceal her baby bump.

"The wedding was incredible and, ironically, suited to my friend's tastes. I thought I had been making choices based on what *I* liked, but I realized I had been making them based on what others expected of me. Now I make decisions based on my own needs. No one else's."

He admired her moxie. She could have gone the other way and abandoned her dreams and goals in order to stay married to that toad. Or she could have allowed her doomed engagement to make her doubt herself. Instead, she'd grown a Jack's beanstalk of a business from one humble little bean.

"At the reception for my friend's wedding, I was approached by her cousin and a bridesmaid about their future weddings. They wanted to hire me to be their planner. I agreed on the spot, had some business cards printed and started my business. I moved from Texas to LA, and have been working nonstop ever since."

"God, Rylee." Awed, he shook his head.

"What?" Her smile was tremulous.

"You're incredible."

Her fair skin stained pink. She looked down at her wineglass. "I traded a fiancé for a career. I don't know if that makes me incredible, but it does make me scrappy."

Hell yes, it did. He had friends who would curl up and die if they'd had a fiancée dump them a few months before the wedding. And he had at least one other friend who would have trashed his future rather than embrace the newfound freedom and the opportunity to grow.

Rylee had gone from being a distractingly attractive rule-follower to a plucky, do-whatever-it-takes woman. She was take-charge and in-charge. She might have started out following her family's plan for her life, but she'd ended up chasing her own dreams. He was enamored. Enthralled.

Turned on.

"So, there it is. My tale of a passionless engagement

and recycled wedding plans. And now you know I'm one of the snobby rich." She cupped her wineglass but didn't drink from it.

She was waiting for him to make a joke, perhaps at her expense. Instead he did what he'd wanted to do since they sat down at this table.

He leaned in and kissed her.

Nine

One minute Rylee was trotting out the scandalous and sordid tale of how she'd ended up planning the Noble-Ramos wedding, and the next she was being kissed thoroughly by the man who'd intended to crash it.

Trick's hands were cupping her face as his lips moved softly but firmly over hers. He didn't invade her mouth, but instead teased her lips with the very tip of his tongue. Abruptly, he backed away, ending the kiss too soon.

He didn't let go of her right away. He lingered, peering into her very soul as his mouth spread into a cunning smile. A smile that had her nipples pebbling inside of her bra, and warmth gathering between her legs.

"You're so fucking sexy I can't stand it," he murmured, his voice husky. "Sorry to attack you, I just…couldn't help myself." His throat bobbed with a laugh as a slightly chagrined look crossed his features. As if he'd been overcome by her and had taken himself by surprise.

Same.

She liked that he hadn't been fully in control of his faculties. Passion had been in short supply in her life. Partially because she was raised in a prim and proper environment. Rarely had she seen her father offer more than a demure peck to her mother's cheek. Affection had been tempered in her household.

She glanced around the restaurant, half expecting someone to be gaping at her very public display of affection, but no one was paying attention.

"I'll refrain from further lip-locks until you give me permission," he promised. "Your turn."

"My turn?"

"I promised to tell you something no one else knows. Or you can ask me anything."

She put her hand to her head. She'd forgotten they were in the middle of a conversation. "Right. I, uh, lost my place."

Grinning, he eased back into his chair. He wore smugness well.

"Did you go to college?"

"Ah, a softball."

"We can start slow." The comment held a charge. She could practically feel the hum in the air between them.

"Slow is good for me, Peaches." He cleared his throat. "College. Yes. Film school, actually. The idea of becoming a filmmaker was a straight shot from childhood to now." He arrowed his arm out in front of him. "I always knew I wanted to be an entertainer. I connected with the films I watched as a kid. I've wound up in front of the camera, but my original goal was to be behind it."

"You're good at what you do. Although, I'm not a fan of pranks you used to pull in your older videos."

"Most of those were Todd's ideas. Not to lay blame, but he's not here to defend himself, so let's blame him."

"Was he a friend from film school?"

"Yeah. He's a good guy. I drew the line at humiliating people. No one likes to be made fun of."

"Tell me about it." While she'd had a fairly secure childhood, she recalled plenty of times she'd felt set apart from her friends. Her best friend Monica had been a wisp of air compared to Rylee's curvaceous build. "I never managed to slim down to the size of my closest friends. A few well-meaning but hurtful comments are still embedded in my memory."

Trick's mouth pulled into a frown.

"You know, because of..." She mimed the shape of an hourglass with her hands. "I should have asked, but I didn't hurt you when I fell on you, did I?"

"Are you fucking kidding me?" His tone was sharp, disapproving.

"N-no. I mean, I did fall from a considerable height."

He leaned in closer. So close she could make out the stubble pressed deliciously against his jawline. "I can handle every neckbreaking curve and hairpin turn on your body, Rylee." He made a low appreciative sound in the back of his throat before blatantly checking her out. "You're perfect. Insanely, distractingly perfect."

She hadn't been fishing for a compliment, and as a result had no idea what to do with one. Since those tender teenage years, she had accepted her body type and size. Rejoiced in it. She was active, healthy. She was also proud of the way she looked. But it'd been a long time since she'd taken her clothes off in an intimate act. The idea of being naked with Trick sent a barrage of tingles over her skin. She wasn't nervous, but *excited*. She'd al-

ways been self-conscious around Louis. He hadn't out-
right criticized her, but neither had he openly praised her.

"I'm so comfortable around you," she told Trick, awe-
struck by the realization. "More than I was with my fiancé. That's strange."

"Is it?"

"I guess not. Everyone else is at ease around you.
Charm is one of your gifts. You don't have to try at it."

"Believe me, Peaches, with you I'm trying. I'm holding back so I don't scare you off."

"Scare me off? Do I seem easily frightened to you?"

"Fuck, no! You seem like the type of woman who is
burned once and doesn't allow a second chance. I am
well aware that I'm on borrowed time."

"Accurate." They stared at each other, soaking in the
possibility of more. At least, she hoped he was contem-
plating more. She sure as hell was.

"I bet you've decided never to get married."

She inclined her head. "You are correct."

"Never getting married but planning weddings for
others."

"It's an updated version of *always the bridesmaid
but never a bride*." She sipped her wine and then asked,
"What about you? Is there wedded bliss in your future?"

"Definitely. I always wanted to share my life with
someone else. Being alone sucks."

She laughed, finding his easy admission startling. She
would have put money on him being a total playboy.
"That's a rare opinion for a guy. Of the weddings I've
planned, 'cold feet' on the part of the groom was a real
and diagnosable affliction."

"Yeah? How many of them bailed?"

"One," she answered. "But he came back."

"Let me guess, you hunted him down and talked some sense into him."

"His brother, the best man, did most of the talking. But I was there to facilitate."

"Of course you were. You couldn't let a groom with cold feet wreck your plans."

"True story." She took a breath. "Louis never viewed our relationship as a partnership. It was always him on top with me bringing up the rear."

She heard the double entendre too late. Trick raised both eyebrows as she covered her cheeks with her hands in an attempt to cool them down. "Oh, my god. I can't believe I just said that."

"You said it, not me."

They both laughed. He was so easy to hang out with.

"I did. I can't believe it, but I did. Ugh. Let's talk about something else. Will you have a huge wedding?"

"I guess it depends on my bride, doesn't it?" he asked, thoughtful. "But if I have a say, I've always pictured a wedding on a cliffside with, like, four people in attendance."

"My parents would die of culture shock if I dared to have a small wedding. Seeing and being seen is practically etched into our family crest."

"They wouldn't *die*. They recovered after you built a career rather than marry Mr. Personality, didn't they?"

"They are alive and well." Her smile was unstoppable. Her wine was also gone. For the first time in a long, long time, she wanted to order another glass and blow off her responsibilities. So, so tempting. Impossible, but tempting.

"You sound like you have good parents. They didn't

give you too hard of a time about the wedding falling apart, did they?"

"No, actually. They were supportive. I wonder if they had second thoughts about Louis and his intentions. Though my mother would love to be bouncing a grand-baby on her hip right about now."

"Plenty of time for that."

"What are your parents like?"

"My dad is a mason and a complete jokester." He pointed to himself to show that he'd inherited that particular skill set. "My mom tried acting, but ended up a costume designer instead. She used to take me to the set with her. I fell in love with everything around me. It was a cool way to grow up."

"Sounds amazing." His upbringing was wild and unexpected whereas hers had been mapped-out and boxed-in. Had she grown into the woman her parents had cultivated, or had she chosen her own path? Spontaneity was a rare trait in the Meadows family. The idea that she'd been popped out of a mold of their making bothered her. Sure, she'd had a mostly good childhood, but no one wanted to believe they'd been crafted in a laboratory like Edward Scissorhands.

Trick polished off his beer and set the empty glass on the table. Their night was coming to a fast close.

"It's late." He checked his phone. Then he opened the app where literally millions of strangers followed him. What was it like to be admired by that many people?

"Did we go viral yet?" She didn't know how she felt about being on his social media channel. Excited? Weird? Both?

"Not yet, but there are no shortage of comments." He

lifted an eyebrow. "Most of them encouraging me to kiss you."

"They saw that coming."

"Guess so." He continued scrolling. "And—"

"Don't tell me any bad ones."

"There aren't any. But I have good moderators who delete them for me." He winked. "I was going to say that someone has offered to replace your shoes."

"Seriously?"

"Yup, and... I don't know if you want to know this."

"What? What is it?"

"There are a lot of peach emojis. A *lot*."

"Oh, god." She shielded her eyes. "In reference to my ass, I'm guessing."

"Well, I did refer to you as Peaches. But in their defense, you do have a fantastic ass, so probably." He chuckled, wily and wicked. Both of those attributes were doing it for her tonight. That was a first. "I assume you have to go back to your room soon."

As much as she hated to admit he was right, she had a million things to do. Reluctantly, she pushed out of her seat and collected her purse. "It's probably the best idea to call it a night."

"Far from the best idea," he argued as he stood with her. "I'll walk you to your room."

Ten

"Floor?" Trick asked as they entered the elevator.

"Six."

He pressed the button.

"Are you on six, too?"

"Four." He cleared his throat, uncharacteristically nervous. Rylee, unlike most people he encountered in his day to day, intimated the hell out of him. It wasn't her wealthy upbringing, either. Trick had been in the company of famous people on-and-off in his life. Hell, he'd crashed more than a few events where celebrities had been in attendance.

No, the intimidation factor with Rylee was that he didn't want to blow his shot with her. He couldn't tell where her head was, and found himself guessing instead of knowing what she wanted. Confidence was his baseline, but she'd knocked him off balance. He'd been on the balls of his feet since she'd walked into his tailoring appointment.

They arrived on her floor. He stepped out of the elevator and walked with her in silence down a corridor. She turned right. He followed. Her room—a suite—was set apart from the other rooms for privacy. A note hung on the handle and she lifted it to read the message.

"My package arrived from Ariana. She sent me a gift. So thoughtful." Rylee slapped the notecard against her palm, a nervous gestured while lingering at the door. "Do you—"

"Yes." They'd had a phenomenal day, and evening, and he wasn't ready for it to be over.

"You don't know what I was going to ask," she said around bubbly laughter.

"Do I...want to see the gift? Do I want to have a nightcap? Do I want a kiss before I travel two lonely floors to my own room?" He shrugged. "All yeses."

"You'll get a kiss, at least, Trick." She let that tantalizing comment dangle like bait on a hook as she let them into her room. Correction, her *suite*. It was easily three times bigger than his own room in the Bellamy, with an office area, a living room, and of course, the bedroom. He followed her to the desk, glancing over at the crisp white comforter covering the bed mere feet away.

She opened the shiny black box wrapped in white ribbon to reveal a selection of products Ariana had chosen for her. "Wow, what an amazing selection. She picks the best stuff."

"Most lifestyle brands do." He grabbed a bottle of massage oil from the box. "Are you a fan of guava?" He showed her the label. "It's edible."

"Stop! Are you kidding?" She took the bottle and read the label for herself. Then she dug through the crinkle paper tucked around the products and held them up one by one. "A sleep mask, tea, a pocket massager. Exfoliating facial masks... What on earth did she expect me to do with these?"

"I instantly have a hundred and one ideas." Every last one of them involved Rylee out of that dress and in his arms.

She fiddled with the elastic band on the black silk sleep mask. He half expected her to fling it at him, or playfully punch his arm. Instead, she stepped closer to him, invading his space with her soft floral sent and the bluest eyes he'd ever seen.

"Well?" She hoisted an eyebrow. A dare. He recognized this version of Rylee from their first kiss. And so, he threw her words back at her.

"What am I waiting for?"

"Exactly," she whispered.

Hand on the back of her neck, he towed her in. Unlike the kiss at the tapas bar, he didn't have to be polite. Without an audience, there was no need to cut the kiss short. He took his time, molding his lips to the shape of hers, drinking her in—an attempt to slake his thirst for her.

Not possible. But he was going to try.

She kissed him back, pressing her body to his, her breasts bumping his chest. He cupped her butt with one hand and gave the cheek a squeeze and she instinctively tipped her hips forward. She couldn't think of anything except how she wanted every part of him touching every part of her.

He smiled down at her. "Peaches."

"Don't make fun of me."

"I'd never." He dove back in and lit her on fire. His warm wet tongue stroked hers and she clinched her thighs. Partially to assuage the throbbing there. She had yet to stop imagining his mouth on her body. On *every part* of her body.

She wasn't typically plagued with sexual or even romantic fantasies. While she'd had a coffee date here or there, none of those dates had prompted the idea of a second. And the kisses, with Louis and since, had been forgettable. A blur of gray.

There was nothing "gray" about Trick. He was fiery red and burnished orange, sunny yellow... She was awash in summery tones as heat saturated her bloodstream. His tongue stroked hers, and she emitted a helpless whimper.

He tightened his hold on her ass and pressed her hips to his. They lined up too well. His hardness, her softness. The levity dancing in his dark eyes had shifted to molten desire. He watched her from beneath drowsy lids as he said, "Give me the mask."

She'd forgotten she was holding the sleep mask. Black silk with a tiny diamond star in one corner. He took it from her and then reached for her hair clip, letting her fair hair fall into loose waves. Then he covered her eyes with the mask.

She felt his breath against her lips when he invited, "Ready to have some fun?"

"Overdue," she breathed, only half joking but pleased when she heard his raspy laugh.

"God, I hear you."

She assumed his dry spell wasn't as kindling-like as her own. Ever since she'd dared him to kiss her today, she'd been justifying to herself that it was okay to like him. More out of habit than anything else. No one had demanded she explain herself. Hell, Dee had practically told her to go for it after her own opposites-attract love story had turned out so well.

Which was *not* what this was about with Patrick, Rylee reminded herself. He was from an entirely different world than she was. She was in no danger of falling in love with him. Trick was a good-time guy, and he was willing to have a good time with her. For once she didn't want to plan and overthink.

He grasped her hand and lead her in the direction of the bedroom before backtracking to rifle through the box she'd opened.

"We're going to need some of this stuff," he said. "Hell, maybe all of it."

Her heart thrashed excitedly as he walked her from the suite to the bedroom. She felt heat emanating from his body when came around to stand before her. She heard him toss the box aside.

"Changed my mind." He removed her mask. She blinked, her eyes adjusting to the dim light of the room. "I want to see those blues."

He kissed her again, but his hands didn't stay in one place. They roamed, down her ribs and up again, where they cupped her breasts as his thumbs played over her nipples. They were peaked to the point of pain, begging to be free from the bra she'd worn for way too long today. As if in answer to her silent request, he drew down the zipper of her dress. Inch by agonizing inch, he opened the back of the garment and then smoothed the sleeves off her shoulders. His lips left hers to place a soft kiss on the top of one shoulder, and then he flicked open the front clasp of her bra.

"Tell me your nipples are peach-colored too and I'll die a happy man." He parted the material of her bra and cupped her generous D-cups with his palms. "Goddamn, Rylee. You are so fucking beautiful."

He suckled one nipple into his mouth, swirling it with his tongue as his fingers plucked the other. She gripped a handful of his thick hair, arching her back in response to the sharp pleasure spiking between her legs.

He raised his head, barely giving her a chance to take a breath before he lowered his mouth to the other nipple and sent her on a repeat journey.

"I knew you'd taste good everywhere." He freed her from the bra straps and then dropped her dress to the floor. On his knees in front of her, he took her shoes off one by one. "To be sure, though, I have more exploring to do."

He peered up at her, on his knees, his eyes hooded, his smile lazy but confident. He was still completely dressed, which seemed unfair since she was only wearing her underwear. He tucked his fingers into the waistband of those next, complimenting her on the pale pink color that matched her discarded bra. He rolled them down, past her thighs. She shifted her hips, excited and nervous in equal amounts. Once she'd stepped out of her panties, he held one foot in the air and gently draped her leg over his shoulder. Now she was open to him, the crook of her knee hooked on his shoulder, her center open to his perusal.

He took a long look as her heart hammered and her fingernails dug into his shoulder. Then, his hazel eyes on hers, he leaned forward and dragged his tongue along her folds.

"Oh, god." She hadn't meant to speak. The slick, wet feel of his tongue on her most sensitive part had drawn the words from her without her permission. She continued moaning as she rode his mouth—that talented mouth—

musing that he was every bit as good at this as she'd assumed he would be when he'd kissed her.

His hands roamed, one cupping her ass, the other reaching up to play with her nipple, hardening in the air-conditioned room. He plucked and laved in tandem while she moaned her approval. She said his name a few times, and "oh, god" a few more times. The rest of what she uttered was nonsensical gibberish. She was beyond caring. Nothing had felt this good. *Ever.*

Her orgasm shimmered on the horizon, growing closer like a speeding train on the tracks. It came into view, glimmering in the moonlight, and she voiced it with a long, appreciative moan. With her hands in his hair, she rode out her release, weakened by the sheer strength of it.

Trick held tightly to her thighs as he savored every moment of her release. He finally relented when she weakly begged for him to stop. She was swept up into his arms and then being lowered onto the bed. Her body sank into the pillowy white comforter while her mind floated miles above it. Part of her was lost in the afterglow. It pulsed through her, keeping time with her heavy heartbeats.

She flopped an arm over her closed eyes, mumbled something about how gifted he was, and then his mouth was on hers. When he moved her arm aside, he was the very picture of a smug male who had done exactly what he'd set out to do.

"Let's hear it," he said. "Scale of one to ten."

"A million?"

His sexy grin broadened. It was high time he removed the clothing he was still wearing. Weakly, she plucked at his shirt. "Take that off. I'm too tired."

"Yes, ma'am." He stood and pulled the shirt over his head, revealing a sculpted chest with a tasteful smattering of hair in all the right places. His pecs were round and thick, his biceps impressive, but then she'd been ogling those earlier, hadn't she? She refocused on his abs, the smooth bumps that led to a belly button and a trail of wiry hair that disappeared past his belt.

"Those, too." She snapped her fingers for effect. He gave her a stern look, which still managed to look playful on him, and then undid the belt and lost the pants. She didn't have to lecture him about taking off the boxer briefs. He slipped out of those too, freezing the next command on her tongue in its tracks.

His cock was tall and proud, grazing the top of his belly. He reached for it, gave it one stroke, then two, and her mouth literally watered. She couldn't look away. It was like seeing a sunset for the first time. Or a unicorn. My god, it was beautiful. Thick, too, which made her thighs squeeze together in delicious anticipation.

"We have more to do before the finale, Peaches." He crawled onto the bed and laid next to her. She rolled over to argue, reaching for the appendage she wanted inside of her as of two minutes ago.

He snatched her hand away and pinned it to the pillow over her head. He repeated that move with her other hand. Once he was over top of her, told her the score. "First the mask. And then the massage oil. Maybe that vibrating thing."

She bit her lip with her top teeth.

"No one wears a *yes* the way you do, Rylee." He kissed her on the lips, instructed her not to move, and then he grabbed the oil.

Eleven

Trick had focused his massaging techniques on her nipples since the oil was edible. It didn't taste half bad. Although he supposed when slicked over those peach, pert points, any flavor would have sufficed.

The mask covered her eyes, and her hands rested over head as he'd instructed. Each time he backed away to look at her body spread out before him like a goddamn dessert, her breathing would increase ever so slightly.

Rylee Meadows was *not* used to being out of control.

He'd enjoyed how she'd let go with him. How she'd said yes to him when her first instinct had been to turn him down. How she'd relinquished control tonight. Done with the oil, he tracked his fingers over her body, starting with her arms and then to the breasts he wanted to build an altar to worship.

"You have the most gorgeous breasts." He touched each of her nipples and watched as they tightened. Her body responded to him instantly, which was the most amazing thing. "And thighs."

He gripped each thigh with his hands and then spread her legs open. Forget the massager. He wanted to touch her here.

"Can I see you now?" Her hands were free, but she didn't remove the mask. Seemed as if the woman who was in charge of everything was reveling in the opportunity to be told what to do. He could understand that. He'd watched her, even from afar, as she'd planned and scheduled, delegated and answered. If he had her career, he'd need a vacation every other *week*. The worst part was, she hadn't enjoyed the parties she'd planned, but stayed at the ready in case something went wrong.

No fun.

He took the mask off. Her gaze went straight to his dick, the hunger in her eyes unmistakable. She pushed herself up, her smile wonky and relaxed, her cheeks rosy. Then she sat up and pushed him onto his back. He let her, easing onto the bed and propping one arm behind his head.

"I'm not the only buffet in town, buddy." God, she was cute on her knees in front of him. Especially while lowering her mouth to his favorite part of his body. She lifted his erection, painfully hard at this point, and circled the head with her tongue. Then she took him into her mouth and he said a quick thank-you that she hadn't tried to make him wear the mask. Missing out on watching her plush pink lips take him in and slide away would have been a crime.

He swore as he palmed her flaxen head. His fingers stroked and then clutched when she swallowed him down again, leaving nowhere for him to go—not that he wanted to be anywhere else. She let him loose with a *pop*, then sat back on her knees, resting her palms on her thighs. Her large perky breasts beckoned, so he pushed himself up to meet her.

"I wasn't done yet."

"Oh, you're done." He reversed their positions, her beneath him, those dimples punctuating her cheeks as a throaty laugh exited her lush mouth. He kissed her and then left in search of his pants, where he hoped to god there was a condom. He opened his wallet, said a prayer and—*yes*! Actually, he said it out loud.

"I hadn't thought that far ahead and you have one in your wallet?"

He checked the expiration date. "Yeah. Still good, too."

"Well that's a relief. I was about to call the front desk."

"No need." He tore open the condom, amused to notice that his hands were shaking as he eased it over his aching girth. Steadying his breathing, he positioned himself over top of her. "I'm going to try my best to last as long as you—*Fuck*."

She didn't let him finish his promise before she guided his cock deep inside her channel. Surrounded by tight warmth, he again vowed to last as long as she needed him to.

"I don't care about long. I care about *hard*. Can you deliver?"

"Yeah. I can deliver on hard." Sweat broke out on his forehead as he lifted her right leg and rested her knee in the crook of his elbow. Angling her so that he was seated deeper, he thrust forward. "Can you handle me?"

Lust had widened her dark pupils, black eating up the surrounding blue. Her mouth had dropped open, her "yes" a barely audible breath.

"I thought you could." He was beginning to think she

could handle absolutely anything. He hated the idea of her trussed up for some stiff who had only wanted a trophy wife. That wasn't her. Rylee was spirited, sexy, wild.

She was *his*.

The thought came, but he didn't push it away. He didn't question it, didn't evaluate it. He'd learned a long time ago that his instincts were a lot smarter than he was.

He started with slow, easy thrusts before graduating to harder, faster. Soon he was slamming into her, the rhythm hectic, desperate. Winded, he released her leg and dropped his hands to the mattress. She wrapped her legs around his waist and her arms around his neck, trapping him there.

"There, there. You feel *so* good," she praised. He worked her into a moaning, squirming lather, each of her compliments going straight to his dick.

"Come, Rylee," he demanded. "Right now."

"Again?"

"Yeah, honey. Again." He reached between their bodies and set his thumb to her clit, adding pressure as he stroked into her, filling her, working her exactly the way she needed to be worked.

Her forehead creased in pleasure-meets-pain pleats. A second later, she scratched her nails across his shoulders and cried out. Embedded deep within her, he felt her inner muscles spasm around him, pulling his own orgasm from him in one long, mind-altering release.

Eyes squeezed shut, he nearly blacked out from pleasure. He rode out the final waves of his release, lost in a sea of sensations. His mind was empty. His arms were full of Rylee. He sucked in a labored breath and some of her hair with it, pulling it off his tongue and kissing her neck instead.

Her arms closed around him while and he laid, silent and still, willing himself, despite feeling as if he was in an entire field full of poppies, *not* to fall asleep.

"Slap me."

Since Trick had murmured that into her neck, Rylee wasn't sure she'd heard him correctly. "What did you just say?"

Eyes closed, he lifted his head and said, "Slap me so I don't fall asleep. I'll never forgive myself if I do." Then those eyes opened and he kissed her firmly on the mouth. "Kidding. But seriously if I start looking sleepy, do it."

Her laughter had never been so carefree.

"Let me take care of this." He kissed her and climbed from the bed. She hugged her pillow and watched his backside flex in the lamplight. Then she sighed to herself, content.

When was the last time she'd felt this comfortable after a physical romp? The answer was swift: *never.* She'd never felt this way with Louis. He'd been the only sexual encounter she'd had, save for a few second-base experiences.

Since Louis was her first =, she'd had no one to compare him to. Now that she'd had a ten-on-the-Richter-scale orgasm, her ex was faring far worse than she'd known. Trick was attentive and, more importantly, *fun*.

Planning weddings might look fun on the outside, but that wasn't the word she'd use to describe her career. Rewarding, yes. Profitable, absolutely. Nothing was as satisfying as helping someone else's dreams come true. But, her vocation had come with a price. Sleepless nights and working every weekend, which made getting together with friends challenging.

When Trick had arrived in Royal, she'd been convinced he was going to ruin Ari and Ex's wedding, and Rylee's reputation by proxy. Instead, he'd been agreeable and helpful. And had taken her from a woman on a mission to a woman in the missionary position.

She chuckled at her own joke as he returned from the bathroom. Gloriously naked and completely confident, he strutted toward her.

"I love that smile." The box Ari had sent was on the dresser. He rummaged through it. "There's more in here we can take advantage of tonight." He unearthed a flat gold box she must have overlooked. "Chocolate?"

He plopped onto his side on the bed, the open box of chocolates between them. He lifted a piece of dark chocolate from its brown crinkly wrapper. "Chocolate roulette. Sure I know it's dark, but anything could be inside. Cream. Coconut." He made a face. "Baked beans."

"Let's hope not," she said through a laugh. Tugging the sheet so that it covered her breasts, she rolled to her side to face him. She closed her eyes and picked a chocolate. They said "cheers" and tapped the candies together before each taking a bite.

"Chocolate cream." She hummed her approval as she chewed.

"Mine's filled with toothpaste. How disappointing."

She almost choked on another laugh , but managed to pull herself together. They polished off one more chocolate apiece, coconut for her and vanilla crème for him.

"Will you change your mind about crashing weddings after this weekend? Or did I ruin your streak since you are technically invited to this one?"

"That award goes to Esther Edmonton." He picked through the chocolates and came out with a small square-shaped piece.

"Who is Esther Edmonton?"

"She's a saucy grandmother I met last year at a wedding I crashed. She asked me to dance with her, assuming I was one of the groom's friends. What could I do?"

"Nothing. Clearly. You were trapped."

"She knew it, too." He ate the candy and sucked a bit of melted chocolate off his thumb. She stared for a prolonged beat, parts of her growing warm at the idea of where his mouth had been tonight. "She used to be a nurse. She told me she was married fifty-two years to a 'wonderful man' who she couldn't wait to see again in heaven."

Rylee put a hand over her heart. "Aww."

"It gets better. Esther regretted never having her own children, so she said she hoped her grandniece—the bride—chose to 'make babies' with her husband. Then she asked me if I'd like to 'make babies' and I told her I was flattered, but I was much too young to consider a family with a woman so out of my league." Rylee giggled on cue. "And then I gave her the real answer. I told her I'd love to have kids, but I'm in no rush."

Rapt, she leaned in.

"Then I asked Esther if I could interview her on camera and we sat and talked for another forty minutes in a quiet corner of the reception hall. I never put the footage up. It felt private, you know?"

He picked another chocolate out of the box and offered it to her. She took it, but didn't eat it right away. "I'm afraid you're about to tell me something sad."

"I am." He offered a tight smile. "The bride—Brittany— contacted me after she found footage of me at her wedding. In the email, she said her great-aunt Esther had passed away. Apparently, Esther had mentioned me multiple times since the wedding, and the fact that she'd been interviewed. Brittany sought out my channel hoping that I'd posted the interview. I explained that I'd kept it private, but I was happy to send it to her." He took a breath before continuing, obviously saddened about Esther's passing. Rylee could understand why. She felt sad too and had never met the woman. "Anyway. I edited a video together and sent it to Brittany. There were so many great moments, little moments that are normally edited out. Those are the best parts. Esther looking off to the side. Losing her train of thought and laughing. Telling me a dirty joke."

Tears in her eyes, Rylee smiled.

"I knew the moment I finished that edit and emailed it off that I was in the wrong business. I had taken a left when I should have hung a right. I started out in film school for a reason, and it had nothing to do with followers, sponsorships or blocking comments from trolls. Ironically, had I not crashed that wedding, I never would have met Esther and found my way, you know?"

"So, what now?" The story couldn't end there.

"I'm in deep, Peaches. Like when someone is in the mob. I have sponsorships I've agreed to that I either need to honor or cancel. I have a video schedule to adhere to, although I'm looking into crashing celebrity charity events to spotlight the charity rather than myself. It's a pivot, for sure. Slower than I'd like, but I've never been patient."

"So, you're going to be a filmmaker after all? Documenting the small moments in life."

"The best moments are the moments that are usually edited out of the final." He picked another chocolate out of the box and tossed it into his mouth. "Like the one we're having now."

Twelve

When her alarm jangled from her phone on the night-stand, Rylee launched out an arm to tap the Stop button like she did nearly every morning at 6 a.m. Instead of her phone, she encountered a muscular male arm. A rogue dart of panic stabbed her chest for a fraction of a second before she recalled the night before.

Trick following her to her room. The basket of self-care goodies from Ari reimagined as props for foreplay. The incredible sex. Eating chocolate in bed. Him mentioning how life was made up of little moments that were often edited out to allow the bigger moments to shine.

"Sorry," she whispered, reaching past him for her phone.

He muttered under his breath. Then his arm lashed around her back and he tugged her roughly against his naked body. His mouth hit her neck and she felt his lips tickle her skin when he rumbled, "Morning."

But that wasn't all she felt. Several inches of morning

wood pressed against her when he shifted his hips. This was definitely an improvement from how she normally awoke each morning. She dropped her phone back onto the nightstand and reached beneath the blankets. She gripped his erection, massaging it once, twice.

He responded by thrusting into her hand as he yanked the covers off both of them. Then he removed her hand and kissed her palm before kissing his way down her body. He paused to flick his tongue over each nipple and her belly button before settling between her legs.

"Trick." Whatever excuse she was about to make about being late was lost on a sigh. She rested her hands on his head, tangling her fingers in his messy hair. The room was dark thanks to the heavy curtains being pulled. Her alarm was off. It was too early for anyone to call with an emergency. She further reasoned that she made her own schedule, and she could do whatever she damn well pleased. Her brain tried to insert a to-do list into the mix, but the man between her thighs must have sensed he was about to lose her. He doubled his efforts, effectively erasing any coherent thought from her head.

Mere minutes later, an orgasm slammed into her without warning, wringing a cry from her lips.

"You're so fucking hot." He bit the inside of her thigh and soothed it with a kiss.

She ruffled his hair, thinking to herself that it was Trick, not her, who was hot. With his dark hair a mess, his five o'clock shadow scraping her sensitive skin, and those hooded eyes that tempted her to laze around all day with him, he was sexy as hell. Add that up with last night and what he'd just done to her? Forget it. He was her ultimate fantasy man.

"How many more do you want?" Her fantasy man's gaze was on her face when he slid his tongue over her clit.

"Do you charge by the hour?"

"By the orgasm, in your case. It doesn't take an hour to start you up, Peaches."

"Ugh." She covered her face in her hands. "More proof I don't know what I'm doing when it comes to one-night stands."

He shifted positions so quickly, she was face-to-face with him in a blink. "What are you talking about?"

"You're my first."

"Your first." An alarmed expression crossed his handsome features.

"Not my first *time*. My first one-night stand."

"Oh." Relief, and then he shook his head. "That's not what this is, Rylee."

"Of course it is. I mean, I know it's morning instead of night, but we're within a twenty-four-hour window."

"I'm in town for a few more days." His eyebrows drew together over his nose. "You're not escaping me that easily. I'm your partner, remember?"

"That was your term, I believe." She kept her tone light, but she was surprised to hear he wanted more than one night. "I'm going to be busy with the final preparations, you know."

"You're also going to be getting busy *with me*." She liked the hint of possessiveness in his voice way too much. "How else can you expect to work off the stress that builds on any given day. He gripped her thigh and massaged it gently. Don't you want to keep your heart healthy? I can help with that." He pressed a kiss between her breasts, right over her fluttering heart. "Last night, tonight, tomorrow, and the wedding night makes this a *four*-night stand."

"I'm not sure we can include the wedding night. I'm usually ready to collapse by then. Don't expect any acrobatics."

He kissed her nipple succinctly and then looped her leg around his hip. "You like to point out your limitations. When are you going to realize I'm far more capable, patient and talented than your country-club boyfriend?"

Oh, she'd already realized that. She played with Trick's unkempt hair, loving the way it stubbornly flopped to one side, refusing to be tamed. A good metaphor for him. Where her ex-boyfriend had been as tame as a pony at a children's birthday party, Trick struck her as a man who couldn't be corralled. Plus, what was the harm in a four-night stand? They were already in Royal together—in the same hotel, no less. It would be silly to stop sleeping together, especially since he didn't want to stop. Frankly, neither did she.

"So, you're not done? With me," she couldn't help pointing out, a hint of disbelief in her tone.

"Peaches." His grin was feral, infectious. "I'm just getting started."

Trick was a lighthearted guy, but it still surprised him when he began whistling his way through the lobby of the Bellamy. That was new.

He passed the tapas bar, smiling as he recalled last night. He had hoped the evening would end with Rylee in his bed—or his in hers, he hadn't been picky—but the resulting night he'd spent having sex with her, laughing with her, and confessing his secret motivation for changing careers had been unexpected.

And not in a bad way.

After they'd sorted out that one-night stand dilemma, he'd made love to her again, effectively silencing any argument she might have made that she would be late for work. She worked too much. Her focus was always on others and not on herself. She deserved a break. He'd talked her into giving him an hour. Incredible sex plus a long hot shower had eaten up that hour up and then some. She'd admonished him, but the smile on her face had never gone away.

He'd promised to make up for lost minutes by picking up coffee, and then he'd dashed down to his room to get dressed. She'd assured him she could be ready in fifteen minutes and would meet him in the lobby. He knew she was organized and punctual, but fifteen minutes was a feat that remained to be seen.

There was a fancy coffee kiosk adjacent to the lobby where an eager barista awaited his approach. He'd expected more people to be in line, but perhaps the Bellamy's residents had taken advantage of the in-room coffee makers instead.

Their coffees in to-go cups, one in each hand, he was angling for a sofa when the elevator doors pinged and opened. Out stepped the woman he hadn't known he'd been dreaming of until he'd set foot in the great state of Texas.

Her super short black dress gave him a stellar view of the legs he'd enjoyed having wrapped around his neck this morning. Her shoes were tall with a lot of straps. Even as he thought she must be swearing with every step she took, he appreciated how damn sexy they were. How damn sexy she looked wearing them. Her confidence accompanied every sharp heel tap, the short ruffly sleeves of the dress lifting in the breeze she made on her way to him.

"I didn't think you could pull off fifteen minutes."

"I have my routine down." She adjusted her purse on her shoulder and smiled, gifting him with those cute dimples. "Plus, I left everything in the office at the TCC yesterday, so I didn't have anything to pack up".

She pushed her bangs off her forehead. Her mid-length, pale blond hair was down in loose waves. Had she run out of time to pin it back? Or had he put her into a loose, relaxed mood that her hairstyle was reflecting? He liked the idea that he could be partly responsible for her literally letting her hair down. He also hoped he'd had something to do with the spring in her step and the bright smile on her beautiful face.

"I didn't think you could look any better than you did naked next to me in bed." He handed over her coffee as she jerked her eyes around the practically empty lobby. "I was right. You look better naked. But you still look amazing."

"Just when I think you're going to be serious." She shook her head, but she didn't appear the least bit upset that he'd teased her.

"I'm completely serious. Do you need me to go over which body parts are my favorite? Which sounds you make that I like best? What about—" She pressed her fingers to his lips, something she'd done before. He smiled against her fingertips, kissing them lightly before she pulled them away. "What's on our agenda today?"

"The usual. Planning a wedding."

They walked into the parking lot to her mother's car that she'd borrowed for the week. On the short drive to the TCC, Rylee detailed the "ten million things" she had to do before the wedding on Saturday.

The list made him instantly fatigued. He took a deep drink of his coffee, glad he'd gone for an extra shot of espresso. His agenda wasn't so much an agenda with a timeline and bullet-pointed tasks—he shuddered—than him waiting for the right moment to turn on the camera. After filming for years, he had a sixth sense about what to shoot and what angles were best. He operated on instinct, not pragmatism. Too much planning gave him hives.

"And then the rehearsal dinner tonight, of course."

Shit! He'd forgotten about that. She caught his alarmed expression as she parked near the side entrance.

"You forgot."

"I didn't. Okay, I did, but I would have remembered way before that."

"Don't worry. You will have a break late afternoon to go back to your room and freshen up if you need to." She patted his cheek. He caught her hand. They sat in her car, keys off, the interior heating in the Texas sun, staring into each other's eyes. Her blues exactly matched the clear sky. Unbidden, the moment took on a different vibe. Serious. *Meaningful.* One of those moments in life that is not to be missed for other seemingly more impor-tant ones. To keep from wading into the deep end far too soon, he rerouted the conversation to sex.

"Not unless you come to my room with me. We didn't use every item in that gift box, you know."

"You're not going to waste a single second while you're here, are you?" The question was rhetorical, he assumed, since she left him in the car rather than wait for him to answer.

He shut his car door and followed her to the building,

the strangest sensation spreading over his chest. What had started out as mind-blowing sex with the wedding planner who'd been his nemesis for the last few months had changed into something more.

And without his permission.

Did they...have a future? A terrifying prospect for a guy who rarely planned ahead. The premonition didn't fade for a good hour or two. He tried not to obsess over what that might mean.

Thirteen

Her morning had started with a bang. Not only was she on the phone answering questions from the caterers about table settings, but while she was on the phone, Ariana had sent texts.

Multiple texts.

For good reason, Rylee calmly reminded herself as she took a deep breath. She'd asked Ari to let her know of any last-minute seating changes so that Rylee could let the caterer know. A cancellation or an additional plus-one was to be expected. What Rylee hadn't expected was *seven* additional guests and a request from a couple in the middle of a divorce to sit at different tables. Now the entire seating plan was thrown off.

"Here we have our cool under pressure wedding planner," Trick narrated. He'd warned her he'd be filming this morning. She forced an amiable smile for the camera, but on the inside she was Edvard Munch's *The Scream*.

Rylee had already phoned the calligrapher, who'd

thankfully answered. The bad news was, she was out of town. As in *Germany*. Rylee couldn't very well demand that the woman stay in the States until after the wedding, but she wondered if she should make that request in the future.

She had explained the seating kerfuffle, asking the calligrapher to pen, scan and email the files. Rylee would figure out a way to print them onto Ari's and Ex's specialty card stock so that they matched the others. Unfortunately, the calligrapher had just boarded her flight and would be staying in a small town without Wi-Fi as part of a "digital cleanse." Rylee had been tempted to swear or beg or cry—or a combination of the three—but in the end had wished the other woman a happy vacation.

Trick swept the camera over the reception area, pointing out the large chandeliers and the dance floor. He mentioned that Colin Reynolds, Irish-born head chef for the local restaurant, Sheen, would be catering.

Rylee shook her head in bemusement as she thought back to her mini meltdown a few months ago. When she'd been wishing Trick would have chosen any event other than hers. Now, she didn't wish that. She found his presence, including his attention to the details she'd so carefully orchestrated with the vendors, soothing.

It was funny how drastically her feelings had changed.

He signed off and tucked the phone into the pocket of his pants. He wore pale-colored trousers today with a deep green T-shirt that complemented his black hair and olive complexion. She no longer saw the wedding crasher hell-bent on destroying her world, she saw the man with his head on her hotel pillow grinning back at her.

It blew her mind that she'd become comfortable being naked with him in such a short period of time, but maybe it shouldn't. Trick wooed everyone within shouting distance, and since he was online daily, that was a lot of people.

A lot of *women*.

Frowning at the rogue streak of jealousy, she quickly slapped on the smile she'd worn for the camera a moment ago.

"What's up?" He narrowed his eyes in suspicion. "I can tell you're faking being happy. You're practically wearing your shoulders as earrings." He placed his palms on her shoulders and gently pushed them down. His touch, his unerring eye contact, and that sideways smirk hinting that everything would be okay calmed her some. "Talk to me, Peaches. Who ruined your day already?"

"The calligrapher," she answered, relieved to have someone to talk to about it. She recapped the seating-chart tragedy and waited for his face to reflect her defeat. That didn't happen, of course. He was Patrick MacArthur, man capable of only good moods.

"Who else can write names on parchment that you know?"

"It's not that simple. They must match *exactly*. The ink color. The penmanship." She lifted and dropped her hands, the problem growing horns and hair and sharp, jagged teeth. "I can't very well have mismatched place cards!"

"Breathe," he instructed. She did, even though the suggestion peeved her. She was more peeved when a few deep breaths took her down a notch. "Did you know that anxiety literally shuts off the problem-solving portion of your brain? You need that part, Rye. So. Who do you know that does calligraphy?"

"No one," she answered automatically. "Wait. My mom."

"*Your mom*? How could you forget something like that?" He chuckled.

"I didn't forget. It's one of her hobbies. Along with painting landscapes, making mosaics from broken dishes and quilling."

"What the fuck's quilling?"

"It's where you roll these little strips of paper into flowers or—you know what? Never mind. The point is my mom has a lot of artsy hobbies. She doesn't do any of them for a living."

"Do you have samples of the calligrapher's penmanship? Can your mom copy it?"

"Maybe." Rylee's heart buoyed. Could the fix be this simple?

"Do they live close by?"

"They do. My hometown is about forty-five minutes away from here. If she's willing to do this for me, I could drive there and be back by this afternoon." Which gave Rylee plenty of time to check on the preparations for the rehearsal dinner and greet Ari and Ex when they arrive. "Let me make a quick phone call."

Her mother was home, and not only was she willing to help with the place cards, she was also excited to try her hand at it. Rylee gathered the box of place cards that were already done, plenty of extra card stock, and headed for the door. As she turned to ask Trick if he needed the office key in her absence, she found him gathering his camera bag.

"Where are you going?"

"I'm coming with you."

"What do you mean you're coming with me?"

"This is behind-the-scenes gold. I'm not letting an opportunity to film last-minute place cards and your mom as the emergency ringer pass us by. You painted this like a Greek tragedy two minutes ago. This is the big save."

"I overreact sometimes," she mumbled, slightly embarrassed for leaping off the deep end when the answer had been right in front of her face. If Trick hadn't been here, she didn't know if it would have ever occurred to her to call her mother and ask for help.

"It's what makes you good at what you do." He took them the long way through the TCC, grabbing a few bottles of water from a cooler on the way. She stopped him before he asked the kitchen staff to whip up a charcuterie board for the road.

"Want me to drive?" he asked as she unlocked her mother's Mercedes.

"No. You film. I'll drive. It'll give me something to do besides watch the minutes tick away." In theory they would return on time for the rehearsal dinner. Barring any unforeseen circumstances that would cause a delay. This wedding had been chock-full of unforeseen circumstances. While she didn't want to jinx herself, she was aware anything could happen. The passenger in her car was all the proof she needed.

"Will your dad be there, too?" Trick asked once they were on the road.

"Possibly. He works from home more often than not these days. He has stepped back some from his position as CFO."

"Certified... Frisbee Overseer?" Trick laughed at his own corny joke. "What's his business?"

"Baird Textiles. My great-grandmother's company originally. Baird was her maiden name. She handed down the company to my dad and his brother, who is the CEO."

"Ah yes, Chief Elephant Operator."

She couldn't help chuckling. "Close. Baird provides luxury fabrics for some of the top industries in the world. Hotels, theaters, awards shows."

"*The* red carpet?"

"Rumor has it." She hadn't been fascinated with her father's business when she was younger, not until she'd started planning weddings and had recognized Baird fabrics seemingly everywhere she went. The more upscale venues were outfitted with Baird drapes, carpeting and even artwork. She hadn't been able to keep from feeling a surge of pride. "I'll introduce you as the videographer when we arrive to avoid any impolite questions."

She could practically hear her mother now. *"Who is this man you've brought home to us, Rye? How did you meet him? What is his family like? Do they have ties to Royal?"*

Her mother, and father for that matter, had always had their sights set on a wealthy beau for Rylee. Until she and Louis had split, she hadn't seen their meddling for what it was. Not quite an arranged marriage, but possibly its cousin.

"I'm not a videographer." She glanced over to find Trick's mouth screwed into a curve of displeasure. "No offense to the people who are videographers."

"If I say filmmaker, they'll ask you what you're famous for," she warned.

"So tell them the truth. Or are you embarrassed to be seen with a lowly social media content creator?"

"*The truth* is that you were famous for wedding crashing and I've been thwarting your advances and preparing for your invasion for months."

"Invasion?" He laughed as he took hold of her free hand. "You didn't thwart me for long. I woke up in your bed this morning, and I'm planning on being in it to-night."

"None of which I care to share with my parents."

"That's fair." He kissed her hand and dropped their linked fingers onto his leg. "Videographer it is."

"Social media superstar," she corrected herself. "Can I leave out the wedding crashing part?"

Fourteen

Trick had shot some footage out the window of the car, but let Rylee know he'd shut off the camera before revealing her parents' house number. She turned into a ritzy neighborhood, each house larger than the last. She navigated a few more streets before they arrived in a cul-de-sac, with a single house on a hill sitting behind a row of trees. He realized when she turned into the driveway that the mansion was their destination.

"Holy shit. You grew up here?"

"I did." She parked in the cobblestone driveway in front of a garage with four extra-wide doors. He had grown up in a nice house in a well-to-do neighborhood, but Rylee's family home was next-level.

They stepped out of the car at the same time two men holding golf clubs strolled into the grass. One was older. One younger. Trick started for the house but soon realized Rylee wasn't next to him.

"What's up, Peaches?"

"That's my dad. And Louis."

"Louis. As in your ex, Louis?"

"Yes. I have no idea why he's here." The older of the two men raised a hand to wave, while her ex-fiancé grimaced as he tugged on a leather glove.

Trick felt the instant pull to protect her, but Rylee had already stepped around him.

"Louis. This is a surprise." She smiled genially, which Trick saw as unnecessary. Then she kissed her father on the cheek. "Hi, Daddy."

Trick sized up her ex in spite of himself. Louis was tall and lanky, with hard eyes and a short, neat haircut. He wore a collared polo shirt tucked into his trousers. Everything about him screamed *boring*.

"Your mother mentioned you'd be stopping by," her dad said. "I thought you were the one at the door, but I found Louis on the porch instead."

"New golf grips," Louis said in explanation, raising the club in his hands and giving Trick an assessing look. Rylee, born and bred into this kind of bullshit disguised as politeness, didn't miss the awkward pause and was quick to fill the silence.

"This is Trick MacArthur. He's shooting video for the wedding I'm planning. He tagged along to film some footage."

Trick tried not to visibly react to the phrase "tagged along." It was clear from the way Louis looked down his nose that he'd already labeled Trick as an underling.

"Trick?" Her father's face scrunched.

"Short for Patrick," Rylee said. "Trick, this is my father, Meyer, and his coworker, Louis. We grew up together."

"We did more than that," Louis grumbled, earning a

look of disapproval from Meyer Meadows and a matching one from his daughter. What a dick. "How long have you been a videographer, Patrick?"

"He's a filmmaker, actually," Rylee interjected. "He has one of the largest channels on social media in the world."

"Oh?" Louis asked, his tone flat. "What's your niche?"

"Weddings!" Rylee said. "If you'll excuse us, we are on a time-crunch. Is Mom in her office?"

"Or in the kitchen, fussing over hors d'oeuvres," Meyer answered before he stepped onto the green front lawn and took a swing with the club in his hand. "You'll have to give me the number of your pro shop," he was saying to Louis. "If new grips shave three strokes off my game, I'll finally make par."

Whatever the fuck that meant. Trick offered a tight nod as he passed by Louis, refusing to make small talk. He already didn't like the guy for what he'd put Rylee through, before dumping her, no less. That her father still employed him was infuriating. No wonder Rylee moved to LA.

"Do you play golf?" Trick asked her as they entered the house.

"I used to. I rarely find the time now." She angled through the foyer, past a sitting room and through a corridor leading to the kitchen. The house was palatial, their footsteps echoing off the marble flooring as they made their way through it. Evidence of the Meadows' wealth showed in every tapestry, fussy vase and haughty design choice. Opulence had its place, but this house, for all of its space, was stuffy.

They approached an older woman who was cleaning off a countertop in the kitchen.

"Hi, Abigayle. Have you seen my mother?"

"In her office. I sent Anya up with a tray of macarons and a pitcher of lemonade."

"Perfect. Thank you." Rylee left the kitchen and led Trick up a set of stairs. They passed Anya on the way, a woman around their age who Rylee hugged mid-staircase. In a long hallway upstairs, Rylee and Trick entered the third room on the left.

The office was every bit as large as the kitchen, and had not one but two balconies complete with French doors. Rylee's mother was standing at a side table, pouring lemonade into glasses. Her eyebrows shot up when she saw Trick. "I assumed when Anya brought three glasses that Louis would be joining us. That doesn't make sense now that I think about it, since he never cared for your hobbies."

Rylee's smile stayed plastered on, but Trick could tell she hadn't enjoyed hearing the career she'd built from scratch being referred to as a "hobby."

"Hello. I'm Regina."

"Trick MacArthur." Shifting his handheld tripod and camera into his left hand, he shook Rylee's mother's hand with his right.

"Patrick," Rylee inserted, and for some reason that bugged him. "He's filming behind the scenes for Ariana and Xavier's wedding and you are about to have a starring role."

"Oh, dear. I should have had my makeup done." Regina fluffed her hair, light blond like her daughter's, but longer. She was wearing a pantsuit with large rhinestones on the sleeves and a pair of shoes that added a few inches to her smaller stature. It was no secret where Rylee had inherited her height. Meyer was a good foot taller than his wife. Trick wondered if it'd been Regina who had insisted Rylee wear high heels with everything.

"Let's go over what I need, and you can practice mimicking the calligrapher's style. Once you're comfortable, if you wouldn't mind Trick, erm, Patrick filming you while you write, that would be great. Of course, he doesn't have to show your face if you want to remain anonymous."

"Don't be silly." Regina had already pulled out a compact and was generously applying lipstick. "Patrick, you'll only film me in the best light, correct?"

"You have my word," he assured her.

After her mother and Trick were comfortable in each other's presence, Rylee excused herself to take a phone call. This one was from Colin, who asked if there were any additional guests expected at tonight's rehearsal dinner. He and his team were doing the cooking for the event. He'd assured her he had plenty of food, but preferred to quadruple-check the headcount.

"I appreciate that quality in you, Colin," she told him as she stepped outside.

"Tell Corynna that." His Irish accent was dreamy, but took on a sensual quality whenever he mentioned the woman who'd once been his enemy and was now the love of his life.

Rylee thanked him for checking in and promised to see him tonight. Her father, looking like a gender-swap of her with his own cellphone pressed to his ear, nodded as he bypassed her and went inside. Work took precedence with him. Not for the first time, she recognized that quality in herself. One that Louis, who regarded her with a frown as he tucked his club back into its bag, had always been quick to point out.

"You look good." His eyes roamed over her hair as if deciding if he liked her updated cut. "Not as professional as you could be. That dress is a little short."

She chuffed her disagreement, but her hand automatically smoothed over the material. "Are you finished showing off your clubs?"

"Nearly. Your father's coming out with me to play nine after his call." Louis tucked his hands into his pockets. "I have a few minutes to talk."

She didn't have anything to say to him, but she supposed chatting about the weather or work was innocuous. "How are things at Baird?"

"Good. The same."

"That's good. How are your parents?"

"They're fine. Are you planning on telling me why you're hanging around with the internet's most infamous wedding crasher?"

She blinked, shocked that Louis had recognized Trick. Maybe she should have omitted his last name from the introduction. Or made one up.

"You're wondering how I knew, aren't you?" He glanced around her parents' estate. "People at work have been talking about the video you were in with him. You fell off a ladder. He caught you. Ridiculous stunt."

"It wasn't a stunt," she found herself defending.

"You hanging out with him sure as hell is. A content creator, Rylee?" He shook his head the way he'd done whenever he'd been disappointed with her. "A bit below your pay grade, isn't he?"

"We're...friends." Not that it was any of Louis's business, but he had made a lot of assumptions and she didn't care for it one bit.

"You mean like we're friends?" He leaned casually

on the railing, never taking his eyes off her. She used to think his blue-gray irises were attractive, but now the color appeared cold. "Forgive me for saying so, but someone should."

"Louis—"

"I can't believe this is the life you've chosen. We had a future planned, Rye. One where I would make enough money for both of us so you wouldn't have to stoop to do people's bidding. My God, you've even roped your mother into handwriting place cards for a talentless celebrity couple."

"They're not talentless."

"It's demeaning."

"No, it's not. She was happy to help."

He shook his head. "I'm insulted. I could've given you anything you wanted and you chose to be a servant. Why do you cater to rich people when you are one yourself? Explain that to me."

"Why do you choose to work for my father instead of start your own business?" she shot back. "Isn't that beneath you?"

He laughed in that condescending way he'd perfected. "Nice try, but no, a three-generation multimillion-dollar corporation is a far cry from you scuttling around counting chairs for guests. When you were with me, did you ever consider the chair you were sitting on?

"Of course you didn't. You were with me. You were taken care of. Anything you needed, wanted, dreamed of having, I provided. I know you've been under a lot of stress with this wedding. Your father mentioned it while we were out here chipping balls."

Well. That was the last time she shared her job stress with her mother. She hadn't thought it'd be relayed to Louis via her father.

"He's worried about you. He wanted more for you too, Rye. He wanted me for you."

"He wasn't the one who would have had to marry you," she snapped. "Let's not forget that you were the one who left, Louis." Her voice crept up an octave. "You were the runaway groom, remember?"

"No need for theatrics." Louis had perfected being infuriatingly calm. He waved a hand in the general direction of the house. "Once this boy is out of your system, you should reconsider the life you left behind. It's not too late for us to try again."

She didn't know which argument to make first. "We split up three years ago."

"Which gave you time to grow up. You tried out a business, you gave living in California a shot, and now you know how many people are willing to take advantage of you." He smoothed a lock of hair away from her face. "Make no mistake, Rye. Trick is using you. He has no intention of sticking around and being the man you need. He doesn't have a real job. He can't provide for you like I can."

When he brushed her cheek with his knuckles, she smacked his hand away. Her throat was full of words to say, but she had too much tact to say half of them. She wanted to inform her buffoon of an ex that she and Trick were having incredible sex, and that he'd taught her things about her body Louis never bothered to learn. Then again Louis might tell her father she said that, which would be horrific on several levels.

Maybe she would point out that there was more to Trick than his online antics, and that his dreams and goals were worthy of pursuit. But before she could arrange any one of those phrases into spoken form, the door swung aside and her father stepped out of it, his bag of clubs on his shoulder.

"Your mother is asking for you. Ready to hit the links, Louis?"

"We're almost done here." She propped her hands onto her hips and faced her ex. "I don't need you to provide for me. I can provide for myself. You are not, and will never be, a consideration. Not ever again."

"Rylee," her father barked.

"You can go now," she shooed Louis toward the steps. "Have fun, Daddy. As much as you can have with him."

Louis's upper lip curled.

"Erm, I'll drive." Her father started for the garage.

Louis shouldered his golf bag. Before he stepped off the porch, he offered a parting jab, "You're better than this. You know it, I know it. *Trick* knows it, too. You know where to find me."

She sure did, she thought as he walked away. Right up her father's ass.

Fifteen

Trick had never seen Rylee so infuriated, which was saying something as his mere presence in Texas had pissed her *way* off at first. Outside of her parents' house, he found her sitting on the white porch swing, pushing herself back and forth. Her hair lifted in the breeze created by the overhead fans. He'd thought at first that her cheeks were red because of the heat, but then he followed her gaze to the retreating car holding her ex-fiancé and her father.

Trick sat next to her on the swing. She didn't take her eyes off the long driveway even though her father's car was long gone. She seemed to notice Trick's presence belatedly.

"All set?" she asked, her smile tired.

"Your mom said it'll take a few minutes for the ink to dry. I'm no professional, but I think she did a great job. She's a perfectionist so it had to be just right. She reminds me of you."

Rylee turned her head. "You sound surprised."

"I am, actually." When Rylee had described how she'd

been raised, he'd assumed the women in her family were robotic servants with the men their controllers. "Pleasantly."

A beat of silence passed. They continued swinging, their feet pushing against the boards. Trick decided to take a wild stab at what was bothering her. "Louis said something stupid, I take it."

She grunted. "Lots of stupid things. Including telling me that I was welcome to come back to him when I'm done being rebellious."

"He sees your business as a rebellion?"

"And you."

He had to laugh, which drew a genuine smile from her. That was good to see. "Men like him have no confidence. It's an act. He's trying to sound big while being small. He isn't aware that you can see through him because he can't admit to himself that you're smarter than he is."

She kissed Trick so fast he never saw it coming. Once her lips pressed against his, though, he responded. Cupping the back of her neck, he deepened the kiss, tilting his head to further drink her in. She tasted like sunshine and capability. Like a woman who would never trade her career for a paltry offering made by an insecure man-baby.

Trick admired Rylee all the way down to those uncomfortable shoes she wore. The more he thought about how much she didn't like them, the more irked he became. As she discovered more about herself, he hoped that she would let go of anything and everything that didn't serve her. Men and shoes in particular. He also hoped that he wasn't part of what she cast off, even as he acknowledged that he didn't want to explore that thought too deeply.

He tried to stop kissing her, honest to God, but the moment her tongue touched his, he forgot why. He set his equipment on the swing to free his other hand. Now he could cup both sides of her face. *Perfect.*

If she was using him as a way to release her pent-up emotions, he would gladly give her what she needed. She'd become a safe place for him as well, an uncommon occurrence in his world. When she'd brought up a one-night thing this morning, he'd been offended. Strange, considering he'd never before argued with a woman about keeping things light.

Rylee was different from any other woman he'd known. They naturally melded together. Spending time bouncing ideas off of each other was easy, and fun. He didn't know how to define what was happening between them, but he knew what they were doing was the *opposite* of a one-night stand.

Lips tingling, he surfaced from her mouth at the same moment he heard the delicate clearing of a throat behind them.

Rylee unwound his arms from her body and jerked away. He instinctively knew they hadn't been interrupted by one of the house staff. When he turned his head to look over his shoulder, Rylee's mother was standing in the doorway, a small flat box in her hands.

"Sorry to interrupt." Her mother's voice held a note of amusement disguised as a singsong lilt.

While Rylee wouldn't have expected her to be clutching her pearls, she had expected Regina Meadows to offer censure for what she'd witnessed.

"I have your place cards ready. Trick agreed that I matched the handwriting of the originals quite closely."

"You have talent, Regina," he said with warm familiarity. What had those two talked about upstairs while

Rylee had been listening to Louis be a butthead? She had expected her mom to be cordial to Trick, but she hadn't anticipated them chatting.

Rylee had never brought home a boyfriend her parents didn't know. Trick, as it turned out, was the first man in her life that had required an introduction.

"Thank you, Trick. I pride myself on my penmanship, so that means a lot." Her mother's mouth twisted. "I suppose your father and Louis are on the golf course. I do not know why he continues to be loyal to the man who broke your heart."

"Louis didn't break my heart, Mom" Rylee was quick to argue. "He broke our engagement."

"You don't have to downplay it, darling."

"I'm not. I didn't love Louis in the way a wife should love a husband." Rylee frowned. This wasn't an epiphany she'd had before, and she wasn't entirely sure where it had come from. It sure as hell felt true, so she continued with her stream of thought. "I don't know if I dated him because he was convenient or because I was shuffling along a chosen path."

"Ultimately, you un-chose that path." Her mother sounded almost defensive before she added, "I'm proud of you for speaking your mind. Your father and I were less than thrilled to hear that the wedding was called off, but only because we assumed you were happy. Then you started your business and we saw what happy actually looks like on you."

"Thanks," Rylee said, meaning it.

"Does she seem happy to you, Trick?"

To his credit, he didn't shift under Regina's scrutiny. "She does."

Rylee puffed her chest. Trick had seen the real her. Not

as a perfectionist who worried herself ragged over every detail, but as a strong woman who knew her own mind. How many times had he poked fun at her for wearing shoes she hated? Like he'd been daring her to kick them and go barefoot. Too many to count.

"Try not to take your father's behavior personally. You know he'll golf with anyone." When her mother's comment failed to lighten the mood, she added, "For all of Louis's faults, he *is* a good employee. Not CEO material, though. Despite what he thinks, he will never be in charge."

"I suppose that stick in his ass comes in handy. You can prop him in the corner during long meetings," Trick said.

Regina, her hand on her chest, let out an unladylike guffaw. Rylee wasn't sure what was funnier—Trick's quip or her mother losing her composure.

"Trick, you must come back and visit." Regina handed the box of place cards to Rylee. "Bring him for dinner the next time you're both in town."

Rylee swallowed the argument that bringing him to dinner wouldn't be possible. This was a four-night stand, not a relationship. But her mother didn't need to know the gory details. She stood from the porch swing. "We should be going. Thank you for this. You're a lifesaver."

"You're welcome. It was fun to be a part of a couple's special day. Trick, I enjoyed talking with you."

"I enjoyed it as well." He kissed her mother's cheek and then he and Rylee stepped off the porch and angled toward the driveway.

Before they got too far, Regina called out, "If you ever need a calligrapher in the future, feel free to consider me!"

Trick's eyebrows sprang to his forehead when he exchanged glances with Rylee, who offered a clumsy, "Oh-okay. Sure," in answer to her mother's offer.

Sixteen

Ariana and Xavier were due to arrive at Sheen well after the seven o'clock rehearsal dinner, so Rylee was at ease as she glided through the restaurant and into the kitchen where Colin was bustling about with his staff. He finished instructing one of his sous-chefs before dashing over to her, his eyes wild.

"Last minute change-up, Rylee," he said, his Irish brogue thicker than usual. Maybe stress amplified his accent. "The dinner is now a cocktail party, so we've reimagined the menu."

"A...cocktail party?"

Colin went on to describe the small plates he'd whipped up last minute, developed from ingredients that were originally going to make up a five-course dinner.

"Xavier called right after I talked to you. He said Ari wanted a casual cocktail party with tapas, and that they extended invitations to out-of-town guests." He stroked his beard as he studied Rylee with his penetrating green stare. "He didn't call you?"

"Um. I, uh, must have missed a text." She slapped on a smile.

"Well, it shouldn't change anything for you. Corynna's setting up the flowers now. If you see her, can you send her back?" His sous chef called out and Colin answered succinctly before swiping his brow. "It's a bloody madhouse."

"Is there a message I can pass along to her to save you a few seconds?" The kitchen was literally vibrating with activity. "You seem to have your hands full."

"Yes." He gave her a handsome smile. "Tell her I need the edible flowers for the gorgonzola and fruit plate. Thank you."

"You're welcome."

Rylee left the kitchen projecting much more ease than she felt. Another last-minute change from the bride and groom? She hoped there weren't any more surprises to come in the next few days.

She checked her texts, but didn't see one from Ari or Ex. Odd. Then she noticed she had zero texts. *Then* she noticed the little airplane symbol in the corner of her screen. Her phone was on airplane mode? Panicked that she'd missed more messages than she cared to acknowledge, she turned off airplane mode and waited for the flood. Three texts came through, and her email showed ten unread messages. Not great, but not a disaster.

Ari's text to Rylee read, "We are switching up the menu for tonight but Ex called Colin personally. See you at Sheen!"

Rylee's heart was leaping out of her chest, unspent adrenaline zipping around her bloodstream. She pursed her lips and blew out a breath. While tonight was an upset she hadn't seen coming, everything seemed to be under control. Shoulders back, she replied to Ari and scanned the other incoming messages to make sure there were no more emergencies to head off.

Over the next hour, guests poured into the private seating area in the rear of Sheen, more than the originally planned-upon bridal party, but still a reasonable number. Rylee greeted everyone with a smile, and a few friends with hugs, including Dionna who had come directly to her.

"You are exquisite." Dee held Rylee's hands out to her sides and admired her coral dress.

It was fitted, cocktail-length, and had a decorative bow on the shoulder that normally would have been a bit much for her. But it had seemed the right vibe for a rehearsal dinner…even one that had turned into an hors d'oeuvres and cocktail party.

Dee cocked her head. "What's different?"

"Um. Nothing?"

"Your hair is down. Your dress is brightly colored." Dee's eyes popped wide. "You slept with that hunk of yummy wedding crasher, didn't you?"

Rylee shushed Dee, but the other woman did not oblige.

"I knew it!" Dee hugged Rylee, saying into her ear, "Your secret is safe with me."

Once that mini interrogation was done, Rylee found Corynna, who appeared half as harried as Colin. She relayed the message from the chef, and Corynna hustled outside to gather the edible flowers she'd brought over from her shop.

Rylee wasn't quite in Relax Mode yet, though. As more guests arrived, she had to slip out of the private area to alert Sheen's staff that they needed more chairs, and at least one more table. Both were delivered quietly and efficiently, and with as little disruption as possible.

The waitstaff, dressed in black, served wine and champagne as well as some sort of puff pastry that looked amazing. Her mouth watered at the thought of a nibble of one of Colin's last-minute creations, but she didn't want to take food from the guests. Best to wait and make sure everyone was fed first.

A warm hand slipped around her back and gently tugged her close. She knew it was Trick without turning. Not only because of the faint scent of his cologne, but also because she'd come to know his touch. Gentle but firm. In a few short days, he'd become so familiar to her.

She relaxed against him, realizing that she'd been holding tension in her shoulders for the last few hours.

"Welcome to the rehearsal cocktail party," she said to Trick as she waved to Sasha, Ari's sister, who was on the other side of the room.

"No dinner? I'm starving." He held up his cellphone and angled the camera at them, never taking his hand off Rylee's back. "Smile pretty, Peaches. We're going live."

Before she could protest, he hit the red button and gave the camera a wide grin. "Hey, Tricksters," he greeted his fan club. "I'm here with the beautiful, beguiling Rylee Meadows, resident wedding planner and savior of celebrity nuptials. You asked for more, and here she is." He faced her, his jovial smile going a long way to soothing her nerves. "You look stunning. Who are you wearing?"

She laughed at his shtick. The way his eyes twinkled when he looked her up and down hinted that he liked what he saw.

"This is one of Keely Tucker's earlier designs. You

might recognize it. Didn't you leak some of her stuff to the public at one point?"

"And she's feisty," he said, never taking his eyes off hers. "I'm going to shake a few trees and find out what Ari and Ex's guests think of Sheen and Colin Reynolds's culinary creations." He removed his hand and tilted his head. "I'll find you later, Peaches."

That rumbled promise left a trail of tingles down her arms. She watched as he made his way across the room, stopping to say hello to Dee and Tripp first.

With a spring in her step that wasn't there before Patrick had come over to say hello, Rylee walked over to greet a pair of new arrivals.

Trick thanked Dee and Tripp for their time and shut off the camera. One of his series on his social media channel was a three-question interview with the guests. Typically he saved it for the reception, but as he wouldn't be filming any of the wedding or reception, he'd been forced to be creative.

He cast a glance over at Rylee, who couldn't look hotter unless she were holding the tray of flaming baked Alaska that was being whisked across the dining room of the restaurant. She was also calmer than usual. Oh, sure, she was hiding stress beneath a stunning smile, but he could tell she was no longer fretting over the party.

She lifted her foot and adjusted a strap on her gold high-heeled shoe, grimacing the entire time. He shook his head, and then had an idea...

His phone buzzed in his hand with an incoming text. Then another. Then one more. "What the...?"

Todd, via group text was the first. Yo, Trick! We're in Royallllll.

Yee-haw! came Rusty's reply to all.

James chimed in with a gif of a cowboy riding a Mustang into the sunset.

We're staying in a fancy-ass hotel called the Bellamy. Planning on crashing the Noble-Ramos wedding. Let us know when to sync up.

Following Todd's text was a photo of the three of them—more acquaintances than friends now that they no longer ran a social media channel together. Trick hadn't hung out with his buddies in at least a year. Why had they crawled out of the woodwork to fly to Royal?

Not sure on timing yet. Beer tomorrow, Trick texted back. He looked over his shoulder at Rylee. He couldn't very well explain to his friends that there would be no crashing via text message. He'd have to tell them in person.

On his channel, he'd maintained that he was filming the pregame, but he hadn't let his fandom know that he would not be sharing any of the Noble-Ramos wedding or reception. Frankly, he hadn't decided if he would or not. He was filming an interview with Ari and Ex tomorrow. There was an outside chance of gaining their blessing to shoot footage of their big day. Asking for permission was weird, but not in a bad way. Trick was looking forward to showing up invited rather than crashing an event where he didn't belong.

Tonight! Rusty argued via text.

Shots, baby! James replied.

Shit to do, Trick answered the group, but he had to smile. As boneheaded as they could be, they were good guys. He hadn't shared that he was radically changing his public content, so it wasn't their fault they didn't know. He texted over the address of a cantina in town and suggested that his buddies grab dinner and drinks there *without* him.

A few texts followed with middle-finger emojis and good-natured razzing. Trick ignored them. Tomorrow, he'd straighten it out and let them know what was up.

Applause filled the room and Trick looked up to see Ari and Ex walk in. Looking every inch the celebrity in a skin-tight pale gold gown, Ari waved. Ex was in a suit and tie, sans jacket. He took a bow which elicited more applause and laughter from friends and family.

Rylee materialized at Ari's side and directed them to a table that had been reserved for the bride and groom. She then attempted to fade into the background.

For Trick, she hadn't faded a bit. Or maybe it was that she *couldn't* fade. Wherever he was with her, Rylee glowed like the north star, far outshining the wealthy entrepreneurs in their midst.

He knew why he was looking forward to showing up invited to this wedding. Because Rylee had been the woman to invite him. She was the main reason he was looking forward to Saturday.

Maybe the only reason.

Seventeen

Rylee was exhausted. Her feet ached. A tension headache was forming between her eyes. She was tired of smiling. She was starving. She wanted nothing more than to go back to her room, finish eating the box of chocolates and then collapse on her bed and sleep for twelve hours straight.

She regarded her watch. It was nearly 11 p.m. She'd have to settle for five or six hours of sleep. *Sigh*.

She'd lost Trick at some point during the evening. He'd been filming and chatting with the guests, conducting interviews like the ones Rylee had watched on his channel before. The questions were innocent, ranging from favorite flavor of ice cream, to whether the interviewee would prefer living near the ocean or in the mountains.

She'd felt his hand on her back at least one other time during the evening and that had been when he'd handed her a plate of assorted hors d'oeuvres. He must have noticed she hadn't sampled the trays being passed around. Was there anything the man didn't notice?

Ari and Ex were making their way to the door. Rylee was glad they had thanked Colin for the last-minute arrangement. They might be particular about their preferences, and change their minds more than any couple she'd dealt with in the past, but they were also polite and kind, and never took advantage of the people helping them.

"Rylee." Ari smiled, a glimmering goddess in gold. "You were right about that wedding crasher. Everyone loved the interview questions. They thought Ex and I cooked them up."

After the happy couple had been seated at their reserved table, Rylee had informed them of Trick's plans for the rehearsal party. She'd assured them that their fans would love participating in the behind-the-scenes extras, and promised that there was nothing offside about Trick's plans. Dee happened to overhear and had backed Rylee's claim.

"Everything turned out great," Ex said now. "We'll see you and Trick tomorrow, I take it?"

"Six o'clock sharp."

"It'll have to be sharp. I want to get a good night's sleep, and we're planning on a long, hot bubble bath afterward." Ari walked her fingers up Ex's tie before kissing him. All Rylee could think about was how wonderful a bubble bath would feel right now.

She saw the couple out, waited until the last guest followed and then nearly collapsed. Not before thanking Colin and Corynna, who were in the kitchen faux arguing over which edible flowers tasted better. The kitchen staff was in cleaning mode, their pace moderately slower than earlier. Rylee said goodbye and thanked them collectively, and then left via the rear exit.

Outside, Trick was leaning against the door of her borrowed car, his legs crossed at the ankles, tripod on the ground, his hand on the hilt. She came to a stop as her pinky toe wailed in agony. This was the first and last time she was wearing these damn shoes.

"I thought you'd gone hours ago," she said, wearily making her way to him.

"I left and then came back. I had an arrangement to make."

She regarded him with suspicion. "What kind of arrangement?"

"It has nothing to do with the wedding." He held out one hand. "Keys."

She dropped them into his palm, happy to sit on the passenger side. "I'm at your mercy."

He turned on the car. "I like how that sounds."

"Don't be too excited. I'm half asleep already." She laid her head back and shut her eyes, the entire day washing over her in one draining wave.

Two more days. Just two more days. This was crunch time, always the most challenging part of planning a wedding. But each item she ticked off the list brought her closer to the grand finale. Once the reception was winding to a close, she was home free. Then this wedding would be in the history books, another success story to add to the testimonials page of her website.

"You don't have to stay awake for where we're going. In fact, falling asleep might be considered a compliment."

He didn't give her any more hints than that. She watched out the window as he drove them back to the Bellamy Hotel. Hopefully he would tuck her in for a nap before attempting any sexual acrobatics tonight. They were running out of time to spend together, but even that ticking clock hadn't imbued her with her the *oomph* she needed.

She joked as they strolled through the lobby that she required a coffee before any of her clothes came off. He stayed quiet, holding her hand and leading her past the elevators and down another corridor.

"Where are you taking me?" She perked up when they stopped in front of a darkened window. "The spa? It's closed."

Trick leaned in, his voice low. "You said you could pick a lock, right?"

"Oh, no. No, no."

He grinned and then produced a keycard from his pocket. He swiped it and depressed the handle, holding the door open for her. "Relax, Peaches. I wouldn't ask you to burgle the hotel spa. Come on."

A million questions cluttered her mind as they stepped into the shadows. Manicure stations were tidy and silent, rows of nail polish lining the shelves like colorful soldiers. They passed massage rooms and a room marked "sauna" before coming to a room with a pedicure chair.

"Thank you, Janice," Trick said to himself as he stepped into the dimly lit room. The tub at the foot of the leather chair was bubbling away, steam floating up from the basin.

"What did you do?" Rylee asked as he lowered to his knees. "What are you doing?"

"Giving you exactly what you deserve." He unbuckled the dainty straps around her ankles and removed her uncomfortable shoes. A deep sigh worked its way up from her throat. "Have a seat."

She sat, anticipating a pedicurist to materialize from the doorway.

"No one's coming." Trick slung a towel over his shoulder. Then he sat on a short stool and lowered her feet into the water one by one. "Just me."

"You're—I can't let you do this." She started to pull her foot from the water, but he placed a hand on her knee below the hemline of her dress.

"You have to. I spent an hour here with Janice, the manager, and learned what to do."

"How?" She couldn't wrap her head around what was happening. Not being in a spa alone afterhours, or Trick sweet-talking the key from the manager, or the fact that he had taken one of her feet from the water and was squirting oil onto his hands. "She let you in here unsupervised?"

"Well, I had to promise we wouldn't have sex on the massage table."

As good as his thumb in the arch of her foot felt, she stiffened. "You didn't."

His grin was mischievous. "I didn't. Relax. That's your only job. I watched you run around and organize everything for everyone else tonight. It's time you allowed yourself to be pampered, don't you think?"

She eased back into the chair. He finished massaging her foot and then traded one for the other. He poured a scoop of scented sea salt with tiny, dried roses into the tub. Slowly but surely, Rylee allowed herself to relax.

Earlier when he'd stopped in to talk to the manager of the day spa, Trick had asked if there was anyone available for a pedicure very late tonight. Janice regretfully declined, explaining that her employees were coming in early tomorrow with appointments, and that she had a family dinner tonight she couldn't miss.

Trick hadn't given up. He'd had a pampering session in mind for Rylee. He'd watched her leap hurdle after hurdle today. She'd catered to the bride and groom, who had thrown another curveball her way, and she'd handled it with the same grace and poise with which she'd handled everything else. Including him.

Rylee deserved to be spoiled.

"What if I do it?" he'd asked Janice. The manager broke into a small laugh that had crinkled her eyes at the corners. He'd gone on to explain who he was, and had shown her a few of his online videos. When he offered to mention the spa to his subscribers, he won the other woman over. She'd been looking for a unique way to advertise, and him offering to do it for free had been too good to pass up.

Janice had given him the key card and asked him to stash it in the front desk drawer when he left. She'd given him a basic rundown of how to give a woman a relaxing foot treatment, teasing that she didn't have adequate time to teach him how to polish Rylee's toes.

"I never had the chance to ask you the interview questions I asked everyone else today," he said now, digging his thumbs into the wide part of Rylee's foot. Her eyes were half-open, her body sagging on the cushy chair. "If you are coherent enough to answer them."

"You could talk me into anything right now." She moaned, a sound he felt in his groin. He reminded himself why he'd done this rather than take her back to her room. Because she'd been obligated all day today. He wasn't about to obligate her further.

"Don't tempt me," he said anyway. "Okay, question

one. What is your favorite relaxing pastime? Foot massages from sexy strangers doesn't count."

She smiled, her lashes casting shadows on her full cheeks. Her lipstick had faded, her hair had gone limp and she still looked amazing. Nothing short of edible.

"You mean besides being fed chocolate in bed after being thoroughly sexed up and down?"

He groaned under his breath. There was a definite stirring below the beltline he couldn't alleviate any time soon. "Yes, besides that."

"It's boring."

"Humor me."

"I like to reorganize my pantry and spice rack."

He nearly laughed. Of course she did. But he didn't want to insult her, so he kept going. "Question two."

"Wait, what's your answer?"

"This is my interview."

Her forehead creased. "I want to know."

He'd never been asked, but he didn't have to think about his answer. "The beach, a cold beer and a sunset."

"That sounds nice." Her expression was one of longing. "I could use a vacation."

He swallowed the offer to treat her to an evening like it. "Question two. Who is your favorite person on the planet?"

"At the moment, it's you." She gave him a wonky smile.

"Nice try." He drained the tub and dried off her feet with a towel. "It's probably hard to pick from the thousands of friends you have."

"I don't have many friends."

He laughed, assuming she was kidding.

"I'm serious. Until this wedding, where I've befriended

several of the vendors, the bride and her family, I realized I don't have many friends. Any, actually. I should make some more."

"You should," he agreed, smoothing lotion onto one of her legs. He'd expected her to struggle to pick from the people who loved her.

"My mother. Is that lame?" She wrinkled her nose.

"Not lame. My answer is my sister, Cassie."

"That's sweet."

"She's great." He stopped short of telling her she'd meet his sister one day. Would she? They hadn't spoken about what would happen once they returned to their separate lives in LA, and now didn't seem like the right time to bring it up.

"Last question. Other than water, what is the one beverage you could drink for the rest of your life?" He waited for her to say a peach Bellini. Expected it, actually. In his mind, this question was a deal breaker. He and the woman he was seeing could disagree on the first two questions, no problem, but the final one was nonnegotiable. There was only one practical answer.

"Coffee."

"What did you say?" He paused mid-massage with his hands on her calf, his pulse quickening.

"Coffee. It's the possible answer. What about you?"

He stood, offering his hand to help her up. "Same exact answer."

On her feet, she gazed into his eyes. "Thank you for this."

"You're welcome." They both looked over at her discarded shoes. "Want me to carry you to your room?"

Laughter shook her shoulders. The tension in her body was a memory. He'd wanted to treat her, and she'd let him. He'd come here with the most noble of intentions, but now that she was looking at him with a twinkle in her eye and those dimples were on display, well, hell. How could he keep from wanting her?

"You don't have to carry me there." She wedged her feet into her shoes, but she didn't release his hand. Squeezing his fingers in hers, she said, "But you should join me."

Eighteen

The second she stepped from the elevator, Trick wrapped his free arm around her waist and gave her a hard kiss. Their tongues tangled as they stumbled in the direction of her suite. She didn't take her mouth from his as she blindly fished her key card from her purse. Or maybe she couldn't.

Warmth slid through her veins as he made out with her. His lips were firm and unyielding, like the firm erection pressed against her. Her pulse sped, her nipples tightened. She nearly forgot where she was—in the hallway of the elite and luxury Bellamy Hotel. Had she ever been so turned that she didn't care where she was or if someone caught her?

Easy answer. *No.*

Trick seemed equally overcome as they half tripped, half walked down the corridor. She smiled against his smile but the levity died quickly when they reached her suite. After she made three clumsy attempts to insert the key card, he took it from her and successfully disengaged the lock. They spilled into the room, him pausing to set aside his gear and her purse on the desk before steering them to the bed. He stopped kissing her long enough to hang the do not disturb sign on the door handle.

She kicked off her shoes and he rushed toward her. He wasn't smiling now. She preferred the intense version of him. The man who couldn't wait to strip her naked and put his lips on her body. She'd appreciated the version of him downstairs, too. The man who'd gone the extra mile to treat her.

He had a reputation for being a nuisance and a bad boy, but she'd seen a different side of him. Patrick "Trick" MacArthur had more tricks up his sleeve than showing up where he wasn't invited.

Illustrating one of them now, he shimmied her dress up and over her hips, bunching it at her waist. He flattened his palm and slipped it into her panties, stroking her folds with the tips of his fingers. She'd been slick the second his tongue had touched hers. It was like her body had known what was coming and had readied her for his exploration.

She reached behind her and unzipped the top of her dress, pulled it over her head and tossed it aside. Inside-out, no less. A fleeting thought about how it would be unforgivably wrinkled and require prompt dry cleaning vanished when he set his lips over the lace of her bra. He suckled her nipple through the fabric, leaving it damp and warm, as he stroked her below. He complemented each stroke with his thumb on her clit. By the time he lightly grazed her nipple with his teeth, she was shuddering.

The orgasm rushed over her like a tidal wave, clearing her mind of her to-do list, her schedule, and the worry over how much sleep she'd lose tonight. There was only the feeling of sparks dancing on each of her erogenous zones.

"Goddamn." He kissed her mouth—or tried, anyway. She could barely muster the strength to pucker. His voice was rough and raw when he complimented her. "That was the most beautiful thing I've ever watched. Do you have any idea how gorgeous you are when you come?"

Her hands in his hair, she played with the longer strands. "I love your hair." She kissed him. "I love your mouth." She kissed him again. "I love your fingers."

"Thanks, Peaches." His voice was strained. Perhaps because she'd rerouted her hand to his cock and was stroking him through the fabric of his pants.

"I want you. Right now. Before I come down from this incredible high. You're so hot."

He laughed, a low raspy sound. "Okay, okay. You don't have to convince me."

He shoved her hand aside and slipped out of his pants. A moment later she was steered toward the bed and pushed down onto it. He joined her, unhooking her bra and setting his mouth to her breasts. She was hovering in a hazy, gauzy post-sex veil. That was new for her. That probably meant something. Not that she had the energy to sort through it now. There would be time to think later. Right now all she wanted to do was feel.

Chest to chest, he placed a kiss on her throat and whispered into her ear. "Give me those blue eyes, Peaches."

Lazily, she gazed up at him. Her vision was filled with dark hair and piercing hazel eyes. After watching his videos, she'd admitted to herself that he was handsome. What she saw now far surpassed that. He'd become more. Without her permission and without her realizing it.

"I want to watch your face this time, too." He tilted his hips and slid past her folds. Once he was nestled deep inside of her, he paused to allow both of them to appreciate the snug fit.

She couldn't stop staring. He made no effort to look away. It was like they were each witnessing something neither of them had expected.

"Ready?" he asked, his voice hoarse.

She nodded and he began to move. He thrust into her, his gaze locked with hers, his arms tight around her. He heeded her request for "harder, faster" as another orgasm galloped to the drumbeat of her heart.

She shouted her release, losing herself in the vivid colors that sprang to life on the backs of her eyelids. Holding on tight, she soaked in every bit of what he gave her. She felt dampness from his brow when he dropped his head onto her chest. And pressure when he came inside her, his hips pumping helplessly as he finished.

His back muscles had tightened and she hugged him close, holding him together after she'd flown apart. A heated breath coasted along her neck followed by one word. "Fuck."

"I love that part of you the best." Her voice was a froggy croak. She needed water. She needed sleep. She needed another orgasm. Hell, maybe two.

Or maybe a lifetime of them.

"You're magical." She turned her head and kissed his ear, running her fingers through his thick hair. "Has anyone ever told you that?"

No one had ever told him he was magical.

At least, not in bed. He'd never thought of what he did between the sheets as the equivalent of making someone disappear. Though he could admit that he wasn't 100 percent present at the moment.

Each time she'd pointed out what she loved about him, his chest had caved in a bit more. Now it was dented and dinged. Another blow might shatter it completely, and then she'd find out what was inside.

What *was* inside?

He wanted to watch her come again. He wanted to whisper dirty words into her ear and watch her expression while he did it. That's why he'd wanted her to look at him. Then she did, and he'd no longer been in control, but careening out of it.

He'd been overcome. Overwhelmed. Who was this woman? He'd thought he'd known. She was the four-night stand wedding planner. Lover of peach Bellinis. Wearer of uncomfortable shoes. But Rylee had become more than a quick lay or a temporary fling.

What the fuck did *that* mean?

"You used a condom, right?" she murmured. "I seem to remember hearing a packet being torn but my brain isn't firing with all cylinders."

He had to look down to double-check, but yeah, there it was, thank Christ. "I got you, Peaches. You just lay there looking like every wet dream I've had in my life. I'll be right back."

He didn't feel as light and playful as he sounded. Though he could appreciate how hot she looked, naked on the hotel bedding, her breasts a pair of tight peaks in the room's cool air. When she tucked a hand under her cheek and batted thick, dark lashes, his heart literally skipped a beat.

Shit. He was losing it.

He offered her what he hoped was a smile before he

stepped into the bathroom. He splashed his face with cold water and then eyed his dripping reflection.

"You're okay," he assured himself. "Nothing has changed. Go back out there, curl up next to her and go to sleep. When you wake up in the morning, blow her mind all over again."

He nodded. His reflection nodded back. It was a good plan. Solid. He and Rylee had two more days together. He was going to make every moment count before he never saw her again. Staying the night was the best decision. He didn't want to miss that sweet, sleepy look in her eyes first thing in the morning.

"Solid plan," he reiterated. Then he dried his face with a hand towel and opened the door.

Despite having convinced himself to stay, when he reached the bed, he heard himself tell her he couldn't. He pulled his clothes, muttering excuses about how she needed to sleep and how he'd had a long night as well. It sounded like bullshit to him, so he could only imagine how it sounded to her. Ultimately, he kissed her goodnight and left.

He refused to categorize what he'd done as running away. He simply wasn't prepared for the heavy emotions that had ridden sidecar with making love to Rylee. He didn't want to think about the future. He liked plans with an "*ish*" attached. Dinner at six-*ish*. Nightcaps at nine-*ish*. He liked surprises. He liked things up in the air. He preferred to act on instinct, whim.

Rylee wasn't that way. She was a planner. She made plans twelve, eighteen, hell, twenty-four months into the future. He'd convinced himself that he'd won her over to his way of life. *Don't think too far ahead. Go with the flow. Let it ride. Relax and enjoy.* She'd loosened up, but what if she'd also rubbed off on him?

Was he ready to be a planner?

He'd die before he turned into a rigid cyborg like her ex, Louis. That sort of pinned down, propped-up lifestyle didn't appeal. Trick didn't want to be a drone. Was that what a woman like Rylee expected? God knew her father did.

This was why he didn't have romantic relationships. They hampered his lifestyle. He couldn't make last-minute plans and do whatever he wanted when there was someone other than himself to consider.

He stepped into his dark hotel room and sat on the edge of bed, mindlessly checking the footage on his camera. Amidst the interviews of the guests tonight there were shots of Rylee. Faraway. Close-up. Sometimes she smiled, other times she looked pensive. Still others, unsure. Her smile was a bombshell that rattled his chest walls.

"Patrick MacArthur," he muttered. "What have you gotten yourself into?"

He shook his head. Not because he didn't know, but because he did. He was in deep with a woman he didn't want to walk away from. A woman he *had* to walk away from. There was only one word to describe his situation, so he said it out loud.

"*Fuck.*"

Nineteen

Rylee should've woken feeling light and happy. She should be floating through her day without a care in the world. But after Trick's hasty departure last night, she'd barely slept. Instead, she'd lain awake and thought over around and through what had happened.

Coffee in hand, she made her way to the hotel lobby, expecting to run into him and carpool over to the TCC for another busy day, but she didn't see him in the elevator or in the lobby. Or the parking lot. She hesitated, her thumb over the text message icon on her phone, before deciding not to contact him.

Last night had been amazing, life-altering. There had been a moment where an understanding had passed between them. An unspoken promise neither of them had vocalized.

Or so she'd thought.

When he'd come out of the bathroom, she'd been lying on her side waiting for him, anticipating him sliding in next to her and curling around her for the remainder of the night. She'd already begun looking forward to this morning. But he hadn't stayed.

"Peaches," he said, his smile relaxed and easy as he placed a kiss on her lips. She hummed, waiting for what came next. More chocolate in bed, maybe? "I'm heading back to my room. You're fading fast and I've already kept you up too late."

It hadn't been a question, so she hadn't answered. He'd pulled on his clothes, not appearing the least bit shaken, which was why she'd been so confused when he said goodnight and then walked out of her suite.

Odd behavior, for sure. She hadn't had a lot of experience, but after sex that good, why would he leave? Unless he was preparing to leave her permanently. Which had always been the plan, she supposed. She certainly hadn't started sleeping with her nemesis in the hopes of building a life with him.

And yet...

There was more between them than mere physical attraction. They should be able to talk about it openly. Honestly. Frustrated by her own inability to soothe herself or make a decision about where to go from here, she drove to the Texas Cattleman's Club. She parked near the side entrance, confident about her decision to show up and face Trick.

But as she entered her darkened office, her fortitude began to crumble. The way he'd run out on her last night hadn't made her feel sexy or wanted. Trick had made her feel used, just like Louis had suggested.

The wedding cake arrived at 11 a.m., delivered by a woman named Ebony and two men introduced as her "helpers." Rylee showed the trio to the kitchen where space had been cleared in the refrigerator to house the tiered cake. The two guys headed back out to the van, and Ebony and Rylee walked to her office to sign off on the safe-and-sound delivery of the cake.

"It's a masterpiece, truly," Rylee said as she scribbled her name on the invoice.

"Thank you." Ebony pushed a thick braid over one shoulder. "I wish I could be here to see Ari and Ex's reaction."

"Trust me, they're going to love it." Rylee walked Ebony to the door, chatting about the heat and how challenging it must have been to transport the cake without it melting. She'd been paying such close attention to the other woman's story about a time when the refrigeration unit stopped working in the van, that she didn't notice Trick until it was too late.

On the sidewalk, he was chatting with Ebony's helpers. Well, more than chatting. Laughing and addressing the camera while he filmed them.

"That's Trick MacArthur," Ebony said.

Rylee waited for the smile, the mention of how big of a fan Ebony was, or for her to swoon over how attractive she found him. Because who didn't? It seemed everyone he'd met worshiped at his altar.

Instead, Ebony wrinkled her nose. "I don't trust that guy."

Rylee snapped to attention. "Excuse me?"

"Sorry if you two are close. Ever since I found out he was running a hoax, I can't support what he does."

"What hoax?" Rylee's stomach clenched. What was Ebony talking about?

"The one where he pays the bride and groom to let him 'crash' the wedding. He's been spotted leaving a thick envelope full of cash money on more than one gift table. It was all over The Dallas Duchess's website."

The mention of The Dallas Duchess gave Rylee pause. It was a known gossip website, hardly the evening news, but that didn't mean there wasn't a nugget of truth to what was reported.

"On camera, he appears out of the ether, winning over guests at the reception one by one. We assume everyone falls in love with him, but in reality they've been paid off. Not even reality is real any more. It's a shame." Ebony shrugged and then gave Rylee a professional smile. "To each their own, I guess. Have fun at the wedding tomorrow."

Fun. Sure. Rylee nodded absently.

Trick finished with his camerawork, and then shook both of the other men's hands. Once the van pulled away, he strode over to Rylee. Was that a glimmer of uncertainty in his eyes, or was she imagining it?

"Morning." He was standing farther away from her than usual, which was making her suspicious. "How'd you sleep?"

"You *pay* the bride and groom to crash their wedding?"

That wasn't how she'd intended to greet him, but wasn't sure she was ready to discuss him running away from her last night. If that's what he'd done. *God.* Had she ever overthought a situation this much?

"What are you talking about?" He shot a thumb in the direction of the van driving down the road. "Is that what she told you? Where'd she hear that?"

His tone was clipped, which made her wonder if there was some truth to the accusation. "Do you?"

He ran a hand through his hair, blew out a breath and looked at the ground. Then he met her eyes and said, "How the hell did someone find out about that?"

* * *

Rylee wasn't quite fuming, but he had a feeling she would be if they'd been in the privacy of her office. Outside of the TCC, she maintained her composure. Barely.

"You let me believe that you won over the people you met at the weddings you crashed. Now you're telling me it's prearranged? You've been lying to me."

"I've never lied to you." To himself, sure. Like last night when he freaked the fuck out and left her alone in her hotel room bed. This morning he woke up feeling like a horse's ass.

He wasn't accustomed to planning for the future. His superpower was living in the moment. He'd intended to apologize to Rylee for leaving the moment he saw her. The truth was, he should have stayed and woken up with her this morning. When it came to her, he wanted to stay in the moment with her rather than panic over an unforeseen future.

But this morning he'd suffered his own bout of "cold feet" when he stepped into the elevator. Rather than go up to her floor, he pressed the button for the lobby. He'd been killing time since, shooting B footage and gathering his thoughts. It seemed he'd finally run out of time.

Her arms were folded over her breasts, one fair eyebrow raised while she waited for him to explain himself.

"The bride and groom don't know about the money." He kept his voice low. "No one does. I leave the cash anonymously, sliding it in with the other cards and gifts. I'm a wedding guest. I should bring something, right?" He offered a sheepish smile as he palmed the back of his neck, unsure how to take her blank expression.

"You're not a guest, technically."

He dropped his hand. "This isn't what you're really upset about, is it?"

Her mouth tightened. She turned on her heel and strode away from him. He followed her inside, catching the door before it shut in his face.

"Rylee. Wait. Last night—"

She spun on him, her eyes flashing a warning. "Keep your voice down."

"You're not escaping me this easily."

"Why not? I let you escape easily."

He sighed. That was fair. He gestured to her closed office door. "Please?"

She watched him for a truncated moment and then huffed her acquiescence. "Fine."

He pulled the door shut once they were inside. He wanted to kiss her, give her the apology she deserved... make love to her on the desk. Unfortunately she looked as if she might take his head off, so he decided to explain himself first.

"Last night, I left."

"No kidding."

"I shouldn't have."

Her features softened slightly. "Then why did you?"

"Because I—"

A knock at the door drew her attention.

"Don't answer that."

"I have to. This might be a fun little adventure for you to check off your bucket list, but this is my career." She pushed past him to open the door. One of the catering staff stood in the threshold saying something about a flatware shortage.

"At least nine place settings." The kid appeared to be around seventeen years old and looked like he might puke on his shoes. Probably because Rylee was shooting laser beams out of her eyeballs at him. Not the kid's fault. Trick was mostly to blame for her foul mood.

"I wonder—" she snatched a single gold fork from the kid's hand and tapped it against his nametag "—Rodney, if there is anything left that could go wrong at the last minute."

"Peaches," Trick started. It was the wrong thing to say. She aimed those laser beams at him next. He didn't flinch. "We'll fix it."

"*We* are not going to do anything. *We* are not a 'we.'" to Rodney, she said, "Is there someone else I can talk to? Someone who might have a contact at the vendor who supplies the flatware?"

"I—I don't know, ma'am." The kid sought out Trick for help, but before he could intervene, more unexpected company appeared outside of Rylee's office.

"Trickster!"

No, no. No, no, no.

Trick stepped into the corridor as his friends, Todd, James and Rusty, were barreling toward them. Todd grabbed Trick's shoulders and shook. "You owe us a beer!"

"How did they get in here?" Rylee directed that question to Trick.

"I don't know."

"You know." James nodded. Then to Rylee said, "He knows."

"I don't know." Trick shrugged off Todd's hold. "What the hell, you guys?"

"You said we were having beer. We're here for beer."

"It's barely noon," Trick said, which sent the three of them into fits of laughter.

"And to discuss our plans for Saturday," James said, not bothering to hide his intentions. Trick was supposed to meet with them today to explain that no one would be crashing the Noble-Ramos wedding. He hadn't expected them to ambush him at the TCC.

"We understand if you've been busy." Todd scanned Rylee top to bottom. "But you can't avoid us forever. We are here. We are ready to party."

"Get your *boys* out of here before I call security. On all of you." Rylee's tone was borderline lethal. She was already convinced that Trick had lied to her about paying off the brides and grooms of the weddings he crashed, and now his so-called friends were making it seem like he'd planned to include them in just that.

Rylee locked her office and clipped away from him, young Rodney at her heels.

Out of options, Trick pointed his friends to the nearest exit so he could handle at least one of his problems. "Let's go."

Twenty

After Trick and his guests had rolled out of the TCC in a plume of cologne, Rylee had followed Rodney back to his manager to discuss the flatware issue at length. The catering company had scoured their own inventory and had come up short, and the vendor they typically used for the gold cutlery hadn't been able to locate any backup sets as of yet.

Rylee was trying not to panic. A voice in her head reminded her that mismatched flatware wasn't the end of the world. Annoyingly enough, that voice sounded a lot like Trick.

He'd claimed to leave money for the couple anonymously. It irked her that she'd instantly given him the benefit of the doubt. She was trying to be mad at him, dammit. After the way he'd left last night, she should be upset. Right?

Cellphone in hand, she was tempted to contact a friend and ask her opinion. Dee came to mind. Ariana came to mind. Even Keely. New friends, but they would be honest with her. But she didn't want to burden them with her problems.

Instead she tapped in the phone number she'd secured earlier for the vendor. When a woman answered, Rylee introduced herself. She calmly explained the flatware issue, ending with a request. "If you could give me any information you have about the brand, style, and where and when you found it, I'd appreciate it."

Her friendliness had gone a long way. Rylee jotted it down the details the vendor shared onto a pad of paper on her desk. She finished the call, opened up her laptop and set her fingers to the keys. She wanted this handled by the time she met with Ariana and Xavier for their interview with Trick later. She would find the missing gold cutlery for the couple's wedding reception before they knew it'd been an issue.

The hours passed in a blink and Rylee, after several frustrating phone calls and redirects, hadn't come up with a solution. She'd even reached out to Colin Reynolds, who was using his fame and reach to contact his friends in the restaurant world. He'd struck out as well.

Shuffling along the hallway, Rylee paused to adjust her right shoe. Her pinky toe throbbed painfully, but she did her best to ignore it. A quick glance around the lounge showed no sign of Ari and Ex, or Trick.

A text from Ari pinged Rylee's phone. It read: We're at the Silver Saddle. Where are you?

Rylee responded that she was waiting for Trick in the TCC lounge, where she thought they were supposed to meet. She apologized and promised to be along shortly. Ari's "No problem!" seemed sincere, but Rylee was angry with herself for dropping the ball. It was ultimately her responsibility to double and triple-check the details to avoid miscommunication of any kind.

Halfway through typing a text to Trick, she heard his voice. He was twenty minutes late. She assumed he'd been partying with his friends this whole time.

"What'd I tell you about those shoes, Peaches?" He stuffed his hands into his pockets, and watched her through clear, hazel eyes, which made her question her assumption.

"Ari and Ex are at the Silver Saddle waiting on us. I must have had the location wrong."

"I saw them as I was leaving the Bellamy."

"Pardon?"

"I saw them in the hotel lobby. I swung by and asked if we were meeting at the tapas bar and they said yes and told me you were waiting on me at the TCC. So, here I am." He smiled like the change of plans was no big deal.

"Why didn't you call me so I could rush over?" she practically shouted, already angling for the exit. He gently grasped her arm and swung her around to meet him, face-to-face.

"Because I also asked Ari and Ex how much time they had and they said enough that I didn't have to rush. So. I'm not rushing." He gestured to a seating area with a coffee table surrounded by a sofa and cushioned chairs. "Can we talk?"

"Now? About what?"

"About us."

Rylee sent a longing glance at the exit before deciding she could use a moment to calm down. It wouldn't be good for the bride and groom to witness her this upset. She sat on the sofa, both wanting and not wanting to address the issue that had been on her mind since she woke up this morning.

Trick sat next to her and took one of her hands in both of his. "This isn't what it started out being."

She agreed. "Which was a one-night stand."

"*Four*," he corrected with a completely captivating smile. "Four-night stand. I like you, Rylee. I think you know that."

"I like you, too."

He hesitated, stroking his thumbs over her hand.

"Well? What's the plan?"

Sure they both lived in LA, but her work took her all over the country. She assumed he traveled quite a bit too. Whose career would win if they decided to keep seeing each other?

"I don't like to talk about the future," he started, and she readied herself for a *but*. Something like *But I can't deny we have one*. What he said next was so far off she thought she'd misheard him.

"Let's not make a plan. Let's...wing it."

"Wing it?" she bit out.

"Yeah." The ease of his grin offset her tightly pursed lips.

"But you want to keep seeing me?"

"Hell yeah."

"Then we have to make a plan. Otherwise, when will we see each other? I work every weekend. What's your schedule like? How often will we be in the same state? I don't even know where your house is in LA."

"Slow down." He squeezed her hand. "Peaches, you were never part of a plan. Plans ruin everything."

Offended, she shot off the sofa. "Plans are what my life is built around. Plans are the reason you have weddings to crash. Plans are what we make with the people who are important to us."

"Plans are also chains tying you to an obligation when you'd rather be doing something else. Like right now." He stood. "I'd rather be taking you up to my hotel room or yours than interviewing the bride and groom."

"But they're the entire reason you're here!"

"They used to be. Things change. You changed everything."

Worry skittered over her bare arms like an army of ants. She wasn't sure what he was trying to say. She couldn't picture their future together, not that he'd painted one for her. He was offering her everything and nothing at the same time. How infuriating.

"Not making plans doesn't work for me."

"It might. Give it a shot." He leaned close, his lips on their way to hers. She wanted to kiss him and forget this entire stupid conversation. She wanted to relive last night. From the pampering session to the incredible sex, it'd been amazing. But if he couldn't acknowledge that they had real, concrete issues to work out—like his schedule and hers—how would they ever make it?

"It's not enough to say we'll take it as it comes, Trick," she told him before his mouth touched hers. "I need to know what is going to happen when we both go home to LA."

"Why?" The first wrinkle of frustration appeared on his brow.

"Because I am a planner. I love planning. Planning makes me feel safe."

"Plans are not guaranteed," he pointed out. "You had plans with Louis. Those fell through. What good did your plans do then?"

"That's different."

"How?"

Because Louis had told her that he loved her. He'd proposed. They'd had an engagement party and had met with vendors and caterers and photographers. Trick couldn't bear to stay in her hotel room last night after sex, and now he thought their relationship would simply work itself out? Ludicrous.

"We don't have time for this. Ari and Ex are waiting. Like it or not, you made a commitment, Trick. One you're late for because you decided to show your out-of-town friends a spur-of-the-moment good time. But then, they're probably allergic to plans, too, aren't they?"

Rylee and Trick arrived at the Silver Saddle five minutes later. Ari and Ex were sitting at a wide round table in the corner, with what looked like one of every appetizer spread out in front of them. They offered to share, saying that the chef had given them the spread for no charge as a wedding gift.

Trick dug in, laughing and joking as if he and Rylee hadn't just argued about their future together. She watched the interaction through narrowed eyes. How was it that he got away with absolutely everything? He crashed a wedding and the guests and couple fell in love with him. He barged into town, his sights set on the Noble-Ramos wedding and their wedding planner invites him to record the festivities.

It hadn't taken much more than a peach Bellini and a smile for her invite him into her bed. He'd had Dee and Tripp, Rylee and her mother, and now Ari and Ex eating out of his hands.

He was also notoriously generous. He left envelopes full of money as wedding gifts—okay, fine, she believed he did it anonymously—changed tires for stranded couriers, and turned complete strangers into fast friends. He was confounding.

Trick set up his tripod and camera while chatting with Ari and Ex about the questions he was planning to ask them. He advised them not to worry, that this wasn't a live feed and they could yell "cut!" and start over if they needed to.

After Ari took a sip from her glass of rosé, she tilted her head. "I have to admit, Trick, we weren't sure your intentions were pure. If it hadn't been for Rylee, you'd have been kicked out of the TCC the moment we spotted you."

"Out of the great state of Texas," Xavier corrected with a smile.

"I owe a lot to her." Trick looked Rylee's way and she plastered on a smile for the sake of Ari and Ex. They didn't need to know about the drama going on behind the scenes. As far as they were concerned, there was no issue with the gold flatware or between Rylee and Trick.

"I have a question before we start." Ari leaned in. "It's been eating me up inside."

Trick mirrored her position, leaning forward as well. "I'm all ears."

"Why weddings? Why interlope on a stranger's happiest day? I don't ask out of malice, just curiosity."

Trick nodded slowly. "I know it might appear that I'm there wreaking havoc." He waved his hands in front of him to illustrate. "The truth is, I'm a romantic at heart. I'm there to capture the moments that go unnoticed. Everyone films and photographs the dancing, the cake, the bouquet toss. What about grandma crumbling her napkin in her fist as she remembers her own wedding sixty years ago? What about the first time an aunt holds her newborn niece? Lots of unexpected—" he slid his gaze to

Rylee "—and *unplanned* moments happen at the wedding reception. Those are what make each wedding unique."

"That's so true." Ari, and now Ex were hanging onto Trick's every word. Rylee knew that he was speaking from the heart, which made it that much more annoying to hear. "I'm so glad we invited you to ours. Will you be catching those small moments on film?"

"I'm under strict orders not to film the wedding or the reception. Unless you override your wedding planner, my hands are tied." Trick's affable manner was boiling Rylee's blood.

"What about your friends who crash weddings with you?" Rylee snapped. "Would you like to explain to Ari and Ex why they showed up this morning, howling about how they couldn't wait to crash the wedding with you?"

Twenty-One

Rylee had been resolutely quiet since they'd sat down at the Silver Saddle, which was unlike her. Apparently, those unspoken comments had piled up, and she'd gathered enough steam to erupt.

"Is that true?" Ari asked, a worry line bisecting her brows.

"It's true," Rylee said. "Trick left with his buddies to go day-drinking and discuss your wedding. Which was why he was late meeting me, and why I was late meeting with you."

Ari blinked and exchanged a look with Ex.

"I'm sorry." Rylee shook her head, meaning it. "You trusted me to corral him. I believed he was sincere when he promised not to ruin your big day. Evidently what I say, or *plan*, means next to nothing to him." Challenge flashed in her eyes, as if she was daring Trick to speak up in front of the almost-married couple.

Challenge. *Accepted.*

"They showed up without telling me," Trick explained, keeping his eyes on Rylee. He pivoted to face Xavier and Ariana. "I don't work with them anymore. And you don't have to worry about them coming to the wedding or the reception. They showed up thinking they could jump in, since the Noble-Ramos wedding is the most trending social media topic on the planet, but I set them straight. They're on a plane to Vegas as we speak."

"Las Vegas?" Rylee's expression was pure chagrin.

"Yes, Peaches. Las Vegas." He addressed Xavier when he continued. "We were close in college. They don't know me as well now. They used to be part of my crew and we did dumb shit to gain online views and followers. They broke off to do their own thing, but used to pop in for cameos every once in a while. Until today, they didn't know my plans to go legit, or that I'm giving up crashing altogether."

"Are we your last wedding?" Ari arched an eyebrow.

"At first I was going to taper off, maybe crash one or two more, but actually...yeah. This is it for me." He blew out a breath as he digested the words he'd finally spoken out loud. He'd thought a lot about making this wedding his last, but he hadn't had the courage to admit it.

"Leaving behind the thing you're known for isn't the easiest transition to make." Ari, actress turned producer, knew of what she spoke. "The public tends to view you through one narrow lens. They rarely accept evolution."

"I know." When he moved from the good-natured prank-style videos to wedding crashing, he'd experienced an initial dip in viewership.

"If you want to grow, it's the risk you have to take," Ari said.

"I'm proud of you, baby." Ex slipped a hand around his wife-to-be's back.

"We bring out the best in each other." Ari leaned in for a kiss. Trick sneaked a peek at Rylee, who was studying her water glass as if it would tell her the future.

Future. He shook his head. That was why they were in this mess. His resistance to it and Rylee's need to plan for it. She probably wished she was clairvoyant so that there would never be any surprises. He didn't want to know how everything turned out in the end. There'd been too many pleasant surprises waiting around corners for him. Knowing the road ahead was different than anticipating the road ahead. Knowing took all the fun out of it.

"I wasn't late because I was *day-drinking* with my friends. I had an errand to run," Trick explained, needlessly at this point since Ari and Ex were gazing into each other's eyes. "I'll be attending the wedding and reception alone and invited. Unless it would make Rylee more comfortable if I skipped the event."

"Of course not." She inclined her chin proudly. She affected an expression that was as plastic as the straws poking out of their water glasses. "I'd never take that decision away from Ari and Ex. It's their big day."

He figured. What was Rylee doing if not making sure everyone else's life ran perfectly while ignoring her own preferences?

"We want you there," Ari told Trick. "And if you see any of those small, special moments that need to be captured on film, I want you to shoot them."

"I'd be honored," he answered, meaning it.

"Now that *that's* settled." Xavier said. "Let's get on with the interview."

"If you'll excuse me, I have a few last-minute preparations to handle." Rylee stood and pushed out of the high-backed chair. "I'll see you both tomorrow bright and early!"

"Thanks, Rye!" Ari gave a cheery wave, and Rylee scuttled for the exit.

Trick pretended to adjust his camera settings as he watched her. She sent one last look over her shoulder at him, and then she was gone.

Two hours later, Rylee locked the door to her private office at the TCC. She'd finalized everything there was to finalize, with one glaring exception. The gold flatware situation had not been resolved. She had gone through several stages of grief over the debacle: anger, denial, bargaining. She hadn't rounded the corner to acceptance yet. There was always tomorrow.

She was going to be out of bed at five in the morning to do research and call any potential suppliers in the area the minute they opened. She didn't have time to do that, but she wasn't about to have mismatched cutlery. Not on her watch.

As she walked to the reception area for a final once-over, she thought about Ari and Ex's interview. She hoped it had gone well. Trick was a pro, both tactful and entertaining. He also had an answer for everything. He'd had no trouble coming up with a plausible explanation as to why his rowdy friends had crashed the TCC with ulterior motives.

She'd believed him at first when he'd said they'd flown to Vegas, but over the last few hours she'd begun to have her doubts. Louis's, and even Ebony's, comments about Trick had parked themselves in the rear of Rylee's skull. She thought she'd seen a different side of Trick, but had she? What did she know about him really? For all she knew, he'd been playing the long game—his most extravagant prank yet—and was planning to crash the wedding with his bros after all.

You don't believe that.

She didn't. Not really. But she had come to another decision about the two of them.

"Hey."

Startled, she let out a shriek and spun to face the double doors she'd just walked through. Her hand on her chest, she admonished her visitor. "You scared me half to death!"

"Sorry." Trick, a box in his hands, eased the door shut behind him. He looked tired. He looked wonderful. Like the person she wanted to curl up with and fall asleep next to tonight.

"How'd it go?" She fussed with a place setting instead of looking at him, lining up the ends of the fork and the knife so that they were even.

"Great. Ari and Ex are naturals on camera. Their public will love it."

"We should stop this now," she blurted. If she didn't admit it now she never would.

"Stop what?"

"*This.* Us."

He set the box down at the guest book station, the feathery plumes blowing in the breeze created when he walked to her. "Why would we do that?"

"Because we have a fundamental disagreement about how to move forward. You don't want to make any plans. I want to make *all* of the plans."

"Again with this? What's under your need to plan everything half to death? I've admitted I'm more comfortable not knowing the future. What's your excuse?"

"You have no plan for your career! How will we know when or where *or if* we'll see each other? Are you telling me you're going to stick close to home? Because I'm not. I have a busy life. The weddings I plan take me out of town periodically."

"I'm not going to stop traveling, either but I'll be close to home for a while. As you heard me confess earlier, I'm done crashing weddings. I have hours upon hours of footage to edit and compile into content. I am so backlogged I could spend the next six months catching up."

He reached out to grip her arms. She let him. It felt good to be touched by him. To be comforted. Even when he was saying things that scared her.

"So far all we've done is argue how we should move on, not if we should move on. You want to be with me too, don't you?"

"There is no guarantee you won't show up tomorrow and pull a stunt you cooked up tonight." She shook off his hold and walked around the long table, needlessly straightening flatware as she went. "Every problem you cause can't be solved by leaving behind an envelope of money or flashing one of your charming smiles." She paused, opposite from him. "We were only supposed to last one night anyway."

He nodded so slowly it was almost imperceptible. He looked hurt, but she refused to feel guilty. He hadn't offered her anything concrete. There was nothing more to say.

"I understand that you're scared, Rylee. So am I. At least I can admit it. You know me. The real me. No one else in Royal can say that." He let out a small laugh.

"Hell, not many people at home can say that. You want me to wedge myself into some tidy column because you aren't comfortable acting on impulse? Not going to happen. I couldn't follow your rules if I wanted to because every time I turn around there is a new one." He gave her his back.

"That's not true." She should have let him leave but what he'd said had etched itself into her skin, leaving her feeling raw and vulnerable. "I've been the one bending to your will, not the other way around."

"Was that so bad? The Bellinis and the kissing and the sex and the foot massage? Eating chocolate in bed?"

"Waking up alone after you walked out on me without an explanation."

"I overreacted. I owned it. But right now? This? This is you doubling down on your fears. If you stay afraid, Peaches, we'll never have a shot at more."

She wanted to scream *How much more?!* but the words wouldn't come. The truth was she *was* scared. She wanted guarantees, promises, assurances. She wanted to know that the bottom wouldn't drop out from under her if she allowed herself to get her hopes up.

"This is for you." He tapped the medium-sized cardboard box he'd carried in. "Inside is the real reason I was late to the interview. See you, Rylee."

She let him go. She didn't want to show up at the wedding and reception tomorrow with any unexplored issues between her and Trick. She had a job to do, and he'd already distracted her from doing it. She tried to blow out a sigh of relief, but the truth was she didn't feel better. Nothing had been resolved. If anything, their relationship was *un*resolved. It had ended, but with an ellipsis.

The unmarked cardboard box he'd carried in was

holding what, she had no idea. It could be a new pair of shoes—flats, she thought with a sad smile—or a nest of fake rubber snakes.

Hesitating over the closed flaps, she thought again of him asking for "more." She loved the idea of more. More friends, more weddings to plan. When it came to her romantic life, she hadn't warmed to the idea of more. The one time she'd reached for that golden ring—quite literally—she'd ended up returning it to Louis.

Trick's presence in Royal had changed her over these last few months—the rumors of his antics had preceded him. She'd gone from a hyperactive, fretting perfectionist to a woman who wore her hair down. A woman who stayed up past her bedtime to make love rather than answer emails.

Unable to stand the suspense, she opened the box. When she moved the tissue paper aside, her eyes filled with tears. They spilled over and ran down her cheeks.

Inside the box was the exact match for the gold flatware she'd been fruitlessly searching for all day. She wouldn't have to wake up early tomorrow after all. She wouldn't have to burden herself or worry about everything matching. As she moved to a back table and set the box onto the waiting folded napkins, she spotted a square handwritten notecard.

In spite of your best laid plans, one issue seems to have worked itself out. ~Trick.

Back in her room, Rylee didn't sleep. She stared at the ceiling, asking herself how a guy like Patrick MacArthur had turned her head. He was her exact opposite in nearly every way. He made no sense. *They* made no sense. Who entered a relationship planning no further ahead than tomorrow? And who accepted an open-ended future without the promise of more?

Hands over her eyes she felt the heat of fresh tears on her palms. A bout of clarity swept through her. Despite her best efforts to prevent it, Rylee, like everyone else who had encountered him, had fallen head over uncomfortable high heels for Trick.

The woman who'd prided herself in having a plan for every possible situation, had never seen it coming.

Twenty-Two

Rylee discreetly positioned herself near the bride and groom as they made their way to an undisclosed entrance.

The guests were making their way to the main entrance, where signs and helpful staff members pointed them toward the reception area. Rylee had checked the room again this morning to ensure nothing had hopped up and run off in the middle of the night. She'd been pleased to find that everything was exactly as she'd left it, but with the addition of fresh flowers from Corynna and her assistant, Hannah.

The blueish purple buds of the blue bonnet were beautifully complemented by the crisp cream tablecloths and shimmering gold accents—including the gold cutlery, a complete set.

The outdoor ceremony had been lovely, and they'd been spared too much heat thanks to clouds blotting out sun. Along with the near-perfect weather, a gorgeous backdrop of mountains and the field of thick, green grass,

Ariana was stunning in her bridal gown. On the hanger had been one thing, but seeing the bride in her dress for the first time had been a whole other experience.

Ari, her cropped hair styled and her jewelry understated, had floated down the aisle. The white dress dipped in to accent her trim waist and flared out at the hips. Blue bonnet flowers had been sewn into the skirt but managed not to distract from the bride herself. When Xavier saw her for the first time, Rylee could practically hear him swallowing past the lump in his throat.

Once Ari had reached the end of the aisle and her father had taken his seat, Ari and Xavier hadn't broken eye contact. Even when the officiant addressed them directly, the bride and groom had spoken only to each other.

Ariana Ramos and Xavier Noble had recited their vows. The kiss was the best part of any wedding ceremony, hands down. Rylee had dabbed at her eyes with a tissue, accustomed to choking up during that tender moment. And then the moment had been upstaged by a very young man in a very expensive tux.

The ring bearer had taken it upon himself to leapfrog up the aisle preceding Ari and Ex when they were introduced for the first time as husband and wife. The boy's mother intercepted him and wrestled with the croaking, leaping child. Before Rylee could panic over the ceremony being ruined by the unexpected display, Ari and Ex had thrown their heads back and laughed.

Their reaction had been contagious and had spread to the guests and even the officiant. Rylee had joined them, the stress of the last few months melting away. She'd laughed so hard, she'd snorted, which had made her laugh even harder. At that moment, she'd met eyes with Trick across the aisle, who had been laughing with her. For a prolonged moment, they'd simply stared at each other, grinning like loons.

And then the moment had been over. The guests had stood to follow the bride and groom off the lawn, and Rylee had circled behind the crowd so that she could greet Ari and Ex inside.

She held the door open for Ariana now. Xavier helped his wife with her dress, leaving room for the short train. He made a comment about how the "kid could have thrown in a ribbit or two in order to sound authentic" which made Ari and Rylee giggle over the incident again.

"I guess I'm unable to plan for every possibility," Rylee said.

"Well, it's on video, so we'll play it at his wedding and show him how it feels," Ari said with another laugh. Her buoyant mood was permanent today. "How long until we are introduced?"

"At least ten minutes. We'll give the guests some time to settle in."

"Perfect. One of these gorgeous blue bonnets is tearing loose from my skirt. I know you have a sewing kit on hand."

"I do." Rylee reached into a pocket of her pale pink bag, an almost exact match for her dress.

Ari spun to face Ex. "Could you fetch me a glass of water *husband*? I am parched."

"Sure thing, *wife*." He said the word on a growl into Ari's mouth and then pressed his lips to hers. Rylee busied herself unzipping the sewing kit, the intimate moment stinging more than it should have. Their intimacy reminded her of her own short-lived romance, which had been as unexpected as the ring bearer turning into a bullfrog.

Ex vanished down the hallway in search of water, and Ari rested one manicured hand over Rylee's. Ari's expression was pure concern. "Why are your blue eyes bluer than usual? What's got you down?"

"I—what do you mean?" Rylee slapped on a broad smile. This was Ari's day and Rylee refused to ruin it with her wayward emotions. "Everything is wonderful. Now show me where the threads have popped and I'll do my best to repair them."

"Are you kidding? This is Keely's design. Not a thread on this dress would dare pop without her permission." Ari rested her hands on her hips, looking like the in-charge, take-charge producer more than the demure bride minutes after she'd said *I do*. "Talk to me."

Rylee tucked the sewing kit back into her bag. "Your only concern is to go into that reception hall and be doted on by everyone. Don't worry about me."

"You're my friend. I want you in that reception hall smiling, too."

"I am smiling."

"Like a robot." Ari palmed one of Rylee's arms. "Nothing can ruin this day for me. It's unfolding as it was meant to. Now tell me why you're upset. Is it Trick?"

Rylee debated lying, her mouth opening and closing and opening again before she said, "How did you know?"

"These two eyes." Ari gestured to her face. "And Dee mentioned you two had hit it off. Talk about opposites attracting."

Rylee forced out an explanation that would satisfy any friend. "We spent some time together. He's a good person, but ultimately we weren't cut out for forever. I wish him well, though. He's so talented."

As she waited for the lie to land, her smile faded. That

BS would satisfy any friend, except, as it turned out, Ariana. Ari's eyebrows craned upward in disbelief. "Really?"

Rylee dropped her shoulders. "Okay. The truth is—"

"Finally!" Ari raised her arms, bouquet and all.

"The truth is," Rylee restarted. "Trick is good at making people fall in love with him. He is charming and fun, and he has a way of giving someone exactly what they need before they know they need it. Like peach Bellinis, charcuterie boards, a foot massage. Forks." Her vision blurred with tears as she recalled the many, many gifts he'd given her in the last couple of days.

"Forks?"

"Uh, never mind. My point is, everyone falls for Trick. Including you and your husband. I can't trust my feelings when I could very well be part of his shtick." His great-in-bed, feed-her-chocolate, kiss-her-senseless-in-the-hotel-hallway shtick.

"I admit, Trick is likable. I never imagined inviting a wedding crasher to my wedding," Ari said with a headshake.

"I'm sorry. I shouldn't have suggested that."

"Don't be sorry. I was worried for months about nothing. He's wonderful. That interview was from the heart. He can turn it on, for sure, but no matter how great Trick is at his job, it doesn't change the fact that you're wrong."

Rylee's head jerked on her neck. "I'm wrong? About what?"

"I was charmed by Trick. Ex was charmed by Trick. Dee and Tripp were charmed by Trick. Every one of our guests who spoke with him at the rehearsal cocktail dinner was charmed by Trick." She poked Rylee in the arm as she made her point. "But not you. You were the one who *fell in love* with Trick."

Rylee was silent for a beat. She'd been called out. Ari was right. Rylee had fallen in love with Trick. Which was insane, made no practical sense, and had *not* been on the agenda.

"I—That's ridiculous. You can't fall in love with someone in a few days," Rylee argued. "Plus, he doesn't want to talk about the future. I need to talk about the future. He wants to take it a day at a time, see where it goes. I need assurances that everything will go according to plan."

Ari's smile softened with knowing. "You mean the way everything in our wedding went according to plan? What about when our rehearsal dinner turned into a rehearsal cocktail party with an entirely new menu? Or the color-scheme change or the addition of last-minute guests? What about our ring bearer stealing the show when he became an amphibian?

"There is no way everything will go according to plan, even with a plan as rock-solid as Rylee Meadows's plan. But look at Xavier and me. We're married. As planned! Nothing changed that outcome."

Rylee was beginning to see her friend's point. No matter how firm the plans had been, many, *many* things had changed during the course of planning this wedding. But in the end, it'd all worked out.

"Here you are, sweetheart." Ex appeared with a water glass in hand.

"Thank you, darling." Ari took a sip as the announcer spoke from the other room. "That's us!"

"Meet you in there." Rylee said, taking the glass from Ari, but her friend wasn't done dispensing advice yet.

As Ex positioned himself beside his wife, she whispered, "Remember, Rylee, magical moments happen at weddings."

"Everyone welcome the bride and groom!" the announcer said.

Rylee pulled open the door for them, and Ari's words echoed through her mind. She'd used the word *magical*. The very word Rylee had used to describe Trick.

She silently closed the door on the couple as photos were snapped and flashes popped. Then she looped back to the corridor and slipped in through the front.

As she angled for her own chair, by itself in the rear of the room, her heart lifted. She half expected to find two chairs instead of one, and Trick waiting for her to arrive.

Instead, she'd found the table exactly as she'd left it. With her planner next to her own set of gold cutlery, and her place card on the center of the dinner plate.

Twenty-Three

The meal was exquisite. Each course came out on time, with every garnish in place. Not that Rylee had checked every plate personally, but as she was positioned near the kitchen, she'd peeked as the servers had whisked by. While she appreciated Colin Reynolds's talent with food, her heart hadn't been into enjoying it. As each course was served, her heart sank lower and lower. Trick hadn't come.

She didn't understand. He'd been at the wedding. He'd laughed. They'd locked eyes. Ariana had pointed out that Rylee had fallen in love, and then had practically promised her a happy ending tonight with that "magical" comment.

During the cake cutting and Xavier and Ariana's first dance, Rylee kept watch for Trick. Ariana threw the bouquet directly to Dee, who caught it with a flourish. Rylee had smiled and clapped along with the other guests, hoping she'd effectively hidden her true emotions. She was a professional, here to serve the bride and groom. Today wasn't about her happily ever after. No matter how badly she wanted one.

Ariana and Xavier were married and enjoying their reception. That had been the goal. Rylee's work was technically done the moment that Dee caught the bouquet, but she couldn't seem to make herself leave. Even as the band played a slow song and warm amber lights swirled on the dance floor.

She watched from afar as Ari and Ex's friends paired up. She kept smiling despite her own empty arms. Her heart ached. Whether or not something magical happened to her tonight was of no consequence. Magic was all around her, and that was a enough reason to celebrate.

Even if Trick had left Royal, Texas, without telling her goodbye.

A member of the waitstaff offered her the lone glass of champagne on his tray.

"Thank you." She accepted the flute. As the waiter zipped away she realized it wasn't *just* champagne. The orange hue exactly matched that of her favorite cocktail.

"Peach Bellini," came a rich, low voice next to her left ear.

She turned around, her heart in her throat.

"Hi."

"Hi," she said, breathless.

"What's wrong? Did you think I wasn't coming?" Trick, dressed in the same navy-blue suit as he'd worn at the wedding, was a literal a breath of fresh air.

"I wasn't sure."

"Well, shame on you. I was invited, after all." He pulled his cellphone from his jacket pocket. "I was wondering if you would take a look at something for me." He swiped the screen. "I've been working hard on it, but it's not quite finished."

"Oh, of course." She swallowed down her yearning and focused on the task. Today wasn't about them. Trick knew that as well as she did. "What, um, what is it?"

"It's a video of those unexpected moments I'm always going on and on about." He rolled his eyes in an adorably self-deprecating manner. "I compiled some for the week, but I wanted your opinion. Unless you're off the clock."

"Have you seen these shoes?" She pointed her toe. She was wearing the gold strappy pair she'd sworn never to wear again. She hadn't been able to resist since they'd paired so well with her dress.

He turned the screen horizontally and played the video. Rylee expected stolen moments featuring the wedding guests to pop up on the screen, but there was only one person featured on the video.

Her.

Trick had filmed her without her knowing. While she had been talking on the phone, or walking around the site. When she'd sneaked a shrimp off a platter at the rehearsal cocktail party when she'd thought no one was looking. He'd filmed her kissing friends hello, and later when she'd hugged them goodbye. And there were several clips of her slipping off her shoe to rub her sore pinky toe.

"What is this?" she whispered.

"Video evidence of every little thing you did that made me fall in love with you." She looked up at him but his eyes were on the screen. "I have hours of footage."

"Trick…"

"I know. I'm as shocked as you are." He pocketed the phone and offered his hand. "Dance with me?"

She placed her hand in his. He set aside her Bellini,

promising that she could finish it later. Then he walked with her to the dance floor and began swaying to the music.

"I thought you went home." She was dazed, her voice hollow.

"Without saying goodbye? What kind of jerk do you take me for?"

"I was terrible to you. I never thanked you for finding the gold flatware. How did you do that, by the way?"

"I can't tell you all my secrets, Peaches. Some mystery is healthy for a budding relationship. And you haven't been terrible. You've been you. And as I've established, I love you. See? Told you it would work out."

She had to laugh. "Nothing's worked out. There is no pl—"

He pressed his index finger to her lips. "Don't say the *P* word. Besides, I have one."

When he moved his hand away, she said, "You have a plan?"

"I do. I'm going to film events and clip together video montages like the one I just played for you. How does MacArthur's Moments sound?"

"Cheesy," she said with a confused smile What was he talking about? She was still wrapping her head around the *I love you*, and now he was...*starting a business?*

"Yeah. That is pretty bad. I'll poll my fan base and see what they think. They're very smart. Most of them believe that I'll end up marrying the wedding planner I met in Royal, Texas." He shrugged. "I'm not sure she'll have me, but we do have one very important thing in common."

"Wha-what's that?" she asked, her mind tripping over the word *marrying*.

"Coffee. You answered my deal-breaker question correctly. What more do we need to work out?"

She shut her eyes, information and proclamations coming too fast for her to process. "Trick, what is going on?"

Wordlessly, he let go of her and dropped to his knees. Before she had a heart attack in the middle of the wedding reception, she realize he wasn't proposing, but removing her shoes. He tossed them to one side and stood to applause from the crowd. They adored him—no surprise there. Barefoot, she stood a few inches shorter than him and felt a million times more comfortable.

"Now for a proposal unlike any other. I promise to love you and make a maximum of one plan per month." He faked an eye twitch that made her laugh. "*If* you promise to stop wearing shoes you hate and let me hang around with you on a permanent basis."

"Permanent?"

"Maybe you can tack on my video services as a part of yours? Or if not, I could still join you at the weddings you plan as your date."

"And if you're not invited?" she teased.

"Hmm. I'll find something to do. Do you know anyone who can teach me how to golf?"

"*No,*" she said with meaning. "Do you know anyone who can teach me how to take life as it unfolds instead of planning for every possible circumstance?"

He sucked air through his teeth. "I'm not sure you can be taught."

Her mouth dropped open. "I can so! I've done everything you've asked me to since you showed up in town uninvited."

"That's true. You are a quick study."

She wrapped her arms around his neck and hugged him close. "Do you know what else I'm a quick study on?"

"What's that?" He embraced her, pulling her flush

against his body, and making her want to be alone with him as soon as possible.

"You. I have you down. You charm anyone and everyone you meet."

"True."

"You are able to solve any problem with a smile and a conversation."

"Guilty," he agreed.

"And you made me fall in love with you, even though I never planned on it."

Whatever smart-aleck remark he'd reserved never made it out of his mouth. His eyes heated. He dropped his forehead onto hers. "You fell in love with me?"

"I'm afraid so."

"Seems fair. I never saw you coming." His eyes jerked to the side. "Except for the times when I went down on—"

She pressed her lips into his to keep him from finishing that sentence. Then she whispered, "Let's talk about that later."

"Let's go back to your room and talk about it *now*. Are you free, or are there any other unforeseen emergencies you have to circumvent?"

"I'm suddenly free. This great guy I know handled the last of my problems."

"Well, he sounds like a keeper."

She tilted her head and prepared for another toe-curling kiss. "He is. He really is."

Epilogue

Rylee blew out a breath and steeled herself. She'd planned lots of weddings, but over the last year, none had been as significant as this one. She smoothed her dress with one hand and peered into the cathedral where the pews were packed with guests.

"Is it bad luck to see you beforehand?" Trick whispered into her ear.

Startled, she spun to face him. "That rule is only for the bride, not her wedding planner." He gave her a kiss, and butterflies took wing in her belly. "Besides, we don't have bad luck."

"Mmm. Good point." He kissed her again. "Was this the most challenging wedding you've ever planned?"

"Not even close. That prize belongs to Ari and Ex, and you had quite a bit to do with that."

He raised their joined hands and kissed hers. "Where do we stand for this part?"

"You"—she pushed him toward the side entrance—

"go over there and film those unforgettable moments you promised the bride and groom you'd capture."

"What about you?" he asked as he checked the settings on his camera.

"I will wait back here and make sure the wedding party and the bride make it to the end of that aisle."

"So you can head off any disasters before they occur?"

"Exactly."

"Lens check." He lifted the camera and pressed Record. Rylee was used to him asking for her help with lighting tests.

She posed and sent him a cheeky grin. "How do I look?"

"Like a woman who is being proposed to."

Her smile dropped. "Excuse me?"

"We've already combined our lives and our businesses. Why not make it official?" With his free hand, Trick produced a ring from his pocket and extended his arm. "I can't let you continue to be the wedding planner who hasn't planned her own wedding. And I can't bear the idea of going one more month without knowing you'll be part of my future."

"The man who never plans is planning for the future?"

"*Our* future." He lowered the camera, but kept it facing her, the red light on. "You bring out the best in me. You always have. What do you say? Will you marry me, Rylee Meadows?"

"Cliffside wedding?"

"You're the planner. You tell me."

She rushed to him, bypassing the ring to plant a kiss on the center of his mouth. "Why don't we plan it together? I'm flexible."

He grasped her waist and squeezed. "You proved that last night."

Against his lips, she laughed. She liked knowing she'd be laughing with him for years to come. Sometimes the best-laid plans weren't planned ahead.

No matter where they held their wedding: on a cliff-side, at the Texas Cattleman's Club or on a space shuttle bound for the moon, Rylee had faith in Trick and in their future. A future that *didn't* have to be perfect.

The best things in life rarely were.

* * * * *

COMING SOON!

We really hope you enjoyed reading this book. If you're looking for more romance be sure to head to the shops when new books are available on

Thursday 8th June

To see which titles are coming soon, please visit

millsandboon.co.uk/nextmonth

MILLS & BOON

LET'S TALK

Romance

For exclusive extracts, competitions and special offers, find us online:

- **f** MillsandBoon
- 🐦 @MillsandBoon
- 📷 @MillsandBoonUK
- ♪ @MillsandBoonUK

Get in touch on 01413 063 232

For all the latest titles coming soon, visit
millsandboon.co.uk/nextmonth

MILLS & BOON

THE HEART OF ROMANCE

A ROMANCE FOR EVERY READER

MODERN
Prepare to be swept off your feet by sophisticated, sexy and seductive heroes, in some of the world's most glamourous and romantic locations, where power and passion collide.

HISTORICAL
Escape with historical heroes from time gone by. Whether your passion is for wicked Regency Rakes, muscled Vikings or rugged Highlanders, awaken the romance of the past.

MEDICAL
Set your pulse racing with dedicated, delectable doctors in the high-pressure world of medicine, where emotions run high and passion, comfort and love are the best medicine.

True Love
Celebrate true love with tender stories of heartfelt romance, from the rush of falling in love to the joy a new baby can bring, and a focus on the emotional heart of a relationship.

Desire
Indulge in secrets and scandal, intense drama and sizzling hot action with heroes who have it all: wealth, status, good looks…everything but the right woman.

HEROES
The excitement of a gripping thriller, with intense romance at its heart. Resourceful, true-to-life women and strong, fearless men face danger and desire - a killer combination!

To see which titles are coming soon, please visit

millsandboon.co.uk/nextmonth

JOIN US ON SOCIAL MEDIA!

Stay up to date with our latest releases, author news and gossip, special offers and discounts, and all the behind-the-scenes action from Mills & Boon...

 @millsandboon

 @millsandboonuk

 facebook.com/millsandboon

 @millsandboonuk

It might just be true love...